**Praise for the novels of**

"Herrera is consistently one of the most prescient, thoughtful romance writers today, always finding compelling ways to weave vital topics into her scorching-hot love stories."
—*Entertainment Weekly*

"Herrera excels at creating the kind of rich emotional connections between her protagonists that romance readers will find irresistible."
—*Booklist*, starred review

"Sweet and thoughtful, but delightfully filthy, too."
—*New York Times Book Review*

"Herrera's work remains compulsively readable. She crafts lively Latinx characters with instant, electric chemistry that sings on the page, and handles realistic obstacles in a relatable manner."
—*Publishers Weekly*, starred review

"Incisive and modern, navigating the complexities of privilege, purpose and power, all while exploring intense passion."
—*Washington Post*

"Herrera...deftly charts the struggles of finding love and friendship in unexpected places."
—*Library Journal*, starred review

"Adriana Herrera writes romance with teeth—you'll laugh, you'll cry, and you'll be refreshed and inspired to fight even harder to create the vibrant, welcoming America in which her books are set."
—*New York Times* bestselling author Suzanne Brockmann

"[Adriana Herrera] is writing some of my favorite Afro-Latinx characters and giving us beautiful love stories along the way."
—National Book Award winner Elizabeth Acevedo

"Herrera masterfully combines the fun, gooey, interpersonal, romantic stuff with plots that are firmly grounded in reality and involve social justice. The result is contemporary romance that matters, stories that reveal an abundance of inconvenient truths about society."
—*Book Riot*

# ON THE HUSTLE

## ADRIANA HERRERA

carina
press

carina
press®

Recycling programs
for this product may
not exist in your area.

ISBN-13: 978-1-335-60082-0

On the Hustle

Carina Press
22 Adelaide St. West, 41st Floor
Toronto, Ontario M5H 4E3, Canada
www.CarinaPress.com

Printed in U.S.A.

To my sister, Lorena.

A hustler like no other. Scholar, dogged researcher, firefighter, adventurer, and a truly phenomenal tía.

# ON THE HUSTLE

# *Prologue*

## ALBA

Julia: You can do this amiga! Drop that motherfucker like a bad habit and break free from that eight-pack addiction.

Nobody should have to put up with this much wiseassery from their best friend at five in the morning, but here we were. The eight-pack in question did not pertain to beers—or anything I was allowed to consume—but rather to my boss's extremely off-limits abdominal muscles.

Alba: Julia what the hell are you doing up this early? It's like four in the morning in Dallas?!

Julia: I set an alarm, boba! You think I was going to run the risk of you going to see that pendejo without a pep talk?

Julia had not very good feelings about my employer and had been hounding me to quit my PA job for months…and it *was* mostly my fault that she hated his guts. The man frustrated me to no end and Julia, even though she now lived many states away in Dallas, was still my number one go-to venting safe space when it came to the man. And she was right. I did need a talking to this morning.

Alba: I'm ready though. I'm doing this.

Julia typed a series of fire and fist-in-the-air emojis. Then a GIF from Hamilton with Lin Manuel Miranda mouthing "take my shot."

Julia: You got this ma!

The three dots stayed on the screen for a beat and before the words popped up on my screen I knew what she was going to say.

Julia: And you're still visiting right?

Though I knew it was coming, the question kicked up the anxious pounding in my chest. She wasn't asking to confirm, she was asking because the four other times I'd promised to visit I'd canceled on her at the last minute.

I had a hard time leaving New York.

Between my three jobs and my family, I constantly felt like whenever I left the city I only came back to a string of fires to put out. But I had not taken a weekend off in a year and I was running on fumes. Also—and I really was ashamed of this part—Julia had been in Dallas for almost two years, and I had yet to visit. My friend had gone and made a whole-ass life for herself in Texas. New friends, new job, new man. She was happy, and though I was proud of her and so fucking happy that she was killing it down there, I felt like if I went and saw what she'd made, that I'd start comparing. That taking stock of what I still didn't have would make me bitter.

But things would be different after today. I was finally doing the thing. I'd put this off for too damn long.

Julia: Am I going to need to get on a plane and force you to go on vacation, Alba Serena Duarte?

Maybe this bitch *could* read minds?

Alba: Damn, chill, Julia. I already have my ticket. I'm packed too. I'll let him know today and fly to Dallas tomorrow. Be ready to pamper my ass like your place is the Ritz-Carlton.

Another GIF, this time of Michelle Obama clapping.

I was glad that she couldn't see my face. Julia would make me in a second. Even typing those words *let him know* set off a cold sweat through my entire body. This was why I kept chickening out, because whenever I set out to do it, I'd go into a full panic. Fear that nothing would work out the way I wanted. That I'd fuck myself over by leaving a secure situation to strike out on my own. Fear that once I walked away from a steady—and generous—paycheck there would only be me to blame when everything went tits up. But I could not keep delaying things any longer. The future I wanted for myself was riding on me bossing up and doing this. I was not going to let fear fuck with my dreams anymore.

Julia: Ahhh! I can't believe I get you for a whole week! We're going to have so much fun. The Gotham Exiles are all dying to meet you. They all feel like they know you already.

I grinned at that as I forced myself to take deep, calming breaths. Julia's friend group was a crew of ex–New Yorkers living in Dallas. Most of them worked for Sturm's, the department store that owned the foundation Julia and her man worked for.

**Alba: I'm excited!**

I wasn't lying. I'd FaceTimed enough with all of them over the last couple of years to feel like I knew them too and was genuinely looking forward to meeting them all in person.

Right then my phone—provided by my boss, so he could keep tabs on my ass whenever I was on the clock—pinged with my thirty-minute warning. Immediately my stomach did that flippy move it did whenever I was in proximity of the reason I was up and out in the streets of Queens before the sun was out. You'd think after three years I wouldn't feel like ants were running a marathon over my skin, but you'd be wrong. It had to be some kind of trigger or an allergy. Yeah, it was mostly likely some kind of emotional allergic reaction. That *had* to be a thing.

**Alba: Okay I have to go. TTYL**

**Julia: Next time we talk you will be free from the clutches of that big-ass Greek-Dominican nightmare you work for.**

I winced, picturing the brooding, perfect face attached to those six feet and three inches of hard muscle encased in delicious caramel skin, and with determination pushed through the doors of my boss's building.

I was ready. I would be fine. It was my time now.

# Chapter One

## ALBA

*Alba Serena Duarte doesn't have bad days.*

This is what I chanted to myself in a loop as I hustled across the lobby of a Long Island city high-rise, then shook my head like Marimar, my abuela's poodle, after she gets a bath. What kind of asshole talks about herself in the third person, even if it's in her own head?

That didn't make my mantra any less true though. I didn't have bad days, or more specifically I couldn't afford them. Not while juggling three jobs and managing a seemingly endless stream of family demands. It wasn't even that I was self-righteous and thought having bad days was beneath me; it was just my way of dealing with the fact that whenever I did have a bad day, I still had to work.

It's a trick you learn when you can't have something you really need. You start telling yourself you don't want it anyway. You reframe, you pivot, you spin. I was really, *really* good at this particular form of mental gymnastics. Which was why I'd convinced myself I just didn't have bad days. I allowed myself the occasional "we'll try again in the morning" days. I could even do "let's try to focus on the bright side" days...or my go-to "you're a bad bitch and you can handle this" days.

But never *ever* a Bad Day.

Bad days implied taking breaks, time off to recharge, and my schedule did not allow for that, which meant I was exhausted. Wrung out down to the marrow of my bones. But hustle culture doesn't come to a halt just because I'm feeling like a piece of chewed gum stuck to the pavement. That bitch keeps churning like a merry-go-round on steroids and you can either handle your business or get tossed on your ass, with your dreams right alongside you.

So I stayed on, even if some mornings I did it by the skin of my teeth. My dreams were worth losing a little—a lot of—sleep over, and what's more I was slowly—very slowly—making them come true. Despite the utterly endless grind of the past three years, that thought brought a smile to my face. I was on the cusp of achieving a huge milestone. I just had to get through this morning—or more like the next few weeks, and I'd be there.

"You better hustle, Alba Duarte!" Nico the doorman called as I punched the code for the elevator. When I looked over my shoulder he lifted his wrist, tapping the brand-new Apple Watch he'd gotten from our boss last Christmas.

"I know! I'm going!" My feet responded to the playful urgency in his voice and I jogged in place, making him laugh.

"Dile a la Natasha que le mando saludos!"

I rolled my eyes and shook my head at his request to deliver his daily romantic overture to my coworker.

"I got no time to play middle-school love messages game with you, Nico." I flashed him with deuces and stepped into the elevator. It was 5:30 a.m. and I was already five minutes behind schedule. Which wouldn't be a big deal if I didn't work for the most fastidious, demanding, punctuality obsessed man on planet earth.

Theodoro Anibal Ganas, *heir* to the Ganas real estate empire—and I meant that literally, the man's father owned hundreds of apartments in Manhattan, Brooklyn and Queens. The senior Ganas was a former Greek nuclear physicist trained at MIT who instead of, as he put it, "making bombs for some dictator," in the '80s began buying condemned buildings and renovating them himself with the help of a friend. A decade later, Achilles Ganas was a bona fide mogul with dozens of properties. As his star was on the rise he met a lovely Dominican flight attendant while on a business trip to the DR. That relationship was not one of Achilles's most successful ventures, but it did yield my pain-in-the-ass boss. You'd think me being Dominican would give some kind of favor with the man.

Well, you'd be wrong.

Theo Anibal Ganas did not give a fuck about our shared ancestry. Where I was a little militant about my Dominicaness, Theo barely acknowledged it. To be fair, he didn't seem to care about being Greek either. Theo was…taciturn. Stoic. *Contained.* After years of working for him I could recite every detail about what the man did from the moment he woke up until 6:00 p.m. every evening, but I had no idea how he felt about *anything.*

Okay, maybe that wasn't exactly true. I knew he loved his little sister, Zoe. I knew his best friend was his stepmother— which was not as weird as it sounded since she was only like five years older than him. I also knew he was a generous and fair boss. But other than that, Theo Ganas was a mystery to me. A large and imposing, ruthlessly serious mystery that I wished I cared a lot less about deciphering.

And I *had* tried. I'd told myself it was part of the job. That being a good assistant meant you had to know your boss enough to anticipate his thoughts. So I'd tried to mine him for anything I could use to get a bead on the man who paid my salary. My efforts had not produced much. For fuck's sake, it took six months for me to even realize he *was* half Dominican and that only happened because I brought some breakfast to the office—mashed plantains with fried cheese and salami, my ultimate comfort food. Natasha—his other assistant—recognized the DR staple and commented that Theo's mother was Dominican. When I asked him why he hadn't mentioned it, all excited that we had *something* in common, he looked down his infuriatingly straight nose at me and told me that not everyone had to act like a walking, talking ad for Dominicans in New York.

*See?* Asshole.

The annoying thing was that despite Theo being a broody prick to me at all times, everyone in the office loved him. It seemed that a charming, warm, funny Theo Anibal surfaced regularly, as long as I wasn't around. Natasha had been working with the Ganas family since he was a teen and basically worshipped the ground he walked on. But I had never seen any evidence of this lovable version of Theo. What *I* regularly got was a scowling despot—no, that was not too harsh—who didn't even deign to make eye contact with me.

That first Christmas after I started as his PA, when I still thought I was working for a sentient human, not an evil droid encased in an insanely buff skin suit, I naively left a bottle of my abuela's ponche on his desk with a very festive red ribbon tied around the neck. I even attached a little sprig of artificial mistletoe with my glue gun. It was adorable and sure, I might've been trying to score some points, but that ponche is the fucking nectar of the gods. It is extremely sought-after in all of Corona, Queens. How was I supposed to know the only person with Caribbean blood running through their veins that didn't rock with ponche was Theo?

I still squirmed remembering that morning when I watched my boss walk into his office, stand in front of his desk for a full minute then walk right back out with the tip of the bottle pinched between his two fingers like it was an active explosive. And because sometimes I was that dense I smiled, thinking he was coming to gush about the present, and blurted out, "Don't try it on an empty stomach it's got a lot of rum!"

The grin and thanks I thought were forthcoming did not happen. Instead he placed the ponche on my desk and without even bothering to look at me said, "I don't accept gifts from my assistants," then walked off.

*Such* a comemierda.

*He won't be your boss much longer,* I reminded myself, trying to shake off the lingering mortification of that memory. But instead of relief at the thought of no longer having to deal with Theo Anibal looking right through me on a daily basis, that weird sensation like I'd swallowed a bunch of ice settled in my stomach again.

It had to be nerves. It made perfect sense to be a little nervous that the leap I was taking on my own was a huge one and losing the security of a job with full health benefits was understandably spooking me. It wasn't like I'd miss him, that would be… Well, it didn't matter what it was because I was *delighted* to be quitting this job.

It wasn't even about Theo, really; being a PA had always been a temporary plan. I had a degree in interior design from the New School and a master of architecture from Columbia, which I would be paying for until I died. Making macchiatos for surly millionaires wasn't what I was destined to do.

Hell, this job was supposed to be a six-month gig to help my mother through one of her many "money is tight" spells while I was in grad school. It was a one-year-tops situation, and here I was almost three years later, still getting yelled at for not getting the right biscotti for a man with a degree from MIT with access to the same food delivery apps I had.

For over a year now I'd let my mother's warnings that "decorating bedrooms for your friends isn't a secure job" keep me from taking the leap. And it was true that a few hundred thousand followers on TikTok didn't exactly warrant success for my business, but I'd never know if I didn't try.

That thought kept me going as I ascended to the twenty-eighth floor of the Ganas Tower. Eyes closed, sucking in air through my nose and exhaling slowly out of my mouth for a few seconds, I pushed down the urge to talk myself out of it. As I neared my office I shut the door right in the face of the smug little devil perched on my shoulder whispering in my ear that the Duarte family could not afford to take one more risk. That I was going to fuck up and waste my savings. That no one in their right mind would pay me to renovate their house. That people might hit like or comment on TikTok, but they would never actually shell out thousands of dollars and entrust me with their entire homes. That decorating bedrooms in the theme of someone's favorite book could never work as a viable business. That I would be back here in a few months begging for my job. I shut all of that out, swallowed every ounce of doubt and imagined it being crushed to dust in my gut. Hesitation was not part of the program today. I had to stick to the plan.

Finally launching my business, the only thing in my life that I was proud of: Bookish Boudoir.

While in grad school for fun I started doing book-themed budget bedroom makeovers for my friends. They'd give me a thousand bucks and I would turn their room into an homage to their favorite story. Julia—who honestly always had the best ideas—suggested I do before and after posts on Instagram. I tried it and it kind of blew up. I was a whiz with the sewing machine and knew every trick in the book when it came to DIY, and soon I started making custom designs for my clients. When word started getting around a bunch of other grad students wanted my makeovers. I even had people sliding into my DMs, asking to book me. Since then, I'd been steadily building it up.

But for the money to really be good, I needed to focus solely on BB. Which was hard while juggling three jobs. Whenever I wasn't managing Theo's life, or doing makeovers, I took on freelance work from architects, which left me barely enough time to eat, shower and sleep a few hours. Something had to give and for once I was going to do the thing that made *me* happy.

I took out my phone and scrolled until I found my latest makeover. A suite inspired by a wildly popular fantasy series. I had read the books and loved them and went all out on recreating my vision for the Night Court where the protagonists reigned. The post for it went viral and it had given me the last push to finally strike out on my own. As I read the positive comments, I began to feel calmer.

NightCourtFayrie: I am in awe. It is perfection.

BookWorm151: It's the wallpaper for me.

I grinned, nodding at the wallpaper comment. That one I was particularly proud of. I'd sketched matching thrones with silver silhouettes of a winged king next to his queen on midnight blue matte paper. The room, which was for a friend of my cousin, looked like I'd conjured it right out of the pages of the book. The reading nook I'd done in the colors of the Spring Court with bright pinks, yellows and greens. That corner of the room bled into the Night Court theme, which was done in deep blue, slate and silver. Light to darkness. I'd even thrifted an amazing Chesterfield armchair at a swap meet and ended up upholstering it myself in floral fabric with hints of gold that looked perfect next to a small, brushed metal table. Little details like that were what made my renovations so popular with clients. I took their passion for their favorite books very seriously, because I was the same way. I knew what it was like to find refuge in a book. To have every emotion pulled out of me by a story. I knew there were books that could touch something inside you like nothing else could. It was something so magical you wanted to be surrounded by it. Which was why when a client trusted me with a design, I made sure to give them their bookish haven.

"Okay, not to brag," I told my reflection in the elevator. "I'm a fucking genius."

I made myself believe that. For three years I'd been living on five hours of sleep and wrangling more than any person should. Three demanding jobs, finishing grad school, and helping my mom deal with the debt she'd been repaying for the last decade. But I had stayed focused, saved, planned, strategized. All on my own, every step of the way.

As the elevator pinged I took one more deep breath. I opened my eyes on the exhale and stared at myself in the spotless mirror. Kelly green pantsuit, white T-shirt, vintage-style wire frame glasses, and my brand-new white Adidas—because this man had me running all over the five boroughs, and I was not doing it in three-inch stilettos. I turned around so I could see myself from the side: yep, chin-length curls popping, hoops dangling in my ears, face beat perfect. It was now or never. I tapped on my Alba La Jefa playlist and blasted "Money" by Cardi B into my AirPods for an extra pep in my step.

I strutted into my office and dropped off my backpack, a little more in control of my morning. I looked up at the enormous clock on the wall—it looked like one of those digital banners in Times Square and almost as big, but when you worked for a time-obsessed maniac, you did what you had to do—I was cutting it close. After a quick scan of my desktop monitor for any Code Red Post-it messages I rushed across the hall to where Natasha was already at her desk.

"Is he—"

She nodded before I could finish. "He's up there," she confirmed. Not that I expected the man not to be on schedule. Theo Ganas was a fucking machine. Woke up every day at 5:00 a.m. and fifteen minutes later he was cutting across the water on his climate-controlled rooftop swimming pool. Fifty laps every morning. At 6:05 a.m., on the motherfucking dot, I had to walk into the pool area with his coffee and his daily schedule, and I did not want to be running behind on the day I would deliver the news that would alter his ever-important routine.

"Dammit!" I grumbled, as I put on the Starbucks barista apron Natasha had gotten me as a gag gift a couple of years back.

"I already took out the beans for you and I picked up his voice messages," she said, moving her hands in a shooing motion.

"You're my favorite person, Nat!" I bussed her on the cheek, making her squeal. Natasha was in her fifties, but you could not tell from looking at her. The woman was like a cross between Sophia Loren and Elizabeth Taylor with the same curves, eyeshadow and hairstyle choices. Natasha Djurovićhad never met a wrap dress in a jewel tone she didn't like and to be fair, she bodied them. But I didn't even have time to compliment her on today's fit because I had to focus on the science experiment my boss called morning coffee.

Theo Ganas didn't even caffeinate like a regular person.

His daily dose of joe was in fact a daily test on my sanity. When Natasha first walked me through the ritual during my "onboarding" I almost quit on the spot. The only thing that held me back was the siren song of that all-cash end-of-the-year bonus I'd been promised.

First there were the beans, which I had to special order and pick up in person on the Upper West Side. Half Italian Espresso, half Sidamo, which I had to mix by hand because the two beans could not comingle until they were about to be ground. Once they were appropriately pulverized, I had to make his triple shot espresso, and froth his oat milk to perfection. The beverage was poured into his *three-hundred-dollar* coffee cup then placed on a gleaming silver Tiffany & Co. tray, next to a crisply starched linen napkin. On a small plate I served him one—never *ever* two—piece of almond biscotti, which Carlos, my go-to courier for Upper Manhattan and the Bronx, picked up for me at the boss's favorite bakery on Arthur Avenue. If you asked me, the man had the tastes and sleep cycle of an Italian octogenarian with mob ties, but I was not paid to have opinions.

I tossed back my own double shot of very premium java—one of the perks of the job—tucked the iPad with my boss's schedule under my arm and turned in the direction of the elevator.

"Are you telling him today?" Natasha whispered as I breezed by her desk. I bit my lip, glancing down at my wrist on instinct. I had five minutes to get up to the thirty-fifth floor.

"Yeah," I said, as my heartbeat picked up speed.

"Good." She nodded in my peripheral vision, an encouraging smile on her face. "Then you better get up there and do it!" She swatted my butt. "Do not let him detract you with that sculpted chest!"

# Chapter Two

## ALBA

Seven floors hardly took a minute and I walked into the pool area with thirty seconds to spare. Which meant I was an audience of one for the sexiest fucking ten seconds known to humanity, aka Theo Ganas emerging from his pool just as the sun was coming up over New York City. Almost three years of getting this same show five times a week, and my pulse still rose to dangerous levels whenever I caught a glimpse of him punching out of the water like a Poseidon with better hair and a double dose of melanin.

I could not move if I tried.

My legs were rooted in place and my entire range of vision was swallowed up by all that sinewy power. Typically I'd let myself look for just a few seconds before I focused on something else, but today my eyeballs took him in with reckless abandon. I raked my gaze over the ridiculously massive thighs encased in navy blue spandex, glistening with droplets of water all over an expanse of bronzed and sculpted everything. A buzzing started in my head when I gleaned the world's most erotic treasure trail. It was enough to make me swallow my tongue. Jesus, my eyelids were sweating.

*One one thousand, two one thousand. Grab the towel, Theo. Wrap it around your hips for fuck's sake.*

One perk of not working for him anymore would be getting the blood flow in my body back to normal. Each morning I had to witness this man get out of that fucking pool, every ounce of liquid in my body rushed to parts of my anatomy that had no business being activated in a professional setting.

"Good morning." I stepped to the side as his wet feet slapped on the concrete and handed him his robe, which he took with a grunt. He gave my outfit a cursory look, his eyes stalling for a fraction of a second somewhere between my shoulders and my face. Nothing that could be considered lascivious or inappropriate. Theo Ganas was much too controlled to ever display any sort of interest in his lowly assistant. He would never compliment my outfit either. That would require words, and he was very economical with those. I kept my sight on the far wall, avoiding the rippling muscles just inches from my face at all costs.

Not that I actually wanted him.

Great body, face, eyes, mouth, hair, voice, hands and feet aside, he wasn't my type. I preferred people who were more adventurous, more spontaneous, who weren't afraid of showing a little—or any—emotion. I stared because it was impossible not to. It was like stumbling upon one of those massive flowers that only blooms once every hundred years—it was impossible to look away.

I mean, sure, someone who *was* attracted to him would definitely think that his pecs looked good enough to lick and that the dick print in his wet swim trunks was thick enough to be launched like a motherfucking war missile. Someone who liked that sort of thing might feel her vagina clench at the sight of those massive thighs. Not me though. Because that would be highly unprofessional.

"You're late," my boss said in that apathetic tone of his.

I breathed through the annoyed comment itching to come out of my mouth and reminded myself I was about to ruin his day, which *did* bolster my spirits.

"Actually, I was thirty seconds early, Mr. Ganas."

He responded with an irritated sound. Theo absolutely hated to be called Mr. Ganas.

"Theo," he ground out, and I bit back a grin.

I loved fucking with him. It was the only thing that got me on that elevator some days.

"I have your messages," I said as he took his first sip of coffee. I held my breath as he did, remembering those early months after I started when he'd hand me back the cup, lips pursed, and order that I make it again. That hadn't happened in years and this morning he only groaned happily as he drank.

The grunts and groans were an occupational hazard, but I'd trained myself to at least not visibly respond to them anymore. I tapped the iPad with the stylus as he drank, knowing that once his caffeine levels were at "human interaction" levels he'd prompt conversation.

"So?" A raised sable eyebrow was sent in my direction. "How was yesterday?"

"It was fine, thanks for asking." I smiled awkwardly. I'd taken the afternoon to go look at a shared office space I was considering leasing, but I'd told him I was going to help my mother with something. Every once in a while Theo got curious about my personal life and would ask questions. Just my luck that this morning would be his annual moment of realizing I was a human being with a life outside of arranging his dry cleaning and setting up his dentist appointments.

I scanned the messages Natasha had typed up for me in our shared Google Doc. Nothing I couldn't deal with myself, except for one. I suppressed a sigh and opened my mouth, already knowing what he'd say.

"The producers from Star Renovations called again, and they—"

"Tell them I'm not interested." He cut me off before I could even finish the sentence.

"All right," I said with a tight nod and miraculously suppressed the judgmental tone that was burning to come out of me. Every few months for the last year one of the big reality TV production companies reached out to Theo and tried to recruit him for one of their home renovation shows.

Star Renovations was behind a very popular series that paired celebrities with a knack for design with a professional. Typically, the makeovers went to deserving families or non-profit organizations. Theo wasn't exactly a "celebrity" but ten years ago he'd won two Olympic medals for swimming while he was still in college. That in and of itself was a huge deal, but he'd also become a bit of an internet sensation— much to his chagrin it wasn't due to the races he won silver and bronze in, but because videos of him drying off after his heats had gone viral. Once the public learned that the swimmer in question was New York City royalty and an engineering student at MIT things went nuclear. His pecs had their own hashtag: #OlympicNips…which had provided me personally with hours upon hours of entertainment.

Of course, Theo loathed all of it. I, on the other hand, would've killed for a chance like that. To be able to showcase my design skills on that scale could literally change my life.

"What?" The challenging tone in his voice made me snap my head up. Theo was not a man one would call *impassioned*. *Deadpan* was the most one could get out of him, but he was looking at me so intensely, I wondered if I'd spoken out loud.

"Nothing," I lied, laughing awkwardly.

"That scowl on your face doesn't look like nothing."

I opened my mouth but nothing came out. I didn't even know how to respond to my boss even acknowledging I had emotions, much less him apparently being sensitive to that fact. I was still trying to come up with an answer when he spoke again.

"You think I should do it?"

I'd never been exactly encouraged to be candid in this job, but once again reminded myself I was about to quit. "I mean, *I'd* do it. It's a good opportunity."

I stopped there because a more elaborate answer would almost certainly get me into oversharing territory and I'd never told Theo about Bookish Boudoir. I didn't exactly hide it, but the man prided himself on being honest. More than once his "feedback" had almost brought me to tears, and I didn't think I could handle him putting down my business. Besides, I knew he didn't care. I wasn't sure where this sudden burst of interest came from, but I'd guess boredom. Theo Ganas didn't care about me or my life in the slightest. To him, my only functions were getting his schedule managed and his coffee done right.

"A good opportunity," he echoed a long time after. "What kind of opportunity do you think I need exactly?" He didn't actually sneer, but it came through loud and clear in his voice. "The business is doing fine. I can hardly keep up with the demand."

I kept the eye roll inside of me because this was par for the course. Humble was not one of his traits. Theo Ganas was the poster child for BTE… Big Taurus Energy. Self-possessed and commanding were his entire personality.

And it wasn't like he was lying; the Ganas empire had been thriving since he'd taken over for his father two years earlier. He'd made a lot of changes, including building greener, more affordable housing, which seemed to be important to him, even if it made him butt heads with his dad. The se-nior Ganas only seemed to care about getting as many lux-ury high-rises off the ground as possible. More than once I'd seen them argue over decisions Theo made that Achilles didn't agree with.

"Maybe a show like that could be a way of establishing your own brand, separate from your father." It popped out of my mouth before I had a chance to really think about what I was suggesting. He stiffened at my comment, sitting up straighter as he took me in. Like he was only now getting a first good look at me.

"Is that what you think I should do?"

Maybe I knew even less about Theo Ganas than I thought, because that response surprised me. I expected him to blow me off, or even tell me to mind my business. Even more puz-zling was the fact that he actually seemed to want me to say more. "Do you think I should go off on my own?"

I could just say I'd spoken out of turn and get back to quit-ting, but to say this man had never asked my opinion about his business would be an understatement. Finally telling him what I really thought was too much of a temptation.

I shrugged as I came up with a not-too-harsh answer. "I think you should do what you're passionate about and I don't know if building ten-million-dollar lofts for oligarchs is that for you."

"Hm," he groaned in answer and leaned back on his chair, a contemplative expression on his face. The urge to keep my thoughts to myself around Theo was so ingrained that I felt a little sick for saying that little bit. The uneasiness only grew when he kept staring into space without saying any-thing. Those usually flinty gray eyes were now glowing with whatever was going through his mind. I was close to bursting when he finally responded to my outburst. "But what about the couple thing?"

"The *what*?" I grimaced at my almost yell, but I was fully on edge at that point. Of all the freaking days for Theo to develop awareness about other people's inner lives.

"About the fact that it's a show for couples," he explained. He frowned when he looked at me, probably given the look of astonishment on my face. Eventually what he said sank in. The couples for the show. Although it technically wasn't a requirement, it did seem that part of the secret sauce for Star Renovations' shows involved a dash of romance. Almost every season, even when the co-hosts started out hating each other, by the end they were "involved." The internet loved a hot reality TV ship like nobody's business and the producers knew it.

"I don't think you're required to be a couple," I hedged, still not quite believing we were having this conversation. "Besides, you're filthy rich, smart and have an irritatingly perfect body." His mouth twitched, but I knew he couldn't be smiling, so I figured the caffeine must have been kicking in. "I don't think you'll have any trouble finding a twenty-five-year-old with a viral charcuterie board Instagram business to pretend she's dating you if it came to that." To my utter amazement he actually cracked a smile. Something wobbled in my stomach, likely shock from seeing all his teeth at once. His gray eyes journeyed over me, that mildly amused expression causing weird things happen to my body.

"Would *you* do it?"

Huh? I resisted the urge to turn around and see who he was directing this question to.

"Would you pretend to date someone for something like that?"

*Would I?* I mean, I was well-versed in the subtle art of deception. It was the only way to navigate being a sexually active bisexual while living with your entire Dominican family. But getting creative about where you're spending the night is very different to pretending you're in a relationship with someone in front of a camera in order to push ahead your career. And as much I was always willing to go the extra mile for some good D, P or any other body parts I was partaking in at any given time, I had never lied about my feelings for someone out of self-interest. Then again, being on a show where Bookish Boudoir could be exposed to millions of people had never been part of the equation…yeah, I'd do it.

"In a New York minute, Mr. Ganas." I made myself sound a lot less conflicted than I felt about it.

"I didn't know you to be such a ruthless businesswoman."

The comment rubbed me the wrong way. Because that was such a "dude" thing to say.

"Just because I'm not scowling at everyone all day and drinking coffee thicker than petroleum—" He scoffed at that but I ignored it. "Doesn't mean that I wouldn't do whatever it takes to be successful." I pinned him with my most intense gaze and he stared right back. All this eye contact was freaking me the fuck out.

"So testy today, Alba Cassandra."

I swallowed down a roar of irritation while his satanic eyes danced with mirth at my fury. "Alba Serena," I reminded him for the twenty millionth time.

I ramble when I'm nervous. My ramblings are almost always overshares about my family. During my interview for this job, for some ungodly reason I word vomited for five minutes about how I was named Alba after my mom's mom and how all of my cousins where also named Alba and whenever the ten us were together it could get chaotic, then I proceeded to recite every single one of our names. Theo Anibal

Ganas's favorite game was calling me by the wrong middle name. Mostly he used names from Greek mythology, and he did it constantly, because psychologically torturing me was the only source of joy in his life.

At least my annoyance was suffusing my nerves about quitting. I should've known I'd be ready to walk out on the spot by the time I told him.

*"Anyway."* I stretched out the word long enough to turn it into a verbal eye roll. "I'd do whatever I had to if it meant I could go after my dreams, and it's not like the Ganas brand couldn't use some goodwill." That last bit I would've never uttered had I not been planning to peace out in the next couple of weeks. "The show does a lot of renos for deserving families or for nonprofits," I said pointedly. Theo *was* a very conscientious businessman, but his dad had been kind of a weasel landlord for a while. Only in the last decade, since Theo and Cecilia had taken on more of the day-to-day, had they managed to clean up the man's bad reputation. "It *could* help with the family image."

A raised eyebrow was all I got back.

"What do I have this morning?" he asked, clearly done with my hot takes. I smothered the nasty comment begging to come out and dove into my boss's very complex schedule. Twenty minutes later we were done and the last item on my to-do list for the morning was still glaring at me like a beacon on the screen.

*I quit.*

My breath started coming a little short as I prepared myself to say the words. Tremors coursing through my body as they did when I was stuck somewhere too cold without a jacket. I clenched my teeth to keep them from chattering, tapped on the Instagram icon on the home screen and glanced at my latest Bookish Boudoir post in an effort to bolster myself.

"Anything else?" The undisguised impatience in his voice made me look up.

"Mr. Ga—" The constriction in my chest was hard to speak through, but I managed. "Theo, I have something to tell you."

He shifted his body so that he was not fully facing away from me, which I took as his way of saying *go ahead*.

I opened my mouth and a cough came out. My body still trying its best to sabotage me.

"I…um. I…" I scrambled, my brain suddenly foggy. I was nauseous from nerves.

"You?" he asked impatiently, turning his hand around in a wheel, which honestly did nothing to help me focus.

*You're ready for this*, I told myself as I tried to conjure up the sketches I'd done for my upcoming makeover, a bedroom inspired by *Bridgerton*. I was already in business, I just needed to own it. And even if I was throwing up in my mouth a little this *was* the right decision. Yeah, he would be pissed, but he could find someone else to make him his copies and handle his biscotti order.

"I wanted to let you know that I have decided to…" I clamped my mouth shut, reconsidering how much information to divulge. "After I come back from my vacation…"

"Yes." He was looking less amused by the second and I could see the window about to slam shut. If I didn't get this out now, I was never going to do it. "I will only be working here for another two weeks."

I kept my eyes on the floor while I broke the news, but even if he was a rude asshole about eye contact, I actually had home training. So I looked up. I expected to encounter absolute disgust in his gaze. There was nothing that Theo Anibal despised more than having his ever-important routine disrupted; to my surprise when I looked he seemed…

pleased? Or maybe this was him pissed and I'd seen such rare displays of emotion from him that I couldn't tell them apart.

"I'm quitting," I said into the silence, the only sound in the room the whirring of the pool heater. After what felt like an eternity he nodded, crossing his legs.

"All right." His voice was almost breezy when he spoke, but other than that there was absolutely no reaction. No feigned regret, no *I wish you the best*. Not a fucking thing.

This *motherfucker*.

After all this time the least he could do was *pretend* he cared I was leaving my job. "You'll need to find another assistant." This was voiced a little more sharply; I was unable to disguise my annoyance. When he ignored me, I opened my mouth again. "I could train them. And Natasha could help with posting the job and setting up interviews while I'm out." That part I said because I was a fucking mess and probably had Stockholm Syndrome.

He looked at me for a very long time, so long that I started squirming in my chair.

"What are you doing after this?" He locked his eyes with mine and I realized then that it was a blessing that the man rarely looked at me, because I was having a hard time breathing. "Are you going to an architecture firm?" He asked it casually, but the way his icy gaze narrowed a little as he asked told me he was interested in the answer. Theo's gray eyes were flecked with brown. It was such a weird hue and at certain times of day or depending on what he wore they could be almost a honey color. And I needed to fucking focus.

I considered how much to say. It wasn't like he wouldn't find out. I was friends with Natasha, and Cecilia, his step-mom, knew about Bookish Boudoir. She'd even said she wanted me to do Zoe's room for her birthday as a surprise. They would blab about what I was doing if he asked. Not that I ever imagined Theo would give me a second thought once I was gone.

"I'm starting my own interior design firm."

If he was surprised he didn't show it. He just kept me pinned under that icy stare. How can a person be that imposing while wearing a terry cloth robe? "I've been doing some freelance jobs for the past couple of years, and it's taken off. I've saved up a few months of salary and enough to lease a workspace for a year."

He nodded, with an odd expression. Was he *happy* I was quitting?

I stopped talking and waited for his response and after a moment he stood.

"Congratulations, Alba. I wish you the best." He rose from the chair after that and without a backward glance he walked away. This was our usual routine, after the morning check-in, he'd go to shower and dress while I went down to the office to get my day started. But I just sat there stunned. Was he really not even going to say he was sorry to see me go? My stomach got that icy feeling again as I watched him stride to the elevator door, but this time it was all humiliation.

"And two weeks is fine, we can find someone by then," he said right as the doors closed while I sat there with my head swimming.

The phone buzzing in my pocket snapped me out my trance.

Julia: So?

I breathed through the constriction in my throat and tapped a message.

Alba: It's done. Get your guest room ready.

An explosion of emojis appeared on the screen and though I smiled I could feel the strain of it, like the stress on my face was going to make something snap. For the rest of the day, I didn't let myself think about why the idea of leaving a job I hated and no longer working for a man I couldn't stand made me want to cry.

# Chapter Three

## ALBA

*One week later*

"Oh my God, Alba Serena, just do it already!" my best friend and biggest instigator said over my shoulder for the tenth time in the last thirty minutes.

"Dame un momento, Julia!" I cried back with my eyes frozen on my laptop. I scanned the words again, the succinct explanation, the dates, the note letting my boss know that I was not coming back to fulfill my last two weeks like I'd promised. "I don't want to burn bridges," I whispered feebly, as I stared at the words again.

*I regret to inform you that I will not be able to return for my final two weeks. But as you said when I gave my notice, you should not have much trouble replacing me. I've been presented with an opportunity out of state that I can't pass up.*

Conflicting emotions warred in my gut. Excitement at the amazing opportunity that had landed on my lap only days after arriving in Texas and the weird sense of loss dogging me since the moment I'd told Theo I was quitting. The day and a half I'd been at the office after telling him I was leaving had been painfully awkward. So much so that I'd been practically counting the hours to get on the plane to visit Julia.

And the visit *had* been wonderfully recharging.

She'd been right that I needed distance from the grind of my life. Then, as if to confirm that perhaps I was well overdue for a full life reboot, the designer the Sturm Foundation hired for the renovation of a community children's library they were sponsoring quit at the last minute and I was offered the job. A whole new chapter of my life was ready to begin, if only I reached for it. And yet, I'd been avoiding sending this email for a full twenty-four hours.

"Do I need to pull up the two dozen DMs you got in just the last two days asking if you're going to start doing Bookish Boudoir makeovers in the DFW area?" Julia asked, clearly ready to launch all the ammunition available to her.

"No, thank you!"

I'd made a quick post when I'd gotten to Dallas asking followers to send me their ideas for Texan bookish makeovers and the floodgates had opened. I'd had no idea I had so many fans down here. For all that quitting had been harder than I imagined it would be, I was potentially sitting on a gold mine. And now with a two-month gig at Sturm's, it felt like I was really on my way.

Right then, as if she could sense that I was making major life decisions without her knowledge, my phone flashed on the desk and a photo of me and my mother appeared on the screen.

"I should tell her first."

Julia responded with her "I am this close to losing it on you" sigh. It wasn't that Julia didn't love my mother. But she also knew that my family put a lot of pressure on me and I was incapable of saying no to them. I hadn't even gotten the courage up yet to tell her that my seven-day trip to Dallas was about to turn into a short-term living situation.

"Why don't you do this email first and *then* talk to her?" Julia suggested, plucking the phone from the desk. "You know I love your family like my own, but you've put off your own needs a lot for them, Albita. And they *are* doing okay right now."

I knew she was right, but after the last ten years it was hard to shake off the feeling that there was a disaster lurking around every corner. That anything good that came our way would be promptly followed by a chaser of something horrible. Ten years earlier when I was a sophomore in college, my father had died unexpectedly, leaving my mother in a financial nightmare. It took years and me, my grandmother, and even my little brother working to help her to catch up to years of unpaid taxes and credit card debt. My mother had blindly trusted my father to manage their finances and he'd betrayed her. At nineteen I'd become her rock through all that, and in many ways I still was.

"It's hard for me, Julia, you know that." I glanced at my phone, which was still in her hand. Julia sent me one of those pitying looks I hated.

"You can take this time for yourself. You can be away from them and things won't fall apart." Intellectually I knew that Julia was right. My mom and abuela were healthy. My mom's business was stable...finally. My siblings were thriving. We were hanging in there. Still, I worried that a call with an emergency would come in the middle of the night, like it had that night ten years ago, and I wouldn't be there with my mom to help her.

"Alba..." Julia's warning tone told me she knew exactly the kind of mental math I was doing. "You are entitled to take this step because it's what you want, and it's what's best for you, without feeling guilty or selfish."

I closed my eyes and exhaled, as warring thoughts swirled around in my head. Julia was right and I also couldn't bear knowing I was a cause for my mother to worry. It was just so much easier when it wasn't me. Which was why I had turned down a full ride to Savannah College of Art and Design but wrangled a yes out of my mother for my sister to go to UCLA next year when she got in this past winter. It was also why I didn't take the job offer in Boston after grad school but pushed my little brother to take a position in Connecticut so he could be closer to his boyfriend when things between them got serious. It was the reason I'd delayed taking the plunge to start my own business for years, kept working for Theo, and living at home in case my mother needed me. My dreams were always the easiest to defer, but this time I knew I was being given an opportunity I could simply not pass up.

"Ay, okay," I grumbled, taking the phone from my friend. "I'll just tell her I'll call her later. You know she'll just keep calling until I confirm that I'm not dead in a ditch." Julia chuckled in commiseration knowing her own mother was not that much different.

Alba: Ma, I'm fine.

Reassuring my mother that I wasn't in an emergency room because I had not responded to her call within seconds was first and foremost.

Alba: I'm just finishing something up with Julia. I'll call you back in a few minutes.

Mami: I thought something had happened to you! Can you help me with the bank? I can't get into it. You know I don't know how to do it.

The flare of annoyance and guilt coursed through me, but I resisted just hitting the call button. My mother was almost sixty years old and had run her own home cleaning business for twenty years. She would have to learn the password to access her own damn money. It was time.

Alba: Ma, text Miguel, he'll help you.

Mami: Ay, I don't want to bother him for that.

Again I smothered the frustration and tapped my phone.

Alba: Ma, it's his job to do that!

After years of tag teaming my mom we'd been able to convince her to hire a bookkeeper, but she still acted like she was asking him for a favor whenever we needed him to do something.

In any other circumstance I would've just done it for her. But today it seemed critical to take care of my needs first.

Alba: I'll text Evie to help you and I'll hit you up when I'm done over here.

Without waiting for an answer I fired off a text to my sister Evangelina.

Alba: Yo! Could you please get your ass out of your gaming chair and help mom get into the bank account?

Evie: Argh! I told Mami not to text you for that shit while you're in Dallas. She's so terca!

That made me smile because though my little sister could be a brat, she'd been militant about letting me have my time in Dallas to myself. I was grateful for her willingness to help, but it was also not easy for me or for my mom to let go of the roles we each had in the family. Evie was the baby. I was the one who took care of things for everyone.

Evie: I'll go help her, but you owe me and by owe me, I mean you better show up here with a bag full of designer clothes from that fancy store you're going to work in.

Evie and my abuela already knew about the offer to renovate the library. My mother…that was another story. But first, I needed to send this email.

Alba: Greedy! Thanks for helping Mami. Luh you.

"All set?" asked Julia, who had been patiently waiting behind me while I took care of family stuff. After more than fifteen years of friendship, she knew the drill.

"Yep." Finally I turned back toward the monitor. "I would be pissed if this was how my assistant decided to end her time working for me." Without needing to turn around I knew Julia's scoff probably came with a matching eye roll.

"You gave that man your all for the entire time you worked for him, Alba. You don't owe Theo Ganas a damn thing." I didn't. I really didn't, then why the hell was I was hesitating? "Babe, it's okay to feel conflicted."

"It's not that," I immediately retorted, shutting down what I knew would come next.

Julia was convinced that I had feelings for the man. I mean, *obviously* I had pants feelings for him. Who wouldn't? Theo was physically perfect, but just because I *occasionally* had fantasies of him licking me until I cried for mercy on that pool deck, didn't mean I had *feelings*. Because falling for a man who couldn't remember my name and barely looked me in the eye would be fucked up and sad. Truly dumb. And I was a lot of things, but I was not dumb.

Click. Send.

"Done," I announced, rushing to stand up before I was tempted to hit the undo button.

"Yes, bitch," Julia cried as she wrapped me up in a bear hug twerk combo. "Fuck, I'm so excited for you, babe. Bookish Boudoir is going to be the biggest thing in interior design." I was still a little dazed and the nausea just would not quit, but seeing Julia this happy for me did let excitement for the future edge out the ball of anxiety lodged in my gut a little bit. My best friend let go of me after a couple more squeezes only to cup her mouth with her hands and bellow out, "Latinas in the motherfucking house. Bookish Boudoir is about to put Insta Karens on notice."

"You're a mess!" I cackled as we grinned at each other.

"I'm happy for you, friend," Julia said, more soberly, as tears clogged my throat. "And I'm a little selfishly glad that I get to have you here for a couple months."

"Dammit, Julia, you're gonna make me cry!" I blustered, now feeling that little spark of excitement roaring to life and burning off the nervous jitters in the process. Who knew what else Dallas could have in store for me? "And speak for yourself, only having your bossy ass to hang out with is going to be exhausting," I lied, and she gave another kiss on the cheek as we walked to her living room.

It *would* be good to have her close again, even if she was really the only person I knew here. In New York I had people everywhere. My mom, my siblings, my cousins, my tias. They were around the block or only a few stops away. But if I was honest, in the last few years I hardly saw them. I was so busy all the time that the friends who used to call me on Fri-

day nights had eventually gotten tired of getting shut down.
Some of it was family stuff. A lot of it had been work. And
though I'd rather cut my tongue off than admit it, I'd miss it.
I already missed him, even in the few days I'd been in Dallas. Which only told me how sorry the state of my life was.

The doorbell rang while I brooded and Julia perked up
in that way she did when she had something up her sleeve.

"They're here!"

They're? Who was *they're*?

I didn't have to wonder for long, because in the next moment Julia opened the door and the entire crew of her Dallas friends walked in the door.

"It's official: we get Alba for the next two months!"

"Fuck yeah, my new work homie!" Dani, the Cuban-Ghanaian bona fide Instagram celebrity, was the first to say
hello. Dani was fancy as fuck and was a full-on Manhattan
prep school kid. He leaned in to buss me on the cheek, a
bottle of chilled Veuve in each hand.

"Dani always understands the assignment," Julia said happily as she took the bubbly from him. Next I got tackled by
José and Tariq.

"Did you quit on that asshole?" José asked giddily before
high-fiving me when I answered with a sharp nod. "I love
that journey for you," he yelled, making the whole room
bust up.

"Technically I had already quit."

"Yeah you had, kicked that dead-end job to the curve,
future lifestyle mogul over here!" Tariq called from across
the room. Both Tariq and José were Bronx boys but the two
could not be more different. While José was short and lean
and always dressed in colorful prints, Tariq was tall, *very* muscular and wore fits I referred to as Uptown Chic. The boy
loved a Yankees hat and Air Force Ones combo in match-

ing colors. They were obviously crazy about each other, but
as far as anyone knew they were just friends.

"Salome," I called as the one person I knew from New
York came closer.

"Girl, I've been wanting you to quit that job since the day
you told me about that asshole's coffee." Salome and I hadn't
been exactly close, but I'd known her from my time at Columbia and we'd always gotten along. When I heard she'd
taken an academic job in Dallas I told her to look up Julia.

I smiled at her words, but again that weird cold spot
bloomed in my stomach. It was almost the feeling I got when
someone talked smack about my relatives. Even if it was the
same stuff I gave them shit for, I still didn't like people who
weren't family talking about them. Which was crazy, because
Theo's coffee obsession was ridiculous and also why was I
getting all defensive on his behalf? I needed to get a fucking grip. But Salome wasn't new and when she pulled back
I could almost see her antennae twitching.

"Hmm…what's with the droopy face, Ma?" She whispered it, as the others huddled in the kitchen pouring bubbly.

I lifted a shoulder, feeling weirdly exposed.

"I am excited, it's just…" I trailed off.

"You're just going to miss that sexy, rude motherfucker
even though he was a nightmare to work for?" José finished
for me, as he handed me a champagne flute. I side-eyed him
and took a gulp, then slumped on the couch.

"Girl, we are not judging," Salome said, throwing me a
bone. "Whom amongst us has not gotten overly attached to
something pretty that wasn't exactly good for us?" José threw
up praise hands like he was at Sunday service.

"Except most people at least get to enjoy the offerings," I
blurted out before I could stop myself. Julia and Tariq joined
us on the couch, and my best friend put her arm around my

shoulder. "I don't even like him, why am I all guilty and weird about ghosting him?"

"Because you, like all of us here, were trained to do your job, even if it's killing you. We don't know how to walk away from a steady check even when doors are opening for us somewhere else." All the heads in the room bobbed in agreement. "It's the immigrant thing, baby."

It was true. I had hesitated to take the plunge with Bookish Boudoir for much longer than I should've not just because of Theo Ganas's eight-pack. Still, I hadn't expected to feel...sad.

"It wasn't all bad," I surprised myself by saying out loud. Not talking about it wouldn't make it less true, and there *were* things I would miss. But before I disgraced myself by listing all two of Theo's redeeming qualities, the buzzing in my pocket made me jump off the couch. "Shit, I forgot to call my mom." I slid my phone out of my pocket, then I saw the number on the screen and tossed the thing on the rug like it had turned into a hissing snake.

"It's *him*," I whispered frantically, pointing at the offending device.

"Don't pick up!" Salome yelled at the same time that Tariq offered, "I'll talk to him!"

It was true that I didn't have to pick it up. I'd said what I'd said. I *was* done with this job and with Theo Ganas forever. But three years of being conditioned to respond to the man's calls instantly were not going to go away because I was having my boss babe moment.

I summoned strength and tapped on the phone screen with Julia's "Don't do it, Alba!" trailing behind me.

"Hello," I said, a little too breathless for having only walked the twenty yards to Julia's home office.

"Where are you?"

When I heard the voice on the other end I had to pull

the phone away from my ear and look at the screen again to verify that this was in fact my former boss. Theo's usual tone of bored indifference was completely gone. He sounded like he'd guzzled down a pint of gasoline before he called me. In three years, I had never heard this man sound more than mildly annoyed at pretty much anything. And right now, on this call, he was straight up shouting. But I had nothing to lose and my true self broke through the usual pushover façade I used with him.

"Sorry…" I muttered, in a thick Dominican accent. "No habla pendejo."

A mighty growl came through the line a second later, and I'm not ashamed to admit I got a little wet. "Alba Serena, I am not playing games with you."

Where was all this even coming from? I knew Theo didn't like to lose, but the man had two assistants who could take care of his day-to-day while he found someone to replace me.

"Oh, *now* you know my name," I retorted, which only elicited more furious sounds.

"Of course I know your name," he bit out, and I could almost hear his molars grinding in agony. "Are you really going to end your time here with *an email*?" I frowned at the way he said it. Like he was offended. But I knew that couldn't be it, since he'd barely blinked when I told him I was quitting. Theo didn't care I was leaving. This was just about his control freak ways. I had changed the plan on him and he couldn't cope.

"Yes, I am," I confirmed, enunciating every syllable. I was pissed now, his recriminations burning through my guilt like a ball of fire. "I left everything in order for the next person and you have Natasha and Mike to help while you find someone, which you told me should be *super* easy." Yeah, I was still mad about that, and so what if I let him hear it. I'd taken pains to never let him see how his indifference got to me. But I didn't care anymore. "Besides, I don't know what you're so mad about, you accepted my resignation, I'm just ending earlier than expected."

He was silent for so long I thought he'd ended the call. When he spoke again that weird hole in my stomach opened up again.

"You didn't say you were *leaving* New York." Was he—? No…nope, absolutely not going there. Deluding myself that my quitting meant something to this man other than being an inconvenience was going to take my mind places it had no business going. Still, he sounded so off.

"I wasn't planning to," I admitted. "I was going to rent a work share space in Astoria, but then a great short-term opportunity came up." For a second I hesitated. This was all so weird. In three years this man had not expressed any interest in my life and now he sounded on the verge of losing his mind. But what could he do? I was like ten states away. "I have an opportunity to renovate a children's library, and I'm going to take it."

The door opened while I pressed the phone to my ear waiting for his response. Probably Julia coming to make sure I wasn't booking my flight back to New York.

"How much?" Theo croaked, as I held up a finger to my best friend's questioning look.

"What?"

"How much do you want to come back to work?"

Pure unfiltered fury exploded in my chest.

"Excuse me?" I made myself infuse those two words with as big a *fuck you* as I could relay over the phone. "I didn't do this so you'd offer me more money," I said through gritted teeth. "I know this might be hard for you to believe but getting you coffee is not exactly my life's goal."

"If you want to do a renovation, I have jobs I can give you. I could—"

"No, Theo," I interrupted in the sharpest tone I'd ever used on anyone. "I don't want to work for you or for anybody. I want to start my own company." Air filled my lungs when I spoke the words, and realized I'd never said this out loud. Even though it was exactly what I'd been working toward, I hadn't voiced it. Not to myself or anyone else. What Theo didn't get, was that this wasn't just about me not wanting to be his PA—I wanted something that was mine. Something *I* got to call the shots in.

"This library renovation can help me get visibility for Bookish Boudoir," I explained, and when he didn't respond I kept going. "It could even lead to a partnership with some lifestyle brands. Get my name out there as a bespoke interior designer. Can you do that?"

He was probably locking his jaw so hard it was sealed together by now. Theo Ganas did not like to hear the word *no*, and I was kind of digging this newfound freedom to deploy it in his direction as much as I fucking wanted.

"Is that what this is about, exposure?" He said the word like it was a brand-new concept I'd just come up with.

"Listen, Theo," I said, before he could say more shit to make me mad. "I have to go. My sister will bring by my work phone and keys this week. Good luck with everything." I heard him taking in a breath, probably to try and wear me down with another round of yelling, but I ended the call before he could.

"What was that?" Julia asked, her eyes locked on my phone like it was an explosive.

"*That* was the heir to the Ganas real estate empire calling me to ask how much money it would take to get me back to New York."

"Coño, that comemierda," Julia said, then twisted her mouth to the side.

"I said no, Julia." My best friend opened her mouth, likely to trash-talk my boss a little more, but seemed to think better of it.

"Good for you." She pulled my hand and we walked back out in silence to where the rest of the crew was imbibing more comped bubbly courtesy of Dani. "I know it's a lot but you made the right decision," she told me in an attempt to reassure. I knew she was right, and still that queasy feeling wouldn't quit.

"It's...just, yeah. It's an ending."

"Endings can be scary," José said, and leaned over to squeeze my hand.

"But you have an exciting beginning here," Tariq, who I had already labeled the designated optimist, said as he clinked his glass with Salome's.

And it was, and I was going to make the most of it. This job for Sturm's could be the chance I'd been waiting for, and I would do whatever it took to keep it. And if my heart felt a little bruised at the idea of not seeing Theo Ganas again, then that was just one more thing that I was going to have to leave out to dry in the Texas sun.

# Chapter Four

## THEO

"Why are you not taking my calls?" my father demanded before bursting into my office without so much as a hello. The man was supposedly retired but insisted on driving from the back seat on everything relating to the company I was technically in charge of now. In the mood I was currently in this interruption was bound to turn into a shouting match.

"I am not at your beck and call, Dad. I am busy." I still had my phone in my hand, though it had to be at least a half hour since Alba informed me she was staying in Dallas and I could go to hell.

I was scattered, reeling from the realization I'd lost her before I even had a chance to tell her how I felt. I'd let my frustration get the best of me and blown the first interaction we'd had without me being her boss hanging over our heads. I'd had the chance to show her I saw who she was, that I respected what she was attempting to do for herself, for her career, and instead resorted to the tactics I loved to quietly judge my father for. The last thing I needed was his entitled ass coming here to make demands.

Alba's words from that day when she'd given me her notice still rang in my ears. In the time she'd worked for me she'd occasionally slide in an observation, but she'd never been as candid as that morning. Her canny insight about my indifference to the legacy my father had handed me wasn't an unfair one, but it had stung. I'd been raised to do my duty, to be grateful for the empire my father had built from the ground up and handed over for me to run, even if the work left me numb. And it had been easy to use that as an excuse not to question the apathy I felt about my work.

My needs or my wants had never been part of the equation. I'd done everything my parents had asked of me. My mother pushing me to be the best swimmer, the best student, the best son so that my father would see she'd given him the perfect heir to his empire and stick around. In the end, none of it had mattered. He'd left her and then she'd left me.

I'd always accepted their selfish expectations as a fact. Never questioned their insensitive demands of me. I'd been numb to my life for years. Right until a curly-haired tempest with a mouthwatering ass walked into my office to interview for the PA position I reluctantly agreed to fill. Alba Duarte barreled into my world with combustible energy. Ready, eager, launching herself into things in that unflappable way of hers, and for the first time since I could remember I'd *wanted*. From the moment I set eyes on her, I'd craved her.

But I knew my place and I knew hers and I would never betray my position or my power just because I was attracted to my assistant. She'd said she would stay for a year, and so I told myself I could wait. I'd let her get what she needed from the job and when I was no longer her boss I'd tell her how I felt. A year turned into three and still, I waited. Until I finally had my chance, and I'd blown it.

"Are you listening to me, Theo?" My father barked, snatching me back to attention. I prided myself on my ability to keep a cool head. Almost fifteen years of competitive swimming had taught me to never allow my emotions to hinder my ability to perform. Emotions were only a reminder that I was letting myself be distracted. A trigger forcing me to refocus. But right now my head was in a fog. I wanted to run out of this office, get on a plane to Dallas and bring her back so we could start over.

"The Valle Mar lawyer just emailed; they've got cold feet." A frisson of concern traveled up my spine at the way he said it. When I glanced up, he looked...worried. "Sounds like they found out about Hunter Gardens."

"Fuck," I bit out, dread pooling in my stomach. No wonder my father looked like he was about to puke. And even though my mind and body were raging at me to get the fuck out of this office and go find Alba, my need to appease my father was very hard to break.

Valle Mar was our first big project outside of residential buildings. It was a deal with a Costa Rican company to build four environmentally friendly luxury hotels on the Pacific coast of the Central American country. Cecilia and I had courted the family who owned Valle Mar—and the beach-front land where the hotels would be built—for a year before they agreed to hear our pitch. They'd turned down some of the biggest developers in Europe and the States, but my step-mom and I had leaned in hard to our Latinx roots and the fact that Ganas was also a family business and managed to woo them. We were only a month away from closing the deal. It was my—and Cecilia's—baby. The first big negotiation we'd done without my father in the lead. Except it seemed that his shady landlord past was coming back to haunt us.

"What do you mean?" I asked, as I forced myself to release my phone from my hand before I cracked it.

"They want the official report on what happened. They want the paperwork from the settlement." My father's shoulders slumped and I could see there was more bad news coming. "They're worried if any of this resurfaces when we announce the deal that it could affect their brand."

I ran my hands over my hair as I tried to smother my annoyance at my father. It had taken me and Cecilia years to put my father's shitty past dealings behind us, but there was always something that cropped back up. Hunter Gardens was one of Ganas Corp's first properties. My father's business partner had managed it. It was a twenty-unit building in Woodside that had gone up in flames when a space heater a family was using to keep their apartment warm had caught fire in the night. It was bad enough that they'd been callous enough to let those families go without proper heating in the middle of winter, but it came out that the tenants had been filing dozens of complaints with the city about the lack of heating that were never addressed.

It had been a huge fire in the middle of February and though everyone had gotten out without incident, the families had been traumatized. My father parted ways with his old business partner after that and settled with the families to repay them for their losses. But he also acquired a reputation as a negligent landlord that almost twenty years later he still couldn't fully shake.

"This is going to take some finessing," I bit out as my mind reeled. This was the last thing I needed right now.

All I wanted was to get on a flight and go tell Alba how I felt about her. But I knew that would get me nowhere. She was there to make a go of her career and it would be selfish and terrible of me to distract her with my bullshit. I needed a plan. I needed a strategy, but there was no way I could just fuck off to chase after Alba and leave Cecilia on the hook for whatever disaster was brewing.

"Did you hear me, malaka?" my father called, annoyed, which only made me angrier.

"No, I'm not listening," I roared, irritated at his tone when it was his fault we were even in this situation. "I'm trying to think of how we fix this. Did you tell Cecilia?"

"No, not yet."

"Dad, I'm not talking about this anymore without Cecilia in the room—"

My father's mouth scrunched up like he'd just bitten into a lemon. The man adored my stepmother. I had no doubt about that. For years she had been his most trusted advisor for the business, but the moment he retired at fifty-five and she expressed interest in running things with me, he'd turned into some regressive, antiquated asshole. I imagined it had to do with the fact that my stepmother was twenty years younger than him and he felt insecure in some ways. But Cecilia loved my father and he was not helping himself by not giving her the place she deserved in the business. Hell, Cecilia wanted all this a hell of a lot more than I did.

*Again* Alba's words buzzed in my ears. What if I could walk away from all this?

"Did someone say my name?" Cecilia asked, her impeccable timing saving me from the fight that was already brewing between me and my old man. She strode in on her ever-present three-inch stilettos, dressed a little more casual than her usual today in designer jeans and a red sweater.

"Hey, Papi," she said happily when she noticed my father standing against the glass wall in my office—I was about to make the gagging sound I typically did whenever she called my father Daddy but the moment she got a good look at him she stopped in her tracks. "What's wrong?"

I winced and my father sighed, but I was not even entertaining the idea of keeping her in the dark. My stepmother was only about five years older than I was, which honestly was fucking weird, but I respected her more than almost anyone in the world, other than Alba. She'd met my dad when I was sixteen and she was twenty-one and now, at thirty-two and thirty-seven she was my best friend. The one who knew all my secrets, including that I had feelings for my assistant. Although at the moment her expression was definitely not motherly; she knew something was up and that she was out of the loop. Cecilia did not tolerate being kept out of her own business.

"Valle Mar heard about Hunter Gardens and they're worried it will damage their reputation if it gets out," I explained, looking at my father dead in the eye.

"Everyone got compensated," my father grumbled. "Am I ever going to get out from under this?" A flash of resentment burned in my chest at his whining. It was true that he'd made sure people were taken care of *after the fact*, but if he'd done what he was supposed to in the first place it would've never happened.

"How do we fix it?" Cecilia asked, taking my father's hand. I could see how just that gesture bolstered him. That no matter how much he tried to be the big macho real estate mogul, Cecilia's love, her strength, was indispensable for him. A niggle of yearning flickered in me as I saw the way he looked down at her, like he'd fight his own selfishness every day not to let her down. "We'll figure it out, baby," she whispered.

"Can you two please…" I pleaded when she leaned into him and he grabbed her ass. Cecilia laughed. But she got a good look at me and frowned. "What else is wrong with you? Did you talk to—"

I was not getting into the conversation I'd just had with Alba in front of my father, so I just shook my head and glared at my dad. "We need to do damage control. Figure out a way to get some good PR lined up for when we announce, something splashy enough to calm the Valle Mar people."

The intercom to my office blared as my father leveled me with one of his "don't you dare talk to me that way" stares. Typically that went a long way to mollify me, but today I resented not being able to prioritize my personal crisis because Ganas Corp always came first.

"Mr. Ganas, it's Sarah Billings from Streamflix."

"Not again," I said with annoyance. "When are they going to give up on this? They just called like a week ago," I growled over the speaker to Mike.

"Yes," he answered meekly. Unlike Alba, my other assistants did not sass me when I was pissed. "They wanted to talk about a new project they're filming in the next month." Next month? Was this a joke? "She said it's a limited series." I rolled my eyes, ready to say no again, when Mike offered an uncustomary opinion. "If you don't mind my saying, sir, she sounds very interested in talking to you. The location is..." He trailed off like he was reading something. "Dallas?" He read the word like he was having a hard time comprehending why anyone would leave the tristate area for any reason.

"Just let them know that I don't..." I froze in midsentence as my brain finally registered the one word I'd missed in my rush to say no. "Did you just say Dallas?" I asked, recalling the challenge in Alba's voice as she'd let me know what she had in hand and what it would take for her to come back to me. A reality show where she could show her skills to the world, where millions could see her designs—that would bring her more exposure than anything she was doing for the Sturm Foundation.

I turned to my father, who was looking at me with that perennial impatient irritation of his, and everything locked into place in my mind. A reality show that gave renovations to worthy causes could be the exact kind of PR we could use after the Valle Mar announcement.

"Sir, are you there? Should I tell her you're not available?" Mike asked, snatching me out of the barrage of thoughts running through my head. Immediately I picked up the receiver, holding a finger up at my father when he opened his mouth.

"Actually, Mike," I said, winking at my stepmother, "put her through. I'd like to talk to her."

"What are you scheming?" Cecilia asked, while my father looked between us, eyes scrunched in confusion. My heart raced as I remembered the ravenous glint in Alba's eyes when she told me that given the chance to be on a show she'd do whatever was necessary.

"Doing a pro bono renovation would be an excellent way to convince Valle Mar that a deal with Ganas would improve their brand, not damage it." My stepmom's eye glinted with approval, but my dad didn't look convinced.

"Tell me more," Cecilia encouraged.

"What is this about?" my father finally asked.

"Streamflix has been after me to be in one of their reality renovation shows. I've never gone for it, but now—" I could almost see the gears turning in my father's head.

"We could use this for some good publicity," I clarified.

My phone buzzed again and I hit the speaker. "Miss Billings, good to hear from you, would you give me a second?" I asked briskly.

"Of course," the woman said, sounding promisingly pleased to actually have me on the phone.

I pressed the mute button and pinned my father with eyes that I knew were the same exact shade of gray as his. "Doing this will almost certainly get us enough goodwill to make Valle Mar happy. But I have conditions." My father *did not* like being told what to do. He also knew this could likely save our ass.

"Fine."

I ignored the grudging tone in his voice and turned my attention to Cecilia, who was looking at me with a surprised expression. I was never this stern with my father. Him being the only parent I'd had since my mother had taken off... I had my fair share of daddy issues. But this was happening on my terms.

"I will call the shots, they are interested in *me*, you get no say on how I do this." He opened his mouth to protest, but I shot him down again. "That's not all. I'm probably going to be out of town while filming and I want Cecilia, *and only Cecilia*, to run point for Valle Mar. She's done most of the heavy lifting for this deal anyway, and when I come back..."

I could see my father's molars grinding under the skin, but he nodded.

"I want to explore doing some solo projects and I'd like for Cecilia to head up the day-to-day." My stepmother liked to pretend like my father's bullshit didn't get to her, but I could see the eagerness in her eyes.

"We'll have to discuss this further," my father offered in place of a yes. "I'm not getting bullied by you." I moved my hand like I was about to hang up the phone and he threw up his hands. "Fine, if Cecilia wants more responsibility that is fine with me," he conceded like he didn't know it was the right thing to do. "But you have to be back here in a month for the signing." I knew not to expect him to just let me have something without making demands of his own. "I don't want absolutely anything jeopardizing this, Theodoro Anibal."

"I'll be here for the signing," I agreed, and Cecilia's smile got wider with every word. In my head I was already laying things out. Streamflix was eager enough to have me that they'd likely agree to bring on a designer I suggested. I just had to sell them on the idea. I could do that. I was usually a very effective negotiator…unless said negotiating was with my former PA.

I hit the button for the speaker phone as my father and stepmother slid out of the room. "Miss Billings, Theo Ganas here."

"I am surprised you took my call." She got the dig in, but she didn't sound mad.

"Timing is everything, Miss Billings," I told her in my smoothest tone. "I'm all ears today." She laughed, but again it was friendly. I relaxed. And just as only minutes ago the idea of doing a reality TV show was repulsive, now I was willing to say anything I needed to in order to make this happen.

"I know that we've offered you more traditional renovation shows before, but this might be something you may be more amenable to. It's a new format where we have celebrities host a renovation for a nonprofit in more of a documentary style. The designer and the host, that would be you," she clarified, "walk us through the process in four episodes. We do interviews with the communities benefiting from the project as well as with the staff and leaders of the agency. It's much less scripted than other iterations we've done and the filming timeline is much shorter. We expect the whole thing to take about four to six weeks."

"Interesting," I bluffed, like I hadn't been ready to say yes the moment she'd opened her mouth.

"You would have to work with the designer of course, there would be a lot of conversations between the two of you regarding vision for the projects and behind the scenes stuff. But the format is not nearly as involved or, frankly, as dramatic as in our other shows. The story is more about helping the community and the larger program than the hosts."

"Wouldn't you want a local builder?" I asked, genuinely curious.

"We have one, but we'll rely on your expertise in construction to relay the information to the audience."

"Essentially I'm there to look pretty and talk shop in lay terms," I joked, but Miss Billings was ready.

"We do need to lure in viewers with a bit of star power, Mr. Ganas."

I appreciated that she was not trying to bullshit me.

"And this would be filmed in Dallas," I prompted.

"Yes," she delivered the word very quietly, like she almost wanted me to miss where it was I needed to go.

"I'll do it."

Miss Billings sighed loudly, which was exactly where I wanted her, but before she started popping champagne I delivered the deal-breaker. "*If* I can pick the designer and the project." My heart slammed against my ribs waiting to hear Miss Billings's reaction to my demand, then she answered.

"All right, what did you have in mind?"

I sat down and filled her in.

"So," Cecilia asked moments after I ended my call with Sarah Billings.

"They went for it," I told her. "Looks like I will be going to Dallas to film a limited series for Streamflix. I need to be there in a week."

"Dallas…" She said the word like it was the first time she'd ever heard it, then crossed her arms over her chest and leaned in on the chair. "Now tell me what else is going on before your father barges in here." Her expression softened and I knew something feelings related was about to happen. "And thank you for before."

"You should be running this whole thing," I said, honestly.

"You're right, I should be, but stop stalling and tell me what this is really about." She spoke with the certainty of someone who knew too well that unless there was a life-or-death reason I would never do something like this willingly.

"What makes you think there's anything else going on?" I hedged like she couldn't see right through my bullshit. "I'm just as committed as you are to see this Valle Mar thing happen. This was a good and timely solution." I gestured at the phone that had just sealed my plan for the next two months.

"Theodoro Anibal, do you think I was born yesterday? I know Alba's in Dallas, pendejo." Lesser men would've crumbled under that sweet as honey accent of my stepmother's but I had fifteen years of building up resistance to it. "So what's the deal."

"Alba's not coming back," I admitted, and instantly that constriction in my chest returned. It was like she'd taken all the air to Texas with her. "She sent me an email this morning saying she was staying down there. Apparently she got a job offer and...she's not interested in coming back." Cecilia's expression went from concern, to realization, to something very akin to satisfaction.

"Good for her."

"Thanks for being on my team, damn."

My stepmother didn't even blink. "Oh, shut up, Theo. That girl should've left this job ages ago. You've seen what she does with those bedrooms, she's a genius and she couldn't wait around for you to get your dumb ass together."

"That's not very nice."

"Pssh." She waved off my comment dismissively. "Who needs nice with tits like this."

"Please stop," I pleaded sincerely, and she just laughed at me.

"Seriously though. I told you so many times to just let her know how you felt."

I pinched the bridge of my nose. Not this shit again.

"I could not just start hitting on my assistant like some

old creep." As soon as I said it I realized my poor choice
of words, since Cecilia met my father while serving as his
translator during one of his business trips to Havana. But
she waved me off.

"Please don't start. Your father couldn't resist all this," she
asserted, waving a hand over her torso. I could only shake
my head. And she was a beautiful woman: dark brown skin,
a riot of ebony curls and a regal air about her that turned
heads. But to me she was the mother I wish I'd had.

"You know I was waiting for the right moment with
Alba," I explained for the hundredth time. "I didn't want to
make things weird in her last two weeks here. She was finally ready to start her business and having me try to get all
in there and be like all 'hey I'm obsessed with you' would've
definitely made shit weird." I sighed and dropped onto the
couch in my office with my head in my hands. "I had a whole
plan. I was going to wait until her last day then call her to
ask her out to dinner. Start slow. Romance her," I pointed
out, since she was the one who always told me women liked
being wooed. "*Court* her."

"Well, you fucked that up good." This was accompanied
by dramatic click of her tongue.

"Gee thanks, Mom," I deadpanned, but didn't argue because she wasn't wrong.

"So what are you going to do when you get to Dallas?
Other than save our asses for this Valle Mar thing?" Cecilia
prompted with a flurry of her hand.

I didn't even have to think about it. The words formed in
my brain of their own volition.

"I'm going to get her back."

# *Chapter Five*

## ALBA

"Maybe you can bring me back one of those vaqueros?" my abuela suggested unhelpfully as I drove into the parking lot of the Sturm Foundation for a meeting with Mitzy and Muffy Sturm, the co-CEOs.

"Mimita, I don't think I'm going to have time to go cowboy or cowgirl hunting while I'm here." I stressed the *cowgirl* part because although my grandmother had been unwaveringly supportive when I came out, she and my mom sometimes conveniently forgot that me bringing a girl home was also an option.

"Maybe you can call back that potro you worked for and get yourself a millionaire instead." My heart did that flippy thing where it dropped to my feet at the mention of Theo. Yeah, because apparently Theo, who once asked me why I couldn't just sleep at the office on the days I worked for him, had driven to my mother's house with the small box of stuff that I'd left on my desk, which he could've given to Evie when she dropped off my phone and keys.

"I don't have any business left with Theo Ganas. He was my employer, and now he's not, so there is no reason for us to talk ever again." I pressed a hand to my stomach; that nausea was probably from having two granola bars for lunch.

"That boy looked like he thought his business with you was far from over, Albita," my grandmother whispered in my ear with the same exact tone she used when she was catching me up on the latest drama of her favorite telenovela. Apparently, he also tried to interrogate my grandmother about my situation in Dallas and when I'd be back. Probably because he couldn't figure out when to scratch his ass without me putting it on his schedule.

"Mimita, I don't want to talk about Theo Ganas, that's old news." The mere mention of the man's name made our last conversation pop back into my head. Just like it had ten times a day since we'd talked. A confusing cocktail of regret and satisfaction churning inside me as I recalled the yearning in his voice. If I didn't know the man was a cold-stone bastard I'd almost believe he missed me. I forced myself to re-direct. Today was too important to get bogged down by my confusing feelings about Theo. "I called to ask if you have someone to take you to do the compra today."

"Yes, querida. Your little sister said she'll take me after school today."

"Oh," I said, surprised. I'd mentioned it to Evie and was certain she'd flake on it, but it seemed she had it under control. "That's good." Every Thursday—my day off—I'd take my grandmother on her tour of every food retailer in Corona, Queens, aka grocery shopping. My abuela didn't just got to the ShopRite and get her food. Oh no. She had a place for the meat, another for the fish, the Korean market for the produce, the Dominican spot for the sazón, and don't even get me started on the expeditions required to purchase paper towels and cleaning products. I loathed food shopping with every fiber in my being, but it was also my quality time with her. It felt odd to know that my sister was now going to do it with her. It was incredibly dumb to feel slighted by the fact that my family seemed to be doing okay in my absence, but I was all over the place these days. Still, I was glad that my sister would take her. Evie was on track for the three-jobs-plus-school life and I knew making time to take Mimita shopping was likely costing her a shift somewhere. I should text her and ask her how she was doing.

"Mija, you still there?" my abuela asked as I fretted about my sister.

"I'm here, just thinking."

"Querida, don't worry," my grandmother niggled. She knew better than anyone that worrying was my only and favorite hobby. "We're doing fine. We miss you, but I want you to have fun over there without worrying about us. We have things under control until you get back, meanwhile don't spend all day working, Mija." Her voice turned salacious then, and I braced for it. "There's always time for a little fun between the sheets."

"Mimita! Oh my God!" I yelled, horrified as I powered off the car.

"Que fue?" she asked all innocent like she hadn't just said what she'd said. "What's all that youth good for if you're not going to let a man, or a lady—" I grinned at that, because my grandmother was the fucking GOAT "—give you a night or two to remember."

Yeah, I needed to get off this call.

"Okay, Mimita, I need to go find some bleach for my brain now, so I'll talk to you later."

"Ay tan dramatica. If I hadn't let your abuelito have his way with me, you wouldn't exist, niña."

Kill me now.

"Bye! Love you." I took a couple of minutes to gather my thoughts after that horrifying interlude as I sat in my rental.

Ciara's "Level Up" came on the speakers, which went a long way to helping me get in the right mindset.

No, I had not done any tumbling between the sheets since I'd gotten to Dallas. For one, my living situation didn't exactly allow for that. I wasn't going to bring some rando back to Rocco and Julia's place. I also hadn't felt like it. But that had also been the case these past three years. I hadn't been exactly celibate, but sex had always been complicated for me. Though I enjoyed the flirting and the building up to it, once things got going I could never quite shut my brain off. Even with my ex Nicole, who I'd really liked, things had been more about companionship than "burning up the sheets." Julia thought it was because I was a control freak, which was fair enough.

I'd just never found anyone who could keep my attention long enough to make me really lose myself in the pleasure. I could bring myself off like a pro, but with a partner I couldn't let go. When Julia started seeing Rocco she'd tell me about the way he talked to her during sex, how he would say the filthiest shit to her all while making her feel cherished. Like she brought out the most primal parts of him. The protector and the aggressive lover. I'd never had that, and I knew a lot of it was that I couldn't fully trust anyone to give me what I needed. Hell, the only person who got me out of my head—with rage—was Theo, and that was definitely not the makings of a healthy relationship. And none of this ruminating on my nonexistent sex life was going to get me ready for the extremely important meeting I was now risking being late for.

I got my ass in gear.

"Okay, Alba Serena, you can this. You are a fucking boss," I recited as I took stock of my reflection in the glass doors to the foundation. Beat was on point. Eyelashes luscious, winged liner perfect. That smoky eye flawless. Nude lipstick making a statement. My fit today was head to toe Sturm's employee discount greatness. It screamed *I'm a classy bitch, and I can handle business.*

I breezed through the reception, waving at the receptionist who knew me by this point, and hopped on the elevator. Within minutes I was in front of Mitzy and Muffy Sturm. I fucking loved those two. They definitely gave off that "kooky rich lady" vibe, but that was just window dressing—they were sharp as hell. It was a bit surreal how much they looked alike. They even shared an office at the foundation. It was an enormous room overlooking a community garden they'd built. The designer in me was also in awe of how they'd done the space.

The left side where Mitzy's desk sat was very minimalist and modern. It was done up in sleek dark wood in a mid-century aesthetic. Jewel tones in blues and greens for the upholstery. A few touches of gold at the base of a lamp or a clock on the wall contrasted beautifully with the walnut tones of the furniture. It was understated and luxurious all at once. Meanwhile Muffy's space was an homage to the Southwest. She had used Talavera tiles for an accent wall, her armchairs were covered in a caramel leather that felt like butter to the touch, and a gorgeous Pendleton rug sat under a hand-carved Texas live oak coffee table. Her desk, she'd informed me, was an heirloom that their maternal grandfather commissioned from a furniture maker from Tlaquepaque, Guadalajara, in the '50s. Very much exuding cowboy culture, while still managing to look refined and elegant. Such different approaches should've clashed, but the styles blended together seamlessly. Proof that if you had taste and enough money you could pull anything off.

"Darling, you look lovely today," Mitzy said, reaching to pat my hand as soon as I walked in.

"Thank you." These ladies' fashion game was next level, and I preened at the compliment. Mitzy was in a killer emerald green pantsuit today. The slacks were wide legged, almost palazzos, with a crease I could slice cheese with. Her sister, who always dressed in colors matching her twin's, was rocking a vintage Dior sheath in chartreuse.

I'd made sure that I looked the part today. It had not taken long in Texas to realize that the usual "gym chic" I sported most days working for Theo would not cut it at the Sturm Foundation. Today, because my legs were deal closers, I'd gone for a skirt and top instead of a pantsuit. An ivory Kobi Halperin pintuck blouse with an open collar that made my boobs look amazing, tucked into a Dries Van Noten skirt in a bright pink, blue and turquoise palette. My nude peep-toe Louboutins on my feet. To finish off the lewk, my "stunt on 'em" Chloe bag—purchased at full price on Fifth Avenue because that's what a bad bitch does on occasion—looped on the crook of my elbow and I was ready for this.

"So shall I give you an update?" I said after a round of kisses and "hey y'alls." But instead of the yes I was expecting, Mitzy and Muffy did that thing where they seemed to be communicating telepathically and then turned to me beaming.

"We would love to hear it later, but right now we have incredible news to share with you!" Mitzy clapped excitedly while Muffy shook her shoulders like she was auditioning for the role of the Chiquita Banana lady. The twins were usually pretty bubbly, but this was straight up ecstatic levels of excitement. I got excited too because if I knew anything it was that rich people only got this hype about money, so I clapped along hoping that meant my paycheck situation was about to get an upgrade.

"We've been approached by a network to do a four-part limited series about the renovation," Mitzy informed me.

"And—" they exchanged another one of those long looks, but this time it was a little more guarded "—they specifically asked about you." For the life of me I couldn't stop my head from whipping to the side or my eyes from narrowing at them when I heard that.

"They asked about *me*?" I jabbed a finger to my own chest while I attempted to get my wild-eyed stare under control. Something was up. I could feel it.

There was a chance someone at Streamflix had researched the library renovation and had seen my name. And I knew Sturm's had done a press release a couple of weeks ago mentioning me as the lead designer. But if I had this much luck, at least one of the ten thousand lotto tickets my grandma had made me buy for her over the years would've won something. My suspicious ass knew the other shoe was about to drop.

"They want you to be one of the hosts," Mitzy clarified before I could ask. "Which we think is a fabulous idea. You *would* be an excellent representative for the foundation and our mission."

"That's..." I trailed off, as a feeling of unease crawled all the way up my spine. "Incredible." Intellectually I knew that this was very good news, but that prickle of alarm would not quit. Something about this was off, for sure. But I also didn't want them to think I was an ungrateful cunt, so I smiled wide and showed some teeth. "Thank you for that," I muttered awkwardly. I loved to talk shit like I'd always be on deck to shoot my shot, but what I was feeling was not eagerness... unless eagerness manifested itself as armpit sweat and nausea.

"We wouldn't think of working with another designer; we have fallen in love with your vision for the library." Mitzy sounded sincere and I relaxed a little. These women did not fuck around with their foundation. If they thought I could represent them on this show—*What the fuck, I was going to be on TV?*—then I would run with that. "Now, we know this is a lot to sort of drop on your lap with zero notice, but things have happened fairly quickly. They only contacted us about a week ago." That prickle was more like a burn now. One week, this had all happened in *one week*? "They will bring in some of their own vendors, but they'll allow us to keep the contractors you've hired." Interesting. I'd heard for this kind of thing the network usually had a crew.

"I've never really done anything on this level." It had to be said. "I mean I do my videos for my bedroom makeovers, but that's like with my phone."

"We understand," Muffy told me, looking motherly, but also low-key bloodthirsty. "The network has a team that will give you all the support your need. This could be a boon for us," she said, taking my hand while I hyperventilated on the inside. "For you and for us. This kind of visibility for our work could bring in funding that honestly could change thousands of lives. And as for you...this could open all kinds of doors. You deserve the world to see how brilliant you are. And it comes with more money, *for you*." Mitzy winked as her sister delivered that little piece of news.

"On top of my salary from you?" I had to get clarity on that because I did not play when it came to checks. With a sharp nod Mitzy grabbed a sticky note, scribbled a number on it and slid it over to me.

*Four episodes. $10,000 per episode.*

Fuuuuuck.

I mean this was all sudden, and I knew shit like this never ever happened without some serious strings...so the enthusiasm levels were not as high as they could be, but for all those zeroes, baby I could buy some.

"Okay, sure. Yes." I straightened my shoulders, nodding at them. "What do I need to do?"

"That's exactly the kind of attitude we love," the sisters said in unison. It really was in unison too. Lots of people could finish each other sentences, but these two could harmonize their speech. It was deeply weird, but they were about to put me on TV, so I wasn't going to throw too much mental shade.

Mitzy was smiling so hard her cheeks had to hurt and Muffy was bobbing her head hard-core. "This is all so exciting. We'd reached out to them months ago about collaborating on something, but gave up the idea when they never got back to us and then out of the blue they were back on." That all sounded super fabulous, but why did I feel like the floor was about to disappear from under me?

"There's just one last thing." And…there it was. "The co-host would like to meet with you one-on-one."

I was not always this paranoid, but every nerve in my body was at full alert. "Sorry, what network did you say the show was from?" Oh, that twitch in Muffy's eye was definitely not a good sign. My stomach twisted again, and I had to rub a thumb over all those zeroes on the sticky note to calm back down.

"Streamflix…" Mitzy said slowly, like she was opening a can of soda after shaking it hard for a full minute. That prickle at the back of my neck upgraded to a stabbing-like sensation and my legs popped me off the chair on their own.

There was no way this could be…no. *No.* I wasn't even going to think it.

"So." Mitzy cleared her throat and Muffy was now fully impersonating Jack Nicholson as the Joker. "We do want to let you know that the co-host they'd like you to work with is someone you know."

Before she even said it, I knew it. *That fucking…*

"Someone I know?" I asked very calmly, because it wasn't

their fault that I'd been working for Satan for years without knowing it.

"Yes, you didn't tell us your former boss was an Olympic swimmer!" I was starting to really fear I was going to combust from fury. I could even feel the hair follicles on my scalp contracting I was so fucking mad. If that *assface* was here to ruin this for me because I refused to go back to work for him, I was going to end up in jail.

"It slipped my mind," I said after I managed to unclench my jaw enough to make words. "Is he actually here now?" The way my heart was slamming itself against my ribs had to be blood rushing to my extremities, getting me ready to dick punch my former boss until he passed out.

"He is!" Mitzy confirmed happily, and that's when I had to reach for the edge of the table so I didn't collapse.

"They suggested a restaurant." Muffy was no fool and from the way she was narrowing her eyes I knew she could see I was not happy. "We thought it best if we kept things to a professional setting. He's in one of the meeting rooms." I could only nod. My brain was struggling so hard to process what was happening I half expected steam to come out of my ears any second.

*Think of the money. Think of the money*, I told myself. Those numbers were enough to set up Bookish, finish paying the last of what my mother owed in taxes, and even help my sister with her first year of college expenses. This could change everything. Theo knew it and he was using it to fuck with me.

The next thing that happened was unexpected but went a long way to help me get myself back together. Without any hesitation Muffy looked me dead in the eye.

"Now, he seems to be a perfectly nice man, but we also know perfectly nice, ungodly handsome men can be predatory assholes. He had nothing but good things to say about you, but if you have *any* reservations about working with or even meeting with him, we will call this whole thing off." My chin wobbled, not because I thought Theo would get creepy or greasy on me. He'd had more than ample opportunity to do so while I worked for him and the man had never so much as looked at me the wrong way. I was just grateful that these women were not putting their own interests ahead of my safety. This was not something I would ever take for granted.

"Thank you," I said sincerely then fought to come up with a smile. "I'm fine to talk to him. He's never been anything but professional with me." At least when it came to slick behavior. Acting like a jerk and trying my patience...that was another matter. In truth, him grabbing my ass was not my concern—me taking my hoops out, flying at him and wringing his neck...that was a more realistic concern.

"If you're sure," Muffy said cautiously.

"I am." I was not sure about a single thing, including what the hell Theo Ganas was up to. But I also would not just let a chance at being on TV slip away because he was playing games. If anyone was going to look like a little bitch in this scenario it was not going to be me. "Let's do this," I said with a clap of my hands, getting the twins in gear. I could not wait to call Theo Ganas's bluff.

"It's just here down the hall," Muffy said as our heels clacked on the marble floors. "I know this is not exactly the right moment, but honey, that man is a tall drink of water."

"Shoulders for days," Mitzy concurred, and despite how pissed I was I had to bite back a smile at the thirst these two refined Southern belles had for my former boss. Fine-ass fucker.

"There." Mitzy pointed at the larger meeting room at the end of the hall. The rooms were all glass, so there was a clear view of him even before I went inside. I actually blinked my eyes shut for a moment, trying to delay seeing him.

I didn't feel ready.

"Do you want us to go in with you?" Muffy asked, as I stood in front of the door staring at the back of his head. Was he wearing…a leather jacket?

What the fuck?

"I'm fine," I assured the pair, who were standing behind me like Chanel No. 5–wearing sentinels. "I'll check in with you once we're done."

"We'll be waiting."

"What the fuck do you think you're doing, Theo?" I said the moment I walked in. My entire body was vibrating from seeing him again. It was just nerves, or rage—definitely rage.

"I'm here to get to know my co-host for our renovation show," he said all casual and shit as he turned to me.

Had this asshole gotten hotter?

"With all this hard staring I might start to think you missed me, Alba Solange," he said all fake nice before standing up to his full height. In my three-inch heels I was still half a foot shorter than him. I took two steps back because I would be damned if I was going to crane my neck to look up at that fuck face.

"Sorry, I was just taken aback by your demonic eyebrows. Guess you're not getting to those waxing appointments now that you don't have your Google Calendar bitch to make them for you."

He frowned at my jab, which only made the little peaks at the center in his eyebrows that much more pronounced. A warm feeling of contentment surged through me knowing I'd put a wrinkle in his plan to mess with me today. "You forgot that I know all your little vanity secrets, Theo."

My former boss's one little flaw, the one thing he was vain about. He was adorably self-conscious about his eyebrows, and I was pissed enough at him in that moment to tease him about them.

"Is that a bit of a Southern drawl I detect, Alba Galathea?" he asked, not taking my bait.

"Oh, cut the bullshit, Theo. What the hell are you doing here? Are you trying to fuck with me because I didn't run back to New York?" My temper started to get away from me the moment I started talking. "Are you so unable to hear the word no that you'd sabotage my fucking career because you didn't get those last two weeks out of me?"

That last part made him flinch. I mean a flinch for him, which for other humans was like an eighth of a blink.

"This isn't a punishment," he assured me all cool, easy and calm. Like he didn't know what he was doing was absolutely crazy. "I can see how you would think that."

"How sensible of you," I practically spit out. I was so mad and still my eyes could not stop roaming over him.

Theo Ganas's beauty didn't just hit you, it grabbed you by the back of the neck so that you could not look away. The thing about my former boss and current waking nightmare was that he was almost too pretty. Skin the exact color of caramel and the face of a fallen angel. The contrasts of him were what always distracted me. Hard muscles, sharp angles. A body that had been honed like a weapon to cut through water at speeds that no man should reach. And then you looked up at his face and the beauty of it was almost impossible: soft pink lips, long lush lashes and those soulful eyes.

"What the hell are you wearing, Theo?" I seethed, trying to keep the fires of my fury by focusing on his extremely confusing fit.

I'd been under the impression he didn't know about denim. In the entire time I'd worked for that man I had never seen him wear anything other than those swimming spandex things and suits. Never mind *color.* This asshole was wearing a red sweater that looked like ClingWrap, molded as it was to his chest, never mind the sexy-ass leather bomber jacket over it. Was he bigger too? Like more ripped? His hair was longer and I could not even fucking cope with the beard he'd grown.

"Is my choice of clothes really what you want to talk about?" No. But I couldn't get past it. I don't know why that of all things was what set me off, but my mouth was running before I could stop it.

"Red looks stupid on you." He chuckled and licked his lips. Licked. His. Lips. I swear on my life I felt the ghost of that tongue on my nipple.

God I *hated* him and yet, the air around us sizzled with more than animosity. It was mostly my dogged, ill-advised, unrelenting, extremely self-destructive, inevitable attraction to him. There was something different about him though. Even in this short time I could see he was a more relaxed— and more rugged in the hot way—version of the man I'd worked for. He was all loose-limbed and at ease. It was fucking unnerving.

"Are you really trying to ruin this for me because I bruised your ego?"

"You should sit," he suggested in place of an answer, gesturing to the leather armchair across from his then sat back down in his own chair. I kind of dug the idea of having the height advantage over him if I stayed standing but everyone could see us in this glass box.

"Fine." I sat down and did not miss his own double take at what I was wearing.

He gave another exploratory glance to my legs and his nostrils flared a little. I worked real hard to act like every inch of me was not aware of the attention. "You look good, Alba Luisa."

"That's not my name, cabrón." I flipped him off for good measure, spitting mad all over again, then remembered anyone walking by could see us and switched it to a thumbs-up. He laughed at me like I was his own personal rodeo clown. "Why are you here, Theo? Because I don't believe for one second you just happened to end up on this show."

He looked so pleased with himself, I wanted to slap him.

"I took your advice," he explained, to which I responded with a wave of my hand indicating he would have to do a lot fucking better than that. He just smirked and winked. I lifted my hand to my face and scratched my nose with my middle finger.

He clutched his chest like I'd blown him a kiss. "Always so sweet."

"Fuck you, Theo."

He laughed then, a real one, and my stomach wobbled.

"It is true that I took your advice," he said once he'd had his chuckle at my expense. "Right after you and I spoke that last time, we heard the Valle Mar deal was at risk because of some past less-than-stellar dealings of my father." Yeah, Ganas senior had been a straight up slumlord at one point, but Theo and Cecilia had worked hard to turn all that around. "Streamflix happened to call as we were figuring out damage control and it became clear it would be a great way to get good PR." He tipped his head toward me. "Like you'd suggested."

I narrowed my eyes at him and chewed the inside of my cheek, then quickly grinned and waved when I saw one of the twins' assistants walk by. My brain was like a pinball machine in my skull.

"That's cute but it doesn't explain how you ended up in Dallas and in the middle of my new job, Theo. There's no way that out of all the renovations in the world Streamflix happened to pick this one."

He uncrossed his legs then and widened those massive thighs before propping his elbows on them. He leaned in, so close to me that I could see the flecks of brown in his light gray eyes.

"No, Alba, *that* was definitely not a coincidence. Me being here is very much on purpose."

Something about the way he was looking at me made my throat go bone-dry. I remembered how one of the twins had said that handsome men could be *predatory*. And though the word came to mind right now, it was not at all in the way they'd meant it. Even when I knew Theo was just toying with me. A wolf with playing with his prey before he gobbled it up in a couple of bites.

"What are you even going to do? We already have a contractor."

"Dallas Green Renovations?"

"Yes?" I said it like a question, because he looked smug enough to let me know I was about to get even more pissed.

"The Villedas were happy to partner with me. Their son, Luis, who currently runs the company, does not want to be on camera. He was more than happy to let me be in the limelight as long as their brand gets to be side by side with Ganas."

I would've loved nothing more than to swipe that grin off his face.

"I am not going back to work for you, Theodoro Anibal Ganas." I enunciated every syllable of his name, as he kept that mildly amused gaze on me. My eyes were basically slits, I could barely see him. His were half-mast, but very much in the sexy Disney villain way, which was also not helping matters.

"You think I'm here to drag you back to be my assistant, Alba?" There was something in the way he said *assistant*, like even the possibility of me thinking that was completely idiotic.

It was on the tip of my tongue to say something insane like *then why are you acting like the melanated version of Christian Grey, bro?* But I didn't because I really wanted this thing to work, and I had been grinding in this late-stage capitalist game long enough to know that the millionaire was going to get what he wanted. And if dealing with this oversize, perfect-faced jackass was what it took for me to get my entrepreneurial glowup then so be it.

"Then why are you doing this?"

"Because I want this to go well, and to do that I need to have the best. *You're* the best." My entire body lit up like the Empire State Building from the praise. I was a lost cause.

"You don't even know my work, Theo! You've never seen anything I've done." His eye did that twitch thing, and I narrowed mine.

"I don't need to. I've seen *you* work for three years and know whatever you put your mind to you will knock out of the park."

"This isn't middle-grade kickball, you asshole," I yelled, no longer caring who saw me losing my shit. "This is my career. What has gotten into you? You're not impulsive. How are you okay with just winging this?!" I decided to reason with him, remind him that he was a cunning, calculating bastard, because appealing to his common sense was clearly not going to work.

"I'm not winging it."

"If you mess this up for me, I will never forgive you." I had a reckless mouth and there was only so much I could do to keep myself in check under this level of stress.

"I want what you want." He said it all sagely and cordial and shit like he didn't know he was completely mindfucking me.

"I seriously doubt that, Theo." He didn't even flinch when I said his name like I meant to say *Satan*. "I don't know what you're up to, but I am going to do this renovation and I'm going to fucking kill it on that show, and you better not just stand there and fucking scowl the whole time like an overgrown Greek statue and bring my vibe down."

"I have no doubt of that, Alba Medusa."

"You know what—" I was about to rip him a new one when he opened his mouth and once again threw me the hell off.

"What do you need me to do to make you feel comfortable?"

"What?" I asked, off-kilter, my mind once again playing catch-up to Theo's games.

"I don't want to make things harder for you, but I'm here. It's happening." He shrugged, like he was just rolling with it, and not the fucking architect of this whole fiasco. "The sensible thing is to clear the air, figure out what you need from me to make this easier for you and get on with it."

Easy peasy, then.

I growled and leaned in too, so that our noses were barely inches apart. He smelled like chlorine and that woodsy aftershave he used. I almost pinched my nose to keep from inhaling.

"What I need is for you to get out of my way." If either of us tilted our heads our mouths would get smashed together. Why was the word *smash* even in my vocabulary right now?

I rubbed my forehead hard and sighed. "I can't even think right now."

"It's almost like looking at me makes you lose your focus." The amount of restraint it took for me not to clamp my teeth on his face was superhuman.

"You wish, asshole," I seethed, leaning back. "And the only thing I need you to remember is that you're not my boss in this scenario. We are equals. I'm not going to be running around like your errand girl, that shit's done." He seemed genuinely surprised at that, as if the last ten minutes of whatever the fuck we were doing had clearly put us on a level playing field. "This is not some game for me, Theo. I will not get a chance like this again."

He got all intense again, his hands fisted on the arms of the chair.

"I would never do anything to hurt you or your business. I want something good to come out of this for both of us." I was a damn fool because I believed him.

"Fine," I breathed out, feeling completely wrung out when I knew that barely a quarter of an hour had passed. "I assume there will be a million meetings and things to do for this to happen, so I better go check in with Dani." I took out my phone, figuring the most sane approach would just be to get to work. Dani was my point guy for most logistics things and he needed to be filled in about this development. "I'll probably have to keep him here all night getting everything ready."

I whipped my head from my phone when I heard something very much like a growl coming from the direction where my ex-boss was sitting. In the three years I worked for him I became what one could call an expert in the complex science of Theo Ganas's many unhappy noises. This was one I had not heard before, but I *could* tell it was in the "distress sounds" category.

"What's wrong?" I forced myself to loosen my shoulders since I was no longer paid to care about any of this man's many discontents.

"Who's Dani?" He looked pissed, but I was not deluded enough to think this was jealousy. Just Theo's control freak ways kicking in. He could insert himself fully in the middle of my professional life without warning, but how dare a person exist without him knowing about them.

"Dani is the liaison for the renovation. He used to work for the store, but last year he moved to the foundation and he's helping me."

"Do you pull all-nighters a lot?"

I rolled my eyes at the way he said *all-nighters*.

"Not that it's any of your damn business, but no. I've had a couple of late nights when I was preparing the designs, but Julia and Rocco's guest bedroom is also their home office so I worked there."

"That's where you're staying?" His voice was all rough, and I would absolutely not try to figure out why. I nodded while I grabbed my purse, ready to stand up. Being in this small space with Theo wasn't helping matters and I needed like a two-day-long time-out to get my head straight before I had to face a whole fucking month of being within touching distance of that eight-pack all day. My nerves were already shot and we hadn't even started.

"None of your business, Theo." I walked out, without another word.

"Did you know about this?" I whisper-screamed as I breezed into Julia's office.

"Know about what?" Julia asked, her eyes wide as I paced the small space in front of her desk. "The twins have been all hush-hush about this 'new development', but no one knows what it is."

José, whose office was right next door and only divided by a large glass wall, noticed my less than quiet arrival and hustled over to us.

"Why are you so tight? Did something happen with the renovation?"

I stopped my pacing before I wore tracks into the carpet in Julia's office and stared up at the ceiling. "Looks like Streamflix wants to do some kind of documentary about the library renovation."

"What?" José shrieked, his perfectly groomed eyebrows perched high on his forehead. "That's amazing! Wait a minute…" His gleeful cheers cut off abruptly when he realized I was not as jubilant as a television opportunity warranted.

Julia beat him to the punch. "What's the catch?"

I breathed in once, let the air puff up my lungs, then slowly let it out. I had to prepare myself to say it, because Julia knew me better than anyone and she would see, *she would know*, probably before I did exactly just how messed up this had me. Because Theo Ganas was here. In freaking Dallas. And we were going to work together.

"It's not a full-on renovation show, but more like telling the story of the project and the community it's for. You all will be interviewed too, but the main hosts will be me, as the designer, and a washed-up has-been as the 'celebrity' co-host."

"Okay," José urged, his hands clutched together in front of him, like a little kid waiting to rip into his birthday presents.

"It's him."

It took Julia a second, but whatever she saw on my face got her there.

"When you say *him*…" José inquired, looking between me and Julia, who now looked like a robot that had malfunctioned.

"My ex-boss, Theo Ganas," I moaned, clutching my head in my hands.

"Doesn't he run a huge company in the city?" I couldn't help smirk at José's *the city*. Like Manhattan was the only urban area that merited the word.

"What the fuck is happening?" my best friend yelped, her

system apparently fully rebooted after the glitch my news caused.

"What's happening is that Theo Ganas is here and we're doing this show together, over the next month, because he's a prick and his hobby is ruining my life." I started pacing again. It was like a swarm of bees chock-full of adrenaline were flying around inside me. It was either that or doing sprints around the building.

"Olympic Nips, that's who we're talking about, right?" José contributed as he pulled out his phone, which he tapped and showed me. "This person." He had a photo of Theo in the Olympics as his home screen.

"Jesus, José," I said, a surprised laugh escaping my throat. "You are so fucking thirsty, and stop calling him Olympic Nips."

Our pint-sized friend pointed at the brown nipples in question, then looked back up at me. "You can't tell me you don't think those deserve a gold medal."

"Let's reserve this particular judging for later, José," Julia said, her voice laced with humor, then turned to me. "That man is here for you, you have to know that, right?"

"No," I said, shaking my head so hard I got dizzy. "No, he is here to *fuck with me*. To *mess* with me, because I said no to him." That could be the only possibility, because anything else would be just...no.

"That's what he said?" Julia asked with a very generous helping of suspicion.

"No, he claims he's here because he thinks the show would be good PR." I made air quotes on the *PR* and kept the fact that I'd been the one to give him the idea in the first place to myself.

"Albita, this would all be so much easier if you admitted

you have the hots for that tall, gorgeous asshole," Julia, my soon to be ex-bestie, declared in exasperation.

"Well, one." I held up a finger. "You're officially the worst best friend ever, and two." Another finger went up. "Any regular person with seeing eyes would find that much ripped muscle at least somewhat enticing. That doesn't mean I have the hots for him."

"*I* have the hots for him," José volunteered.

"*You're* a thirsty hoe," I retorted, to which he responded with a shrug and toothy grin.

"Name-calling is not going to change the fact that you're stuck with this man," Julia quipped. "Because I assume you're still doing it."

"I really wish I would've made different choices in middle school when it came to my interpersonal relationships," I said, pressing a finger into one of my eye sockets. "Of course I'm going to do it. This is a once-in-a-lifetime chance and there's money, a lot of money." I sighed, and used my other hand to massage my temple, but Julia smacked it away and started doing something magical to the back of my neck. "Don't stop. Fuck that feels good," I groaned, ready to forgive her if she just kept hitting that one sore spot on my shoulder.

"You can submit my name to the Best Friend Hall of Fame later. So what if you have to deal with Theo Ganas while filming this show? You've said yourself that he's always been a professional, and it's not like he doesn't know his way around a construction site."

This was true.

"I just don't get why he's *here*," I lamented, even as I gave Julia more room to really get into that massage. "Stream-flix has been after him for years to do something with them. They would've come to him in New York."

"Maybe he *wants* to be here," Julia told me suggestively,

as she made muscle-melting circles at the top of my spine. "Maybe he wants to work with you in a different setting. Maybe he—"

"Don't say it, because it's not true," I stopped her. "Theo has no interest in me. He had three years to express that and never did."

"He was your boss," José reminded me, but I just could not go there. Theo was here for his company. To keep his father happy. To make his money. That was the only thing he cared about.

"Theo being here for me would imply he knew me enough to care I was gone. The man barely batted an eyelash when I quit." Julia sighed. "He told me he would have no trouble replacing me."

"Okay, so he's an asshole, but it does seem like there's some unfinished business between the two of you."

Julia's words hit me a lot harder than I wished they had. Not because they surprised me, but because of how bad I wanted them to be true.

It was so foolish. *So reckless*. And it was pointless, because no matter what, I would never risk my business over a relationship. I was bad at romance. No, I was terrible at it. But I was a fucking Jedi Master at shutting everything else out when it came to getting the job done.

# Chapter Six

## THEO

It turned out reality TV was real in all the wrong ways. We were only halfway through our first morning of filming and things were already going south.

"Sorry, you want us to do what?" Alba asked Chase Cooper, our showrunner and enormous pain in my ass. Her voice was panicky enough to make me push off from the portion of wall I'd commandeered by the kitchen of the penthouse the show was providing for me and went to see what he'd said to upset her. Today we were supposed to do on-camera interviews. We'd been told those would be separate—which, given Alba's extra iciness toward me, I assumed she preferred—but so far they'd only dragged in lighting and set up one camera and microphone in front of the love seat in the living room.

Chase, whose claim to fame was running a successful franchise of reality TV shows about B-list celebrities who seemed to despise each other, was, in one word, an asshole. On that first phone call with Streamflix a few weeks ago I'd been told the showrunner would be a Latina with a great reputation in the business, not that I wouldn't have signed on anyway. But right as I was set to come to Dallas they'd informed me she'd just taken extended medical leave. Which left us with Chase, who at the moment was standing over Alba, his pointer finger only inches from her face. I could see her almost trying to shrink before my eyes while he glared at her. Alba, who just two days ago had risen to her full height of five feet and five inches and threatened me with bodily harm if I ruined her plans, was cowering under this greasy dweeb who couldn't even grow a goatee.

"Is there a problem here, Chase?" I managed to keep my voice neutral, but I knew there was no helping how my face looked.

Alba looked nervous. Her face flushed with red and Chase was about a foot too far into her personal space than I was comfortable with.

He did a double take the moment he got a look at me and took a step back. "No problem, Theo. Just going over a few things with the designer," he said cheerfully, even though I could see from her body language that wasn't the truth.

He'd tried to get in my face too, and I'd quickly made him aware that he needed to watch his mouth with me. He'd stormed off mumbling shit under his breath, but he'd kept things civil since then. I should've known he'd just find someone else to bully. But if he thought that would be Alba, he was in for a very rude awaking.

"You need to take another step back from her, my man." It sounded like a threat because it was, and thankfully Chase's sense of self-preservation seemed to be in working order.

"Sure, man, no problem." He laughed it off and turned his pointy face up to me, as if to say *happy now?* I was not a jerk about my size usually, but it was satisfying to see this asswipe need to tip his head up to look at me.

Meanwhile Alba stayed quiet in the corner and that just made my blood boil for some reason. I just didn't get it. Alba had never been disrespectful to me, but she did not cower.

She stood up for herself. Seeing her like that, meek, I fucking hated it.

"I was just asking about her designing experience. It seems like she hadn't really done big-scale jobs like this one, so I wanted to get a sense for how much help she'll need with managing the crew."

"First, Alba's standing right there. And second, making that judgement is not your job, Chase," I bit out, which made Alba look even more uncomfortable. "Sturm's hired her for the design job. All you have to do is film it."

Chase looked like he'd bitten straight into a lemon.

"Well, showrunning is a lot more than just 'filming it.'" Motherfucker actually did air quotes. He was wearing a fanny pack and for a second I fantasized about wringing his scrawny neck with it. "I need to make sure that everyone looks their best. And part of that is putting the most competent people on film."

I'd watched an episode of the last show he'd done, and as far as I could tell the entire forty-five minutes consisted of discussions involving which kind of ice was the best for wine spritzers. This dude was entirely full of shit.

"I just wanted to get a sense for her history since we're doing the getting-to-know-you sessions today. We should get on with those. Alba can come with me first."

From the corner of my eye I saw my co-host stiffen, but still she didn't say a word. I didn't know what was going on with her, but Chase was not going anywhere alone with her.

"That's not going to work," I told him in a tone that managed to be polite, but also let him know I had no problem fighting over this. "We can do it over there on that couch together. Or get Mona to do it with Alba." Chase's assistant, who Chase loved to yell at, was professional and nice. And most importantly did not give off "greasy creep" vibes.

"Sure. I'll find Mona." Chase smiled tightly and turned around with his phone pressed to his ear.

"Can I talk to you for a second?" Alba asked the moment Chase was out of earshot. Her voice was tight and she was sending serious daggers with her eyes. But if she was going to be mad because I was not letting that asshole get her alone, so be it.

I extended a hand toward the hallway leading to the rest of the penthouse.

"After you." She cut her eyes at me and took off. I made myself not look below her shoulders, but it wasn't easy. She was wearing white jeans that were honestly a public hazard and a flowy light blue shirt with a lacy thing underneath. It was so different than how she dressed when she worked for me. She dressed nice for the office, but none of it really gave off any sense of her personality. Here she was colorful and vivid. My train of thought was interrupted when she took a hard left into the library and got in my face as soon as the door closed.

"What are you doing?" she asked with her gigantic coffee mug clutched to her chest.

"Are you sure that's big enough?" I pointed at the half-gallon-sized thing in her hand. It smelled like fake vanilla and hazelnut. "I guess you need to drink a lot of that watery coffee to get properly caffeinated."

"I don't know who the hell you're trying to be right now, Theo Ganas, but if you're trying to sabotage this for me, I will never forgive you." That caught me off-guard.

"How is me telling that guy to find an assistant if he wants to be in a room with you sabotage?"

For a second she seemed uncomfortable, but then she shrugged. "I don't want him to think I'm difficult. I was late already this morning, and—"

"The commute would be a lot easier if you moved in here," I interrupted, and for a second I thought she'd spit her coffee in my face. The penthouse had been offered to the two of us, but Alba had shot that down in a second when I suggested it.

"The last thing you want is me being anywhere I could smother you in your sleep," she shot back, and I had to bite the inside of my cheek.

"How did I never catch on to this violent nature of yours, Alba Cressida?"

"Fuck you," she said sweetly, then got right back in my face, milky coffee sloshing around in her giant cup. "Chase already made sure to tell me his wife was supposed to be the designer for this project but got bumped off because they went with our renovation instead. That was his hello to me this morning." It was going to be a miracle if I managed a month in Dallas without punching that asshole. "He'd love nothing more than to get me kicked off this set."

There was still not a scenario on earth where I was letting him get Alba in a room alone. "You're not the one asking for him to get Mona. I am." She rolled her eyes at that like I was the stupidest dimwit on earth. Which was ironic, because she was the one who had made me more mindful of stuff like this when she worked for me.

"Alba, you're the person who made me include a policy in our office asking staff what settings they were okay with as part of their onboarding. And now you're telling me to ignore the fact that this guy makes you visibly uncomfortable? I can't believe you didn't ream him out for even suggesting it."

She grimaced then took another swig of that enormous coffee mug.

"This is different," she finally said.

"How?" I was legitimately confused.

"Because *I* can't mess this up." The frustration practically spilled out of her. "I can't afford to be contrary on day one." Her voice dripped with frustration. Like I was dense as fuck for not understanding that Chase getting to treat her however he wanted was just the way things were. "I'm not saying doing the show isn't important for you." She straightened the collar of her blouse. Smoothed a hand over the front, as if she was gathering herself. "But for me, this is life changing. If I have to put up with one more man ego-tripping at my expense to use this opportunity for all it's worth, I will do that." Her voice shook just a little when she said *at my expense* and I felt sick from the need to go out and put the fear of God into Chase. She narrowed her eyes at whatever face I was making and waved a finger. "No, Theo. You cannot be glowering and getting in his face, because of me. That is not your job and that is not your place."

In theory she was right. But I could not let this go. It was the way she looked right now. So alone, like she had the weight of the world on her shoulders.

"What if this was someone else? What if this was Natasha or Zoe and I could make sure nothing weird happened while they were working, would you tell me to back off?" She looked almost resentful that I'd managed to come up with that.

"It's not them though, it's me. And I am asking you to *butt out*." Again, the simple solution would be to back off and let her handle her business, but every cell in my body was spurring me on.

"I'm not going to let that weasel get you alone. I'll stand here and argue with you all morning, Alba." She closed her eyes and rubbed her forehead like I was giving her a migraine, but I was not budging on this.

There were so many things I didn't see for so long. But

the one glaring at me right now was that I'd never stopped to think about what it cost Alba to be strong all the time.

"We can do the interview together then. That way no one needs to be in an awkward situation," I conceded.

"Fine." She said it all pissy, and my body reacted to that sweet little growl in her voice almost involuntarily. "I don't know why you're so into this idea," she snapped, sidestepping me to open the door. "They're probably going to ask us personal questions about each other and you're just going to look like a clown."

Why did this woman calling me a clown feel like foreplay?

"It's physically impossible for me to look anything other than hot and brilliant," I replied, hot on her heels as we headed back to the living room. My co-host only scoffed.

"Didn't you hear the hard-on Chase has about us 'having a history'?" Her whisper echoed across the hallway. "The moment they ask you something about me, you're going to show your whole ass on that video."

"We'll see about that," I said. "You know a lot less about me than you think you do, Alba Fantasia."

"I know that I know a lot more about you than you do about me," she informed me over her shoulder.

"You don't know where my Olympic tattoo is." There was no keeping the satisfied smile off my face when she stumbled and drops of creamy coffee splattered all over the floor in front of her.

"Motherfucker, I'm wearing white jeans!" She spun on me so fast I had to step back and the scent of that fake hazelnut and vanilla with a bit of her nervous sweat got me a little hard. "You're making up fake tattoos now?"

"I'm not making it up." I could tell she was pissed that she had to look up to glare at me, so I stepped close enough to make her crane her neck a full ninety degrees.

"You *are* making it up," she bit out, cocking her head to the side. Ready to debunk the fake news of my tattoo. "I saw you get out of a pool half naked five days a week for three years and you don't think I'd notice an Olympic ring tattoo on your body?"

I took my time dragging my eyes over her face. She was hot with me. Her shoulders straight and that button nose scrunched. I stayed on her lips a moment too long, and licked my own right where I wanted to taste her. I wondered if that milky sweet drink would taste better from her mouth. Her chest rose in a sharp intake of breath when I leaned down, not quite to her ear, but close enough so she could hear exactly what I whispered next.

"It's not in a place you've ever gotten to see, sweetheart."

"I despise you." Those brown eyes burned with absolute loathing, making my cock pulse. Fuck, I wanted to take her right there. "If you're trying to throw me off my game, you're going to have to work a lot harder than that," she huffed, then spun on her heel and strode back into the living room with that pert ass swaying in a way only a woman who had grown up swinging her hips to bachatas could.

"Glad you could rejoin," Chase drawled as we walked back in. Alba responded by sending a "this is on you" glare in my direction.

"What did you say?" I asked Chase with more than a little hostility in my voice and was glad to see that he paled before muttering a "nothing" under his breath.

I was not in the mood to be fucked with.

"Chase and I were discussing that it might be fun to do a joint Q&A first," Mona, who seemed a lot smarter than her boss, told us as she stepped up with a pleasant, if strained, smile on her face.

"Awesome idea." This time I was the one sending a "see, I

was right" look in Alba's direction. She mouthed "I hate you like poison" in Spanish at me, then smiled placidly at Mona.

"That sounds great!"

"We usually do a little *getting to know you* thing at the beginning of the show," Mona explained, while Chase scowled. "Just an informal Q&A where our producer sits down and gives you some prompts so the audience can get a feel for your background, your history, your personalities. We don't typically show the whole thing at once but will use snippets of it throughout the series as filler. Just some fun little moments of levity."

"Think of it as an icebreaker," Chase said in a tone that very much said *it's going to happen so just deal with it.*

"An icebreaker should be fun," I said, which elicited a murderous glare from my co-host.

"Since when do you like icebreakers?"

"I love icebreakers." I lied to her face and waited for the explosion I knew would come.

"You literally banned them at the last employee retreat, and the year before you walked out until we'd finished." In hindsight, her previously withholding those growls of hers was a blessing in disguise. My self-control would've snapped a month into her working for me.

"That's not how I remember it." I was being completely shameless, but at least she wasn't nervous anymore. She looked like she wanted to murder me, but that was an improvement from her looking spooked by Chase. She probably would've kept reaming me out, but Keli, the other producer—and the one I actually liked—walked in.

"This is so great," she exclaimed, apparently delighted to see Alba trying to take my head off over icebreakers. "The viewers love the banter. You know what?" she asked, turning to Mona. "It might be fun to have them answer some questions about each other." Alba's eyes lit up at that, probably thinking she had me.

"Let's do this then." She clapped, suddenly all smiles.

"I never knew about this petty side of you, Alba Dulcinea," I teased, and she smiled wider, coming closer.

"Bite me, Theodoro."

"Just tell me when," I told her under my breath. "I have a few spots all picked out already." She bared her teeth, and I had to adjust the front of my slacks.

"The first ones will be pretty easy ones," Mona assured us, unaware of the threats my co-host was muttering in my direction. Keli was all smiles, seemingly ecstatic that Alba hated my guts. Chase stood back and watched us with an ugly sneer on his face. I at least gave him credit for realizing he was close to getting his ass beat and staying out of my way.

"This should be a cakewalk for the two of you," Keli chimed in. "Since you've worked together for years." Alba shot me a smug grin like she couldn't wait to watch me fuck up.

What Alba didn't know was that I paid attention to everything she did. I may not have known her childhood history or even the names of her siblings, but I knew Alba Serena. I could write a fucking dissertation on the way she scribbled tulips in the margins of her ever-present notepad whenever she had to sit through one of my business conference calls. I could give a TED Talk on the way she would turn all the capital Os into smiley faces when she was in a good mood. I may not have known where she went for elementary school or who her prom date was, but I could tell you what kind of day Alba Duarte was having by the way she handed me my macchiatos in the morning.

"First question," Mona announced, and Alba sat up straight.

"Teacher's pet," I muttered, and she responded with more death threats in Spanish.

"Stop flirting with me, Alba Athena, it's unprofessional," I mumbled back, which rewarded me with more promises of my impending demise.

"You guys have such chemistry." Mona clapped again.

"See?" I angled my head toward the PA while I kept my attention on my costar. "Mona enjoys my wit, and it seems we have great chemistry."

"So did the atomic bomb."

I actually chuckled at that one and she preened.

"So," Mona said, bringing our attention back to her. "You put in long hours in the office. What's your favorite music to work to, to liven things up?" She didn't say who the question was for, but Alba answered before I could.

"He hates music," she said smugly.

"That's not true."

"Okay fine, he hates *fun* music."

"Pssh." As far as comebacks went, I could've done better. But she seemed to be on a roll and I wanted to hear.

She sent me a wiseass smile, then returned her attention to the camera. "He has the music taste of a ninety-year-old abuelito." Mona and Keli both chuckled at the look of disgust on Alba's face. "Nothing but old boleros on that geriatric shuffle of his."

That hurt. What the hell?

"Those are *classics*. What did Beny Moré ever do to you, Alba Penelope?" I protested then saw the smart-ass smile on her face. She was fucking with me.

Mona frowned and looked down at her clipboard. "I thought your middle name was Serena."

"It is!" she shot back, arms splayed in front on her in a "see the bullshit I deal with" gesture. "He thinks it's cute to call me the wrong name." She mouthed "cabrón" and then turned to Mona, who was looking at us like she'd hit the reality TV jackpot.

"You guys are really cute together." I know I didn't imagine the gagging sound coming from next to me, but Mona was eager to bring out more of our bickering and turned to Alba.

"And what about you, Alba? Who is constantly playing in your AirPods?"

"She listens to everything," I said, before she could answer. Alba rolled her eyes and whispered "nailed it" under her breath. I leaned back in my seat so I could look at her in my periphery while facing the camera and proceeded to blow her mind. "It does depend on her mood though." She pursed her mouth and shook her head like I was embarrassing myself. "She listens to Bad Bunny when she's tired." She didn't say anything, but her eyes widened just a little. "When she's in a funk it's Selena or old-school stuff, like José José and Juan Gabriel. If she's happy, old-school Merengue, '90s hip-hop and Cardi B. But Cardi is also for the days when she needs extra motivation." She was so quiet I would've thought she had fallen asleep, but for the stare burning a hole into the side of my face.

"I love that, is it true?" Mona asked my co-host. Alba nodded very slowly like she was digesting what had just happened. It took her so long to answer I almost thought she would deny it, but eventually she dipped her head.

"Yeah, it is."

I turned to look at her and found more than surprise there. It was as if she was just noticing some vital pieces of me for the first time.

# Chapter Seven

## ALBA

Theo Ganas knew my music tastes. I was still ruminating that late in the afternoon after the crew had finally left and instead of getting my shit and heading back to Julia and Rocco's I was sitting at the breakfast bar, staring at my laptop screen while Theo went to "get comfortable."

Logically I knew it was not that surprising that my boss could've picked up on what I liked to listen to. I kept music on in my little office next to his whenever I was there, and though I made sure to keep it at a low volume, in three years he was bound to become aware of some of my favorite artists. It's not like I didn't talk about Cardi B and Rihanna like they were my personal friends.

It was *how* he'd said it. That he'd noticed when I listened to certain songs, and more surprisingly was the fact that he could tell when my mood was low or high. I'd been under the impression Theo Ganas didn't have anything beyond a superficial awareness of me while I worked for him. I could've sworn on my life that as long as I did the things he required of me, he didn't have a single reason to give me a second thought. But one didn't discern the music listening habits of another person with that degree of accuracy unless they were interested in them. Right?

The pounding of bare feet on the floor replaced my anxious overthinking with that weird roll of nausea and anticipation that accompanied Theo's entry into a room. He was wearing jeans again and a gray T-shirt, which had no right looking as good as it did. The thing was practically ripping at the seams from his big-ass triceps.

"Where are you going?" I asked because my home training filters had run out of batteries somewhere around hour five of filming.

"To the store," he said, sliding his feet into a pair of leather sandals. "I need to go raid a 7-Eleven or wherever it is they sell the vanilla-flavored dirt you use for coffee and the fake milk you pour on it."

How did a person manage to be that thoughtful and that much of a jerk at the same time? Still, I had to work hard not to smile.

"My coffee is delicious." I ignored his scoff and fake retching sounds. "And you don't have to get me anything." I didn't know if it was the habit of getting things for him for years that made the thought of him going to the store just to get me something feel weird.

"Do you even know where to buy regular human coffee?" I asked before I could stop myself.

He shrugged those massive shoulders that had been on the cover of the *Sports Mag* Body issue *two years running*, and I could see the cuts and dips under his tight T-shirt. "There's a Target like ten minutes away. You're going to be here a lot, it makes sense to have some essentials." He held up a hand like he knew I was going to gripe, but he surprised me by offering an invitation. "You could always come with me if you don't think I can handle buying your caffeine-infused sawdust."

"I have to go home soon; it'll take me forever to get back to Julia's," I hedged as he walked over to where he kept his keys.

He made a noise of disapproval and turned to scowl at me.

"You *could* just stay here and reduce that stressor from your life. There's plenty of space."

"And deal with your stench and freak big toes?" I looked down at his feet and pretended to be horror stricken. "No thank you," I joked, but the possibility of rooming with this man was no laughing matter.

Theo Ganas was a temptation even when he behaved like a heartless, selfish ass. This thoughtful, funny, flirtatious man who had arrived in Texas could be potentially disastrous. I could not get caught up in whatever game Theo was playing with me. Not when I was so close to getting what I wanted.

I didn't think I imagined him calling me "malcriada" under his breath, but he didn't push the issue.

"Are you coming or what?" he asked, sliding his phone into his front pocket.

On one hand, being in a car with him was probably a terrible idea. On the other, I had checked the pantry earlier and the snack situation in there was a fucking nightmare. If I was going to spend hours upon hours here for the show, I was going to need better stuff.

"I don't go food shopping voluntarily," I informed him and he raised an eyebrow. "I have to take my grandmother once a week and that is as much as I can deal with."

"Then I guess you have to eat whatever I buy for you." He thought he was so fucking smug.

"Oh my God, fine, I'll come." I popped up. "But only because the dry pellets you seem to enjoy just don't do it for me."

"You could just tell me what you like."

"Please," I scoffed. "You can't be trusted. I know what you eat. You're practically a two-legged alpaca." He made a choking sound, which when I looked up I realized was a laugh.

"My snacks are fine."

I waved a hand toward the pantry, before walking over and opening it. I pulled out the supposed food that Theo had purchased. "This looks like bird food, and everything is brown."

"Those are high-protein options, you could eat those crackers with some of the hummus in the fridge." He told me haughtily.

"Not on your life." I cringed before returning his cardboard bites to the pantry. "I'm going with you and getting some Cheez-Its and Oreos, the kind of food nature intended us to stress-eat with."

He kept his face very serious as he shook his head in disgust, but he was smiling with his eyes.

"Fine, but I'm driving," he informed me, grabbing his wallet then sticking his sunglasses on the collar of his shirt, which shouldn't be nearly as hot as it was. I really had to stop getting turned on by everything he did.

It wasn't that I'd never noticed the almost inhuman hotness that was Theo Ganas on a regular basis when I worked for him. There was no ignoring a body like that, but so far it had been hotness like Henry Cavill was hot. Something any human could appreciate, but no normal person could actually possess. When the only two sides I ever saw of him were Mr. Ex-Olympian and real estate mogul in five-thousand-dollar suits I had no problem compartmentalizing. I could keep my professional distance while dealing with perfectly groomed millionaire Theo. This smiling, leather flip-flop and faded jeans wearing man was one I could definitely fuck with.

"You all right there?" he asked as he opened the passenger door to his rental Tesla SUV for me.

"I'm fine," I assured him, but he must've caught something in my answer, and his face turned deadly serious. We were standing together in the space between the open door and the seat, his bigger body looming over mine. When I looked up at him, attempting my best placidly detached smile, the evil glint in his eyes told me he saw right through me.

"Are you still mad about me knowing the music you like?"

He didn't even try not to be all cocky about it. God he was so big. It was like being cornered by a building.

"No," I said, making sure that my nose got nowhere near that dip at the base of his throat. He always smelled a little bit like chlorine, no matter how freshly showered he was. It was familiar and comforting—and disorienting—because Theo's smells had never been my smells. Nothing about this man had ever belonged to me, but I *knew* him, and since he'd shown up here in Texas the lines of who we were to each other kept getting blurred. I couldn't afford that kind of distraction right now. "I was just surprised you could name artists born after the Great Depression," I fibbed before scrambling into the passenger seat. He didn't call my bullshit, just stood there staring at me too hard and too long, until I had to look away.

"You're thinking about my tattoo, aren't you?" He pushed off the side of the car and closed my door before I could react.

"I am not!" I balked as he got in on his side, hoping my face would do me a solid and not get super red. "I was making a mental list of what I need at the store."

"I thought you only wanted Cheez-Its and Oreos."

"Yes, but—" I spluttered, making him laugh that new sexy Dallas laugh, which had a worrisome effect on my privates.

"Just admit you were wondering where it is?"

I huffed and turned my attention to the window.

"How had I never noticed you're obnoxiously conceited?"

"It's on the notch of my hip. In the front."

"I did not want to know," I lied, squeezing my eyes shut. I tried very hard to keep the image from forming in my head. But it was impossible. It was in full color right behind my eyelids. All that smooth tan skin with the colorful rings etched onto it and only inches lower his…

"You're imagining right now, aren't you?"

"I loathe you. If I didn't need my face for this stupid show,

I'd hurl myself out of this car." I was all short of breath and he was loving it.

"Oh, Alba Phaedra, am I getting on your nerves?" How had I completely missed the man was a full-fledged clown?

I would never admit it, but I liked this playful version of Theo. He was always so forbidding in New York. Like there was a wall between him and everyone else. It wasn't that he didn't do his job well. He was relentless and brilliant. But he was always disconnected from everything. Like he excelled not because he cared, but because he didn't know to do anything other than to win. He'd even been a good boss in some ways. But he wasn't warm. The only times I ever saw some softness in him was when dealing with Cecilia and Zoe.

"Was going to the Olympics something you decided?" I heard myself ask. I'd wondered about that since I started working for him. He'd won two medals, one bronze and one silver, which I'd expected to see hanging in a frame in his office or in his house. But they were nowhere to be found in either place. When I'd asked Natasha about it, she told me he kept them in the box he got them in, in a drawer in his house. All those years of work to not even display his achievements. It seemed so odd to me. Still, I didn't actually expect him to answer.

I couldn't see his eyes behind the sunglasses, but I knew his "deep thoughts" face. His eyebrows got really flat and he'd gnaw on the inside of his bottom lip.

"I'm really good at swimming." What a weird fucking answer.

"A lot of people are good swimmers, but they don't make it to the Olympics." I was pushing him, but he seemed to be into answering my questions.

"True, but my family had the money to train me to get to that level." He stopped talking as he got us through a particularly busy intersection and took a turn onto a street that looked residential.

"I like this neighborhood," he told me as we drove through a series of beautiful homes with big yards and lots of green grass. One blue Craftsman cottage with green shutters caught my attention.

"I could live there." I pointed to it, figuring we were done talking about his Olympic days. He turned his head slightly to look at it and grunted. "Looks like a place a person could be happy to come home to after a long day." I didn't know why I said that, but he seemed to understand what I meant.

"It's nice," he agreed, and then went back to driving. "I think mostly I kept going with it for my parents," he surprised me by saying. "We had the resources to hire the best coaches, tutors, whatever it took so I could spend every waking moment making myself into an Olympian." I noticed that there was not a single word in that explanation about him actually *wanting* to be one. "To my father if you're good at something the only option is to keep going until you're the best." To his father. Not to him.

"Did you want to do it?"

He lifted a shoulder and the side of his mouth tipped into a smile that seemed to have a jagged edge to it. "Who doesn't want to be an Olympian?" From the look on his face, I was guessing him. I really thought he would leave it there, but he kept going. "I wanted to make my father proud. My mother wanted my father to be proud of the son she'd given him. And I was good at it, I like doing things I'm good at. I like to push myself to do things other people think impossible," he admitted, and I recognized that drive. But there was also the resignation in his words, as if he understood that his very existence was not because his parents wanted a child, but because they wanted a human trophy. It made me sad for him. Made me wonder if I didn't know Theo anywhere near as well as I thought.

"Why don't you hang your medals?" As soon as I blurted that out I regretted it. His expression, which had not been quite open but at least somewhat amiable, shuttered.

"Why didn't you ask that this morning?" he asked in answer.

"This morning?" I didn't have a clue what he was talking about.

"When Mona asked you to say something that surprised you about me."

Oh...*that.*

Theo had always been perceptive, so him realizing I'd held something back wasn't exactly a surprise. The question *had* stumped me, not because I couldn't rattle off something silly and minor, which I had, but because what had come to mind first was a morning about six months into working for Theo.

"No, that wasn't it," I admitted. "I was going to tell them about the time when you had knee surgery," I told him, still a little embarrassed even after all this time. "I didn't think you'd want that side of you being aired out to strangers." He looked at me again, and this time there was something there I could not quite discern. Maybe he didn't like me rousing up that memory.

Back then he'd been recovering from pretty intense surgery and was working from home, except on Thursdays when the cleaning lady came to his house and he came to the office. He'd been barely able to walk but insisted he didn't want to be in the house with her. When I asked him why, he was brusque and cagey. I was livid, thinking he'd rather risk hurting his knee than talk to the woman who cleaned his house. By the third week, when he practically dragged himself from his place to the office ten floors below, I'd had enough.

I ranted to Natasha for a full five minutes about how

fucked up it was, and then she told me. She explained that he did it because he didn't want to make the cleaner uncomfortable. He'd been hiring staff from a back-to-work program run by a local domestic violence agency and he always made sure he left in case they felt unsafe alone with a man in the house. I'd practically crumbled from mortification in front of Natasha. I'd been so nice to him after that he'd yelled at me to quit talking to him like he was a time bomb.

"You're right, I wouldn't have liked that getting out. It's personal." His voice was quieter than it had been. And it occurred to me that for all his arrogance, Theo was not one to boast about the kindnesses he did.

"You used to do a lot of work with them, the agency," I said after a while, and again he seemed to weigh his words for a long time before answering.

"I did." The first year I worked for Theo his dad was still running things at Ganas, and though my boss was the second-in-command he'd had all kinds of side projects. He was passionate about more environmentally sound construction and he'd doing more builds for communities with housing insecurity. But once he'd taken over after his father's retirement he'd let all that go to focus on running Ganas Corp like the patriarch expected.

"What does your dad think about you coming to do this?" I expected him to shut me down at any moment, but he kept surprising me.

"He wants the Valle Mar project to happen. I'm supposed to be there in a month for the deal closing." The reminder that this would all be over in a month did not grant me the relief I hoped for.

"Right," I responded awkwardly. Then got lost in my head again. Maybe he really was just here to smooth things over with Valle Mar. Maybe this was just one big coincidence. Or maybe he wanted to work with me because he thought he could steamroll me. Or maybe I was overthinking everything way too much. Whatever his reasons were, they weren't my problem. My only job was to make myself look as good as possible.

"We're here," Theo announced as he pulled into one of the spots in front of the store. Once we were out, he went around to the trunk and collected a handful of reusable bags.

"So domestic, Theodoro Anibal," I teased him.

"I have to get food for a few days and need bags, Alba Carmelina," he told me in a very serious tone that was a striking contrast to the smart-ass grin on his lips. Smart-ass or not the man was fine as hell.

"You sure you can fit your pints of blood and pig hearts for your vampiric feedings in those little bags?" That only made him laugh.

"Does that mean you're curious about my fangs?"

My entire body flushed hot and cold at that image, and I reverted to what I did best. Get bossy.

"Is this going to take long, because I have to get back to work on my presentation for the team."

"I have a list, so no."

"Okay good, because I need to review my notes for the team meeting."

"You'll be fine." He said it like he was aggravated by my whining. "Where's *your* list?" he asked, and he looked serious too. Like he was certain they'd make us leave if we dared enter the store without an itemized inventory of what we'd buy.

"All in here." I tapped my temple as I pushed a shopping cart through the automatic doors.

"I guess we'll just go to the junk food aisle and you'll arm sweep shit into the cart."

"How did you know?" I smiled over my shoulder and

noticed that his eyes were very much in line with the swell of my ass.

"Are you ogling my assets, Theo Ganas?"

"I've always been captivated by a solid asset." He winked… *winked* as he totally checked out my butt.

"You're kind of a dirtbag."

"And I can cook too," he added, like I'd just extended him a compliment. He sped up past me then and I had to haul ass to catch up with him.

"What are you making for dinner?" I asked when he gently placed a parcel wrapped in butcher paper in his cart.

"You asking for an invitation?"

I responded with a disgusted scoff.

"What, you need to rush back to that dinner of Red Bull and Cheetos?" He was looking pointedly at my cart when he said it.

"Those are snacks!" I protested and he rolled his eyes like a jackass. "Besides, I don't know your skills. I don't want to end up with food poisoning."

"Oh, I'm a great cook," he informed me as he moved on to avocados. When he found a few that met his exacting requirements, he pulled out a little mesh bag he'd brought and put them in there. "I'm braising those short ribs I just got in a red wine sauce, maybe sauté some mushrooms with them. Delicious."

My damn traitor of a stomach growled and he laughed.

"You can stay for dinner, you know."

Staying for dinner would put us in "friendly territory" and I didn't think that was advisable. I needed to go home and process all the new sides of Theo Ganas I'd seen in just the one day we'd filmed together. Or take care of the new requests I had for Bookish makeovers, look over my slides for the presentation, check to see if my mom had figured out payroll…so many things to do. But none of it seemed quite as compelling as hearing more about these ribs Theo was planning to make.

I stood there, clutching the handle of my cart when he settled next to me. His hips bumping my elbows. "You don't want to pass up those ribs. They're my specialty."

"Psshh." I added an eye roll to really hammer in my skepticism regarding his cooking.

"It's true." His voice lowered, and suddenly it was all raspy and deep. It made something hot flash through my entire body. "It's all about patience when it comes to good meat." A breath skittered out of me, because for some reason that had sounded utterly filthy. "I like to take my time…really coax out the juices slowly. Simmer it low and slow." The tip of his tongue came out and swiped over his bottom lip. My eyes were stuck to his mouth like I was under a spell.

"Okay," I breathed out.

"But the real secret," he confided, as I did grounding exercises in my head, "the true secret is massaging the meat. Work it with my fingers, you know?" I was sweating, but his laughing eyes told me he was just fucking with me.

"Are we still talking about food?" I sounded winded, but he was perfectly cool.

"I don't know? Are we?"

Before he could say something that got me in trouble I pushed my cart past him and barreled to the aisle with ice cream.

"Try to keep up, Theodoro Anibal."

He called my bluff and pushed me and my cart halfway across the supermarket while I shrieked my head off with laughter. In the end I went home and dined on the Cheetos and Red Bull he teased me about, but I did wonder about those ribs, way past my bedtime.

# Chapter Eight

## THEO

"So basically you rode into Dallas on your big horse to claim your lady and she threatened to kill you in your sleep and then fucked off." Cecilia thought she was cute.

"No, that is not what happened at all," I gasped as I stepped off the treadmill in the penthouse gym. "We discussed it and she declined my offer to stay here with me." My stepmother snickered like this was the best comedy show ever. But was staying strong. All in all things had not gone terribly this first week. We'd done a couple more days of filming filler scenes and visited the construction site without too much drama.

"But things are going okay between the two of you?"

My stepmother did not like the noncommittal sound I gave her in answer.

"You know you could just tell her how you feel," Cecilia nudged for the millionth time, and I shook my head as I trained my sight on the glimmering surface of the pool on the patio. The turquoise rectangle was still the one place where everything seemed to make sense to me. If my body cooperated, I knew how to get what I wanted out of that length of water. But people were unpredictable.

"Have you considered she's just waiting for you to ask her out?"

"No, I haven't because I was too busy fending off her promises to kill me." I shook my head like she could see me, as I walked the length of the glass wall separating the living room from the outdoor area. "I want Alba to see a different side of me. And I don't want to make things awkward for the filming with my feelings sitting like congealed word vomit between us for the next month."

"That's disgusting," Cecilia griped disdainfully.

"Exactly, which is why I need to play my cards right. I have a plan. A strategy."

"Strategy doesn't work in romance, bro!" I couldn't help my grin when I heard my little sister's voice.

"What do you know about love, squirt?" I asked, as I heard the rustling of Zoe wrangling the phone from her mother.

"I learned everything I need to know from romance novels. If you want to get the girl, you have to do something unexpected, you have to surprise her."

"Me showing up in Dallas with an offer to get her on a reality show isn't flashy enough of a surprise for you then, sis?" I asked with a laugh.

"Oh please, how surprising is it for you to figure out a way to get people to do what you want?" my fourteen-year-old-going-on-eighty little sister fired off.

"Damn, burn!" That was courtesy of my stepmother.

"Okay, enlighten me, oh wise one," I teased her, although I was kind of low-key curious and definitely desperate enough to use the advice.

"Do something nice for her. Something that's not like buying her a car," Zoe added, in that "I know everything" tone that magically appeared the day she turned thirteen. "Look out for when she's tired or hungry and do something to help. It's the little things," my pint-size relationship guru assured me.

"That's not bad advice, squirt," I told her, impressed even though I knew suggesting to Alba Serena Duarte that she was overdoing it at work would likely get me punched in the nuts. The intercom buzzed, surprising me. Unless I had misread the schedule there wasn't supposed to be any filming happening until the next day. "Sis, I gotta go, there's someone here. Love you, smart-ass. Send me pictures of what you do today!"

"'Kay, and don't make any moves without texting me!" After assuring her she would be in the know of any developments I hustled to the intercom.

"Miss Duarte is on her way up, sir," the doorman announced when I pushed the button.

"What?" Had I missed an email?

"Is that all right?" the doorman asked, while I unsuccessfully hunted for clues in my calendar app. "She's got some suitcases with her," he informed me, and I let the phone drop on the counter. "I offered to come up with her, but she said she didn't need help." I didn't have time to ask more questions, because right then the doorbell rang and my entire body lit up like I'd been plugged into a wall socket.

I looked through the peephole after I got to the door, just to give myself a second to get my shit together, only to realize my mistake too late. The preview of all those curves just got me more riled up. She was fucking delicious in yoga pants and a little workout top that made her tits look amazing, and that was really not at all the kind of shit a man playing the long game should be thinking about.

"Don't say anything!" she growled, dragging two enormous suitcases behind her as I opened the door.

"Good morning to you too, Alba Luisa." Fucking with her was likely not the best approach, but this middle name game had been the only thing that had ever gotten under her skin. When she worked with me, there was nothing that fazed her. My demanding ass could send her on errands to the ends of the earth and she'd just smile, nod and say, "Of course, Mr. Ganas," but the middle name...that always got me a frustrated little growl or a withering glare that I found immensely gratifying.

"I thought you didn't want to stay here. Did the siren call of the penthouse get to be too much?" She curled her lip at me, but she kept her attention on rolling her bags into the middle of the room.

Once she unclenched the handles, she spun on me. "You know what?"

"I am sure you'll tell me," I drawled as I looked down at her. Hands itching to slide a finger over the edge of her top.

"For your information, I am not here by choice. *And* I am not in the mood for more of your bullshit." Despite her irritation, I saw a flash of sheer exhaustion behind her eyes. It was just a second, like she was putting her weapons and armor down for a moment before barreling back onto the battlefield. Everything in me responded to that glimpse of vulnerability. I wanted to cocoon her from anything that would shadow even for an instant the radiance of this woman.

"Rocco's sister had an issue in her apartment," she explained, running a hand over her forehead. "A pipe broke and it flooded. She and the baby need a place to stay for a couple of weeks while that gets sorted. Rocco and Julia's place is comfortable enough for three, but definitely not five."

She sighed and took a step back from me; I had to restrain myself from reaching for her.

"I'm happy you're here too, Alba." I went for a teasing tone, because in the mood she was in, trying to coddle her was bound to piss her off.

"You fucking wish, Theo." I expected her to launch into

another round of insults, but instead she turned in a slow circle, giving me a 360 view of that delectable body of hers.

"We should be able to do this without me wanting to kill you," she whispered, as she bent over to look at a book on the coffee table. I managed to keep my groan inside as I took her in. Images of palming that perfect peach as she rode my dick almost made me black out.

"We need to set up some ground rules," she announced as I peeled my eyes off her ass. Before I could ask what exactly she meant, she lifted one hand, index finger in the air.

"First rule, you need to cover this up." Further explanation as to what "this" was came with a wave of her hand in the vicinity of my torso. "Seeing you half naked all the damn time is no longer part of my job description."

I almost laughed because for all that she'd seen me come out of the pool every morning for years, her eyes still did that moony, crossed thing every time they landed on my pecs. She liked what she saw... I knew that. *She* knew that. My mission for the next few weeks was to figure out if it was more than detached appreciation.

"I was working out."

"Have you ever heard of this new invention called a T-shirt?" God, that smart mouth made me hard, every fucking time.

"So I can't walk around shirtless in my own house?"

"It's not your house anymore," she reminded me while pinning me with another dirty look. "It's *our* house now. And I can't be dealing with you all bare-chested." That was way too easy for me too not jump on.

"Can't handle how sexy I am then?" I asked with a snap of my head. "Got it."

She let out another one of those sexy little growls, small fists tight at her side. I wanted to kiss her until she was out of breath.

"Nooooo." She stretched the word out for what felt like a minute. "I can't handle partial nudity when I'm trying to drink some damn juice in the kitchen."

"That's really specific." I tucked my hand under my chin, in mock confusion. "Are you afraid you'll be so overcome with lust from the sight of my smooth, tanned chest and choke or something?" She didn't answer with words, but her middle finger let me know what she thought of that theory. I recklessly went right back at it.

"Besides what's the big deal? As you already mentioned, you saw my chest five times a week for two years and it wasn't an issue."

"I was getting paid to do that," she snapped. I did not miss the extra-long second those big brown eyes snagged on the area of my upper torso.

"That hurts, Alba Altagracia." She took a step toward me like she was really trying to figure out if she could take me.

"I am perfectly capable of resisting your…" She bit off whatever she was going to say and spun on her heel in the direction of the kitchen. "Never mind."

"Don't worry, I won't tell anyone that you find my body so irresistible you requested I put on a garbage bag to cover it," I called after her. "We're good, Alba Eurydice."

I heard the scoff, but she didn't turn around. "I'm not taking the bait, you know perfectly well that's not my name." She opened the fridge door. "Let me check in here, because after all that spelt and alfalfa sprouts I saw you buy at the store, I need to make sure there's food I can eat." With that she proceeded to stick half her body inside, putting her pert ass on full display for me again.

My reaction to the view told me I should probably start listing some rules too, because I didn't know how I'd get anything done with her walking around in yoga pants and crop tops. A sound of disapproval from the depths of the refrigerator redirected my attention away from the perfect bubble butt in front of me and to its owner.

"What?" I asked, but she kept rifling through the contents without a word.

"No plantains, no salami." She clicked her tongue as I swallowed mine when she wiggled her behind. By the time she popped back up from the vegetable crisper, I had my first rule: no bending over in yoga pants.

"What kind of Dominican are you?" she chastised as she blessedly turned that delicious rump away from me.

"I don't like plantains." That got the reaction that I'd witnessed again and again through most of my life.

"Are Dominicans even allowed to say that?" she exclaimed in what I suspected was not feigned horror. And I couldn't help but feel disappointed. I'd been judged about this for so long. My mother's family in the DR still could not comprehend how I could not like the food that was such a basic part of our diet. It was one of those little things that made me feel like I didn't quite measure up. I didn't belong with my father's family in his native Thessaloniki. The dark-skinned boy he'd fathered in America. And in the DR, I was the light-skinned child with the broken Spanish whose gringo father never came to the homeland to pay his respects to the family. I was a stranger to both sides of my family, never finding my footing anywhere.

"Actually, you know what?" she said after she'd stared at me for a moment. "I get it. I love plantains, don't get me wrong, but I absolutely hate guandules." She twisted her mouth at the mention of the peas that were another staple in Dominican cuisine. "My mom always acts like I need to be exorcised whenever I say it." I had no idea if it was true or if she was just picking up on my discomfort with her judgement, but I took it as the white flag it was.

"I can handle T-shirts if you can live with my hate of plantains."

"Deal." She smiled at that, her lush mouth tipping up as she shook her head at our ridiculous conversation.

"Do you cook?" I asked. Her head reared back at the question like I'd called her a name, and I had to cough to hide my laughter.

"What exactly do you mean by 'cook'?" The air quotes almost took me out.

"Preparing food on the stove or oven to feed yourself."

"I'm not super into that, no." She looked self-conscious for a second but she recovered quickly. "But..." She tapped a finger on her cheek while she assessed her next move. "Since you seem to be obsessed with feeding me, I guess I can do you a solid."

"You're ridiculous," I told her without heat, and decided not to examine too closely the tightness in my chest from her using the words *feeding me*. "But I don't like cooking for just myself," I said, feeling weirdly exposed from that admission. "And you know my schedule, a lot of times I just don't have the energy to cook. In New York, I only had Esteban to make my dinners. The rest of the meals I had to fend for myself."

She narrowed her eyes at that, and I realized what I'd said, then threw my hands up in concession.

"Okay, for *you* to fend for me."

"That's right," she huffed, hands on her hips, and then her eyes widened and her chin turned up. "And before you ask, yes, I will do you a solid and let you cook for me too, since you don't like to do it just for yourself."

"Wow, that is quite a reach, Alba Medea."

She huffed, but her grin was still in place. "I'm going to

let you get away with that one Theodoro, but don't get used to it," she warned with a wave of her finger.

"If you help me clean up after, I'll make us both dinner whenever we're home for the night." It was funny to think the thing that had most attracted to me about Alba was her self-sufficiency. How she never seemed to need anything from anyone. And yet, the thought of making a meal for her was all-consuming.

She slanted those chocolate brown eyes in my direction, like she was trying to figure out what trick I had under my sleeve. After a moment, she nodded, that dubious expression still on her face.

"All right, but I'm not doing any sous chef shit." How had she managed to keep all this surliness under wraps for so long? Suddenly all I could see was Alba sitting at the kitchen island, moaning over food I'd made for her with my hands. Of that sweet little butt twitching in the seat when she took a bite of something she loved.

"Maybe I can give you a few cooking lessons," I told her quietly, certain she would clap back with something scathing.

"If I wanted to learn how to cook I would've paid attention during one of the million times my mother or grandmother made dinner." She harrumphed, and I bit my lip.

"Fine. *But* you have to eat with me." She glared for a moment, her stance straight like a soldier's.

"Fine." She pushed off the fridge door and pushed a pointy nail into my chest. "But no guandules."

I resisted the temptation to tug on the hand pressed to my chest and glue her front to mine, to press my mouth to her ear and tell her to fuck the guandules and the plantains, that the only thing I wanted on my tongue from now until forever was her skin.

I was pumped full of adrenaline. Riled up for a heat. "For

someone so annoyed at me you sure do stare hard at my chest, sweetheart."

The instant I said it, I knew I'd made a tactical error. She was off me before I could backtrack. Her expression cool and detached. "Where are the bedrooms in this joint?" she called over her shoulder and went for her suitcases again. Play time was over then.

"Down there." I pointed at the corridor lined with doors, following her at a distance while I regrouped. "I'm in the first room to the left, there's another bedroom across from me." I pointed to my closed door. "On the other side of the living room there's a TV room, but it's more like a home theater. And on the end there is a library with an office. Oh, and the mezzanine has a home gym."

"What's outside?"

"Patio with gazebo and grill." She made an appreciative sound at that. "And a pool/hot tub combo." She stopped abruptly at the mention of the hot tub and the movement made her ass bounce. I wanted to take a bite out of it.

"I think I'm going to take the room at the end of the hall," she said quietly and picked up the pace.

That was the farthest room away from mine.

"You sure you have enough distance," I said testily, before I could stop myself. She snapped her head up at me, but I couldn't tell what she was thinking. If she was mad or just surprised at the edge in my voice. When she rolled her eyes I got my answer.

"We're going to be working together all day and I feel like it will be good to keep *some* distance."

"We worked twenty feet from each other for three years," I reminded her.

"I'm aware of that," she bit off as she turned the knob on the door. "I'm still wrapping my head around everything. It's weird enough to be doing this with you." She paused then, her luscious mouth flattening into a taut line. "Honestly, I need time to adjust to not having to be at your beck and call all the time. I'm not used to seeing you as anything other than the person whose needs it's my job to fulfill."

I knew what she was saying was fair, but it still smarted that she couldn't see me as anything other her former, demanding boss. "I wasn't that bad."

"Yeah, you were," she snapped instantly.

I opened my mouth then closed it knowing that if I pushed, I'd undo any progress I'd made with her. A man who was too fragile to hear about his shortcomings was not a man who deserved Alba, even if that man was me.

"You weren't a *bad* boss" she said, probably in an attempt to appease me. "*But* you were sort of a terror about having your shit just so, and not very forthcoming in the thank-yous…and I have people pleaser issues, which made it doubly aggravating." She shrugged in a "what are you going to do" gesture. "It's going to take time to wean myself off reacting whenever you look unhappy or asking you what you need."

"I haven't asked you for a single thing, Alba," I reminded her and then immediately regretted it.

"I realize that, Theo," she said with clear exasperation. "But you aren't supposed to be here at all. You wedged yourself into my new job for some unfathomable reason, and now I have to…" She clamped her jaw shut and pushed the door open. "You know what? Never mind. This room is fine. I'll see you at dinner."

She slammed the bedroom door in my face.

# Chapter Nine

## ALBA

Whether my cheapness would end up biting me in the ass for coming to the penthouse instead of getting a hotel was yet to be seen, but I could not deny my new digs were extremely nice. And so far Theo was respecting my boundaries. Since I'd locked myself in my room to unpack, he had not come to mess with me once. All in all my arrival had gone better than I'd expected.

I still couldn't figure out what Theo's end game was. Maybe it was a pride thing. I told him he didn't have anything that could bring me back and this was his way of proving me wrong. He was enough of a headass to do something super extra to make a point. But that would mean I was important enough for him to bother with all this, which I knew couldn't be it. He had been flirting pretty shamelessly with me, but maybe that was because he could now that he wasn't my boss. It's not like I didn't think I could pull a guy like Theo. But he was way too controlled to spend this much time and effort just to fuck around. It had to be the Valle Mar thing, and finally proving himself to his father.

Still, none of that explained the personality transplant I'd witnessed since he'd shown up in Texas. Walking around shirtless and grinning all the damn time...joking about my music tastes, *wearing jeans*. That shit I could not actually explain or honestly handle for very long. Dallas Theo was a conundrum, a mystery. A sexy-as-fuck mystery who seemed weirdly invested in making me food *and* coffee.

"Yo, it's us!" Julia shouted on the other side of the door, blessedly pulling me out of my Theo ruminations.

"Us?" I asked suspiciously, as I went to open the door and got the answer to my question a second later. Standing there were Julia, Salome and José. "What are you guys doing here?" Despite the semi-flustered tone in my voice I *was* glad to see them. I needed all the buffers I could get during the adjustment period with Theo. But one of my least redeeming qualities was my tendency to push people away when I needed them most.

"Obviously we're here to offer you moral support, rude ass," Julia chastised me as she pointedly stared at the two bins full of my stuff Salome was holding. My best friend knew only too well that my "I am an island" thing was usually a cry for help.

"Sorry," I apologized, ushering them inside. "I'm a little tense because of..." I waved a hand in the direction of the living room as explanation.

"We're here for you, babe." José was the first to take a step forward. He quickly gave me a peck on the cheek before nosing around the bedroom. "Girl...this is nice." He stretched out the word making it sound more like "noooooice," making me laugh. And the room *was* baller.

"A professional had a hand in this for sure," I agreed. I was usually a snob about design, but whoever did this penthouse had taste. My room colors were a palette of earthy greens and browns, and even though those colors were a bit more masculine than what I would've selected for myself, it worked. The bed was huge, with a headboard done in a mocha quilted leather that reached halfway up the ceiling. The wall behind it was covered in a gorgeous floral wallpaper in burgundy, gold and dark green. Across from the bed was an outrageously lavish fireplace done in wrought dark metal and shiplap that I was planning to take with me when I left. The balcony was spacious and had two comfy chairs with a table in between overlooking the Dallas Arboretum grounds. It was full-on Texas-style chic and there was no way I could afford a hotel with this kind of room in it, not without hurting my plans for BB.

"This is pretty swanky, Albita, you should not feel obligated to come back to my place." That was Julia, who was already perched on a leather wingback armchair, her feet propped up on the matching ottoman. Yeah, my spoiled ass was not going to leave this place and go to the Holiday Inn just because I could not handle Theo's dick print in those gym shorts. I'd just have to control myself.

"Yoooo, you could have an orgy in that shower." That contribution came from Salome, who'd gone into the bathroom with the bin containing my toiletries.

"Alba, ma, I'd like to file a complaint for misrepresenting the facts," José piped up from the corner he was inspecting. I raised an eyebrow in expectation for the ridiculousness I knew was coming. "You said *He* was tall." The capital-H *he* in question could only be my former boss. "But you didn't tell us he was the size of a small country and had pecs like hubcaps," José said in a fake whisper, and the other two laughed. "I mean I did my due diligence on the internets and knew he was fine, but the pictures were old. Mr. Ganas has been hitting that CrossFit gym regularly since Las Olimpiadas, baby." He actually smacked his lips.

I narrowed my eyes and shook my head. "Is he always like this?" I asked, but José continued undaunted.

"Girl…that man can destroy my life any time he wants." By now he was on his back on the bed fanning himself with a cushion, both legs up in the air. "Whew, I need a cold drink after seeing all that azucar parda."

"Damn, José. I've never seen this dick fiend side of you," Salome cackled.

"You know what… I'll kick you all out of here," I threatened, trying hard not to giggle because José was doing a snow angel on the bed.

"Uh, no can do, sis. We've been invited to stay for dinner." I whipped my head over to where Salome was tinkering with the record player that came with the room.

"Who invited you?"

"Your roomie," Julia said with a shit eating grin.

"Don't you have to go home and help Rocco with your sister?"

"Nope," my best friend informed me, lacing her fingers behind her head. "They're all settled in." I wouldn't put it past her to have made up the flooding, but Rocco wouldn't let her lie her ass off like that. She tapped the very sturdy arm of the chair. "Come tell us how it's going so far because even from here I can tell your head is a mess."

"I'm fine," I lied and sank next to her, then breathed out a long exhale.

"Yo, I know we're supposed to hate him and all, but my man's mad friendly," Tariq said as he burst into the room. "We were shooting the shit about basketball and he knows *a lot* about sports."

"He's an athlete, dumbass," Salome cried, from where she was sitting on the floor playing with a wood puzzle she'd found somewhere.

"Tariq, you think absolutely everyone is friendly," José

said, at the same time that Julia echoed Tariq's sentiments with "Yeah, why do we hate him again?"

"Because I don't know why he's here. I don't know what he's doing," I enunciated, while my friends looked at me like I'd grown horns.

"But does it actually matter?" Salome asked, her face scrunched in concentration as she slid wooden pieces from one side to the other on the board. "I mean. If this wasn't your boss who you had a history with, would you be questioning this at all or just be happy you get this awesome opportunity to do a show as the main designer?"

"And to live in this pimpistic penthouse." We all rolled our eyes at Tariq's extreme enthusiasm for my new place.

I stewed for a bit weighing Salome's answer and the truth was that if Theo hadn't crashed into my party like the Kool-Aid Man I would be living my dream.

"I probably wouldn't have, no." I conceded, turning to Salome. "But it *is* him and I just don't understand what he wants from me."

"Has he done anything to make you feel like he has an ulterior motive?" Julia's face hardened and she slid her legs of the ottoman like she was getting ready to go and kick Theo's ass. "Because you know I'll roll in Rocco's truck ready to hide a body."

I held up my hands when Salome echoed her willingness to commit murder for or with me. "Let's not start making plans for felonious acts, all right? And no, he hasn't done anything. Not really." I mean he had joked about me being obsessed with his abs, which was not exactly a lie. But other than that, he'd been fine. More than fine—he'd been charming, and protective when Chase got out of hand. Hell, he'd been kind of sweet...never mind the flirting at the store. I got hot flashes just remembering the way he'd been looking at my ass. "I just don't like being messed with and I don't see how this could be anything other than that."

"Maybe he wanted to do this for you. You worked for him for years, he must know how much your design work means to you." Except he didn't. I had never, not once talked to Theo about Bookish Boudoir. He'd never asked either. In the three years I worked for him the man never showed even an inkling of caring about my work outside of what I did for him. Which was why him knowing my music tastes made me feel crazy.

In the end, Salome was right—whatever his reasons were, it didn't matter. He was here and I could either take advantage of it. Or I could sulk.

"I'm going to need to vent to y'all a lot over the next month," I groused, slumping further on the chair. Julia gave me a sympathetic pat of the leg.

"I mean, could you do it while we soak in that hot tub I peeped out on the patio?" José asked, making me grin despite everything. And yeah, there was a whole lot of weirdness going on in my life, but if I stopped to think about it, a lot of it was good, including having my best friend in the world here and her friends—who already felt like my friends—to support me if I needed it.

"Y'all are fucking trash for a little bit of fancy, damn," I teased, and would've kept on going but got sidetracked when I saw the photoshopped picture of Darth Vader with Theo's face pasted on flashing on the screen of my phone.

Did he go somewhere and forgot his keys? "Yes?"

"Dinner's almost ready," he informed me, and I could hear the smile on his lips. Why was he so fucking happy all the time now?

"But why are you *calling me*, Theo?"

"The commute to your room is a hike and I have unlimited data." I refused to be amused.

"Whoever told you that you're funny really did you a disservice." He responded with a low raspy laugh that wrapped around my middle like a rope and tugged until I had to suck in more air.

"It was the same person who told me I was hot and charming." I would not grin, I would not smile.

"Are they on your payroll too? How did I never notice you're a certified delusional narcissist?"

"Because I didn't want you to know," he informed me, and I had to resist sticking my tongue out at the phone. "Ask your posse if any of them are allergic to seafood. I'm making Asopao de Camarones." Of course he'd make one of my favorite meals. Damn you, Theo Ganas.

I tapped to end the call and tried not to glare at my friends, who were all waiting expectantly. "Food's almost ready, anyone allergic to seafood?"

A chorus of nopes resounded around the room, and just because I had to take it out on someone I pinned Salome with a death stare.

"Aren't you a vegetarian?" I asked, as we all filed out of the bedroom.

"*Pescatarian*, ma. I am down, down, *down* for free food I don't have to cook. *Even* if I wasn't I might still try it because it smells really fucking good." She wasn't lying, the aroma of garlic, saffron, white wine and sofrito enveloped me as we walked down the hallway into the great room where Theo was moving around, his torso thankfully covered.

"Damn, bro, you want another roommate? I can sleep in the gym!" Tariq called, before slapping him on the shoulder. Theo laughed and tipped his chin in the direction of the dining room table.

"The wine fridge is right there. There's a sauv blanc and a chablis on the top shelf that will be great with the asopao." Tariq nodded and started moving. "Sauv blanc is your favorite, Alba, right?" I didn't narrow my eyes at him because we had witnesses; I just nodded once.

"Chablis for me, hon," José called to Tariq and parked his butt on a stool next to Julia and Salome, while I stood in the periphery of the kitchen like a loser. My friends all looked happy as hell while my ex-boss whipped up a gourmet meal for them. Freeloaders.

I didn't know where to put my eyes, every time I glanced at Julia she kept mouthing shit like "relax" and "you're being a weirdo." But letting my eyes land on Theo was one hundred percent out of the question. It looked like he'd taken a post-workout shower and he was now wearing a white T-shirt that looked painted on and gray sweats that left absolutely nothing to the imagination when it came to his groin area.

"Alba Serena, ven aca." He snapped the words, and crooked a finger at me, and I swore my soul left my body for a couple of heartbeats.

"What?" I asked, still trying to keep some space between us, like taking the few steps to join him in the kitchen would put me biting distance from a caged tiger.

"Come here, I need your help." He employed that commanding tone that I'd heard him use a thousand times—on me, on his other staff. But now, there was something right under the order that made my stomach feel molten. Playful but stern and my body reacted to that call in ways that could get me in a hell of a lot of trouble.

From my peripheral vision I could see Julia and José both making shooing motions at me with their hands, and I decided it was probably best to keep these assholes out of the picture because they were no help at all. I cut my eyes at them and went into the kitchen.

Fuck, he was wearing the aftershave I liked. The one with bay rum and black pepper.

"You scared of me now?" He said it really low, like he didn't want the others to hear.

Not scared of him per se, but definitely a little apprehensive about the proximity to that dick print and massive thigh combo in those tight sweats. "Of course I'm not," I squeaked and came the rest of the way until I was standing next to him in front of the kitchen counter. "What do you need?"

"Just some help mincing this garlic and cilantro. Can you do that for me?" I almost, almost, said *yes, Daddy.*

I needed to calm down before I did something really stupid. The man just needed some shit chopped up.

"This?" I asked, pointing at the bunch of herbs and the head of garlic sitting next to a cutting board on the counter, like I'd never seen either in real life.

"That's all...for now," he confirmed with a sexy slickness that was frankly uncalled for when dealing with herbs and spices.

He reached over on my left side so that his front was right at my back, not close enough to touch, but I could still feel the heat of him up and down my body. He grabbed a small knife from a magnetic strip on the wall and slid it next to my hand.

"Use the cutting board," he ordered, while his other arm appeared on my right and tapped the wooden slab in front of me. It was like being sprayed with flames. "You got this."

He winked then turned his attention to stirring the pot full of the stew like he hadn't just defibrillated my libido. I leaned both hands on the counter, letting the cool granite calm me while I breathed through my nose a few times before turning to Julia and hiking a thumb in Theo's direction.

"See what I mean," I mouthed. My friend didn't answer, just picked up her phone and tapped on the screen and a few seconds later my own buzzed in my pocket.

Julia: We're taking bets on how long it'll be before you two fuck on that counter... I say a week. José says Friday.

Alba: It's Wednesday!

Julia: OH... We know.

I flipped them a shaky middle finger and proceeded to do the shoddiest job of mincing cilantro in the history of humankind.

"Here's the garlic press." That was said right against my ear, and I very nearly maimed myself.

"I don't need that," I said a little more testily than was warranted and slid the garlic press away.

"It's easier," he prodded in an overly amiable tone that put my teeth on edge. I really wanted to fight him. Fight him and then climb up the distance to his mouth and kiss the hell out of him.

"I don't want it," I insisted when he continued to stare at me. "You told me you needed minced garlic, doesn't mean I have to do it like you'd do it," I said through gritted teeth.

"Oh, that's pretty clear," the asshole said, raising an eyebrow at my pile of poorly minced cilantro. This was why whenever cooking was happening in my house I stayed as far away from the kitchen as possible. I was so good at putting things together, at making things. But with food I didn't have the slightest clue. I hated feeling clueless, and like always when I felt inadequate, I lashed out.

"You said you wanted me to help," I said in a quiet unsteady voice. "This is the best I can do; if you want it your way, then you do it." He stiffened at my humiliating outburst, then without a word he moved away. Which only made me feel worse. I wanted to fist his shirt and haul him back next to me. I didn't turn to see what he was doing but I heard the fridge open and close while I frantically chopped cilantro into misshapen smithereens.

"Here." My entire body sprung to attention. I expected him to offer more critique of my less than stellar sous chef skills, but instead a can of guava LaCroix appeared next to my hand.

"You like those," he informed me, in an almost too casual tone.

"Thank you," I said breathlessly. I opened the can and took a sip, and almost wished Theo would keep arguing with me, so I'd be distracted from the warm glowing thing in my chest.

A throat cleared behind me, reminding me we had an audience. When I turned Julia was working on one of those "speaking glances." I mouthed a semi-annoyed "what" as I gingerly picked up the now severed head of garlic. Instead of answering she tapped something on her phone and seconds later Salome, José and Tariq were fishing their own out.

"Darn, you know what?" Julia cried, and I knew for sure she was up to some bullshit. "I just remembered I need to stop by the store to get some peanut butter for Blue." I cut my eyes at her for using Rocco's little niece for her lies.

"You're not going to stay for the asopao?" Theo didn't exactly seem mad at the change of plans. And even though I'd asked them to help me out with my awkwardness around my new roommate I was kind of relieved for them to go. There was something happening in this kitchen with Theo, and I wasn't sure I wanted to find out what it was with an audience.

"Save me some, I'll come by to get it tomorrow." Julia was smirking now.

Tariq chimed in next.

"Yeah, man, I need to get my dry cleaning." He rubbed the back of his neck, awkward as fuck because even though the others could moonlight as con artists, Tariq was way too pure to be effectively deceitful. Soon Salome and José were lying through their teeth too and heading out the door like their asses were on fire.

Theo lowered the heat on the cast iron pot he was using and covered it with the lid then came over to proffer kisses to Salome and Julia and dap to José and Tariq.

"Maybe another time we can have you over for some steaks?"

I was still reeling from the effects of that "we" when Salome responded from the doorway.

"If you include an Ahi tuna steak I'm down."

Theo shot out a "You got it" before looking at me as if I had the final approval of this soiree he was planning.

"Steaks sound good," I mumbled awkwardly and pointed to the door. "I'll walk them out."

When I got back to the apartment Theo was leaning against the counter drinking a bottle of Shiner Bock and staring out into space.

"That was an abrupt departure," he said, and I just nodded, because now I felt guilty that I'd been short with him all day.

The garlic was still sitting there, untouched. And I decided to show some grace and grabbed the press. Except that when I pulled off a couple of cloves I noticed they were too big for it. "What kind of mutant garlic is this?"

He grinned and came over next to me.

"I ordered online and that's what they sent. It said that it's Elephant garlic. I agree it's a little freaky. But here," he said, grabbing a smaller knife than the one I had. He cut the clove in half then handed me a piece. I put it in the press and squeezed. He was so tall he could stand behind me while he showed me. He probably had a bird's-eye view from up there. I was grateful that the knife-handling moment was over, because this much proximity to Theo would almost for sure end with a visit to the emergency room.

"Like this?" I asked, my voice high and a little hysterical. It was annoying how cool and calm he was while I was ready to stick my entire head into the freezer.

"That's great." The praise went through me like an electric current.

"Are you going to be here for the stylist tomorrow?"

"No." I felt him shake his head behind me, his chin grazing me when he moved. "I already saw her."

"You did?" I glanced up at him and found him grinning at me. It almost knocked me out. He smiled so much in Texas, big ones that made a dimple on his chin pop. It was freaking annoying.

"That red sweater you loved so much was from her."

"I didn't love your dumb sweater," I lied through my teeth. "It just kept catching my attention because your chest is the size of a billboard and that bright color was hurting my eyes."

"That's too bad, because the stylist wants to 'capitalize on my physique' so there are lots of tight, brightly colored sweaters in my future." He leaned in again and I squeezed the seltzer can in my hand. "Sorry."

He didn't sound sorry at all.

"Did I scare off your friends?" He turned away from me when he asked.

"No," I said honestly, but he kept stirring, not looking at me. "Don't tell me that you'd care if you did." He went really still then, then turned off the gas on the stove. He moved so he could lean on the counter, his arms over his chest in a mirror image of mine. If my mirror image was half a foot taller and had fifty pounds of pure muscle on me.

"I do care, because I want you to feel at home here."

"That's going to take time, Theo."

He bit his lip, probably fighting the urge to order me to trust him.

"I'm honestly surprised you were up to letting them stay for dinner." I said it before I really thought about what I was implying, but he didn't seem to mind.

"I wanted to meet Julia. She's your oldest friend." I almost laughed at the way he said it, like he was informing me of the fact.

"She is." I sipped from the can of seltzer, just to have something to do while he stared at me like he was trying to get right in my head. He kept gnawing on that lip while the string that had been pulling between us since the moment I'd walked in here this afternoon tightened by the second.

"Since New York," he hedged, like we were doing a fill in the blank game for my life.

"Since middle school in Corona," I clarified, and he nodded like I'd just confirmed a fact for him. "Why are you suddenly so curious about my life, Theo?"

It took him a while to answer, so long I didn't think he would.

"Because I can be now." He said it to go along with another one of those self-conscious shrugs. Because he could be...now? Like as opposed to before when he couldn't because he didn't give a fuck?

"Why didn't you tell me about your book renovations?"

That surprised me. Surprised me so much that I stayed with the can suspended in the air, midsip, staring at him. "That's a change," I told him honestly, and he had the gall to look offended. "I seem to recall being told not to ever discuss personal business unless I was asked." He winced at that, then rubbed a hand behind his neck.

"I can be an asshole."

"Without breaks or lulls for three years straight," I said deadpan, and that seemed to break the tension somehow. The sense that we were inside a balloon that was about to pop eased and I could take deep breaths again.

"How about this?" He pushed off the counter so that we were only a couple of feet apart. His eyes looked like gray marble, flecked with brown and black. He kept finding reasons to get closer, to push on the space between us and make it smaller.

"What?" The question came out breathy, eager. Like I already knew the answer I wanted to hear. Maybe there were parts of me that knew exactly what they wanted with Theo Ganas. Thankfully the parts with common sense remained firmly in charge as he loomed large over me.

"If you tell me more about your business, I'll teach you some hacks for chopping cilantro and mincing garlic."

I don't know why I was disappointed, when he was offering an olive branch. Did I really think he was going to kiss me? This was my problem: I always wanted more than I could have.

## Chapter Ten

### THEO

"Ceci, are you still in touch with Tom Hughes?" I asked my stepmother as I made my way to the first meeting with the design team. I'd planned to offer a ride to Alba, but when I'd woken up at 5:00 a.m. I'd had a text from her with a time stamp of 4:30 a.m. saying she was headed to the office early. I had never met anyone that worked as hard as Alba Duarte. Or anyone sweeter and meaner than that woman. Fuck, she did things to me when she turned that chin up and told me to drop dead. Last night I'd almost kissed her, almost asked her for more, but the fear that she needed more time made me stop.

"Theo!" Cecilia's voice snapped me out of my head. "What do you need from Tom?" I laughed at the question, because this was the second time in a month that I was acting completely impulsively when it came to business. Both times Alba Serena had been the spark that lit the match.

"I just remembered seeing an interview a while back where he talked about an affordable housing program here in Dallas. Something for veterans. I remembered it because he's partnering with two Dominican pro players," I added into the silence. Millionaire Tom Hughes had donated a shit ton of money to build a domestic violence shelter a few years earlier and we'd won the contract. It had been a great project. The kind that I would've loved to do more of, but had not because I'd had to prioritize what my father wanted, which was big projects like Valle Mar.

"Tom is involved with that…" Cecilia's suspicious frown practically came through the airwaves.

"I was thinking while I'm here maybe I could connect with his partners, maybe offer to support the project."

Cecilia made a sound that said, "What are you up to?" but didn't push me. Instead she did what she always did: remained unconditionally supportive.

"I can reach out to him and get you two connected. The last time I talked to his husband, Camilo, he said Tom was flying out to Dallas to meet with the other guys."

The other guys were Giordan Johnson-Mella, the starting point guard for the Dallas Stallions, and Ivan Ruiz, the star pitcher for the Dallas Lonestars. Ivan was pretty candid about his life. He'd come out as gay at the end of his rookie year and done a lot to help fight stigma against LGBT+ youth in Dominican sporting communities. And recently Giordan opened up about his brother's battle with PTSD after serving in Afghanistan. Both Ivan and Giordan were in their midtwenties, much younger than I was, but I respected that they used their platforms and their money to help others. Since Alba had reminded me of the things I'd prioritized before taking over for my father at Ganas, I couldn't shake the feeling that this time away from the obligations in New York was the moment to go back to that.

"I keep thinking that teaming up with some Dominican guys and doing something for communities that need it could be good for me." Even as I said it, I felt fired up. It had been too long since I'd done anything that felt bigger than myself.

"It'll be good for you to do something that's your own."

Cecilia's opinion mattered to me, and the fact that she approved without hesitation told me I was on the right track. "I'll get you that contact information ASAP," she said, before heading out to a meeting. I sat in my car for a moment considering what it would be like to do work I was proud of, and for more than how much money it made us.

Just from the time I'd been in Dallas I'd noticed that there was a big homeless population. Only a block or so from Sturm's, where one could buy a vending machine full of Moët & Chandon, I'd walked by a park that had at least fifteen people sleeping on benches or on the ground in makeshift tents. And though most people didn't have the resources to actually do something to address the situation, I did.

I stepped out of my car feeling more excited at this possibility than I had been at any time about Valle Mar. I grabbed what I'd brought for Alba from the cup holder and made my way to the building.

The moment I pushed through the glass doors my phone rang and I saw my father's number. I thought of letting it go to voicemail, but he'd just keep calling and it wouldn't hurt to encourage him to stay off Cecilia's back as she worked to finalize things with Valle Mar.

"Theodoro Anibal." My father had a gift for making a person feel like they were being arraigned for treason just by saying their name.

"Dad," I answered briskly as I waved to the receptionist.

"When are you going to be done playing games down in that place?" he asked, as I took the stairs and I forced myself to breathe before lashing out at him.

"When the show is done and the Valle Mar deal is locked in, remember?" I kept my voice low, because the moment my father realized he'd me riled up, he'd keep pushing until I exploded.

"I heard that secretary of yours is down there. Is that what this is about? You chasing tail?"

If I got pissed off things would just go off the rails. "My former assistant," I ground out. "She also has a degree in interior design and her own business, and yes, she's the lead designer for the project the show is covering," I informed him as I stepped into the hallway. The conference room's wall was made of glass and I could see Alba clearly even from ten feet away. She was standing by a long table that took up most of the room, poring over a bunch of drawings she'd spread out on the table. She was in one of her Dallas outfits. An emerald green blouse and tight gray skirt. Her curls bounced around her head and I could see just a hint of the lace of her bra as she stretched to slide a paper closer. Focused. Intense. Going after what she wanted with everything she had.

My father droned on about contracts and potential properties to buy, but my focus had already drifted away from him.

Need pulsed through me merely from watching her. This was it, what I'd come here for. This woman who had been here on her own for hours already. Working, chasing her dreams. She must've noticed me, because she popped her head up and looked right at me for just a second. And she looked…pleased?

"Dad, I need to go." I heard the surprised intake of breath and a hole opened in my stomach. That instant guilt at displeasing my father. But I didn't backtrack. I wouldn't apologize.

"I built a kingdom for you, and you act like you're doing me a favor."

"I didn't ask for it."

"What is that supposed to mean?"

Where did I start? I hadn't wanted any of this. Three years ago, I'd been prepared to tell him I didn't want to take over as the head of Ganas Corp. That I wanted something different than what he'd envisioned for me, but then he'd had a heart attack, his third in ten years, and everything changed. I'd taken over the day-to-day operations, hired a third assistant, and told myself I'd help until he was stronger. But one year had turned into three and I forgot that Ganas was my father's dream, not mine. Here in Dallas I'd begun to remember.

"Cecilia can more than handle things while I'm here. You need to learn to let go." And then out of nowhere it was out my mouth. "And you need to be okay with me not being there."

"Where is all of this coming from?" my father practically shouted. The idea that there could be a world where I wasn't at the helm of Ganas in any capacity was something I'd suppressed for so long, it felt almost foreign to think about. But I could see it again.

"I will be there for the closing," I responded, ignoring his question, my vision full of Alba. "I have to go, Dad."

I pocketed my phone and went inside the conference room. It was another room made of glass walls. Everyone who walked by could see us.

"Hey." Why did I sound like I'd been doing shots of gasoline all night?

"Dunkin' Donuts coffee?" She pointed at the cup in my hand. I'd forgotten I was holding it. "I didn't know you were aware that was an option for caffeinated beverages."

"It's for you." I offered it to her, extending my hand. When she narrowed her eyes suspiciously, I said something to get us back on steadier ground. "I told them to put an extra pump of artificial hazelnut-flavored syrup substance in there for you." She pulled a face, but finally reached for it, and when our fingers brushed, that now familiar zap of electricity ran through me.

"Thank you," she told me, bringing me out of my lusty thoughts, then proceeded to take a thirsty gulp. She held the cup with both hands as she glanced at me with a mischievous expression. From the raised eyebrow and the little smile on her lips I figured she was about to make fun of me. I didn't care. I loved seeing her relaxed around me. "You need to keep an eye out for the CSA, they might come pick you up at any moment."

"The CSA?" Her grin got bigger at my question.

"The Coffee Snob Agency." She busted up while I shook my head at her.

"You're a cheeseball," I told her, unable to hide the smile on my face. She didn't fight me on that, since the joke had been terrible, just gave me another one of those sassy grins I'd never seen in New York and kept guzzling her coffee.

"You look good." I kept my attention on her face, not letting it drift down to the swell of her breasts, knowing that little bit of lace was calling to me like a beacon. But she was too preoccupied to notice my staring.

"Looking professional and being prepared is the one thing I can control this morning. The rest…" She didn't have to say that she was worried about Chase. *I* was worried about him. He had been an asshole to her at every opportunity and I expected him to be one this morning.

She grimaced and then jumped when the door was pushed open behind us. I didn't have to turn around to know who that was. Alba's crestfallen expression said it all.

"We thought we'd be the early birds, but it looks like you beat us to it."

Fucking Chase.

"Good morning." Alba's entire demeanor changed the moment he walked in. But it wasn't the usual weariness he brought out in her. She seemed confused…and annoyed.

When I turned around, I could see why. There was a very blonde younger woman with him today. I also noticed that he had his hand on her back. I was about to extend my hand when Chase's companion leaned in to buss me on the cheek.

"This is Theo Ganas," Chase said, somewhat civil to me for once. He completely ignored Alba, though she was standing right next to me. "This is my wife, Kayla."

"I've followed you since your first Olympics!" the blonde exclaimed as she grabbed for me. I'd only gone to two Olympics, but I just smiled and nodded. Chase's wife needed a quick lesson on workplace personal space etiquette, because she was very much in mine.

"I follow all your fan accounts."

"I don't really do social media much these days," I said, stepping back, but Kayla was not taking the hint.

"I'm Alba," my co-host announced, and I didn't think I was imagining that flash of animosity in her eyes. "I'm the designer for the show."

"I'm a designer too," Kayla announced, and something about how she said that made the hackles on my neck stand up. From the scowl on Alba's face, I could see she didn't like it either.

"That's right," Chase said in that overly chummy voice of his. "Kayla has a very successful platform, like you do, Alba."

"Okay." Alba's frown was so deep now she had a full unibrow.

"Since time is so tight, I thought it might be a good idea to bring Kayla on as an extra pair of hands." This fucking guy was really trying to sneak his wife into the show without any sort of warning.

"But I don't need an assistant," Alba bit out. I could see the tightness in her neck as she spoke.

"We already have a whole team already helping, who incidentally are starting to arrive." I pointed at the cluster of people making their way into the room. Chase glowered some more, but he didn't argue. Alba he just ignored.

"I'd like to do my presentation first, before we discuss any changes to the team," Alba requested, a lot more politely than I would have. But I could see from Chase's sneer that he was planning to steamroll right over her. He'd have to get through me first.

# ALBA

"Stop that," I yell-whispered at Theo for the second time in ten seconds. We were still standing in a corner of the room as everyone filed in. I was still reeling from Chase's ambush. The guy had really brought his wife to a meeting. *My* meeting.

"Stop what?" the idiot next to me asked like he wasn't sending murder looks in Chase's directions.

"Stop glaring at him like you want to choke him out, that's not helping." All I got was a scoff.

"I don't like that guy. He's a sleazebag."

"Pissing competitions are not how you win with a guy like Chase, Theo," I muttered, then took a good look at him in his Prada loafers and hundred-thousand-dollar Rolex. "Or at least not for me, it isn't."

"I'm not going to put myself or *you* through an entire month of dealing with his shit."

"But you'd have Kayla your number one fan on set all day?" I had no fucking idea where that even came from, but instead of shutting my reckless mouth, I proceeded to clutch a hand to my chest and fake swoon. "Are your arms sore?" I asked while he shot Chase more dirty looks. "She was kneading those things like a loaf of sourdough." The moment I said that his expression changed. A wiseass grin replacing his murder face.

"Are you jealous, Alba de Los Angeles?" I did not need this shit right now. "If you want some of this you just have to say so." He preened, the asshole *preened*.

Puffed out his chest and ran a hand over the sun-kissed waves of his hair. I knew he didn't use any product in it and when he was done it looked rumpled in that effortless-but-still-hot way it always did. His shirt was open at the collar and the dip at this throat which I'd basically avoided looking at for the first year I worked for him was visible. I knew just below that there was an expanse of hard, caramel muscle. And though I absolutely did not want to touch any of it, the thought of Kayla putting her hands on him made me want to scratch her eyes out.

"You ever gotten dick punched, Theodoro Anibal?" I asked, which was a much healthier way to cope than to examine what had just gone through my head.

Again I'd misjudged Theo.

"If you want to touch it so bad, Alba Ofelia, you just have to say so." His voice was pure sin, and though he was smiling I wasn't so dumb to think this man was playing. I opened my mouth to tell him exactly what I would do if ever got my hands on his balls but was interrupted with a reminder I was in a professional setting.

"All right, I think we're all here," the line producer, Tina, announced, ushering us into the meeting before I could follow through on my threats, not that Theo looked very concerned. On the contrary, he seemed very entertained by my threats of violence. Tina was great to work with and so far did not seem to find any of Chase's bullshit cute. She'd almost bitten his head off when he'd attempted to tug on one of her boho locs. At least I knew I had her in my corner.

Once we were all seated the introductions went smoothly enough. The rep for the show's sponsor, Smithson-Napa, seemed friendly. There were also a couple of other producers, as well as Julio, the foreman from the contractors I'd hired, who was now Theo's counterpart. My former boss was currently leaning over an iPad in Julio's hand while the other man grinned at whatever he'd said. It seemed Julio was one more person in the long list of people who, unlike me, loved working with Theo.

"Let's get started because we have a lot of ground to cover." Everyone turned to Tina at the front. "First order of business is getting Alba, our designer, to walk us through the design elements she wants us to focus on during filming. We can discuss the schedule and see where the contractors—" she tipped her chin to Theo and Julio "—want us to focus. We've got a great team here, full of seasoned professionals."

"Well, not everyone is seasoned."

I didn't give Chase the satisfaction of turning around, but I knew he was likely looking at me. "Some of us have never been in front of a camera and it shows."

"Let's get on with it, shall we?" Tina didn't look too happy at Chase's tone, but she kept things cordial...though I would've liked nothing more than to tear that fucker a new one. But I'd learned the hard way that the only way to survive situations like this was to double down on my politeness. Disgruntled, entitled white men were not a foe I could afford to antagonize when it came to my career.

I was certain Tina had learned that lesson long ago too, so she just sent me a "keep your cool" look and turned her attention back to Theo. Theo, for his part, did nothing to hide his disdain for Chase. Thankfully Tina nixed the stare off and called me to the front of the room.

"Miss Duarte, are you ready?" Tina prompted, and I stood up hoping I looked readier than I felt.

"Yes," I said, as I clicked on the slide displaying my vision for the library. I decided to launch into it before Chase offered any more of his helpful comments. "The building itself is beautiful and for the exterior what we need is just a refresh," I explained, bringing up a photo of the building as it was before the renovation and an image I'd generated with the changes we planned to incorporate. The few sounds of approval in the room bolstered me to launch into my rundown for this phase of the renovation. That and the intense yet encouraging expression on Theo's face I kept catching in my peripheral vision.

"The bigger job has been interior," I told them as an image with a big airy room lined with bookshelves appeared on the screen. The building was in the Spanish Mission style and my most ambitious plan involved turning the courtyard into a climate-controlled, four-seasons atrium. "This will be the showpiece for the library." I pointed with the little red light in my hand. "It will be built for the purpose of providing the community a place to enjoy a good book and some of that famous Texas sunshine."

The Smithson-Napa rep was smiling wide, but I barely got three more words in before Chase interrupted me.

"See, this is what I meant when I said we need someone seasoned. This is much too ambitious for the time frame we have. And that mural? Isn't that a little played out?" He flicked his hand in the direction of the area where the picture books would be displayed. "It'll take weeks."

"Like I said, I already have the artists lined up. They are both alumni of the Sturm Foundation's art program and have promised to finish it in five days, also—"

"So the contractor won't be able to get anything done

in there for five days? That will throw off the entire plan."
He sounded shrill and so fucking smug. I would not let this
asshole make me cry in front of all these people. For some
reason, I turned to Theo. Typically his presence would only
serve to make me even more nervous, but this morning, seeing how pissed off he looked on my behalf helped. It helped
a lot. His brow was furrowed as he stared at the showrunner,
his mouth twisted in a very hostile expression. He looked like
he wanted to slap the shit out of Chase. I was just hoping not
to cry or throw up before the meeting was over.

"We have footage from the area where the atrium will go,
we don't need to get in there until it's further along," Tina
reminded Chase, returning my focus to the conversation.

"It's all laid out in the folders in front of you," I told my
nemesis, gesturing to the packets I'd put in front of every
chair before we started. "There are other areas of the renovation to focus on while the atrium is off limits." Chase opened
the folder with one hand, giving the first page of the ten I'd
typed a cursory glance before he went back to glaring at me.

"And what are these?" he asked, pointing at the swatches
for the wallpaper I'd designed.

"They're wallpaper." I infused as much fairy dust as I could
into my voice, but it was taking everything I had not to
curse this asshole out. "They have quotes from classic litera-
ture from all over the world and will go in the main reading room as well as around the circulation desk. I did the
lettering by hand," I explained, and though Chase was not
impressed, Tina gave me a thumbs-up. I zoomed in on the
swatch and pointed to a sketch of a ceramic mug full of hot
chocolate. The plume of smoke coming out of it was a quote
from *Como Agua Para Chocolate* by Laura Esquivel. I had quotes
hidden in imagery from other books all over the design. "I
know Smithson–Napa has just launched a line of customized

wallpaper." The rep perked up at that, which put a little bit of wind in my sails. "I thought that would be a good way to showcase a new product, by using some of these designs and noting they were made with the customization tool."

The woman opened her mouth to say something, but Chase started up again.

"That is completely niche! The Smithson-Napa clients won't be interested in wallpaper that's about foreign books!"

"*Como Agua Para Chocolate* sold *millions* of copies. There was a feature film made from it." I patted myself on the back for how calm I sounded, because I was truly ready to cut a bitch. "That book, or any of the ones I chose for that matter, will not be niche for the predominantly Latinx community that will be using this library." The Smithson-Napa rep's lips flattened when Chase snorted at my comment, but I kept going. "Who knows, perhaps it could even give those who don't know those books something new to learn about."

"Whatever happened to using things that people actually can pronounce," Chase retorted in that insanely irritating tone of his. "Can't we just do *Snow White* or something? Kayla has some ideas—"

"Can you let her finish her fucking presentation?" Theo roared, his hand slamming on the table as he bolted up from his chair, making half the room jump in surprise.

"I was just making some points." Chase paled and his expression went from thunderous to meek the moment Theo got in his face. I stood there like I'd been sprayed with nitrogen.

"She's the expert here and the designer Sturm's hired," Theo seethed.

"Well," Chase spluttered, and I hoped his self-preservation instincts kicked in because Theo looked spitting mad. "Your family builds high-rises in Manhattan. This is small-scale for you. *Kayla* has worked with some of the biggest reality TV stars. Miss Duarte on the other hand has only—"

"*Miss Duarte* has built a thriving platform with hundreds of thousands of followers without anyone giving her a leg up. Have you seen what she can do?" The question was clearly rhetorical since the next thing Theo did was pull his phone out of his pocket. After a few taps he held it up. From where I stood I could see the after photo of the Outlander room I'd done a few months back. Everyone at the table was craning their necks to get a closer look. By then I figured I was either in a fever dream sequence or the coffee he'd given me had been chock-full of hallucinogens. "She's pulled this off while working three jobs and does them with practically no budget." He didn't even have his phone anymore, since he'd handed it to the Smithson-Napa lady.

"This is great," she murmured, although I couldn't be sure if she meant my work or the drama.

"She's a fucking magician," Theo said, eyes still trained on Chase. He could've been evangelizing, he was so serious. Meanwhile I was still trying to wrap my head around the idea that a man who for the three years I'd known him told me on a weekly basis that social media was the root of all evils had intimate knowledge of my Instagram account.

"Don't even think about walking out until she's done," Theo threatened Chase, who looked like he was about to cry.

There were many things that I could've said or done in that moment. Continuing my presentation while Chase was still subdued being the logical one. It *was* my intention to do that, but my mouth had other ideas.

"Since when do you have Instagram?"

Theo, who just the night before had pretended he didn't know a thing about my business, rubbed the back of his head while the two of us faced off with an entire roomful of people staring at us.

"Zo helped me get on it last night," he admitted, and damn the man for being this fucking adorable. "I wanted to see your work after we talked."

And what the hell was I supposed to do with that? Since I had absolutely no bandwidth at all to deal with the fact that this gorgeous, perplexing, not-nearly-as-surly-as-I-thought man apparently asked his fourteen-year-old sister to help him find my work online, I turned around and finished the presentation he'd threatened Chase to let me finish.

# Chapter Eleven

## ALBA

"What the fuck is happening to my life?" I asked no one as I sat in my bedroom still digesting the events of the morning. In the end the presentation had gone over well, or over well with everyone except Chase, who was still a hater. I'd planned to hunt down my roommate and ask a few pointed questions about his newfound social media presence. But the moment I'd ended my presentation, he'd run out of that conference room like a bat out of hell.

He also hadn't been home when I got back. That, of course, led to some Instagram sleuthing, which an hour later had yielded results I was still digesting. Theodoro Ganas was now on Instagram. It was for all intents and purposes a creeper account since his handle was Theo.Ganas.2576, but he apparently *had* created one. There were no profile pictures, no posts, to be seen, and he was following exactly two people: me and his sister, Zoe.

It was so fucking cute I honestly couldn't cope, but more concerning was the fact the little devil on my shoulder, who looked and sounded a hell of a lot like Julia, kept telling me everything I'd learned today meant *something*. Something I absolutely could not touch with a ten-foot pole until this show was done. If one thing was clear, it was that Chase was just itching to find an excuse to kick me off the set.

Still, what Theo had done for me today, no one had ever done. Gratitude and lust were a very precarious cocktail, but I should at least say thank you. Maybe I should just DM to say thank you...and ask if he's making food. *You CAN text him*, the killjoy in my head reminded me.

Holding my breath, I tapped on the screen and typed his handle into the search bar. His icon was an Olympic pool, and yes, the fact that his one and only follower was his sister would never not be the cutest fucking thing on earth.

"Fuck it," I muttered as I followed him back from my Bookish Boudoir account, then I did it.

**Bookish Boudoir: Mr. Ganas... Imagine seeing you here.**

He saw my message right away and a moment later three dots floated on my screen for a few stomach churning seconds.

**Theo.Ganas.2576: Hey. *hand wave emoji* Sorry it took me so long to respond. I was asking Zoe how to add one of those little faces.**

I pressed my lips together. God, he was killing me.

**Bookish Boudoir: At least you have a good social media consultant. Your sister is a little badass.**

**Theo.Ganas.2576: She is.**

He added a smiley face emoji and I clutched my chest like a fucking sap.

**Bookish Boudoir:** Thank you for today.

**Theo.Ganas.2576:** You don't have to thank me.

This entire situation was bizarre. My relationship with Theo, which I had for so long thought I was completely clear about, kept changing almost by the hour since he'd come here. I didn't want to think too much about what that meant, because I knew that Theo didn't actually want the real Alba. He wanted the Alba who had been his PA. The hustling go-getter who had it all figured out. The woman who never complained, needed no sleep, no rest, no help, and could handle business without ever missing a beat.

But what he didn't know was that the Alba that did all that was worn out. That I lived in fear of saying or doing something that would undo everything I'd worked for. That whenever I saw my mother's number a pit opened in my stomach, because it could be a call that once again forced me to put myself aside to fix problems I hadn't caused. It wasn't that I resented my mother, I knew she'd been dealt a shitty hand too. But for Theo, his striver mentality came with a safety net made up of Benjamins; all I had to fall back on was myself.

Still, no matter what his reasons were, he'd helped me out, and at the very least I owed him my thanks.

**Bookish Boudoir:** I do, actually. Because of you I was able to finish my presentation.

**Theo.Ganas.2576:** Chase is an asshole.

I could practically hear the pissed off growliness in his voice.

Bookish Boudoir: He is.

I really should've just left it at that. Thanked him for what he'd done as a coworker and not bring personal shit into the conversation. But here in Dallas I kept blurring those lines.

Bookish Boudoir: So you've been busy liking my posts, huh?

A couple of beats passed with the three dots jumping on my screen, until he finally answered.

Theo.Ganas.2576: They're brilliant. You're brilliant.

I had to breathe through that one, and then immediately fished for more compliments.

Bookish Boudoir: You're just saying that because you know that it'll upset Chase's spirit.

I was never this thirsty. I was perfectly happy to hype my-self, I knew my work was good, but there was something about praise from Theo Ganas that always left me wanting more.

Theo.Ganas.2576: You want me to show you what I think of you, Alba Serena?

Jesus. Why was I suddenly sweating?

Bookish Boudoir: Yeah… I do.

Less than a minute later there was a knock on my door.

"Come in." I jumped up from the bed, my legs clearly not down with this plan to play it cool.

"Have you eaten dinner?" he asked, the moment I opened the door. He looked good enough to eat himself. He was so big, his head almost touching the top of the door frame even in his bare feet. Tonight he was wearing a pair of what was apparently a collection of soft faded jeans and an old Mets T-shirt.

"No," I told him as I clutched the doorjamb like a lifeline and pretended not to notice his eyes were fixed right on the slice of skin between the hem of my cropped sweater and the waist of my shorts. I didn't ask him to stop and he didn't look away. Inspecting, like he was cataloguing every visible part to make sure nothing had been disturbed in the hours he hadn't seen me.

"Let me feed you then." I knew he wasn't offering to actually feed me with his hands, but I still shivered at his words. I needed to get a fucking grip.

"I'll meet you in the kitchen!" I said a little too loudly, standing awkwardly by the bed while his eyes raked over my body. His arms tight against his chest while he looked and looked.

"All right." From under hooded lids I caught a glimpse of gray eyes, which crackled like lightning. "I'll be waiting, Alba."

Yeah...this "keep things impersonal" plan was working just great.

"What's this?" I squeaked out, pointing at the two plates on the coffee table. There were two cushions side by side on the rug and he'd lit all the candles. It was atmospheric as hell and this meal had just become an endurance challenge.

"I thought we could watch something," he said, as he uncorked a bottle. I stared at the food like it was going to jump off the plate and grab my face.

"Sit," he ordered as he passed me my glass and lowered himself down, but my knees didn't budge.

"They're going to get cold," he grumbled through a mouthful of taco. Seeing him wolfing down food like a regular human put me a little bit more at ease.

"Damn, you're so freaking pushy," I protested, sinking down next to him. He scoffed or maybe some taco went down the wrong pipe. It was hard to know with how much food he was shoveling down this throat. "Also, *rude.* Isn't the chef supposed to eat after the guests?"

"The chef does whatever the fuck he wants," he informed me after washing down a mouthful with some beer. It was so annoying how hot I found his rude ass. "Eat, and if you don't stop putting your ass in my face, one of these days I'm going to take a bite out of it." I almost dropped my damn tacos.

"What the fuck, Theo?" I knew my face had to be beet red. He just grinned and licked his lips, and thankfully I was already sitting down, or my knees would've given out for sure.

"What?" he asked, like I was the crazy one. "I said what I said. Your ass is bitable." He popped the rest of the taco into his grinning mouth.

I had shit to say. A lot of it. But I decided to eat a taco first, because there was still the chance that I'd gone into some kind of low blood sugar episode and was hallucinating. I picked up what looked like a birria taco with one eye on the plate and the other on Theo's slick expression. I dipped it in the little bowl of broth first, then closed my eyes and moaned when I actually took a bite.

"Holy shit!" It was hard to stay pissed at his greasy behind when he provided me with tacos this good. The meat was tender and perfectly seasoned and the broth was tangy with a hint of smoke. My taste buds were in heaven. "Did you make this?" I asked, the ass-biting comment forgotten as I practically came from a second bite of taco.

"Nah." He was smiling with teeth now, like me losing it over a taco was the absolute best thing. "I got it at a spot down the street."

I narrowed my eyes at him. It was kind of fun not having to be pleasant to him all the time. "I thought you were going to cook for me."

The smile from a minute ago was still tipping up his lips. But it wasn't amusement I saw on his face. Not quite. It was… satisfaction. It seemed that me being a brat about him cooking for me was great news for Theo.

"I said I'd feed you," he teased. "Not that I'd make it." I really resented that he could look that hot in just a white T-shirt and jeans.

"Thank you, again," I said through my last bite. Instead of answering he grabbed his beer from the table and leaned back to watch me eat.

"There's nothing to thank me for." It was unnerving to have him this close. Especially when my body could no longer refrain from reacting to his proximity. "You were great this morning."

"I hated not being able to ream out that asshole," I finally said and kept my attention on a smudge on the glass top of the table.

"I was surprised you didn't. You never shied away from going toe to toe with me in the office." He sounded genuinely confused that I hadn't acted with Chase the same way I did with him. But truth was that with Theo, even when he was at his most forbidding, I'd never felt like it wasn't safe to tell him what I thought. Even when I knew he wouldn't like it.

"Chase is looking for any excuse to claim I'm not fit to do this job. I'm not giving him any ammunition by running my mouth. But now that you scared the shit out of him, I assume he'll be watching his back."

"He better." Jesus, that sexy, mildly threatening rumble in his voice. It made my entire lower body turn to water.

"You've got something there," he said, as he lifted one of the linen napkins he'd brought from the kitchen—the man was the poster child for Taurus rising, always prepared— and dabbed the corner of my mouth. That little bit of contact, barely a touch, jolted me. My nipples hardened from the blood rushing to places it ought not go. I bit my lip and his own parted just a bit, a sharp intake of breath lifting his chest. I knew the air couldn't actually be crackling around us, but I could almost swear that if I lifted my hand thunderbolts would shoot right out of it.

He was so close, those gray eyes sparkling, lit up by something that I'd only gotten glimpses of before, but that now he was finally letting me see. There had been occasions when I'd catch Theo looking at me in a way that felt…not so much intrusive, but maybe startled. Like he didn't want to be staring but couldn't quite help it. But since his arrival in Dallas he just let himself linger for long moments. Examining me as if he found the sight absolutely riveting. My lips tingled as he locked his gaze on them. I desperately wanted him to kiss me. I was woman enough to sit with that truth.

I wanted Theo Ganas.

"You never said where the idea for your business came from," he said, breaking the lust spell.

I circled the edge of my glass as I considered how to say this to him without sounding like an extremely sad nerd.

"Books were my refuge." I shrugged, still not looking at him and feeling incredibly exposed, but something about his sober silence made me continue. "They were my safe space, my friends. My escape, really. It's not like things were awful for me," I quickly added, not wanting to give him the impression my home life had been terrible, because it hadn't been. But his eyes held no judgement when they met mine. Just curiosity, and even a hint of understanding. "We came to the States when I was almost eight from the DR and I didn't speak any English." I made a zero with my thumb and index finger and held it up to him. "The school was so big and loud." I cringed remembering the huge concrete building so different from the small school I'd gone to back home. "Those first couple of years were honestly traumatizing."

"Fuck, how did I not know that?" I gave him a sardonic smile and he shook his head. "I'm such an asshole."

I waved that away. Because even if he'd been a more casual boss, this was not a story I shared with my employers. This was something I told friends. Not that I was ready to tell Theo Ganas that I was seeing him in a whole new light.

"Hey, you set good boundaries in the workplace and never got creepy on me. I can't believe I'm saying that after all the times I complained you were a stuck-up ass." I laughed, and he frowned.

"Hey." He looked so aggrieved that I had to bite my tongue not to laugh again. "You just said you appreciated my boundaries."

"I did, I did! It's just you could be a little intense." I appeased him, the corners of my mouth turning up at his apparent dismay. "You want to hear about my childhood trauma or not?"

He shot me another one of those half-lidded stares that made my body throb. "Yeah, I do."

I suppressed a shiver and tried to focus on what I was saying. "My ESL teacher recommended that Mimita, that's my grandma…" I explained and this time it was his mouth turning up.

"Oh, we've met," he said, with a smile that told me all I needed to know about how my grandmother had behaved during their encounter.

"I heard," I said pointedly even though I could barely make myself sound annoyed. He bit his bottom lip and winked, a combo that had a very debilitating effect on me. Taking a sip of the crisp, cold wine didn't help to calm me down. "*Anyway*, the library was it for me and Mimita. Our favorite spot. It's how I learned English," I admitted. Those had been such weird times. I'd felt so untethered, Corona could've been another planet, and there was so much noise, all the time. But the library had been my oasis. A comforting haven when everything else was chaos. A memory of something I hadn't told anyone came to me, and before I knew it I was telling him.

"You want to hear something crazy?" I asked rhetorically and he nodded instantly. His big body leaning toward me, eyes lit up with interest. "The first few times we went neither of us knew we could take the books home and we would just hang out there for hours." It had been so long since I'd thought of that. "We don't have libraries like the ones here where you can borrow books. Not public ones, anyway. And definitely not ones with story time for kids or anything like that." I sighed, recalling those afternoons sitting on comfy chairs reading or listening to one of the staff read a book for us. Even when I still couldn't understand much of what they were saying I'd been enthralled. "It was a magical place. Libraries and bookstores have always felt like that to me."

He stared at me for a really long time. So long I started to squirm, and then he shook his head.

"And now you've turned your passion into your business. You're incredible." I tended to bristle at implications that I'd overcome harrowing circumstances, but his words didn't feel like condescension. And lately, I'd been thinking about how hard it had been to manage as much as I had as a kid. That first year of public school when I thought I'd lose my mind trying to understand what was happening around me, while my parents struggled to make a life in a place they could barely navigate. We were all so scared. For months we didn't leave the four or five blocks that made up our neighborhood. My parents, who had been brave enough to leave everything behind to come to New York, became these meek, docile people. Worn down by the slights and rejections lurking around every corner. That fear had grown inside me too, but I'd fought it. Every day I made myself be bold, even when it cost me so much.

"Thank you, Theo." He winced at that.

"Tell me more." The intensity of his focus flustered me, but I also wanted to keep talking. I remembered that little bit he'd shared about his parents pushing him to swim, and I wanted him to know me better.

"When I was a teen I got into DIYing and crafts. I did all kinds of fun stuff with book cover prints. If a book really got to me, it was all I wanted to talk about. I'd pore over fan art and fanfic, whatever could keep me in that world for a little longer." Even now as an adult nothing had the ability to comfort or shelter me like a good book could.

"I always saw you with your reader," Theo mused. "But I didn't know books meant that much to you."

"Book people, like *real* book people...are sort of hard-core. That's why I started Bookish," I explained, unable to stop the excitement that came through anytime I talked about my business. "I knew there were readers like me out there who thought nothing was too extra or too over the top when it came to expressing their love for their favorite stories. And I was right." I let myself get a little cocky then, because the community I'd created with Bookish Boudoir was something I was extremely proud of. He only nodded and kept looking at me with those keen gray eyes.

"What's your favorite book?"

I gasped in horror at this question.

"That's something a true book person would never ask." I was yelling, but he grinned like he was utterly amused by my horror. "It's impossible to answer!" He laughed so hard the corners of his eyes crinkled and something tightened in my chest. "What's yours, then?"

"I'm not a huge reader," he admitted regretfully. "I used to love Sherlock Holmes when I was a kid though." I'd figured as much, and it was probably for the best. For a man with that face, that body and that bank account to also be a book nerd would be too much.

"I love a good mystery." I almost told him that in middle school I'd tried to decorate my room like it was Sherlock's apartment on Baker Street and my mother had almost killed me, but I was already sharing way too much of my bio. And I didn't want to talk about my parents tonight.

"Are you done?" he asked, looking down at my very empty plate. The conversation had been so easy, I'd eaten every bite and had barely noticed.

"I am," I told him, patting my very happy stomach. "Thank you." *For dinner, for asking me about things that matter to me. For listening like the answers were important.*

"Good, come on then," he said and stood up, then extended his hand down to me.

"What? Where?" I looked around the room, confused. But he kept his hand in front of me. Jesus, his dick was literally in my face and I would not be having more wine.

"I should do some work, we have the meeting with Julio tomorrow," I demurred, my hand limp in his. I opened my mouth to politely beg off, but my roommate was apparently not having it, if that stubborn shake of his head was anything to go by.

"No, work is over for the night."

"Okay, but I still have to—"

"Come up here with me," he coaxed, pulling me to him. "I'll get up early and go over things with you, before the call," he offered with another tug, crumbling the last of my resolve.

"Fine." I gripped his hand, but he pulled me too fast, which landed me right up against his chest. I let out an "oof" when our bodies crashed together, but he didn't budge. Not an inch. He stood strong, one arm around my waist and those stormy eyes burning me up. He felt so good. I wanted to bury my nose in the crook of his neck and inhale the faint scent of chlorine always clinging to his skin. But I could not let myself get caught up in this. This pretend house and man who would be gone in a month.

This penthouse and this life were only real for one of us and everything depended on me not forgetting which of us it was.

"What are you doing, Theo?" I forced myself to ask.

"Watching some TV and sitting on the couch?" He had one eye closed and the other open, and it made him look like an oversize puppy, but I was going to have to start resisting his cuteness. This was too serious.

"That's not what I'm asking..." My voice sounded small and despite myself a little bit of yearning slipped out. Because I could tell myself whatever I wanted, but there was no way to hide how good it felt to be like this with him. If I could not make my own heart get with the program, Theo had to do it for the both of us. He almost looked pained, but then he lifted that big hand and tucked a curl behind my ear.

"I don't think I have the answer to the question. You do."

I didn't know what I'd expected, but him putting things in my court was not it. I almost wished he'd do something I could lash out at. Kiss me or get handsy. Grope me so I could jump off the couch and tell him he was being sleazy. He didn't do any of it. He just tugged me down to the couch with him until I was snuggled up against him. "I just want to watch some TV with you."

I *was* practically on his lap, but he didn't push for more. Just reached over me for the control and when he leaned back against the cushion brought me with him.

"Stay still," he ordered as he manhandled me some more.

"You're so fucking bossy," I protested, even as I tucked myself against his side. "And I'm cold." I whined, arms crossed over my chest. He chuckled, and whispered "brat" under his breath, but still reached for a throw blanket and draped it over my lap.

"It's a little down time, Alba." He sounded so fucking reasonable, while I felt like I was sneaking around when my parents weren't home. I remembered Julia's admonition from the night I'd moved in, about trying to be friends with Theo. And, okay, this was a little bit more up close than I imagined a friendship with him would be, but if he could be a grown-up, so could I.

"Fine, but we're watching what I want." I snatched the control from his hand, then yelped when he lifted me until I was lying between his legs. I knew if I told him to stop he would, but I could not make myself do it. It felt nice having a man, *this man*, touching me like this. "I'm not watching sports either." I looked over my shoulder at him, then reared back when he leaned down, close enough to brush our lips together. But he didn't try a thing. Just kept that big, strong arm around my waist and sighed contentedly.

"I'm down for anything," he assured me, and just to be a bitch, I settled on a rerun of *My Little Pony*.

"If you think Zoe didn't turn me into a Brony during her obsession with *MLP*, you must pay less attention than I thought you did."

Damn it.

"Who even calls it *MLP*?" was my dumbass clapback.

"I'm just watching TV, Alba Aphrodite." The fuck he was.

"Not when you're looking at me like that, Theodoro Anibal." I had my finger pointed at his mouth, and the bastard bit it. "Ow," I cried, and wiggled to try and escape, which only worked to make me grind harder on his dick.

He bucked up into me laughing, while I clenched every muscle in my body. "Damn, culona, chill. I know I'm hard to resist once I turn it on but—"

"Did you just..." I whipped all the way around, which would've been way more effective if it didn't just result in me straddling him, but I was already in too deep, so I got in his face. He let loose that shit-eating grin that my clitoris seemed to have a sonar for.

"You did *not* just call me *culona*." Now I was the one growling and apparently he thought pissing me off was foreplay.

"I like your big ass." He did that lip biting thing and though his hands were at his sides, I could feel the ghost of his fingers on my hips. "Actually." He cocked his head, like he was reconsidering his answer, then tipped my chin up, which gave me the full effect of those gray eyes. "Scratch that."

*Scratch what, motherfucker?* I almost screamed.

"I don't just like it. I'm obsessed with it."

"Hey," I protested even as I pressed said ass to his groin on instinct. He hissed but didn't move. God, he was hard and huge, and I had to stop reminding myself I'd lost count of the amount of months that had passed since I'd had an orgasm induced by another sentient being. The chances of this situation devolving into poor sexual choices were increasing by the second, and instead of running to my room, I rolled my hips again.

He pushed up in response and the friction was enough to have me soaking my underwear. He looked up at me with an expression that said *your move.* And holy shit did I have some moves in mind. Like sliding all the way down his body and finally confirm for myself what he was under his sweats. Or perhaps I'd pull of my sweater and see what he'd do. So many delicious possibilities...but I chickened out.

"Since you seem to have turned into a completely different person, I guess you'll be delighted to hear Julia is planning a whole pool party here next week." He didn't call me on killing the vibe, just looked at me like this was chess and he didn't want to rush his next play.

"That sounds great. I love pool parties."

I scoffed, because the alternative was shaking him and screaming *Who are you and what have you done to Theo Ganas?* in his face.

"This isn't weird for you?" I asked, pointing at the spot where our bodies were pressed together. Because I was practically levitating off the couch while he was breathing nice and easy under me.

"Not at all." He just lifted a shoulder, like all of this was just super normal. "I worked out a protocol to manage what your ass does to me years ago."

"You have a what, now?" Another shrug.

"About five minutes after you showed up for your job interview I decided you would be my assistant." That flutter in my belly had to be the birria tacos I'd inhaled. "And for that to not end in a lawsuit I needed to devise a way not to stare at your ass all the time." The matter-of-fact way he relayed that made my head spin, not because of what he said—because by this point I was starting to believe he might be a little bit into me, even if it was just lust—but how he said it.

"And all that time, I thought you couldn't stand me." It just popped out. This was a motherfucking free-for-all.

"If I couldn't stand you, why would I have let you work for me for three years?!"

"You barely ever looked at me for that entire time!"

"That was intentional." He sounded so outraged. Like my lack of appreciation for his sacrifice was too much for him. "Alba, you've seen your ass. Do you know what it took for me not to ogle you when you showed up in those fucking T-shirt dresses you love?"

He had to be fucking with me. That was the only thing that made sense. He was fucking with me. "If you're just going to mess with me then I'm going back to work." I tried to push off the couch, but he kept me pinned to his chest. Then, like I weighed absolutely nothing, he lifted us both until he was sitting upright, his mouth right by my ear. I was so turned on I couldn't make words.

"Let's get this straight right now, your ass is a work of art." It wasn't a growl this time, it was lower than that and it made my insides buzz with want. His hands were clamped to my arms, and they were the only thing keeping me from shooting right up to the ceiling. But Mr. Ganas was not done giving me the rundown on what he thought about every one of my features. "So are your legs, for that matter. Your tits, your face, your entire fucking body."

I sucked in a breath, my body reeling from the feeling of being bracketed by those powerful thighs. "I need you to

know in no uncertain terms that I have never wanted anyone as badly as I've wanted you." I could feel the ghost of
his mouth brushing my ear, and lust tore through me like
a knife. "I've fantasized about what I'd do to every inch of
your body." A gasp escaped my mouth as he barely brushed
my neck with his lips. "I'd lick you so good, give that smart
mouth something to scream about for hours."

"Oh, God." I arched my spine, pressing into him. I was
needy, desperate. He made a smug sound, and pressed a quick
chaste kiss to my jaw before pulling back. I almost cried
from frustration.

"Tonight we're just relaxing," he informed me while I
panted like I'd run a marathon. "You need a night off."

In the last twenty-four hours Theo Ganas had threatened
violence on my behalf, fed me, and was now whispering in
my ear that he fantasized about licking me. I didn't do drugs,
so it couldn't be that. But I *had* to be tripping.

"Theo, what the—"

"Shh, this is the episode where Spike runs away." He
pointed at the TV with the remote.

He followed up his life-altering little speech about his
thoughts on my body by bringing me closer to him and
handing me my wine, and fuck if I didn't lie back against
that massive chest and sip on my sauv blanc until I passed
out right on him.

# Chapter Twelve

## THEO

"Damn, this place is swank," Dani, the friend Alba pulled all those all-nighters with—yeah, I was salty about it—exclaimed as he walked into the house with the rest of our pool party guests in tow. When I'd agreed to the party, I thought it would be a chance to do something that was not work related with my new roommate. Especially after that night when she'd shared some of her history with me. After hearing about why books meant so much to her, it had taken superhuman self-control not to kiss her, but I was determined to take things slow. I didn't want her to think this was about just sex for me.

Sure, I'd had to jerk off twice before getting any sleep, but it had been worth it to have her lie on my chest for a couple of hours before she shuffled to her bed all soft and sleepy. I hadn't been able to get that conversation about her first years in the States out of my head either. It was hard to imagine Alba as a little girl, hiding out in a corner of a library. Finding refuge in the pages of books because life was overwhelming her. She was strong, the strongest woman I'd ever met, but now that I knew about vulnerability behind that hard-ass façade, I only wanted her that much more.

But in the week since we'd seen each other only in passing unless we were on set. As I suspected, most of my job was to smile and look pretty while I regurgitated the shit that Julio and his team were doing. I wasn't bored; Cecilia had connected me with Tom Hughes about the veterans' housing project and going through the material for that had kept me occupied. But I was determined to get some time with Alba today—if she ever came home, that was. She'd run off at barely six in the morning to do "a couple of errands for Bookish" promising she'd be back in time for her friends to arrive, but she was still MIA.

"Come on in." I grabbed the gigantic charcuterie board Julia had with her while I waved the others inside. They all had their hands full of food and drinks. Rocco had a case of what looked like a mix of local craft beers. Salome had at least four bottles of wine and a bag with disposable plates, cups and cutlery. Dani had steaks and a bottle of bourbon.

"Damn, you all take the BYOB to the next level. I like it," I teased, angling my head to the pool area. "There's a fridge out there, and wet bar."

"Please tell me she's here," Julia said, bypassing me to look around the living room.

"She's not," I told her as I ushered them outside and tried my hardest to muster up a grin. "But you're all welcome to hang out as long as you want."

Julia balked at that. "You're hanging out with us too, right?" It's not like I'd been planning to hide out in my bedroom until Alba made an appearance, but it was nice to be invited. I'd never been very social, but I'd liked having Alba's friends here. Most of all, I'd been looking forward to spending time with her when we weren't both exhausted from a full day of filming. But when she wasn't busy with the show, she had her makeovers.

I knew she had duties and responsibilities very different from my own. Successfully carrying the empire my father had built was no small feat, but Alba was making her own path from scratch. I just wished she didn't feel like she couldn't ever stop.

"I'm calling her," Julia said, frustration clear in her voice. They'd been friends long enough that she had far more experience than I did dealing with this particular issue. But almost as if Alba could sense Julia was about to get on her case, my phone rang. My body stiffened like it recognized the vibrations when she called.

"Your friends are here, Alba Maximiliana. Are you on your way?" I asked, even though from the chatter in the background I assumed my roommate was nowhere near done working.

"Shit! They're already there?" I didn't answer because I could see Julia tapping hard on the screen of her phone, and from the frown and pursed mouth I assumed she'd gotten the update I was about to receive. "I am *so* sorry." She sounded contrite—just not enough to actually come home. "I thought the guys painting this room would be done faster. But only one of them came and I really need to get at least this part done today."

"So are you coming?" I sounded annoyed, and I was. But it wasn't because she was late, it was because I wanted her to be here as much as I did. Which wasn't fair, because like she'd told me a hundred times, I was the one who'd pushed myself into what she was trying to accomplish here. I just couldn't stand seeing Alba drive herself so fucking hard all the time. But guilting her wasn't it either.

"Is that her?" Julia asked as she came in from the pool area. "Let me talk to her." I handed over the phone, deciding Julia was less likely to fuck up in this conversation than I was, and took the beer Rocco handed me with a knowing expression.

"Thanks, man," I said gratefully.

"They will put you through it, but they're worth it," he muttered while his girlfriend spoke to my roommate in rapid-fire Spanish.

By the time we finished putting away food and drinks and everyone had commandeered a chaise around the pool, Julia was done with the call.

"Looks like it's just us for now." Julia and Rocco exchanged a look, then she sighed. "She doesn't know how to stop," she muttered, and almost immediately a regretful expression settled on her face. "That's not fair," she said with a click of her tongue. "She doesn't stop because she feels like she can't." I'd seen that myself. When Alba'd been my PA I'd admired how on her game she always was, how tireless she seemed. Just demanding absolute perfection from herself. But now that I knew the toll it took on her, the amount of shit she had to take from the Chases of the world, all I wanted was to take some of that load off her shoulders.

"How do you like your steak, bruh?" Dani called from the grill.

"Let me help you with that," I offered, sitting up, needing a distraction from getting all the way in my head about Alba, but Rocco put a hand on my chest.

"Nah, man, let us take care of it." He leaned in to place a kiss on Julia's lips then jumped up from the chaise. "You keeping my woman entertained is a hard enough job."

"Hey!" Julia protested, but there was only adoration in her voice. After she thought better of it, she cupped her mouth and called after Rocco. "Babe, make sure Dani cooks mine properly; that boy's been hanging out with these Texans too long." She turned to me with a horrified expression. "The last time he grilled for us, mine practically walked off the plate."

"It's sacrilege to grill meat this good to well-done," Dani lamented.

"I'm Dominican and we like our meat charred, gracias and thank you," Julia clapped back, making the other two snicker. "Don't play with me, Dani. Salome, keep an eye on him," she ordered. Despite the threats, Dani happily starting tossing meat and Salome's ahi tuna on the grill while he talked to—and was supervised by—Rocco and Salome, which left me and Julia alone by the pool.

"I hate that she doesn't give herself a break ever."

It wasn't what she'd said that surprised me. It was the concern in Julia's voice. Remorse cut through me when I thought of how demanding I'd been when she worked for me. On her first day I'd seen how competent she was, how eager to please. I'd expected nothing short of perfection and she'd never let me down. Not once had I considered I was just wearing her out.

"I don't know why you look like I just kicked your dog," Julia said, staring at me from behind her sunglasses. "You didn't make Alba turn into a workaholic—that's been twenty-nine years in the making." I made a noncommittal sound, not fully convinced that I didn't have a hand in it. Not all of it was me. But some of it *had* to be.

"She told me about when her family first got here," I said, surprising myself.

"She did?" Julia asked, surprised. "They moved in right across the street from us. They first landed in the Bronx," she said after a long pause. "But one of Alba's aunts knew the man who owned the house across from ours in Queens and they took the apartment on the second floor." Alba's friend threw her head back, eyes closed like she was conjuring a memory. "She was a godsend. We were stuck at the hip from Day One. Insta besties." Julia laughed, recalling their first meeting. "My grandmother doesn't speak a word of English, and she watched me and my sister while my parents worked so *my* Spanish was pretty good, and poor Alba was hard up."

"Has she really always been so…" *Intense, stubborn, persistent.* It's not like I didn't understand those things. Those three words had been my mantra at one point in my life. But what I saw in Alba was different than my pursuit of an Olympic medal. I'd had to grind, but in many ways the train had been put on the tracks for me; all I had to do was drive it to the finish line. Alba, she had to lay the tracks as she went. She was always *grasping*, constantly reaching for whatever she could grab on to. Like there wasn't a single thing she could let pass her by. As if seizing every opportunity was a matter of life or death.

"Relentless?" Julia finally asked and I nodded. She gave me a lopsided smile and sighed deeply, as if her friend's story weighed on her. "I mean it's not like I don't get it. We are all like that at least a little bit. The immigrant parents, the grind. You know how it is." I did and I didn't. Of course, my dad had lived through that, but by the time I was born, he was a millionaire.

"But that's only part of it for Alba." I raised an eyebrow at that, but from our conversation that night on the couch, I'd suspected that what drove Alba was more than just a strong work ethic. Julia looked at her glass, the clear pink liquid swirling around. "I'm not going to give you her life story because I would never betray her confidence like that."

It warmed me to Alba's friend that she looked out for her, even in this way.

"She's been carrying a lot for her family, for a long time." That was not exactly new information. In the time she worked for me, I'd overheard enough whispered conversations with her mother to assume Alba did more than just help out occasionally. But she never once gave me the impression she was struggling. "It's only really getting easier now." Julia quieted for a moment and frowned like she was considering what to say next.

"Go easy on her, she has the weight of the world on her shoulders. Some her mother put on there, but a lot of it at this point is because Alba can't not fix things for her family. If her sister needs money for school, she offers to pay for it. If her brother moves in with his boyfriend, she's there with the deposit." No wonder she never stopped. "I'm still amazed she finally took the plunge with Bookish."

"How's that?" I asked, and again Julia seemed to weigh her answer. But in the end she told me.

"She's been wanting to go out on her own for over a year now, but with her—" She paused, her eyes wide suddenly, like she realized she'd said too much.

"With her what?" Julia's mouth was clamped shut. Something about the panic in her eyes told me I might have been part of the problem.

"Did it have to do with me? Did she think I would give her a hard time when she left?"

"You're here, aren't you?" Julia retorted, then narrowed her eyes, a pugnacious expression on her face. "Why *are* you here, by the way?" I'd known that was coming. I didn't feel like I could say it until Alba knew.

"I think I'm going to hold on to that answer a little longer."

"Chicken," Julia teased, but she pulled her sunglasses down and winked at me over her the lenses, so she couldn't be that mad.

"Damn, why do the two of you look so serious?" Salome asked as she plopped down on the chaise next to mine. "This is not the kind of vibe I need when I'm living the penthouse pool life."

I chuckled and Julia rolled her eyes. "This is why I don't take these fools anywhere," she said with feigned annoyance and though I wanted to keep talking about Alba, I also knew Julia was probably not going to say much more. If I wanted the secrets of the woman for whom I'd come to Dallas, I would have to earn a right to them.

"So you all really like it down here?" I mused, as I took in their comfortable smiles.

"I really do," Salome said, the surprise in her voice making me laugh. She sat up and brought her knees up to her chest, her wineglass dangling from her hand. She was dressed in cutoffs and a tank top that said "Economist: someone who gets excited about things no one cares about." Her hair was short on the side and long on the top and it was a shade of light blue; with her tattoo sleeves she looked very much like a New Yorker, but she seemed at ease here.

"I mean the politics aren't great," she demurred to which Julia concurred with a hearty *amen*. "The summer is so hot I literally feel like my soul is leaving my body just from walking from my car to the door of my building on campus. But I don't know." She lifted a shoulder, brows furrowed, like she still hadn't figured out how her life had turned out the way it had but she was okay with it. "I sort of made my own rules here for how I wanted my life to be." She put down her glass and picked up the sunblock from the table then sprayed some on herself as she thought things over. And Julia spoke up.

"It's the same for me in a way. In New York it almost felt like everything was laid out, you know? That I had to fulfill some script that had already been written for me. How Dominican girls from 'good families' do." Salome nodded at the air quotes. "Here *I* say what stays on this master plan and mostly I make it up as I go along. But there aren't any gossips on the block looking out for when I get home or don't. Or to point out that this is not what 'we do' or how 'we live.'"

"And these pendejos are fun to be around," Salome added

as she waved a hand toward Rocco and Dani and then to Julia.

"Hey, watch who you call pendejo, pendeja," Julia cried, and they both dissolved into laughter. I stayed stuck on what they'd said. All my life I'd felt like I was born to fulfill a role in my parents' vision for their own lives. My mother wanted to hold on to my father and my father wanted a legacy. When my dad married Cecilia, my mother's hopes with my father ended and she left for the DR and never came back. My father loved me in his own way, but he also needed me to carry on what he'd made. My life in New York had been invented for me by other people. But here…here I could decide what that looked like.

When Dani finally yelled that the steaks were done, Salome and Julia got up, but I stayed behind, needing a moment to breathe through what that short conversation had done for me. I felt unlocked somehow. Like a door I didn't know was closed had been opened for me. What if this place was what *both* Alba and I needed?

"How's it going with the filming?" Rocco asked me as he cut into his steak.

"It's going fine, but the showrunner is a pain in the ass." Dani, Julia and Rocco all worked for the foundation and had had to deal with Chase a couple of times since he'd come on board. So they knew. And from Salome's very sour expression I assumed she'd heard about him too.

"Chase sucks," Dani concurred. "So what are you doing with the rest of your time? You running things in New York remotely?"

I lifted my hand and waved it in a "yes and no" gesture while I chewed. "I'm actually looking into the possibility of going in on a project here."

"Oh." Julia didn't even pretend to be coy; she was very openly about to get all over my business. "Do say more."

"I've been trying to get in on a program that's going to build housing for veterans. Two pro players from the DR playing for local teams are doing it. We still haven't been able to meet up though." This was the first time I'd told anyone about my plan, and I wished Alba was here.

"That's amazing!" Julia said, smiling wide. I wasn't surprised the social worker in the group was all over the idea. "Wait." She cocked her head in Dani's direction. "Is that your friend Gio's thing?"

Dani perked up at that, then nodded. "Yeah, Gio and Ivan are raising capital for a project like that."

"You know them?" I asked, surprised. I could almost hear Cecilia in my head going *See! That's why you need friends!*

"I do! You know what?" Dani said rhetorically as he pulled his phone from his pocket. "I'm meeting them next week for drinks. Rocco and Tariq are coming too. I can introduce you."

"That would be great, man," I said, feeling like this was meant to be.

"We're not invited because ladies are not allowed!" Salome said in a singsong voice. She was grinning so I didn't think it was too much of an issue.

Rocco laughed and Dani shook his head. "*You're not invited* because it's José's birthday and you all blackballed us."

"True," Salome acknowledged in that sort of shameless way she had. I really liked her. Fuck, I liked all these people.

"If you wouldn't mind me talking business in the middle of a night out, I'd love to join you."

Dani waved that off. "I'm happy to help you all connect."

"This is amazing!" Julia cried and leaned over to squeeze

my forearm. "I didn't know you did that kind of thing in your company."

"We used to," I said, finger tracing the rim of my beer bottle. "Alba reminded me the other day of a program I was involved with before I took over for my dad. I thought this might be a good time to try something different. Rewrite some of that master plan," I told her with a wink, and she smiled wide.

"If you need anything at all in terms of figuring out trauma-informed programming let me know. Anything I can do."

"Thanks, Julia." I turned to Dani and extended my hand. "Thanks, man. I appreciate you."

"No big, I'd love to see that project get off the ground finally. And we wouldn't mind you finding excuses to stick around," he joked, but something about the way that Salome and Julia looked at each other told me they were down for that plan. Which Salome confirmed a second later.

"We're working on Alba too. We like having the two of you here." Something hot spread through my chest at the casual way Salome said *the two of you*. It was unsettling how much I wanted that. I'd always had such trouble envisioning my personal wants beyond what had to get done for swimming, for my education, for the business. The only time I'd ever prioritized what I wanted had been this scheme to come after Alba. But now the idea of building something here in Dallas, on a different path than the one my father had set for me, was a very enticing possibility.

"Sticking around for what?" Alba's voice cut through the air and we all turned at once to watch her walk onto the patio. Every gear inside me started to turn faster. Her mere presence lighting up my entire system. There was no idling, no autopilot, when it came to this woman. She engaged every molecule in my body the moment she was near.

"Finally," Julia cried with sincere exasperation as she got up to kiss our newest arrival hello. Alba was smiling but something wasn't quite right. She was also looking at everyone except me.

"Sorry, sorry, sorry!" She threw her hands in the air, before bending down to kiss everyone on the cheek. "Today was a shit show of massive proportions, but I am mostly done with that makeover. Hey, Theo." She sounded breezy enough, but when she turned to me her eyes were guarded, like she expected me to be mad at her.

"Hey, yourself," I said and smiled up at her. Then to really drive home the fact that we were cool, I stood up and kissed her on the cheek. She seemed surprised, but a little pleased too. When she looked up at me, I could still see that little bit of wariness, and all I wanted was to kiss it away. I wanted more than anything to be the resting place for this woman. To be the person she went to when the world outside just got to be too much.

"Thanks for holding down the fort." She was in what I'd come to learn was her usual working-for-Bookish-Boudoir attire. Jeans, long-sleeved T-shirt, work boots and her curls pulled back with a headband. She licked her bottom lip nervously and a wave of pure lust almost leveled me.

"You look adorable in Timberlands." She blushed so sweetly and it was all I could do not to maul her right there and then. "That ass still on point too." That part was whispered, and she inhaled sharply. Today I was ready to push her buttons a little. This taking it slow thing was coming to a head, and I didn't know how much longer I could wait before I made my move. I wanted her too fucking much. I needed to know if all those heated glances I'd been getting meant what I thought they did.

"Go get your swimsuit on." I had to close my hand into

a fist not to slap her ass. Her breaths were coming all short like she was thinking about the same thing I was.

"I'll have a glass of rosé and a plate for you when you come back down."

She eyed me suspiciously, as she popped a grape from the charcuterie board into her mouth. "Why are you being nice to me after I left you to deal with my friends for two hours?"

"Because now you owe me, Alba Encarnacion, and I plan to collect my debt later."

"Is that a threat, Theo Ganas?" she asked with a hitch in her voice that told me I wasn't the only one still thinking about that night on the couch.

"That's a promise, culona."

# Chapter Thirteen

## ALBA

"Alone at last," my roommate declared a little too happily once we'd dispatched our guests. He'd been acting funny all afternoon. I'd expected him to give me the cold shoulder for breaking pretty much all his cardinal rules of human behavior. Not only had I left him alone to take care of *my* friends, I'd been two hours late.

I'd walked in fully prepared to be iced out or reprimanded, but he'd been nothing but sweetness. Hell, he'd been more than sweet, he'd been flirty—poured me a glass of rosé and served me a plate of food. Dallas Theo was a fucking trip and the more of this side of him that I saw, the more my resistance weakened. Since that night we'd watched TV something had been crackling between us that was close to combusting with every touch, with every look we exchanged. Was it smart? Fuck no. But I didn't know how to stop myself. I didn't think I wanted to. A distraction like Theo Ganas could be utterly disastrous to my plans. Not only were we working together on the show, no matter how much I denied it, I knew I could fall hard and fast for him. And love was just not part of my plan.

*But* one thing about me: once I decided to be reckless, I was going to be fucking reckless. And right now, my blood was boiling to do something I'd one hundred percent regret tomorrow. I *should've* been tired, given that I'd been working since six in the morning, but Theo had me keyed up and wired. He was tucked into one of the corners of the deep end of the pool and I was on a fancy float slowly gliding over the water, neither of us saying a word, but I could feel his eyes burning me.

"You're quiet tonight, Mr. Ganas." I pushed my sunglasses up and glanced at him while I took a sip of my drink.

"Just taking in the view, Miss Duarte." That sexy-ass voice of his set off a throbbing between my legs. Since we'd gotten back in the pool a few minutes ago we'd been playing this game where he'd let his eyes roam over me and they'd snag right when he got to my boobs. Then he'd lick his bottom lip and keep going all the way to my toes, but he'd made no attempt to get closer. Every time he did it, lust swirled around inside me until my skin felt like it was on fire.

I wanted him, and now that I knew that he wanted me there was no putting that genie back in the bottle. The intense attraction I'd kept buried under lock and key for years had been unleashed here in Dallas. I'd worked it all out in my head after that night I'd ground my ass on his dick for two hours while we pretended to watch *My Little Pony*.

I could do this with Theo. He wasn't my boss anymore. Sure, he was a colleague, but no matter what we got up to in this penthouse, when the show was over we'd each go back to our own lives. Him to New York, me…well, I hadn't figured that out yet. But the important part was that I could let this happen now. Get it all out of my system. It'd just be a fun way to relieve some stress. An interstitial between chapters of my life.

I just needed to keep my boundaries. Work and play didn't

mix. This could be something I did in the evenings. Like a self-care moment, but with orgasms...that I didn't give myself.

"So where are you going for José's birthday?" His voice startled me and I almost fell into the pool. I was so on edge—and him asking questions about José's birthday was not what I expected after all the eye-fucking we'd been doing.

"How did you know about that?"

"Dani mentioned it when you were gallivanting all over Dallas."

"What kind of thirty-two-year-old man uses the word *gallivanting*, anyway?" My mouth had zero brakes when it came to Theo, but he just laughed it off and reached for my float, tugging me closer to him.

"The kind that makes you wet, that's who."

Jesus. He was looking at me like he was going to tear me apart, those massive muscles bunching and flexing as he pulled me to him. "You don't want me tagging along to your party, Alba Serena?"

What was wrong with me that I was now disappointed when he called me by my correct name? Also why weren't we making out?

"It's a girls' night out, Theo, you're not invited." Why did he have to lick his lips like that? He didn't take my bait though, just ran the tip of that pink tongue over that generous mouth, one eyebrow, which I noticed was starting to grow its little peak for real, hiked high on his brow. Meanwhile I was squeezing my thighs so hard I was going to sprain something.

"Besides, I don't want to talk about my friends," I told him as I took a last sip of my seltzer.

His eyes zeroed in on my mouth as I did my best to fellate the straw. "What do you want to talk about?" His voice was rough and I wanted this man to utterly destroy me.

"Oh I don't know." I tapped a finger on the can, as I pretended to think about it. "I guess you could tell me how you plan to collect your debt." He gave me a hot, hungry look and my heartbeat kicked up to a hammering, because yeah, this was happening. If he was up for it, I was about to cash in on about three years of unresolved sexual tension, *with interest.*

"You sure about this, culona?" he asked, and fuck, why did him talking about my ass turn me on this much.

"Are you stalling, Theo?" I challenged, and he lunged for me.

"Ah," I squealed in protest as he plucked me off the float but then my lower body sank into the warm water. "That's kind of nice actually." He laughed huskily, close to my ear, those huge hands palming my ass.

"Not as nice as this." He flexed his fingers, digging in as I circled my arms around his neck. And this did feel nice. Nicer than anything had in a long time.

"I fucking love your ass," he whispered against my neck, nipping at the skin there, and I ground my hips against him, legs wrapped around his waist.

"Why are you looking at me like that?" I sounded winded. Hell, I felt like I'd run for miles. Like I was right on the edge of a cliff and was on the cusp of leaping right off it.

"How am I looking at you?" Theo leaned in, biting down on his bottom lip and making my muscles clench in anticipation.

"Like you missed a few meals and I'm the only thing on the menu," I teased, and the laugh that came out of him zapped right through me. His eyes were serious though.

"I need to be sure you want this."

"I am. Why didn't you kiss me the other night?" His smile turned evil, like his master plan was finally coming to fruition.

"Because I wanted you to be certain." He was talking with

his mouth pressed to my skin, the heat of his breath making me shiver. "If I'd kissed you like I wanted to that night, you would've regretted it." He was right of course, I would've done it, then felt guilty about it. Punished myself for being impulsive. But now with days of contemplating what he'd offered, of knowing how bad I wanted it, I was walking into this with my eyes wide open.

"I don't want it to get complicated, so don't get any ideas," I told him even as I pushed up, giving him more access to my breasts. His mouth was ghosting over the swell of them and I was burning up, even with my body half in the water.

His gray gaze fluttered up to mine as he traced wet circles on my skin with his tongue.

"I have all kinds of ideas when it comes to your body." He followed up that comment by pulling down the side of my bathing suit with his teeth, revealing more skin for him to kiss. "You want to hear them?"

This was the moment to say *no, because this is really fucking stupid.* Instead I clamped my lips shut in case my common sense decided to cock-block me.

"Do you want to know, Alba?" Every word out his mouth ran through me like electricity. I wanted to obey, beg, get on my knees.

God, his voice had bone-melting powers. I made a sound that was somewhere in the vicinity of "yes" and he ran with it. In a second he'd turned me around and had me with my back up against the wall of the pool.

"First, I want to play with your tits, suck on them some more." I arched my back, so he'd get to it, but he just let out an evil laugh that could probably be bottled and be sold as dark magic. He *tsked* when I moaned in frustration, and when he shook his head the ghost of his lips brushed one nipple. I was almost weeping with frustration.

"Nope." He punctuated the denial by squeezing my ass. "Not yet, I have to tell you the whole plan. You're so good at keeping me on track. I want you fully aware of the agenda." How the man made talking about my planner skills foreplay was a fucking revelation. His dick was a hot brand, pulsing against me. I wanted to pull it out of his trunks and touch it. Stroke it, then guide him inside. My body hummed with need. But he just kept me caged between himself and the wall as he offered a play-by-play of what he'd do to me.

"After I've made you moan for me, I'll carry you to the lanai, take off this little scrap of fabric covering your pussy." He ran the pad of his thumb along the edge of my bikini bottom, leaving me shaky with need. But he was still not done with his presentation. "After that I'll palm the inside of your thighs and spread them so I can see all the cream I know you have for me." He was making circles with his fingers on the underswell of my ass as he talked. A lazy, hypnotic massage that should've relaxed me, but only made me hornier. "After I get a good look, then I'll lick you until you come on my mouth." My breath was coming fast and hard, while I pressed myself tighter against him as he scraped his teeth over my hypersensitive skin.

"Stop teasing me, Theo." I sounded close to tears.

"Tell me how wet I make you," he ordered. His hands kneaded my ass as he rocked into me hard enough to make me see stars.

"Tell me this is not going to make things awkward later," I forced out, needing to make sure, even as my hand gripped the back of his head.

"I don't want to make anything awkward, sweetheart, I just want to make you come." He sucked in a breath, just as his thumb stroked the inside of my thigh. "Slowly first, with just my fingers. And then…"

"Oh, God," I mewled. I was mewling. But his teeth were on my earlobe, then he flicked it with his thumb. I could feel myself getting wetter as he touched me. His clever fingers kneading and tugging until I felt like I was going to fall apart. Was I going to come just from this? "Kiss me." It was out of my mouth before I could stop it. Desperate and frantic just like I was, and he didn't make me wait. That big hand slid up to the nape of my neck and he took my mouth like he owned every inch of it.

"Open up, Alba Serena," he coaxed as he sucked on my bottom lip.

"Now you know my name."

He laughed again, low and dangerous. "If only you knew. Vamos," he urged, rubbing that rock-hard cock right into my clit. "Dame tu boca."

I gave it to him and fuck…did he take it.

He gripped me in place and kissed me deep and slow, his tongue swiftly gliding with mine. Licking and taking. It was earthy and raw, not at all like I'd expected this man to kiss me, but exactly like I needed. Consuming and grounding at once. It was a good thing that Theo Ganas was a man who did not cross boundaries, because if I had had any inkling he had this in him when I worked for him, I wouldn't have lasted a week.

"Good girl," he purred between sliding his tongue along the seam of my mouth and gripping my nape tighter. "This mouth is as sweet as I thought. I can't wait to taste your pussy." I moaned in response.

Our mouths were so close I could feel the words against my lips. With what seemed like very little effort, he lifted me out of the pool and sat me on the edge so that his mouth was level with my crotch. He was looking at me like he was going to make a quick meal out of my body, and I had never been more excited to be someone's on-the-go snack.

"Can I?" he asked with his fingers tugging on one of the strings of my bikini bottom.

I didn't answer, just spread my legs and leaned back on my hands. I watched as he undid one side and then the other before pulling it down. My core pulsed, throbbing in expectation for his mouth. But the bastard took a step back and looked up at me.

"Slide a finger in, I want the first taste from your hand," he ordered hotly, like we were talking about cake. I shuddered out a breath and slid my palm down until I was cupping myself. I kept my eyes on him, but his full attention was on the triangle between my thighs. I gathered some of the wetness there with two fingers, moaning when I brushed my clitoris.

"No, don't make yourself come. Not yet." This was usually the moment when I said something along the lines of *Who the fuck do you think you are?* and made myself come just out of spite, but Theo had me in some kind of a trance. I just did as he said. Fucked myself with two fingers, once, twice, then offered them to him. His eyes were hooded and sultry and locked with mine as he sucked my fingers. He looked like Hades himself.

"I want that dripping down my chin." Yeah, this was definitely not what I'd expected from Theo "my favorite word is *insurance*" Ganas, but I was not going to make that observation when he was licking my fingers and promising to do the same to other, more demanding parts of my body. "Do you know how long I've wanted to eat this?" he asked, as he rubbed his thumb along my furrow.

"How long?" I asked, cupping the back of his head, pulling him closer. I wanted his mouth on me.

"Ages," he told me as he made his way up my thighs with

his mouth. "Some days…" he started to say something, then stopped himself.

"Tell me," I managed to say through the fog his touch had me in. He laughed, a low, dangerous sound, then flicked that flinty gaze up to me, searing. "I wanted to go down on my knees the first day you came into the pool with that ass swaying and told me if the coffee you made didn't cut it you knew a couple of guys at Starbucks looking for side hustles." I grinned at the memory, proud to remember that even though he'd scared the shit out of me, I'd always stood up for myself with Theo Ganas. He wrapped his arms around my thighs and pulled me to him until his mouth was flush against me.

"Can't wait to have my tongue inside you," he whispered as he pulled on the sensitive skin at my opening. I felt engorged, swollen, like all the blood in my body was pounding right beneath his mouth. I widened my legs and tilted up so he could see how bad I needed him. I felt wet and slick as his fingers glided over me.

"Let me see it, sweetheart," he coaxed, and I let one of my hands snake down my belly until the tips of my fingers brushed his lips. "Spread that pretty pussy for me." With my fingers I opened myself to him and the sound he made. It could swallow me up.

"Look at you." He sounded winded and I could almost feel my heart crashing against my sternum. "Like a flower. Brown and pink and red," he whispered reverently, his lips so close to my pussy he brushed my skin when he spoke. "Prettiest thing I've ever seen," he panted, head unmoving as if it was locked in that position. Ready to devour me.

"Taste me, baby," I urged, rolling my hips into his touch.

But instead of doing what I asked, he continued his slow, appreciative examination. "I want to sit you on my face later," he said thoughtfully, his face a study in concentration as a strong hand gripped my thigh and opened me further. "How bad do you want my mouth on you?" He was torturing me.

"Come on, please." I urged him. I was so keyed up, I thought I was going to lose my mind. "Don't make me beg, Theo."

"Okay, shh, I'm going to take care of you, sweetheart," he soothed, and flicked his tongue over my clit, sending an electric shock through my body. The scrape of his tongue on that sensitive part of me was almost too much.

"Ah," I cried, as he lashed his tongue over my oversensitized flesh. He hummed against me like he was tasting something so good he couldn't stop savoring long enough to make words.

"God you're delicious." He went back in this time with hand and mouth. Fingers sliding over my folds, dipping into my heat, flicking, rubbing while he slurped on the tight nub of nerves that sent shocks of electricity through my body. The sounds of it were obscene and the way those broad shoulders looked with him hunched over me were almost enough to make me come. I watched as two of his fingers fucked in and out of me while he swirled his tongue over my wetness, like he didn't want to waste a drop. Inside me that hot, sweet tug began to stretch tighter and tighter and my mouth fell open in a muted scream.

"Oh, I'm so close, please," I cried, pressing myself tighter to his mouth, right on the edge of an orgasm.

"Play with your tits, I want to watch while I eat you out," he ordered, keeping the pressure at my core expertly.

"Keep your tongue on my pussy, Theo," I said through gritted teeth and he laughed evilly before going back in, this time wrapping his lips around my clit and sucking hard. I pinched my breasts in the way I liked and he kept at it, his tongue sliding along the furrow then piercing me. He scraped his teeth along the sensitive skin there and a breath shuddered out of me. He spread me with his thumbs and dove in and took pulls from my clit like he was trying to milk it, my eyes rolled in my head from the hot, angry pleasure his mouth was giving me.

He did it again and again then pulled off. I'd never ever had anyone go down on me like this. I felt like I was going to come apart. Without warning three fingers struck my engorged pussy, the line between pain and pleasure taking me so close to the edge I was sure they could hear me panting ten floors down.

"More, please," I begged even though I had no clue what I was asking for. He sucked hard and the orgasm hit me so hard and so swiftly I almost fell into the pool. But Theo kept tasting and touching me through it until I was wrung out.

"God damn, Alba." I looked down at myself. Chest heaving and bikini bottoms undone, my top pushed under my boobs. Theo's head still between my legs. It was as raunchy as it was perfect.

"I want to do that again," I confessed, before my filters could go back up. He grinned, all smug, but I couldn't even hold it against him. The boy had serious game. Without warning, he lifted himself out of the pool. His dick was hard and tenting his shorts and my mouth watered at the thought of taking him. His wet feet slapped on the concrete and in the next moment he was pulling me up to him.

"I knew you'd be fucking delicious." He pressed kisses over my shoulder and neck while he finished untying my bikini. I looked up at the darkening sky and smiled. God this was so stupid, and there was no way I was stopping.

"I want to go somewhere I can kneel without scraping my knees and suck you off," I told him, and he made a sound like I'd punched him in the gut, then hurriedly pulled me by the hand to the oversize chaise in the lanai. He did not waste time, pushing down his trunks the moment my ass hit the cushion.

"There it is," I said as the infamous tattoo came into view. For a moment he looked a little surprised and looked down at himself.

"Not your cock." I laughed. "Although that is quite an impressive piece of machinery you have there, Theo Ganas," I crooned appreciatively as he pumped it in his hand.

"I can't wait to see you take it all, Alba Serena." I licked my lips in answer. Mesmerized. It was thick at the base and cut. He was big, and I couldn't look away as his hand stroked that taut silky skin of that monster. My walls clenched with need at the thought of having all that filling me. He circled his thumb and forefinger around the pink, flushed head, squeezing a little pearl of liquid, and my mouth watered. I swallowed when he pumped it a couple more times and tugged on his balls. Fuck, he was so hot.

"I want this in my mouth," I said, as I palmed the base.

"You're about to get it all," he promised, before he cupped the side of my face. I thought he was going to feed me his dick but instead he knelt in front of me and started kissing along the inside of my legs, up my calf, licking into me again with a groan. But he didn't linger there, moving farther up my body.

"You're so warm," he said appreciatively between kisses. He pressed his lips to my navel, my belly, and then he sucked lightly on the underside of each of my breasts. He tugged on one nipple, then the other as I gasped for breath. "Those little sounds you make, fuck, Alba." His hands were rough as he touched me. It was frantic and possessive and I felt like I was being pulled apart layer by layer.

I slid my hand down his body and grabbed his dick. It felt huge in my hands, hot living steel, and my core clenched with need. He hissed as I ran my thumb over the head, pressing a nail into the slit. I sucked on the head making a little "ah, ah" sound come out of him. My pussy clenched, empty and needy, but I wanted him in my mouth right now. I lifted my gaze to him as I took him inside my mouth. He was so big I almost gagged on the first try. It had been a while.

"Take it," he groaned as he thrust inside and I relaxed my throat until the head nudged all the way back. He pumped inside a few times as I played with his balls. Then I pulled off and focused on the head. I sucked and flicked it with my tongue until he was panting. "God you can suck cock," he groaned. That only made me redouble my efforts, and soon we were both moaning. We stayed like that for a long moment, him fucking my mouth, while I licked and sucked him. Soon his breaths became louder, harsher, and I opened my eyes.

"I want you to come on my tits," I told him, after I let him slide out of my mouth.

"Fuck, you're going to kill me," he gasped, and pressed his palm between my breasts like he was trying to lock down where he would aim. "You're fucking perfect." He braced himself on one hand and reached down to bring himself off, white teeth biting down hard on his bottom lip. "It's coming." His voice was like gravel. I arched my back in invitation and he doubled over, a litany of Spanglish filth escaping his lips as ropes of semen splashed on my chest. A few more tugs and he was wrung out, chest heaving up and down as he took big mouthfuls of air. I thought he was done. He was not. He leaned to kiss me deep and dirty, his mouth tasting like me, then he slid down my body again.

He slid his palm under my legs and pushed them back before he dove in again. Eating me out with a frantic hunger that had me on the verge in seconds. I shuddered hard through my orgasm, body twitching from overstimulation.

I felt hollowed out in the best way possible.

"Jesus, Theo," I gasped, eyes squeezed shut as I gathered myself. Without a word he scooped me from the lanai and after a quick and surprisingly chaste shower by the pool we dried off in silence. We padded back into the penthouse wrapped up in fluffy towels and by then my thoughts were running a mile a minute. When we got inside I headed to my bedroom, but he pulled me into his.

"When we have sex, you sleep with me," he informed me, as I stood in the threshold of his room like I was about to be pushed off the edge of a canyon.

"We need to lock up," I said in another weak attempt to slow down whatever was happening.

"I'll do it, once I've got you in bed." That was said with his "I'm in charge of everything" voice, and I was too weak to fight it.

I was dead on my feet after a long day and the most intense sex I'd had in years, so when he nudged me forward, I went. I tossed the towel aside and climbed in without protest. When he handed me one of my sleeping shirts I slid it over my head and dropped onto the pillow.

"You look good in my bed, Alba Angelica," he teased, and I flipped him the finger while I tried to keep my heart from launching itself up my throat. He'd put on a pair of sweats after we'd finished in the shower and I watched him move around the room. The sex had been...a lot. Too good, too raw, so much so that I couldn't think about it just yet. If I did it would be the only thing on my mind for days.

Instead I distracted myself by observing Theo Ganas move like I never had been able to when I worked for him. He didn't shave as often here in Dallas and his hair was longer than I'd ever seen it. It was lighter from the intense sun here too. Not quite blond, but a very light brown. Like dark caramel. He was long and rangy, a body honed to perfection. And though I'd appreciated it over the years, now I knew what it felt like pressed to mine. The power in it. The way it could make mine hum with pleasure.

I wanted him again, already ached for it. Right then he turned to look at me, an eyebrow raised in question at whatever he saw on my face. I just shook my head, and he offered me a lopsided smile that made my heart clench.

"See something you like?" he asked, with that new Texas swagger of his.

"Not a thing," I lied, struggling to hide the yearning in my voice. He didn't look like he believed me. I wouldn't have either with the way I was glomming up his chest. Despite only ever letting myself catch a glimpse at a time, three years' worth of glimpses made for an extremely in-depth knowledge of that fastidiously smooth chest. The sculpted pecs and dark brown nipples. I wished now that I'd touched more when I had the chance.

I would next time.

"Since you're not interested in any of this, I might as well get comfortable." His voice made me drag my eyes from the divot between his pecs and down to where his hands where pulling off his sweats. I let out a slow breath when I realized he had briefs on. Black, very tight briefs. "Is that disappointment I see?"

"You're certainly full of yourself," I grumbled, making him laugh. Still smiling he lifted the covers and slid in next to me. He made a contented sound as he brought me to him. His strong arms easily gathering me to his side.

"How do you feel?" He sounded casual enough, but I could hear real concern in his voice. And usually, I was pretty

easygoing about these things. Sex was sex. Some times better than others and *always* casual. But now I felt the echo of
where his hands and mouth had been like they were tiny
beating hearts under my skin.

"I'm fine. I'm great. Just what I needed after a long day,"
I said. Easy, breezy. No feelings being felt here. Absolutely
no overthinking happening inside this skull. But Theo already had my number, if that "yeah right" sound he made
was anything to go by. He flipped us over until we were
spooned together, him the big spoon to my little spoon, and
then reached over my head to turn the light off.

"I'm not quite buying it, but I'll let it go for tonight." His
raspy voice was right in my ear. "Let's sleep, I might want
another taste in the morning." He slid a hand under my panties when he said that and on instinct I made space for him.

I groaned and shook my head. "How did you manage to
hide this extremely filthy side of yourself for so long?"

"Because I had to keep the boundaries very, very firm
with you, Alba. You were much too tempting."

He slid his muscled thigh between my legs and something
swooped in my belly. I'd always been hyperaware of Theo. It
was hard not to be when the man practically swallowed up
the oxygen of any room he walked into. But I'd managed
to convince myself that it was because he was my boss and I
wanted to stay in his good graces. I liked doing a good job,
so it was only natural to be attuned to him. But now I knew
that it had always been more than simply being aware of him.
For three years we'd been circling each other like a pair of
Dominican roosters waiting to see who pecked first. Which
reminded me...

"Some of your Spanish slipped out by the pool." I was still
looking away from him, but I felt him freeze at that.

"You know how it is, it comes out when you're about to explode."

I chuckled, nodding. "No matter in what context, the mother tongue slips out. It happens to me all the time, but I didn't realize you even spoke Spanish." His hands that had been roaming over me stopped, just for a second, and then they slid down my legs again. I'd heard him speaking in Greek to his dad on the phone a ton of times, but I couldn't remember ever hearing him say much in Spanish. Not even to Cecilia, who spoke with a thick accent and fell into Spanish with anyone she knew was bilingual.

It took him a while to answer, so long that I started to worry I'd upset him. Fluency in Spanish could be a sore subject for immigrant kids.

"My mom's English is not good, and I always spoke with her in Spanish," he told me. I recalled that the few times she'd called she didn't even attempt to speak to me in English. "She went back to live in the DR when I was twelve and I was with her for a couple of years."

I turned my head so I could look at him. "I never knew you lived in the DR! Were you in Santo Domingo?" I asked, heart beating a little faster now that I knew we had this in common.

"Yeah, that's where we were." He pressed a kiss to my head and settled us again, so I was tucked under his chin. Who would've thought Theo Ganas was a cuddler. "I came back for high school. So my Spanish is decent. She always gave me shit about it and in the DR I was always 'el gringo.'" He laughed but there was very little humor in it and I tightened my hands over his arms. "I guess I got self-conscious about it and now I feel like I've gone too long without using it."

"I mean it's not like I was looking to take points for pronunciation or anything," I drawled. "I was too busy coming all over your face and all." I felt his shoulders shake behind me, even as his hands brought me closer. "But what you did say sounded pretty good to me."

"No me des ideas, Alba," he whispered and that fluttery happy thing bloomed in my belly again.

"Seriously though, I like hearing you all growly and bossy in Spanish. It's hot."

He made a noncommittal groan and gathered me up again. "Go to sleep, before I give you something to do with that mouth." I was kind of disappointed when he didn't fulfill that very enticing promise, but then I felt a brush of lips against the back of my neck before a strong arm tucked me closer to his hard chest. A hushed "sweetheart" against my ear was the last thing I heard before I fell into the best sleep I'd had in years.

# Chapter Fourteen

## THEO

"You ran off on me," I couldn't help but grumble the next morning as I walked into the kitchen and found Alba fully dressed and sipping on some green juice from a straw. She had her laptop in front of her—I had begun to think about that thing as her security blanket. If she was at the table, she had it out, but right now Alba was reading something on her phone.

"I got up and got ready for work," she retorted, without looking up from the device in her hand. With effort, I reined in the urge to walk up to her and tip her chin up for a kiss and focused on getting caffeinated instead. If she was being cool about the fact that I'd come on her tits the night before, then I didn't need to make it a thing. I also was very aware that pushing her right now would be a mistake. She'd been so hot and responsive last night, but I knew she was skittish. She didn't want anything to jeopardize her job and me getting all possessive was going to scare her off. And if there was something I understood well, it was boundaries. The only way she'd keep the door open for more of what we did last night was if I kept my head and didn't get too demanding. We wanted each other, that was clear. We were fucking explosive in bed, and I wanted a repeat of last night. But I had to take it slow. Ease her into giving me everything. That was what I wanted, all of her.

I thought she'd fight me on sleeping in the same bed, but she'd been surprisingly pliable. I'd woken up a few times through the night and still had her clutched tight to me.

Which was why I hadn't expected to find her side empty when I woke up. Without asking I started making her coffee and moved around the kitchen as she read in silence. Once the coffee was done I went to the fridge and pulled out the creamer she liked, setting it on the counter by her, then slid her favorite mug in her direction.

"Thank you." She tipped her head up and offered me a sweet smile that made my gut clench. "You didn't have to do that," she told me as I poured the dark liquid into her cup.

"Paying you back for all those 6:00 a.m. macchiatos," I told her hoarsely, disoriented by the way taking care of her like this warmed me up inside. She went back to focusing on what she was reading while she sipped her coffee, and the ghost of that smile stayed on her lips the entire time. I suppressed a shudder as she desecrated perfectly good caffeine with such a massive amount of French vanilla half-and-half I almost retched. I was obsessed with the woman, but her taste in hot drinks was appalling.

"You got enough fake milk substance in there, Alba Divina?" The moment those brown eyes landed on me, my dick got hard.

"I like a healthy splash of cream, Theo. I would've thought you knew that by now." She blinked innocently as she gulped it down while I tried not to choke on my own tongue. I reminded myself that this was not a sprint and offering to bend her over the kitchen counter was likely not the proper response here. Courting Alba Serena Duarte was a test in endurance. Still, I was only human.

I leaned in just enough that our faces were inches apart.

"I would be more than happy to supply you with more, you just have to ask." She laughed but didn't take the bait. She didn't say no either, so I took it as a win.

"What are you reading?" I was hoping to distract myself from the way she kept licking her lips after every sip. I was also low-key curious about what she was reading, now that I knew what books meant to her. She slid her gaze from her screen and trained it in my direction.

"A romance novel." She said it with a little bit of sass, arching an eyebrow like she expected this to turn into a verbal sparring session.

"Is that your favorite thing to read?" I was genuinely curious. "Not that I'm judging," I said, when she narrowed her eyes at me. "When she was still here my mother dated a guy who taught English at Columbia for a couple of years." I grimaced in distaste recalling that unfortunate part of my mother's dating history. "He constantly would lecture us about what one read being 'serious business.'" I twitched my fingers like he used to do. God, that guy was an asshole. "Romance novels were his favorite thing to trash. He was the biggest prick I've ever met." She rolled her eyes, seemingly unimpressed, and considered me as she took a pull from her green juice.

"He sounds terrible." She made a face, clearly put off by the man's snobby opinions on reading. "To answer your question, they're definitely one of my favorite things to read. I like that messy, flawed people still get to have an epic love story. It's hopeful and comforting, and hot as fuck. There is very little in my life that's as reliable as a good romance novel." It didn't sit right that this woman who took on so much every day had to look for safety in books because her life felt so precarious. I didn't like the thought of her walking around feeling like the other shoe would drop at any moment. I was also extremely aware that me even implying I could help in any way would get me shot down in a hot second.

I tipped the cup I'd just picked off the cabinet in her direction. "What's this one about?"

"It's about a cursed werewolf and the witch who helps him." Her lips twitched with a smile, but I could see the apprehension in her eyes. She was sharing something she loved and expected people to make fun of. I'd die before betraying what he was giving me.

"Sounds intense."

"Oh, it is," she said, in a self-mocking voice, clearly fully expecting me to tease her.

"So does she like have to cure him with sex?" That made her spit out her juice all over the counter.

"Theo! What the fuck?"

"What?" I threw my hands up, biting back a smile. "I want to know if he makes it. I'm invested." She laughed, snatching the paper towel I handed her.

"Don't book shame me, jackass!" she cried as she dabbed a little dot of juice from her denim shirt.

"I'm not, I swear, and I agree with you. Happiness *is* serious business. In books and outside of them." She shot me a skeptical "uh-huh" but kept her attention on cleaning up. I indulged myself by taking her in.

We generally got clothes to wear from the stylist on set, but Alba showed up every morning looking like she was expecting the cameras to be on her the moment she stepped out of the car. She'd gone for the full Southwest theme today, including silver-and-turquoise earrings shaped like little cacti.

"Are those cowboy boots?"

Her head shot up at that, eyes sparkling with delight. She was shameless when it came to compliments, and I loved giving them to her. "You bet your ass they are!" She preened, and I fell a little harder for her when she giddily hiked up her flowy white skirt and lifted her legs to show me.

"They look good on you." I wasn't being polite either, she was enough to eat in her Texan fashion. I poured her some more coffee, leaving space for the creamer. "Here." I slid it her way and took a sip of my own much saner choice of a double espresso.

"Wow, orgasms, compliments and coffee. I like Texas Theo much better than the Manhattan one." I knew she was teasing, testing the waters. But what she said burrowed deep into me.

*I* liked Texas Theo better too.

Tonight I'd be meeting with Giordan and Ivan for drinks. I'd woken up that morning to a text from Dani confirming it and a couple of emails from their foundation with more information for me to review. The more I learned about their project the more I wanted in. I was starting to think I wouldn't be done with Texas when the show ended. I wanted more time with Alba here too.

We sipped our coffees for a stretch, both lost in our thoughts until she leaped off the stool and closed her laptop.

"I have to go! Remember, today some of the staff from Sturm's is coming to the set." The producers had invited the staff so we could film them going around the rooms that were ready and picking colors for the walls and some of the tiles and stuff.

"I remember," I told her as I tracked her fluttering around the kitchen. "You haven't eaten breakfast."

"I had that green juice," she informed me as she rinsed her hands.

"That's not breakfast. Sit down, I'll make you something." I was standing right behind her and the thought of hiking up that skirt and fucking her in those cowboy boots ran like a fever through me.

"I'll buy something later." She sounded annoyed, but I had to do something with my hands, or mistakes would be made.

"I'm offering to cook for you now though," I insisted.

"Oh my God! All right, Dad!" she teased and turned to walk away, which gave me glimpse of that ass, and I decided another mistake would not be the end of the world.

"Come here," I coaxed, bringing her against me. Her mouth made a little O of surprise, even as her arm snaked around my waist. I raked my mouth up her neck, and bit her earlobe for good measure. "If and when you call me Papi." Her body stiffened at the offer in my voice. "It won't be for my breakfast tacos."

"You think you've got me sprung because of last night." She was a little too breathless to be really mad.

"No," I admitted. "But I'm getting you there." She laughed in my face, but she didn't let go either, and when I bent down to brush a kiss on her forehead she sighed so fucking sweetly I almost proposed on the spot. Her laugh was just a little shaky as I let her go, but not before giving her a playful swat.

"Your obsession with my ass is becoming a problem." It did not sound at all like a complaint.

"Can't wait to take a bite out of it," I growled, digging my fingers into her. She pushed into my touch eagerly, her teeth scraping my jaw. We ground into each other like fucking teenagers.

"Shit, I'm going to be late," my roommate moaned as I slid a hand under her skirt.

"I'll make it fast," I promised as I plucked her thong aside, brushing a knuckle over that delicious heat.

"Mm," she moaned, giving me more access.

"You're so wet," I praised while I slid a finger up the furrow of her. She was slick and hot, and all I wanted was to sink inside.

"Don't smudge my lipstick, Theo!" she cried, even as she spread her legs for me. Had I ever laughed this much with anyone? "I'm serious—" She cut off her protest when I rubbed the pad of my thumb over her clit and then her forehead was on my shoulder as we worked on a rhythm together.

"That's it. Fuck my hand, baby, make yourself come." Little puffs of air hit my neck as I played with her. She groaned as I circled her clit with my thumb, then cried when I dipped two fingers inside.

"Ah," she moaned, fingernails digging into the nape of my neck where she clung to me. Her walls gripped me as she came and those quiet whimpers of hers were almost enough to get me off.

"Como me gustas." My voice sounded rough, worn out. I kept my palm on her heat, not wanting to let go yet. I could hear her breath slowing down after her climax but my blood was still hot. "Este bizcochito." I dipped a finger in, so she knew what I was referring to. "Me lo quiero comer, y cuand—" I was so caught up in my dirty litany that she almost bumped me in the mouth when she jerked back to look at me, her lipstick still impressively intact. Her expression was a mix of confusion and amusement.

"Did you just call my vagina a birthday cake?"

I did still have my hand on said body part and just because I could I tightened it, then made myself leave that warmth and wrapped my arms around her waist, a matching grin to hers tipping up my own lips.

"What am I supposed to say? You know damn well there are no good words for sexy body parts in Spanish!" I complained as she clutched my shirt, almost doubled over from laughter. "I have very little to work with if I want to bring the Español," I protested as she cackled. "And you said you liked it."

"You make sex fun, Theo Ganas. I like it." She looked so relaxed in my arms, and I wondered if she had any idea she'd just cracked my heart open.

"I like *you*," I told her, bolder now that she was looking at me like that.

She nodded, but didn't say it back, then eased my disappointment by going up on her tiptoes and kissing me. "Thank you for the coffee and the orgasm. The show calls."

I was beginning to hate that fucking show.

# ALBA

"There were many things that I'd braced for today, but Theo Ganas playing peek-a-boo with a one-year-old was not one of them," Julia whispered as we stood off to the corner of what in a couple of weeks would be the finished atrium for the Sturm Foundation's community library.

"Girl, you are not lying," I concurred, watching the man that merely hours before that had literally *had me* in the kitchen playing with the daughter of one of the foundation staff.

"I'm not even invested in the man like that, but when he put that kid on his shoulder and pretended to be a horse, I almost texted Rocco and asked him to leave work early."

It figured the universe would throw this little tableau into the mindfuck smoothie that was my brain. I was still trying to get back on solid emotional ground after last night and this morning. Sex with Theo was *not* what I'd expected. Not that I thought he would be a bad lover, he was too much of a perfectionist not to deliver in the orgasm department. What I had not expected was how he'd manage to give me such intense pleasure all while making me laugh. Then there was the way he'd wanted to keep me close. His demand that I stay in his bed. It was all too fucking much, and the last thing I needed was to watch him be all sweet and playful with a baby.

"I thought he'd be all touchy and shit since you let him pet the kitty after the pool party." Julia said it so quietly I almost missed it, then punched her on the shoulder.

"I'm going to stop telling you stuff!" In a post-orgasmic moment of weakness this morning I'd texted her and confessed to what I'd gotten up to with my former boss. I should've known she was going to have her fun with me.

"What? What did I do?" She widened her eyes dramatically and pivoted her head left and right.

"I honestly can't stand you."

Julia just laughed at me. "Hey, it's my job as your best friend to tease you a little when you get up close and personal with the D." She crossed her arms over her shoulder, and assessed me. All business now. "Besides, what the big deal? You said you were both being super casual and doing the postmodern booty-call thing."

That's what I thought too, before he'd come out of his room looking like sex in faded jeans, made me coffee, asked me about my favorite books then fingered me against the kitchen island.

"I was kidding myself," I confessed. "That man is much too dangerous to play games with, Julia. I think I need to quit while I'm ahead."

My best friend scoffed, her attention on the man in question. "Alba, Theo is hot, accessible and, as you've been recently made aware of, a demon between the sheets, why on earth would you cut things off when you've only had a sample?"

*Because he's already making my head a mess and it will only get worse.*

"At least now I can cut it off without getting my heart

ripped out." I kept my eye on Theo, who was still holding the baby while the crew filmed him showing the head librarian around. She beamed up at him as he pointed out various aspects of the grounds. He was so different than the man I'd worked for, so open, so real. Genuine in his warmth, so quick to offer a smile. I didn't dare say it, but I knew then that it was already too late for my heart not to get trampled.

"Damn girl, what's got you thinking so hard?"

"No comment." Julia knew me too well not to know the answer for that. So, I wrapped my lips around my teeth and kept all that mess inside. Next to me my best friend sighed, and when I turned to her she put an arm around my shoulder. Her eyes were all shiny.

"This patio is a fucking dream, Albita." She gestured all around us. I smiled, not just because I was very happy not to talk about my obsession with Theo, but because I agreed wholeheartedly. This place was a movie. We'd redone the courtyard in the center of the building as two separate spaces. The showpiece, my glass atrium in the center of the building, was almost finished. We'd left the original fountain in the middle of it, which would be surrounded by benches and a hanging garden. A climate-controlled oasis for those scorching Texan days.

"It does look kind of awesome," I admitted.

"You are brilliant at what you do. I'm so fucking happy I get to see you doing your thing."

"Thank you, friend." I put my head on Julia's shoulder and for once let myself soak in the praise.

"Doing the skylight was a great idea," Julia said, as we watched Mona instruct one of the families on what to do for the camera.

"That wasn't my idea, it was Theo's," I confessed, and

Julia gave me one of those smug looks she seemed to have on tap these days.

"You two make a good team…" Julia was as subtle as a kick in the head, but I was not taking that bait. Not today when I felt like I was one big, exposed nerve. Thankfully my best friend knew me enough to figure out when she'd pushed me too far. We both kept our attention on Theo as he handed the baby to her mom. My breath caught, just from looking at him. It occurred to me that it was a shame this show only had a couple of weeks left. A few more months here and he might get laugh lines around his eyes. The thought made me ache, because I wished I could see it. But I knew that this place was just an intermission for both of us. The pressures of our lives, of our family obligations would swarm us the moment we got back to New York.

Right then Theo looked up and his gaze landed squarely on me. For a second he almost seemed surprised to see me, then his whole face opened with an incandescent smile as he started walking in our direction.

"Damn girl." Julia fanned herself. "That's a whole fucking mood right there."

"Yeah, a life-detracting, goal-wrecking mood," I muttered miserably while Julia laughed. But despite my supposed distress my entire body responded to Theo Ganas's impending proximity. Limbs loosened, belly fluttered. Lips parted, eager for a kiss that wouldn't come.

"Que lo que, Julia." I grinned despite myself as I heard Theo greet Julia with the Dominican expression. I was a fucking sap.

"Hey, you're looking relaxed." The suggestive tone in my alleged best friend's voice was practically screaming *I know you two fucked* but Theo didn't give an inkling he understood.

"Just admiring our designer's vision." Theo smiled in my direction and my stomach did that clench and release thing.

He was wearing a salmon polo and jeans, which should not have looked good on anyone over eight years old but on him seemed straight out of a fashion magazine summer feature. He looked delicious in that sun-kissed Eros thing he had going on at all times.

"I bet you didn't know you had such a brilliant design goddess working for you for all those years." My friend's voice was sweet enough, but there was a challenge in her eyes. Like she was testing Theo. He straightened his shoulders at whatever he saw in her eyes, but didn't really seem annoyed by the question.

"Nah," he answered, his eyes never leaving my face as he spoke. "From the moment I met Miss Duarte I knew I was in the presence of greatness." My mind kept telling me he was probably just ribbing Julia, but his words still made me unsteady. I was still trying to come up with a response when someone called my name. I turned in the direction of the voice and found the rep for Smithson-Napa, who had been at that shit show of a presentation, heading my way.

"Hey." I waved and the young curvy woman with bomb mermaid hair waved back as they approached. She had another woman with her that I didn't recognize.

"Julia," I began, but my friend was already shooing me off.

"Go, Mr. Ganas will keep me company." I grimaced at the potential disaster that could come from leaving Julia alone with Theo but getting one-on-one time with the Smithson-Napa people was very high on my to-do list. I hustled over to them and got ready to code-switch my way into a major collaboration with one of the hottest lifestyle brands in the country.

"Hi there." I greeted the women with my best "non-threatening brown lady" voice. "Carrie, right?" I said to mermaid hair.

"Yes, and this is Yazmin." She waved a hand to the very tall, caramel-skinned butch hottie in a pinstripe suit next to her. "We've been wanting to speak to you since the presentation. We've been looking through all your book-themed designs on Insta and we're obsessed with them." She really stretched out the word *obsessed*, but I wasn't going to throw shade if she was into my stuff.

"That's awesome! I am so glad you liked my work." I shook their hands and made sure to ramp up my smile to megawatt levels.

"Oh, we more than like it, we adore it." Carrie was apparently the hype woman in the duo. "We'd love to chat some more…" Yazmin cleared her throat and I noticed that Carrie shot a look in Chase and Kayla's direction. The two of them were standing off to the side like sharks waiting to feed. Didn't look like Smithson-Napa was Team Chayla, which was just fine with me.

"Let's go somewhere a little more private," Yazmin suggested, tipping her head in the opposite direction of the showrunner and his wife. Once we were out of the courtyard she spoke up. "We've been looking for an opportunity to launch a joint line with an up-and-coming designer."

"Is that right?" I said, all nonchalant while every drop of blood in my body rushed to my head. I squared my shoulders a little more, to give off that "I am your woman" vibe, and ignored the thumbs-up Julia was flashing me.

"Yes," Carrie, the more excitable one, confirmed, her head bobbing so much her green side bangs were bouncing on her forehead. "We want to work with someone to create an entire new line aimed at Gen Z-ers. We want something that runs the gamut, from hand towels, to wallpapers, to light fixtures." Yazmin nodded in agreement, while I tried hard not to start jumping up and down and yelling *pick me*.

"When we looked through your Bookish Boudoir portfolio and saw everything you do with those tiny budgets, we were floored." I preened on the inside, because I really could stretch a fucking dollar to the max. "Those signature pieces you create from upcycled furniture," Carrie exclaimed. "It's so clever and environmentally friendly." She broke into applause again and I almost joined her.

"Thank you for saying that," I finally managed, hoping my nerves didn't get the best of me. "I am very intentional about reusing and refreshing pieces that the clients already own. I think there is a lot of value in giving people options." Both women nodded, like I was preaching to the choir.

"We could see that. You have a lot of vision, Alba." Yazmin, who so far had been more reserved, was smiling wide. "We knew you are who we were looking for."

Oh my God. This was really happening. *Say something, dummy.*

"Are those fabric designs your own?"

"They are." I nodded, completely overwhelmed, but determined to make the most of this opportunity, even if my heart was literally trying to come up my throat. "I started doing those when a client wanted a noir-themed bedroom. It was meant to be for a comforter, but she loved it so much we ended up upholstering a loveseat instead." The silhouettes of dames in their Mary Janes smoking cigarettes and private dicks in fedoras were such a hit that I'd ended up selling it in my merch shop on cushions.

"I love that." Carrie was practically wiggling from excitement. "We'd love for you to come up with a proposal for a sample line, just five or six items we could show to our executives."

I jumped on that without a second's hesitation. "Of course! I'd love to." This was the exact kind of opportunity I hoped the show would bring. "I've had the idea of a design brand that does bookish-themed home décor. A line for rom-com lovers, another for sci-fi/fantasy readers, cozy mysteries…"

"That's perfect!" Carrie clapped.

"I could create a few prototypes for you that fit with Smithson-Napa's style. Maybe bedding, some bedroom accessory pieces?"

"And the wallpaper," Yazmin requested.

"I could definitely do that." Did not need to ask me twice. "When do you need it by?" When they both winced and stealthily looked at Kayla, dread sank through my body, taking down with it every ounce of elation of the last few minutes.

"That's the tricky part," Yazmin said, while Carrie snuck looks over her shoulder. "We tried to call you this morning to see if we could meet before we arrived on set, so we could have a word with you before the others got here." I didn't have to ask who "the others" were given the very sour look Yazmin was shooting in Kayla's direction.

"Your showrunner has been informally talking to our boss about working with his wife. We wanted to offer you this chance first."

"But we were sort of ambushed when we got here." Carrie's high laugh did nothing to hide what she really thought of Chase and Kayla's shenanigans. Hers was probably the call I'd ignored this morning in favor of talking to Theo. The call I never returned because by the time we were done with… I breathed through my nose as guilt roiled through me. This was exactly what letting myself become distracted by sex would get me.

"I can work with whatever timeline you have," I said once I could speak without sounding like I was about to cry. Not because I was upset. But because I was furious with myself.

"The boss asked to see them in two weeks," Yazmin explained.

I cringed internally, thinking that was exactly when we'd be finishing up production here.

"I can do that." It would mean working around the clock between my obligations for the library renovation and my bookish renovations, but I would make it work. There was no way I was letting fucking Kayla steal this from under my nose.

"I know it's tight, but we want to get your material as early as possible so we can really sell it to higher-ups." This came from Yazmin, and fuck I almost really cried then. Because this woman was going out of her way to make this happen for me.

"Thank you," I said, a little breathless, with a hand clutched to my chest. "You won't regret it."

"We'll be in touch," Yazmin said, before the two women walked away.

"Holy shit." I whistled as my eyes searched for Theo of their own volition. A boulder of regret settled in my gut as he spotted me and gave me one of his Dallas smiles. A little dirty and a lot fucking charming. My core responded to the sight of that powerful body, as it always did.

I wanted to run to him, let him wrap me up in those strong arms that I now knew made me feel so safe. I wanted to tell him that something great had happened. That I was on the cusp of getting what I'd worked so long for. I stood there swaying, my legs aching from the need to move toward where he was.

Then I reminded myself what was at stake, and I made myself walk away.

# *Chapter Fifteen*

## THEO

Alba had taken off on me after her chat with the reps from Smithson-Napa and five hours later she was still not answering texts or calls. The woman drove me up the fucking wall. One minute she was giving me everything, and the next she was looking right through me. I couldn't stop thinking about what it had been like to sleep with her in my arms. It was better than anything I could've imagined. But just as I was starting to feel like we were making some progress she'd pulled away.

I wasn't giving up though. No one had ever felt as perfect as she had, just as I'd known she would. No, it was even better than I'd imagined because this woman that I'd gotten to know in the past few weeks had depths to her I'd never gotten to see in New York. Every new part of Alba I discovered only made me want her more.

"What are you so serious about?" Dani's voice jolted me back to the busy bar where I'd been waiting.

"What's up?" I said, standing to greet Dani and the two men I'd come to talk to tonight.

"Gio, Ivan," he said, waving a hand to me. "This is Theo Ganas."

"Hey, man, I'm glad we were able to connect," Gio said.

I was a comfortable six foot three and this guy loomed over me. Which was probably why he was one of the most popular point guards in the NBA.

"Thanks for letting me crash your night out to talk business," I apologized, but Ivan shook his head and leaned in to slap my shoulder.

"Not at all, we've been wanting to get a chance to meet with you since your people reached out to us. We're hoping we can reel you all the way in tonight," Ivan told me, before he pointed a fist in my direction and rolled it like he was pulling me in with his fishing pole.

"All right, then, hit me," I teased as we got settled at a table. Both guys rubbed their hands together at my request and I grinned at their excitement. It reminded me of the way Alba looked when she talked about her projects. The kind of energy I hadn't felt about my own work in a very long time.

"Okay, boom," started Gio. "Here's the deal. I know Tom told you about the plan for the permanent veteran housing."

"Yeah, the tenement model," I said with a nod.

"Right," Ivan said, giddy as a little kid and again I thought this was the kind of vibe I wanted to work around. People who used their money and privilege for something bigger than themselves. "We're going off a program that we saw in Norway. It's all funded by the government there of course," Gio said wistfully.

"Not so much here," Dani piped in with an eye roll.

"No, but in Norway no one is paying their athletes what we get either, so we figure we can give some back." That came from Ivan and I liked that accountability. Respected it. "So that's basically stage one out of like twenty; we want to build a city." Both of the guys laughed when my eyes widened.

"Well, not exactly a city," Gio hedged, doing calm-down

hands to Ivan, "but more like we'd love to build a safe, subsidized housing complex for homeless veterans with all the facilities they would need for their day-to-day. We're talking physical and psychotherapy, groceries, a place to get their prescriptions," he said, ticking items off with his fingers.

"Trauma-informed group therapy, and support for their families," Ivan added, tipping his wineglass, and Gio nodded.

"Yeah, trauma-informed substance abuse counseling, treatment. And we want to do education as well. Skills adaptation," Ivan explained. I nodded with interest at the ambitious plans these guys had, and all for an amazing cause. "A lot of these guys get a ton of sophisticated training during their service. They have a lot of skills. If they could learn how to adapt them to civilian life, they could have more success in the job market."

"That sounds fantastic." More of that fevered excitement ran through me. These men were big thinkers.

"From the experts we've talked about, for a lot of veterans the tricky part is access," Ivan said. "In the beginning just getting to places is overwhelming. So we'd like to have all of it in one place for them. If they have most of their basic needs met in one location, then they can focus on their healing and recovery." I wanted to be part of this, I knew the moment they started talking. But this project was not something I could dip in and out of. Agreeing to be a part of something like this was a big commitment. I couldn't flake out on this halfway into it, and with the commitments of running Ganas day-to-day once I went back to New York it would not be possible. This was not some side project. This was a massive undertaking, and it would require my all. With all that I was going back to in New York I was in no position to sign on to this unless I made major changes. Still, the question slipped out of my mouth.

"Do you have a builder working with you?" The two guys shook their heads, but their eyes sparkled at my question.

"Not yet," Gio told me, and again that fire of anticipation roared in my chest. "We haven't found the right partner. We want someone who understands and is committed to our vision, and who can be in it for the long haul." That should've been my cue to say that I was based in New York and had to be back there in weeks, but my ass stayed planted to the chair.

"What's the long-term vision for this?" Even I heard the thirst in my voice when I asked the question.

Both men grinned wide before Gio responded. "If this one goes well, we want to keep building them, first here in Texas then other parts of the country."

Next to me Dani whistled in surprise.

"We also would love to launch something similar for former elite athletes." That statement was the last push I needed to jump head first into the deep end.

"Tell me more." They had every ounce of my attention now.

"We'd like to have services and some amount of housing for athletes who have been permanently injured or impacted by the sport, same idea in terms of services." I knew guys like that from my time in swimming. Who had messed up their shoulders, their backs, after years of driving their bodies harder than anyone ever should and were left with just a few medals as compensation.

"I want in," I blurted out impulsively. I knew that this was not as simple as saying yes, that there would be serious adjustments I'd have to make in my life to make this work. I still wanted it though. I wanted to do work I felt proud of. A mission where my own values and the things that were important to me were part of the equation.

Ivan leaned in and clapped me on the shoulder, a big grin

on his face. "We know you're based in New York right now, so there's probably a lot to think through, but if you are up for it, we'd love for you to be a part of making this happen with us." I kept my mouth shut, because I wanted to jump in and this was not how I did things. I had to think this through, no matter how much my gut told me this project could be the future of my professional life. "We have the land and we have the vision, but we won't be moving forward with breaking ground until the summer. We can give you some time to think about it." That was in three months.

"If you want we can go to the site next week," Ivan offered, and again my heart decided for me before my common sense could get his two cents in.

"Yeah, I'd like that. What you two are doing is great, man. I really respect it."

"To whom much is given," Gio said with a grin, and again I *felt* that. I had been given so much. And it was time that I put some of it to use for something other than my family. Unbidden, a yearning to know what Alba would say about all this tugged at me. I wanted a life in which she was the person I went to first. Hell, I wanted her next to me right now. Her words had gotten me here after all.

"Hey, what are you all doing here?" Julia's voice sliced through the chatter around the room and my body instantly reacted to the possibility that Alba was right behind her. I turned so fast I almost knocked my drink off the table, but only found Salome, José and Julia.

"She's not here," my roommate's best friend informed me as she bent to kiss me on the cheek.

"She ditched me on my birthday to go work, it's a cry for help," José lamented, but I could tell Julia was worried.

"Sounds like the women from Smithson-Napa asked her for a pitch and she rushed home to get started." Her deep sigh told me that she and Alba had likely gone a couple of rounds before my elusive lover blew off their plans.

"Did she really have to get started tonight?" I had no clue why I even asked. I knew that to Alba every job was a question of life or death.

Julia scowled, that sour look still plastered on her face. "She was all tight about needing to focus and not having time for distractions when I called her to ask if she was meeting us here." Julia frowned like she wasn't sure she should tell me what was on her mind, but after a sip of her drink she leaned in farther. "It sounds like the executives asked that chick Kayla for a pitch too." The rest of the friends had gone to the bar for drinks, and she tipped her head at José, who was dressed in a neon pink suit for his birthday celebration. "I would've gone to check on her, but I didn't want to ditch J too." She gave me a long look as if waiting for the meaning of her words to land...they did.

If I got up and left after her telling me that, I would essentially announce to the whole group that there was something going on between me and Alba. I didn't care. For all I knew Julia was all up to date on my sex life, and as for the rest of the group, let them know. If I didn't suspect she'd probably fulfill her threats to kill me in my sleep I'd announce to the entire Dallas–Fort Worth Metro Area that I was crazy about her.

"She probably hasn't even had dinner," I told Julia, already pulling some cash out of my wallet to pay for my drink. The woman survived on Cheetos and bad coffee. She needed a fucking keeper, and even with the thrill of this project still pulsing through me, nothing felt more important than taking care of her.

"I'm going to check on her." I pulled my phone out of my pocket, then snapped a picture of José and Tariq book-ending Salome as they twerked to a Doja Cat song booming across the room. I made quick work of DMing it to my roommate on Instagram.

**Theo.Ganas.2576: You really let these clowns out without supervision?**

**Bookish Boudoir: New phone, who dis?**

Smart-ass. At least she was making jokes.

**Theo.Ganas.2576: I was hoping I could buy you a drink. I heard you got good news to share.**

I knew I was pushing it there. Alba had made it abundantly clear to me that her business was none of mine. But something bugged me about her blowing off her friends. There was more going on than her feeling under pressure. I saw the three dots pop up and disappear, then reappear again a few times. Finally, a photo of her sewing machine and the fabric she was stitching popped up.

**Bookish Boudoir: Can't. Working. Finishing up something for Rocco's niece. Then I have to get started on something else…**

I looked closer and smiled when I saw the illustrations of brown fairy-tale princesses. She had what looked like a Snow White with afro-puffs and a Cinderella in crystal espadrilles. It was beautifully done, the love and care she'd put into it shining through. This was more than a job for Alba—this was her calling.

**Theo.Ganas.2576: You want some help?**

Again the three dots appeared and reappeared... I smiled thinking that she'd probably typed a searing "fuck off" then thought better of it and replaced it with a more polite version... along the lines of "leave me alone."

**Bookish Boudoir: Nah. Have fun though. See you in the morning.**

I should've left it alone. Alba had enough on her plate without me pressuring her to give me something she didn't have to give. And yet, here I was sick with want, and needing to see her, more than I wanted to keep my pride. I wanted her to know that I saw how much she sacrificed for her dreams.

"Hey, hermano," I said, leaning over and interrupting Gio, Dani, Ivan and Tariq from their conversation. "I'm going to bounce. I'll be in touch," I assured Ivan and Gio. I meant it too. But first I had to go and see to the reason why I was in this city in the first place.

# ALBA

"You got time for a snack break, Alba Artemisa?"

My hands froze on the stitching when I heard his voice. I could pretend to barely notice he was there, but inside, there was a storm. The storm Theo brought with him whenever he came near me now. But this afternoon, I'd gotten the reminder I needed that I could not get swept into it again.

"I'll eat when I'm done, I have to finish with this." I forced myself to keep the machine going, even though I knew I'd risk messing up the stitching with as jumpy as he made me.

"Look at me, Alba."

I didn't want to look at him. Because I'd take what he was offering and that would sidetrack me.

"I don't have time for this, Theo." I heard his sigh behind

me and then the scrape of what sounded like a plate being slid onto the dresser by the door. I let out an unsteady breath thinking he'd leave, but in the next moment his hands were on my shoulders. Heavy and warm, kneading at the muscles that ached from being hunched over for hours.

"They missed you tonight." It was more of a question than a rebuke. Still, it smarted, making bitter bile rise in my throat. I hated always feeling like no matter how hard I worked I was letting someone down. Myself, my family, my friends. "*I* missed you."

The last part made my resistance buckle. Theo's words always seemed to burrow deeper than anyone else's, effectively chipping away at the walls I'd so carefully erected around the place that yearned for things I could not have. It was better to redirect.

"How did it go with Dani's friends?" On Saturday he'd told me he was going to meet with two Dominican athletes who were working on what sounded like an amazing plan for veterans. He didn't answer my question right away, but when I lifted my eyes to him he didn't look pissed that I'd ignored what he said. He seemed…cautiously excited.

"It was good, it's a very exciting project. They need someone based in Texas to partner with."

"That's going to be a hell of a commute," I joked, but he didn't smile. I waited for him to tell me that he clearly couldn't do it since he was based in New York, but he didn't.

"It might be worth it though?" I asked, unable to help myself. I didn't think I was wrong about Theo's indifference to his work. He was different here and I suspected at least some of that had to do with being away from the demands of Ganas. I knew from experience that as hard as it was to grind for your dreams, it was much worse to kill yourself doing something you hated.

Still, Theo's poker face was top notch, and he gave very little away. He only shrugged and gave me a noncommittal "it might be," and went right back to blowing my mind with that back rub. So much, in fact, that my tongue loosened almost instantly.

"The Smithson-Napa reps want me to pitch them ideas for a bookish-themed home collection."

"That's amazing."

"Yeah." His fingers froze for a moment, like he was trying to figure out what I wasn't saying with my less than enthusiastic answer, but he didn't. He kept massaging my shoulders in silence until I spilled my guts again. "They told me this afternoon, apparently Kayla also weaseled herself in there."

He made one of those murder sounds that usually happened when Chase or his wife were the topic of conversation. "Kayla can't touch what you're going to bring to the table."

"You don't even know her work, Theo!" I cried, tipping my head up to look at him and he raised an eyebrow in challenge. I loved how serious he got when he talked about my work. About what he saw in me.

"I don't need to know about her, *I know about you*." He spoke so confidently, like he'd seen my future and there wasn't a thing to worry about. God, I wanted to believe too.

"Let me feed you, sweetheart, you're exhausted." His fingers curled around my jaw, gentle and firm at once. And it took everything in me not to leap into his arms. Let him take care of me, like he was asking.

"Okay, but I need to finish this for Rocco's niece after." He was up and grabbing the plate in no time. We sat cross-legged on the floor while I ate. I couldn't quash the tight, angry, needy thing in my chest that wished this could be my life. That I had someone who took care of me. Gave me what I needed. But I knew no one could put up with my chaos. He'd get tired of it eventually. "Why are you being so nice to me?"

He made that face like I'd punched him and sighed.

"You deserve to be pampered, Alba. You work too fuck-ing hard."

"A lot of people work hard," I retorted instantly. It came out harsher than I meant it to be, but it was not less true. "I'm not even trying to be contrary." He gave me that "sure you're not" look. "I'm serious. My mother has worked fourteen-hour days, six days a week practically from the moment we got off the plane from the DR and no one has ever pampered *her*. What makes me so damn special?" His nostrils flared at my question like it made him mad it was even a question. He waited so long to say something I thought he would just let it go. Nothing could've prepared me for what he actually said.

"You get it because I want to give it to you." I wished that I didn't react to the fierceness in his voice as much as I did. My body ached to get closer to him. "There's not a single thing I'd rather be doing than watch you eat that sandwich while you tell me about this adorable towel thing you made for Rocco's niece."

"It's a throw blanket," I corrected him, like it mattered, and he smiled at me with that expression I recognized as "What am I going to do with you?" face.

He nodded and took my hand, his thumb making cir-cles on the cramped muscles there. "The throw blanket you rushed here to finish even though you're swamped and over-whelmed. I don't give a fuck about special, Alba. You deserve to be pampered because I say you do."

"Theo." I pressed my forehead to his, shaking my head as I tried to push down all the yeses trying to come out of me. "You're so fucking bossy," I relented, making him laugh.

"What's this?" he asked, pointing to a set of sketches that were on the table next to the sewing machine.

"It's for the pitch for Smithson-Napa," I told him, and he hiked up an eyebrow in surprise.

"You've got this much done already? I thought they only approached you this afternoon?" He ran a finger over my rom-com designs like they had to be magic to even be on the table only hours after I'd been asked to make them.

"Please, Theo," I scoffed, as a little ember of pride burned in my chest at his obvious admiration. "You should know by now that I've had these ready just in case an opportunity came along."

His lips tipped up and he turned those gorgeous gray eyes on me. "Oh, I know there isn't a Girl Scout more ready than you." I knew he was teasing, but that sexy-ass grin still turned me on. It was hopeless—if Theo was around everything else paled in comparison.

"So the idea is that you'll do a line for different kinds of books?"

"Yup, different genres. Romance, sci-fi, mysteries, stuff like that. These—" I tapped the paper next to where his own finger was "—are the ones I did for rom-coms." I couldn't help smiling at the swatch with a pink background and featuring my favorite tropes.

"Don't think too hard there, bud," I teased, when his forehead scrunched up in concentration as he studied my sketch.

"So in romance there are tropes, like a shorthand for the dynamics of the romance," I explained. "Like this one." I tapped a fingernail on a couple staring at each other from either side of a bed. "That's *only one bed*." I'd drawn the figures in a way that their heads were turned in the direction of the headboard. There I'd added three big heart-shaped cushions. One had the word *only* in a loopy cursive, the other the number one, and the third read *bed* in big block letters.

"That's really cool." He grinned. "It's cute but the style is really elegant." I knew he was just talking out of his ass, but I appreciated the effort.

"That's enemies to lovers," I explained, flipping to the next sketch of two figures standing with their backs pressed together, glaring over their shoulders as winged golden hearts floated over their heads. "That one is my favorite." He looked intensely at it for a bit, his face serious.

"This is genius, Alba." He sounded sincere, but I never let myself get too excited about people's opinions of my work. One person liking it, even loving it, didn't mean that a corporation would think it could appeal to a larger market.

"It's just a concept, doodles, really," I told him, while he examined my mystery line sketches. "I have to get them much more polished to present them to Smithson-Napa."

"There is no way they won't love these."

"I hope you're right," I said, revealing more than I wanted to in that moment. But Theo was no dummy and he probably detected the worry in my voice.

"I've never seen you doubt yourself like this." He sounded genuinely surprised. "Besides, even I can see these are amazing." I didn't think he was joking, but there was more to this than Smithson-Napa appreciating my style. To my surprise, I told him what was really bothering me. Something that so far, I hadn't confessed to anyone.

"The thing is, Bookish Boudoir is my baby and working with clients… Of course I have to accommodate what they love, and that's fine because it's theirs. A line like this would have my name on it, and I don't want my name on something that isn't my vision. Or on a watered-down version of it."

"Do you think they'll ask you to do that?"

I lifted a shoulder, not wanting to go down that particular rabbit hole.

"I don't want to start hating it." That came out of nowhere, but after I said it, I knew it was true. Theo looked confused, which, fair. But saying the words gave me some clarity. "I started doing the makeovers because I love books and it was a fun way to blend the two things that I was obsessed with. It made my friends happy and I made a little money so I stayed with it. When it was just me doing the makeovers I felt more in control, but dealing with Chase, I've realized that leveling up will be a challenge in ways I didn't anticipate."

Theo winced at the mention of Chase, and I realized he might feel responsible for that. "I'm being dramatic, this is an amazing opportunity and I should be happy I have it." I didn't want to talk anymore. The more I did the more daunting this would feel. I pushed down the niggling feeling that I'd be forced to give away pieces of myself to make a go out of this. Because the reality was I'd probably still do it.

"I have to get back to this, thanks for dinner." I turned my back to him, like the rude asshole I was.

"I can keep you company." He sounded so earnest, so eager. But that wouldn't last. He'd get tired of the long nights and the stretches when I didn't respond to calls and canceled plans last-minute. It wouldn't take much time before he realized that being good at my job came at the cost of being super shitty at my personal life. "Theo, I can't lose my focus here, and this…" He stiffened as I waved a hand between us. "Is a distraction."

"Alba, If you'd let me be there—" I couldn't let him say it. A memory of my dad saying the same words to my mother, only to resent her later, came to mind.

"I can't offer more than what happened last night, Theo. I can't get involved with you or anyone. There is too much riding on this. I…" I palmed my forehead, all of a sudden feeling feverish, nausea roiling in my belly. "Last night was good, it was great. But I just. I want us to be friends."

"You are under a tight schedule right now and I can understand that—"

My laugh was bitter. I hardly recognized that woman.

"There will always be something else for me. And I will probably jump after that too. This is who I am, Theo." I made myself look at him, curled my lip disdainfully, like he was a waste of my time. All the while I felt like my insides had been scooped out. Hollow. "I'm obsessive about my work, self-absorbed to a fault when it comes to getting ahead."

"You carry a lot, your family…"

I shook my head so hard I felt my earrings lashing the side of my face.

"It's me, Theo. It's *me*. I'm ambitious and I'm okay with that taking precedence over my personal life. It's who I am." He stiffened at the sharp impatience in my voice and finally backed off. I had to dig my nails into my palms to keep from reaching for him.

"If that's what you want." He sounded crestfallen. I hid my eyes from the pain in his.

"It is, that's what I want." After he left the room, I sat down at the sewing machine and worked until I couldn't keep my eyes open.

# Chapter Sixteen

## ALBA

Pro tip: do not schedule a Brazilian wax on a day when you'll be running around doing errands, because you could end up by the side of the road somewhere "rural" with no undies on and a rental with two flat tires.

"I'm sorry, babe!" Julia lamented while I fought back the urge to scream. "I can't come down to get you. I have to go pick up Blue at preschool for Sofia. She and Rocco are in Waco today doing that campus tour."

"Shit, I forgot about that." Sofia, Rocco's sister, had just gotten accepted to an MSW at Baylor University and would be moving there in the fall.

"Did you try Salome? She's usually got a more flexible schedule." I groaned internally, realizing I was well and truly fucked since Salome had been my next to last call, before Julia.

"She's got her department meeting until seven," I reminded my bestie. Salome hated her department meetings with a fiery passion and just that morning had asked us for thoughts and prayers in the chat group.

She clicked her tongue in sympathy, but I knew no offer for a ride was coming. "José and Tariq are out of town. Dani's got that photo shoot for the new beer brand he's partnering with." The silence that stretched between us after that spoke volumes and it was mostly saying *you know who you need to call!*

Fuck. Fuck. *Fuck.*

In the ten days since Theo'd brought me dinner and I'd told him I needed space we'd been giving each other a wide berth. We'd had to film together, but usually with other people, so that had thankfully minimized any potentially awkward-as-fuck conversations. The rest of my days had been consumed with the actual renovation of the library and my side hustles. Between the Bookish gigs and the proposal for Smithson-Napa I was either running around Dallas or holed up in my room until all hours of the night. And even though I'd basically hit it and quit it *then* dined and dashed, he'd still been leaving me plates of whatever he made for dinner. Despite me not holding up my end of our bargain to eat with him when he cooked.

Almost every night he'd make a plate for me and put it on the counter with a note saying what it was and how long I should heat it up. I texted him to say thank you, but in the last couple of days he hadn't even responded to that. Because I was a rude ho who ate his food and didn't even have the decency to eat with him.

"Alba, are you still there?" Julia's voice snapped me back to my current reality, which involved a dirt road and an impending hailstorm.

"Yeah, I'm here." Thunder cracked in the distance and the sky looked really dark. I cringed at the photo of vintage Jeannaret chairs I'd found that morning on Craigslist and were waiting for me only ten miles away. The owner was selling them for eighty bucks for the pair, a steal, but the catch was that I had to drive an hour to get them and be there before 6:30 p.m. Which I would've done without issue if my tires hadn't popped on this stupid country road.

"If you call him he'll come, Alba," my best friend said in that extremely annoying mind reader way of hers.

"That's the problem, Julia," I complained. And it was. Theo already had my feelings all over the place. I couldn't stop missing him even though he was right there. I felt needy and clingy and I hated that. I didn't want to rely on him because he was not mine to rely on. And what I'd told him was true. I was too selfish and absorbed in my work to be a good partner to anyone. As sad as it was, I just didn't trust that there was a person out there that would put up with all that without eventually resenting me. So many times I'd almost knocked on the door of his bedroom, but I'd forced myself to walk away. He didn't need my chaos, and I already knew it would destroy me to see him eventually get tired of my bullshit.

"Babe, that man is literally just waiting on you. Call him."

"I fucked him, ate his food, and then basically iced him out, Julia."

"You can come back from that!" My best friend the eternal optimist. "I believe in you and your magic cooch!"

I groaned as one of those rogue images of his head between my legs by that pool flashed through my mind. "You are the worst cheerleader ever!"

"I'm a *fantastic* cheerleader. Now, go call the man for a ride. It's going to get dark soon and you said the tow company can't get to you for at least two hours."

"Maybe I should just keep trying ShareRide," I sighed as I refreshed the app. And nope, there were still no cars near my location for another thirty minutes.

"Alba, are you, a woman raised in Queens, really considering getting in a car with a random stranger with no underwear on in rural Texas?"

"I don't know why I told you that about the underwear situation," I moaned.

"I swear to God, Alba. If you don't call Theo I'm going to, and I *will* tell him you're out there with your chocha in the wind. So help me God."

"Jesus Christ, Julia! Aren't you at work?" The horror in my voice was not at all fake. "Fine! You're coming off my emergency contacts list!"

"As if." My friend laughed off my threat and ended the call with more of her own.

It took a couple of minutes of giving myself a pep talk before I actually called him. By the time he picked up on the fourth ring a bead of sweat was sliding down my back.

"Alba." Okay, he sounded a little put off, but he did take the call, so that was something.

"Hey, how are you?" *Just get on with it.*

"I'm all right."

"That's awesome," I answered a little cheerier than necessary, and screwed my eyes shut from embarrassment at my own idiocy. "So, are you busy right now?" The silence stretched for so long I actually pulled the phone from my ear to see if the call hadn't dropped.

"What do you need, Alba?" I unclenched my teeth at his assholic tone and reminded myself that I had blown him off and ignored him for almost two weeks and that he was my only shot at getting out of my current jam.

"Well, here's the thing. I was on my way to pick up something for a Bookish makeover and sort of blew out my two back tires." A sound that was a mix of humor and exasperation came through the phone and hey, it wasn't rage, so I could work with that. "I called Triple A but the earliest they can come is two hours. There are no ShareRides around, I tried," I added at the end just in case.

"Am I your last resort, Alba Medea?" *Don't curse him out about the name thing. He's your only hope.*

"No," I lied.

"You're so full of shit. You probably called everyone you know in Texas." He laughed but it was not at all the sexy rumble I'd heard so many times since he'd come to Texas. I missed sexy and dirty Theo, but it was my own fault he was no longer there. He stayed quiet for another long stretch. When he finally spoke, he sounded like he was already moving. "Where are you?"

"Around Midlothian?"

"Okay," he said in that self-assured, alert way of his. It felt like my crisis was on its way to being resolved already. "Send me a pin of where you are." I put him on speaker and did it. "Got it. I'll leave now. I was at a meeting."

"You had a meeting? Are you making progress with the veteran housing thing?" It was out of my mouth before I could stop myself, and I did not miss the scoff that followed my nosy-ass question.

"Yes. I will be there in twenty minutes." Okay, so he wasn't in a sharing mood. Not that I'd asked him how it was going before, since I'd been avoiding him.

"Listen, if you're busy with that I'm sure I can—"

"There's a huge storm coming in like an hour, Alba. I don't trust that toaster with wheels you drive around in even when it's dry. I'm not letting you get back in that thing while it's hailing."

"Hey! This car is fine," I groused, but there was way too much relief coursing through my body for it to have much heat.

"It's a fucking death trap is what it is," he said, ignoring my protest. He sounded put off and cranky and it was making my stomach hurt.

"Look, Theo, if you're pissed at me, you don't have to come," I said, as I pulled the car door open and got back in.

"Alba, I can be pissed at you and still want to help you. I'm not a child. Just because shit between us is weird right now doesn't mean I'm okay with leaving you stranded during a hailstorm." I swallowed down the swell of guilt and gratitude crawling up my throat and let out a long breath.

"Okay, thank you." My voice was so small I could barely hear myself.

"I'll be there in twenty. Stay in the car and lock the doors."

These were the times when everything about my life felt overwhelming. I was mad at myself because I wanted Theo and I was mad at myself because I was mad at myself. I was tired because I kept saying yes to more work, then annoyed for being ungrateful that I finally had what I'd wanted. And mostly I just wished I could take him up on the offer to take care of me for once. To crawl on his lap and watch TV all night. But how would I do that when every second of my day was accounted for?

Never, that was when. I sighed and did what always worked whenever I dwelled too long on the extremely treacherous landscape of my love life.

I worked.

I grabbed my iPad and fiddled with the designs for the Smithson–Napa proposal, which I'd sent to Carrie and Yaz-min that morning—five days early. I was feeling pretty good about beating Kayla on the deadline and hoped they liked what I'd sent them. I was so absorbed playing with color palettes that before I knew it Theo's matte-black Tesla SUV was coming down the gravel road toward me. He rolled to a stop right in front of my small car and it was honestly sad how just the sight of him made the air squeeze out of my lungs. I could try and fool myself that it was just relief, but relief had never made my nipples hard.

There was no effective way to prepare for Theo when he was dressed in full real estate mogul mode. Hair tousled just right, his ever-present Wayfarers covering his eyes. He had Ferragamo loafers on his feet and his pants looked molded to those powerful thighs. The shirt, as always, a crisp white and the sleeves cuffed to reveal his veined forearms. The man was the reason the slo-mo setting had been invented.

"Get it together, Alba Serena," I whispered to myself as he walked toward my car. That was easier said than done given the fact that I could see the outline of his bicep bulging the dress shirt he was wearing from ten feet away. "And for God's sake, don't drool on the man," I added in a Hail Mary as I jumped out of my compact rental to meet him by the very flat back tires.

"Thanks for coming," I said in my most grateful-sounding voice as he crouched to take a closer look. He prodded the deflated rubber and frowned without even acknowledging me.

"I was hoping we could get away with changing one tire and then driving on the other one to the nearest gas station, but these are totally done." Okay, so no small talk. I decided to not make a thing out of it, since he was figuring out how to help me.

"Could we still try that?"

He winced, which was answer enough. "There's no way you can drive five miles on that."

"Yeah, they're in pretty bad shape." I squirmed, clutching the handle of my purse tighter.

"You have everything you need?" he asked, tipping his chin at the back of the car. It was completely empty since I'd intended to fill it up with the chairs I was on my way to pick up. I looked at my watch and saw that I technically still had time to get there, if only...

"I do," I told him extra sweetly, tapping my purse for effect. It was now or never. "Listen, I know you've already done me a super big solid today, but I might need another teeny favor." I held up my index finger and thumb a millimeter apart. He clenched his jaw but nodded.

"The thing is," I hedged, and his mouth flattened in a very unamused expression. "I was on my way to pick up these two vintage chairs from a woman that's selling them for basically nothing."

"Where?" he bit out, and I was so close to telling him to fuck off in his big dumb car. Instead I mustered up another smile and got a little closer because I don't care how pissed he looked now, I had empirical evidence of the effect my boobs had on him.

"It's like another fifteen miles south." He scowled with his hands on his hips. He looked so damn hot it was a real struggle to stay on task. "But it shouldn't take more than ten minutes to get them."

"You're a real pain in the ass, Alba," he growled, then sighed before turning back to the Tesla. "Lock up the car, and let's go." I gulped down the snide comment itching to come out of my mouth.

"I need to leave the key for the tow truck." That I delivered in a more smart-ass tone than was advisable.

"Fine. Leave it in the glove compartment and tell your tow company not to bother coming, I already contacted my service and they'll be here in the next half hour."

"You did what?"

He pinched the bridge of his nose like I was plucking at his last nerve.

"I pay for a service with a concierge who takes care of

this kind of thing. It's quicker and they'll bring the car back to our building afterward." I didn't know why him being nice to me annoyed me as much as it did, but I was pissed.

"I already had it taken care of."

"Yeah, your plan worked great."

"You don't need to be an asshole, Theo."

He seemed to find that funny. "I'm the asshole, sure, Alba." His face was pinched and even though he sounded angry there was hurt in his eyes. And what smarted was that I knew he wasn't wrong. I was the one who had pushed him away and here he was after all that still coming to help me.

"Fine," I said, woodenly, sliding my sunglasses on.

He exhaled, like he had no fucking clue what to do with me, but when he spoke he didn't sound annoyed, or at least not as annoyed. "If the tow doesn't come now they won't be able to get here until after the storm and that might not be until morning. My service is already on its way."

"And your tow company is magically not affected by the weather like mine is," I argued, because I was also my own worst enemy.

"My tow company gets paid generously so they're always available when I need them." Since the moment he got to Dallas I'd wondered how long it would take for New York Theo Ganas to make an appearance and here he was in his full arrogant pain-in-the-ass glory. "If anything, with my service your car won't be unlocked with the key inside for hours."

Dammit. He was right.

I quickly texted the tow truck company, who replied saying they had to go deal with an accident on the expressway and wouldn't have gotten to me for a few hours anyway. That information I kept to myself. I wasn't going to give him more gloating material. Then I put the keys in the glove compartment while Theo watched beside the car like my own personal bodyguard.

"Done."

Without a word he turned on his heel. I thought he was going to get in the driver seat and glare until I got in, but instead he opened the passenger door for me. That was worse than him being rude, because then I could just be mad back. But him being gentlemanly and courteous even when I knew he was irritated was just one of the things that had my feelings all over the place when it came to Theo. Because yeah, he was furious, but he'd still dropped everything to come and help me. And maybe he wasn't happy about me asking for space, but he still made sure I had a hot meal when I was working late. No wonder my head was a fucking mess.

"Thanks," I said quietly and gathered the skirt of my dress so it didn't get blown up by the wind, which by now was pretty strong. He looked at me weird but didn't ask questions. Thank goodness.

I gave him the address and within a few minutes we were on the road. I caved first, not able to stand the stony silence.

"I'm sorry, okay, just stop being mad at me." I was wringing my hands looking straight ahead when I said it, so I didn't have to watch him sneering at me. From my periphery I could see his hands tighten on the steering wheel and I could almost hear him thinking.

I felt the tension between us like an invisible wall of heat. I hated knowing he was mad at me. Absolutely hated it. When I was a kid my mother teased me for being shameless when she was pissed at me. I'd act like nothing was wrong until she gave up and started talking to me again. Not with Theo. Maybe that was why I'd been avoiding him, because I knew that seeing him upset would be too hard. What was crazier was that this pissed off, distant Theo was the one I'd dealt with for years, but just after a few weeks the other one was the one I missed. The one I wanted.

He took so long to say something I was tempted to fling myself out of the car.

"I'm not mad at you, Alba."

"You *should* be mad at me. I've been a complete jerk." I did turn around then and I could see how tightly he was clenching his jaw. He might tell himself he wasn't mad, but he *was* feeling feelings. I wasn't foolish enough to think Theo Ganas was in love with me. But his pride was likely hurt. I'd handled all this so poorly.

"I'm not a kid, Alba." He shrugged, as if it didn't matter much. "I can accept if what I wanted to happen didn't."

"I don't even know if I'm going back to New York," I blurted out, the words bubbling out of me.

He did turn then, probably as surprised as I was. Staying in Dallas permanently had never been even a remote possibility, but now that the words were out there, I couldn't sweep them aside.

"You really thinking of relocating?" he finally asked, and I noticed he didn't sound surprised, just curious.

"I don't know." And I really didn't. This time in Dallas was supposed to be an easy rung in the ladder. A solid step up to the next thing, but I just couldn't figure out what I wanted. Other than Theo, that was.

"It's not like I don't want...that I don't want you," I confessed for some insane fucking reason. "I have too much going on right now, Theo. So do you. It's easier this way."

He did turn then. He'd taken off his sunglasses and I could see a million questions flashing in his eyes. "If that's what you want."

"That's what I want," I made myself say, even as a voice inside me called me every name possible. He let my words hang in the air, then gave me a clipped nod as he stopped the car in front of a pretty ranch house surrounded by a huge field.

# THEO

Alba Serena Duarte tested every fucking rule I'd set for myself to its breaking point.

"I shouldn't be more than ten minutes," she said over her shoulder as she jumped down from the Tesla and headed up to the porch of the house. I didn't even respond because I knew it was beyond me to deny this woman anything.

"So how do you know this lady?" I asked in an attempt to distract myself from looking down at the curve of her ass in that dress as I followed her to the door.

"It's from a website where people post secondhand furniture," she explained vaguely.

"You mean Craigslist."

She cut her eyes at me and rang the bell. "*Yes, Craigslist,* and I'll have you know that I find all kinds of good stuff on there for my makeovers. And these chairs are perfect for the signature piece in this Bookish project I'm working on."

I wanted to ask what book it was inspired by, because even though I thought she needed to cut way back on how much she worked, I loved hearing her talk about those bedroom makeovers. But before I could the door opened and an older blonde woman wearing a pink robe and holding two tiny dogs appeared and pinned her sights on me.

"Well, hello there, cowboy," she drawled, not bothering to hide the very thorough assessment of my person she immediately engaged in.

"Ma'am," I said, having been indoctrinated in the proper Texan salutation etiquette.

"You're a lot to take in on one sitting," she told me in a

pronounced twang. I couldn't say for sure, but I was pretty certain she smacked her lips after saying that. Beside me I heard my companion splutter with laughter. I pinched her ass in retaliation, and she jumped, eliciting a satisfying squeal.

"Hi, are you Miss Susan?" she crooned, after shooting me a nasty look. "I'm Alba. We talked on the phone this morning, I'm here for the two Jeannaret chairs."

"Oh, that's right. You can just call me Susan." The woman smiled, extending a hand to Alba before turning her attention back to me. "What's *your* name, sugar?"

"I'm Theo, ma'am. Just here to help."

"Smart girl," she told Alba with a wink. "You brought yourself a big strong man to do all that heavy lifting for you." She gave a grunt of appreciation as she shook my hand. Alba grinned like she was very much enjoying the show. Once she was done with the handshaking Miss Susan proceeded to not at all subtly slide a palm up my arm. Alba lost it when the woman squeezed my biceps and let out an appreciative sound.

"Are the chairs inside?" I asked, as I tried to gently pry my arm out of her literal claws. Alba just snickered like she was watching her favorite comedy sketch.

"No, they're out in the shed." She pointed a red nail to a structure on the right side of the main house. "It's open and there are still a few things in there that need to go. If you want any of it just let me know. I have price tags on everything."

"Oh, that's so nice of you," Alba said happily. She was wiggling her ass like an excited puppy about to get her favorite treat. My dick throbbed in my pants and I had to hold my breath for a few beats to keep from embarrassing myself.

"Yes, go on and take a look." She gave me another once-over as she clutched the opening of her robe. "I have to go get ready for church bingo, but I may come by to say good-bye. It's so rare to get such…intriguing visitors."

"Okay, thank you," I said briskly, already pulling Alba with me to the shed.

"Oh my God," she wheezed out the moment we were out of earshot while Miss Susan looked on from her porch. "She wanted to take a big bite out of *you.*"

"I'm glad me getting looked at like a prize bull was entertaining."

"Entertaining?" she asked, incredulous, then dissolved into another fit of laughter. "It was fucking hilarious. I thought she was going to check your teeth and smack your ass. She kind of reminds me of Jennifer Coolidge in *Legally Blonde.*" She almost couldn't say the last part she was cackling so hard. I only had a vague recollection of what she was talking about, but I didn't need to worry—Alba demonstrated by bending over on the grass and popping back up. "Miss Susan would've loved to give you a preview of her bend and snap."

"I hate you and be careful of what you do with that ass if you don't want me to swat it." The threat was not an empty one. My hands itched to touch her.

"You wouldn't, and besides—" She stopped talking and came to dead stop the moment we stepped inside the shed. I thought something was wrong, but then she jumped in the air and gave a piercing squeal before throwing herself at a coffee table.

"This is a *cloud table!*" She ran her palms over the smooth birch wood surface with a hungry expression on her face.

"That's good I assume?" I asked, knowing I'd get plied with a detailed explanation of everything about this table.

"Uh, yeah." She pulled a face like I was hopeless, and fuck, I wanted kiss her senseless. "The cloud table is a design that was first done by Neil Morris in the late '40s. His stuff is amazing," she said with a dreamy expression, before crouching by the table and turning it over. She frowned in concentration as she looked at the inscription on the side. "It's a replica," she informed me, those brown eyes bright with excitement. "An original could go for a few grand. But this is perfect for the room I'm doing."

"What book is it?" I finally asked, as she moved to look at the two identical chairs in the corner, which I assumed were the reason we were here.

"The client wants something that evokes the vibe of *The Seven Husbands of Evelyn Hugo*." I'd heard of the book but hadn't read it, though she clearly had if her moony eyes were any indicator. When Alba talked about books it was like she was holding her whole heart in her hands. The joy reading brought her was so pure and honest, it was intoxicating. It was disarming to see a woman who approached so much of her life with such dogged, unstoppable determination be so entranced by the stories she read.

"It's so good." Her smile was huge, eyes bright, and my pulse raced in response to all that emotion. "It's about a Hollywood actress who had this long and scandalous career over like six decades and this super-secret epic love story with another actress. It's a total vibe and has all this old Hollywood glamour. But the story is about much more than that," she assured me as she moved around the room hunting for potential treasure. "It's about the price that women with ambition have to pay for chasing their dreams. The double standards we have to manage. About the cost of hiding your true self." She stopped, her eyes fixed somewhere far away. I didn't even know what to say, the moment felt too volatile to voice what I could see now for the first time. Books were not just a refuge for Alba—they were the place she went to feel understood.

After a moment, she shook herself, as if she was coming out of a trance. She turned a radiant smile my way, but I could see the shadows lurking behind her eyes.

"Wow, I got too deep for a second there." She tapped the back of one of the chairs and looked away. "Anyway, the pieces here are exactly what I need to complete the design." This wasn't the right place or time to air out everything I wanted to say to her, but with every passing day I grew more certain that Alba Duarte was the center of my future.

She kept inspecting the pieces with interest as I watched her. When she got to a corner where there was a stack of crates filled with magazines she yelped with delight. "Whoa!" she exclaimed, picking one up. "Those are old issues of *Look* magazine. I bet I could find a few good ones to put in frames for the walls."

The irritation and disappointment I'd felt in the car was long gone now, replaced by that warm glow in my chest that always seemed to appear whenever I got to see this side of Alba. She was always so harried. It was a pleasure getting to see her enjoy her work.

"What are you so serious about?" she asked, after making her way back to where I was standing by the door.

"I'm not serious, I just like hearing you talk about your work." A pretty pink tint flushed her cheeks, and my hands clenched and unclenched at my side from the need to reach for her.

"Oh." She snagged her bottom lip and my whole body thrummed like it was my own skin being scraped by that row of straight white teeth. "I can get real extra when I start talking about this stuff. I know it can get boring." Her voice was small, like she was actively trying to become smaller. I fucking hated it.

*Nothing about you is boring*, I wanted to say, feeling slightly unhinged from the powerful need to convince her that there wasn't a single thing about her I didn't find utterly captivating. But if I started I'd likely scare her off, so I reverted to form. "Don't be too hard on yourself, Alba Cordelia," I teased and she rolled her eyes.

"Jerk." But there was a smile tipping up her lips. "Do we have space in your truck to take this too?" She pointed to the coffee table and the crate of magazines.

I pushed off the doorway forcing myself to focus on anything other than that sweet little valley between her tits, which I now knew would taste a little salty from her exertions and a little sweet from the cocoa butter she rubbed on her skin. My head and my dick were conspiring to make me fumble this whole scenario.

*Focus, Theo, goddammit.*

"I got space," I confirmed as she started piling the pieces she wanted next to the two chairs we'd originally come for. It was a lot of fucking stuff. "How exactly were you planning on fitting all of this into that matchbox of yours?"

"Stop using hate speech when talking about my appropriately sized vehicle," she huffed as she picked up a wall clock that looked like a constellation and put it on top of the table. She sounded all mean and shit, but when she looked up her lips were turned up in a tiny smile. I wanted her so bad I felt like my skin was on fire. "But you're kind of right." She winced. "There was no way I could take more than the chairs and even that would've been an ordeal. You saved my ass."

I grunted at the mention of one of my favorite parts of her anatomy and went to grab the table. I was arranging the pieces in the trunk so we could fit everything when I heard an alarmed "oh no" behind me.

"What's wrong?" I made my way to her in four steps. It was funny how for years I'd been able to stay cool under pressure in situations that would incapacitate most people, yet two words of distress from Alba had my entire body primed to fight.

"Nothing, the wind's just lifting my skirt." She was struggling to clutch it and keep a stack of magazines in her hands from crashing to the ground. The wind was really whipping now and the hem of her dress was swirling around her knees.

"Here." She handed me the magazines, looking and sounding flustered. "Shit, all of Midlothian is going to see my bare *nalgas*." The moment the words came out of her mouth her eyes bulged and she clamped her mouth shut. This was Alba so I knew better than to assume I'd heard wrong.

"What did you just say?" I came closer, until we were inches apart. It was just the two of us out here, and though Miss Susan had promised to check in, no one was around, so her concern had to be about more than me getting a look at her panties. Still, the mere thought of it had my dick rockhard in seconds.

"Uh nothing?" The *nothing* would've worked had her entire face not flushed a shade very similar to that of a ripe tomato.

"Alba, are you not wearing underwear?" Now, logically I knew there had to be some kind of explanation, but all my brain could process were the words *Alba*, *bare* and *pussy*.

"Not that it's any of your business." She had the gall to look affronted. "But I went to get a Brazilian on my lunch break today." I was grateful I had already put down the furniture I'd been moving because I was certain I would've snapped one of those chairs in two just from the jolt of adrenaline that image sent through my body. "Miss Susan called me in the middle of it," she confessed with a little embarrassed hitch in her voice. "I rushed out and forgot to put my thong back on." She shrugged, adorably self-conscious, and I thought it was really a fucking marvel how this woman in the exact same instant could make me want to ensconce her in clouds of silk *and* fuck her through the nearest hard surface until she blacked out. After a couple of seconds of hard staring and me biting my tongue until I tasted blood, I let her walk past me to the truck.

"Gotta get this stuff in the car before this storm comes in," she reminded me. I would've managed to keep myself in check but, like she was looking to burn through every ounce of my self-control in a single afternoon, she leaned inside the back of the truck, which effectively put the ass that I now knew was naked under that dress in the air. And yeah, there was no evidence of panties. There was also no way I was going to endure Alba ass-up on the trunk of my car unscathed.

"Hey," she grumbled when I stood behind her and leaned down to speak in her ear. "You're too close."

I would've taken the protest a lot more seriously if she hadn't pushed into me as she said it.

The way Alba made me forget myself was almost like a damn act of God. One moment I had my shit together and the next I was trying to nail her in broad daylight, swept under an avalanche of need in seconds.

"Just tell me something, Alba Duarte." My lips were close enough that I grazed her earlobe when I talked. She made one of those horny little sounds of hers and wiggled that ass on my cock in response. One of my hands instinctually gripped her hip, fingers digging in. "Who were you getting this pussy waxed for?" I asked, and a little gasp escaped her lips, stretching my control to its limits.

"Oh, stop acting like you don't know." She sounded so pissed, even as she threw her head back onto my shoulder, eyes closed. My hand hovered right over the apex of her thighs, but I didn't touch. This was already fully outside the bounds of what she'd asked for only minutes ago. But that was how it went with us. We set a line in the sand and then proceeded to literally fuck right over it. "Realistically what are the chances that we're not going to keep doing this?" she grumbled. "The only way I was able to keep myself away was hiding from you."

Relief and satisfaction coursed through me from knowing I hadn't been the only one hard up for the last ten days.

"God you make me so fucking horny," she snapped, but didn't make any move to get away. "I don't even know what comes over me."

"So you lied," I muttered, close to her ear as thunder clapped in the distance.

"What? Theo, it's starting to rain."

Trust when I tell you that in that moment, I was half crazed. My whole body was shaking from wanting to shove her in that back seat and have her ride my cock until we both saw stars. But I *had* the endurance to win *two* medals in the Olympics, and goddammit I would make sure we both knew exactly where we stood before I let this lust fog take over.

"Tell me first," I urged her.

"No, I didn't lie," she snapped. "The rational, sensible side of me knows this is a terrible fucking idea. But I want you and I know you want me, so I knew I'd cave at some point." As far as rationales for a woman being with me went, this was not exactly the stuff that dreams were made of. Still, she was here, freshly waxed and primed to be fucked blind. Which I planned to do as soon as I could get her horizontal.

"I'm going to give you a thorough inspection." I pressed my pelvis into her and her ass rubbed on me just right. I could just undo my zipper, lift her dress and slide inside. "As soon as we get back to the house I'm going to take a look. Get up close and really appreciate the good work that was done for my benefit today." She froze at my filthy promise then melted against me. I kept going, fingers edging closer to her heat as I told her all the things I wanted to do to her. "I'm going to suck on those smooth lips while I finger you. Get all that cream right on my tongue, fuck. I can almost taste you." She gasped and scored the floor of the trunk with her nails.

"God, stop, Theo." Her voice shook as we stood there grinding hard into each other. I knew I'd just need to tap her clit once and she'd go off like a rocket.

"You don't like that idea then?" I said, all fake regretful. "I guess you won't want to fuck my face like you did that night at the pool."

"You know I do." She sounded so pissed. Like everything she did with me was against her better judgement and she didn't give a fuck. It only made me hotter for her.

"Maybe I'll edge you until you beg me to let you come." I whispered hotly. I was considering what the chances were of her biting my head off if I did put her over my shoulder, drove us out to the woods and ate her out in the back seat when Miss Susan cockblocked me.

# Chapter Seventeen

## ALBA

Did I let Theo feel me up on the back of that Tesla? Yes, I did. Was I considering engaging in public acts that would likely get us arrested in the Lone Star State? Absolutely.

"There you are!" Thankfully Miss Susan was a yeller, and made her presence known while she was still far enough away that we could get ourselves together. After taking a couple of deep breaths and hoping my face didn't reveal any evidence of what had almost unfolded in the poor woman's driveway I turned around. Theo stood behind me, probably to hide the erection poking my back.

"I'm glad I caught you before you left," she called, and I waved back as Theo wrapped a possessive arm around my waist while my spine arched into his touch of its own volition.

"You're just taking advantage because I can't knee you in the nuts in front of Miss Susan," I muttered and felt the vibration of his smart-ass laugh. "The moment we're in that car I'm giving you a piece of my mind, Theo Ganas," I hissed, which totally backfired.

"The moment we get in that car I'm going to spread that bare pussy in the back seat and suck the life out of you."

I never got to tell him how I was going to murder him in his sleep because Miss Susan reached us dressed to kill in what one could only call Texas Gym Chic "The Neon Edition." There was so much spandex, fringe and rhinestones, my eyes watered a little, but somehow she pulled it off. She grinned as she lowered her eyes to where Theo's arm was resting on my midriff.

"Oh good, you got some stuff," she said wistfully. "I'm glad it's going to someone who can use it. Most of it was my great-aunt June's."

"Oh, I'm so sorry for your loss," I hurried to say, but Miss Susan waved me off and laughed.

"Oh, she's not dead, honey! She just moved to Arizona. Got one of them 'active living' condos. She's having the time of her life out there." She angled her head then, like she was only now really getting a good look at us, and clucked happily. "Y'all are darling together." Then she leaned in with her hand cupping her mouth. "I'm a little jealous of you," she whispered very loudly. "That man looks like he's the best kind of rough ride." That was delivered with a saucy wink and a shiver like just thinking about playing dick rodeo with Theo brought her all kinds of thrills.

The jackass I was with obviously heard her since he was shaking behind me. His fingers fluttered on my back and I didn't have to turn around to know he was trying not to laugh. And what the fuck was wrong with me that my insides started fluttering just from sensing he was having fun?

"Oh, we're not together," I told her and immediately regretted it when I felt Theo stiffen. Miss Susan's face fell for a second, but she wasn't going to let that detract her from her attempt to get all in our business. In response, Theo let his arm slip away from me, and I had to force myself not to grip his wrist to keep him there. He closed the trunk door and waved goodbye to Miss Susan.

"Thanks, ma'am." He offered her a real smile and my

messy-ass self felt a twinge of jealousy. "I'll wait for you in the truck." This was said to me in a very terse tone.

"Oh, honey, thank you for taking some of that stuff off my hands. If you think of anything else you want, come back and grab it. You can just PayPal me. I'll be gone for the next few hours, but I'll leave the shed open for you," she called after him as he climbed in the truck then clicked her tongue again, this time like things were in a state of emergency. "That man looks at you like he's just come out of the desert after forty days and forty nights and you're the only thing he's been craving."

Yeah, I wasn't going down that path.

"Thanks for everything, Miss Susan." I was grateful to the woman for letting me go without another comment. I watched her climb into her car and drive away as her words rang in my ears. By the time I climbed into the car next to Theo it had started to rain. Fat raindrops started splashing against the windshield as Theo got us on the gravel road leading out of Miss Susan's property.

"My service picked up your car. They said they'd drop it off once they switch the tires." He sounded casual, but there was an unmistakable tightness in his voice.

"Thank you."

He only nodded, his focus on the road. The rain was already pounding the roof and it was starting to get dark. I couldn't see much, but Theo didn't seem too bothered by it. We drove in that tense heavy silence for miles until I snapped, again.

"Theo, you can't be mad at me for telling the truth." He exasperated me with his stoic calm. Made me want to push, say things to provoke him until he finally gave up on this. Until he saw that I was nothing but a future headache.

"I'm not mad." His voice was so calm, so detached. Like

the conversation didn't matter at all. I ground my teeth and kept my attention on the relentless spatter of drops on the windshield.

"You're lying."

He made a sound that clearly translated to *you're one to talk*. And yeah, maybe I was being a hypocrite, but that didn't mean I wasn't right.

"You don't want complications, Theo. You don't need me and my chaos." His jaw moved like he was struggling not to say something nasty, then a sound like a gunshot echoed through the car, making us both jump.

"Fuck, it's really coming down," he said, voice alert. "I need to get us out of this." But if he was freaking out, like I was, you couldn't tell from his calm voice or the easy way he maneuvered the car. Theo, always in control.

I sat there in nervous silence as Theo struggled to keep the car from skidding onto the other side of the road. But he kept his cool. Nothing fazed Theo, not a hailstorm, not a call to go on a rescue mission in North Texas in the middle of the afternoon, not an Olympic freaking competition. And that was part of the problem: as much as I looked okay on the outside, I was a mess inside and Theo didn't tolerate mess. It was honestly baffling that he was even here right now.

I returned my attention to what he was doing when he suddenly veered off the road and made a U-turn.

"Where are you going?"

"I'm going back to Miss Susan's. There was a covered garage next to that shed, we can wait out the worst of this there."

"Okay." Miss Susan had said we could come back if we wanted something else. She probably wouldn't mind if we took refuge at her place until the hail stopped.

"Why aren't you going back to New York?" he finally asked when the turn for Miss Susan's was already in our sights.

"Looks like she made it wherever she was going," I said, ignoring his question, as I glanced at the dark house and her empty driveway. Once we were under the cover of the carport, he powered off the car and turned to me.

"Why, Alba?" This was a lot harder to do now that he wasn't trying to drive us through an apocalyptic storm and could look me in the eye when I answered.

"I like Dallas." I lifted a shoulder as I thought about how for the first time in years I didn't have to resolve a family crisis on a weekly basis. "I have breathing room here, and with me no longer just a phone call away my family has had to deal with their shit for once." He made a sound of understanding but didn't say anything. Didn't try to pick apart my complicated feelings. When lightning cracked across the sky and the pellets ricocheting off the roof we were under intensified, instead of getting on his phone and calling for whatever well-compensated cavalry he probably had on speed dial, he just slid his seat back, and reclined, like he was expecting to be here for a minute.

That was something I liked about Theo: as much of a control freak as he could be, when he had to sit one out, he did. He did not lose his temper or waste his energy on trying to change things he could not control. I guessed that was what it was like for a person who knew he had the resources to alter outcomes he didn't like.

"What if I want your chaos?"

I'd been so deep in my thoughts it took me a moment to really hear what he'd said. Once I did, I snapped my head up and tried to see what I could read from his face in the dim light of the car. When I looked into his eyes, I felt like I could get washed away by all that he was offering me.

"You say that now, but the shine will fade very quickly." I braced for his frustrated response. For him to tell me he was done trying to talk sense into me. But like a bubble popping, all the tension seemed to go out of him and the asshole laughed at me.

Which obviously pissed me off, but then he leaned in, slid his fingers into my hair and brushed a kiss against my cheek. "What am I going to do with you?"

I had an answer, a biting one. It was on the tip of my tongue that I was not his to do a damn thing with. But every word melted away in the heat of his searing touch.

"Theo, we're—"

He took my mouth then, his tongue insinuating its way inside in that languid, drugging way he kissed me. Like he wanted to slither right into the marrow of my bones.

"Mm," he groaned as he undid my seat belt. "I've let this conversation go on too long already when I know what you have for me under this dress." He dragged me onto his lap as he slid the seat back even farther. Once I was astride his thighs his eyes locked on me. It was a tight fit but with the seat practically horizontal we could make this thing work and I could not believe I was actually getting it on with Theo in Miss Susan's driveway. But his hands were like live wires on my skin, sparking electric shocks everywhere he touched.

It was dark but I could make his face out. He looked hungry. In this position with him leaning back and me on top of him, I felt much too exposed. His hands gripped my calves lazily and my breath quickened in anticipation. Desperate to finally do this thing that we'd been dancing around since that first kiss. His palms grazed my skin, the friction making me shiver, as I rocked into him. Once he had his hands on the crease of my thighs, so close to where I ached, he finally spoke.

"Let me see it." It wasn't an order, but with his thumbs teasing up and down right on the sensitive juncture of my thighs I was helpless to deny him anything. And I wanted him to see, to look at me in that carnal, wild way he'd done that day at the pool.

With one hand braced on the seat, I gathered my skirt and bunched it high enough so that he could look. I was wet, I could feel myself getting more and more slippery with every harsh breath he took as his hands explored me. My body knew what he could do with his hands now and I wanted all of it again. But he just kept teasing, running the pad of a finger over the slit without dipping inside, and I was burning with need.

"Theo," I gasped, annoyed that he was making me wait.

He clicked his tongue, shaking his head like the fucking sadist he was. "You're going to show me how wet you are first. Slide your thumb inside." I felt so out of control in that moment, so turned on, so ready to throw all common sense out the door.

"This will complicate things," I threw out, desperately hoping that he would be the one to stop us from jumping down this precipice.

"I'm not afraid of complicated, Alba. And neither are you." It wasn't a surprise when relief washed through me at his words. I wanted to believe him.

His fingers dug into me, bringing my focus back to me. "Be a good girl and do what I asked you."

"Where is this Daddy thing coming from?"

He pushed up so that his denim-clad cock rubbed against me hard enough to make me see stars. I was gasping when he clasped his hand on the nape of my neck and brought me down for a kiss.

"You know you love it," he whispered hotly right against my mouth, scoring my lips with his teeth. I *could* deny it, but that would just be more lies. I could continue going around in circles, pretending like I didn't want him as badly as I did.

That I wasn't turned on by the fact that we were in a truck in the middle of nowhere and I was about to get fucked blind by this man who drove me out of my mind with desire. I could do that. Or I could just...let go. How bad would it be if I showed him everything? If I asked for what I wanted?

"I want you to fuck me," I told him, even as I dipped two fingers inside myself.

"Let there be no doubt in your mind." He said it while his thumb pulled up the top of my slit, exposing my clit. "I am going to fuck you so hard." He rubbed circles over the engorged nub and I moaned, pushing into it. "You'll be feeling it for days." With a hand still on my pussy, he used the other to pull down the hem of my dress and reveal my tits.

"Give them to me," he demanded and I leaned in. He cupped one in his big hand and circled his tongue on the nipple, flicking with the nail of a finger then sucking until I was right on the edge. "So good, I love the weight of them on my hands."

"Undo my zipper," he said as his two fingers continued that pressure on my clit that made my skin feel too tight. It was too good, and I was close to coming with the double assault on my clit and my nipples. When I reached to do what he asked he stopped me.

"No, wait," he said, suddenly sitting up and looking around. He looked as frantic as I felt and a shiver ran through my spine in anticipation of having all that energy unleashed on me. "Let's go to the shed." He fixed my dress, so that my boobs were covered again, while I worked my way out of the sex fog I'd been in to make sense of what he'd said.

"The shed? But Miss Susan..."

"Won't be back until this has died down." He tightened the hand he had on the back of my neck and pulled me closer, kissing his way up from my collarbone to my jaw. By the time he got to my mouth I would've probably let him fuck me in the hailstorm. "I want to sit you on that dresser and put my mouth on you. Suck on that sweet little pearl you've been denying me for weeks. Then I'm going to bend you over and fuck you until you scream my name."

I was ready to beg, my blood boiling in my veins, rushing around in my body like fire.

"Let's go," he said pushing the door open. The door of the shed was covered by the car port and it only took seconds to get inside. He didn't even bother turning on the light. Barely a minute passed before he had me propped on a table and went down on his knees. This all felt so dirty, sneaking around in a shed that anyone could walk into that belonged to a woman we'd met an hour ago. I should've been concerned by it, but there was no work, no renovation, no show, absolutely nothing more important than what Theo was about to give me. What I knew he'd make me feel.

"The light switch is behind you," he whispered, as he hiked my skirt up again. "I want to see you." He cupped my heat and hissed out a curse. "Spread your legs," he ordered and I did what he asked, exposing myself for him. He placed a hand under my knee, and lifted it until it was propped on the edge of the table, leaving me wide open for his view.

"That's so sweet," he whispered, his breath fluttering over my sensitive skin. His tongue snaked out and slid inside. "So fucking wet, dripping for me, sweetheart." His big hands brought me flush against his mouth and he tongued me roughly, getting me close and then slow, as I rolled my hips into his touch. Hands gripped on either side of his head, while I screamed his name. It was frantic and raw and I loved the way I felt with him, like nothing else mattered but what we were doing. My orgasm pummeled me, intense and quick as he tasted me again and again.

"I need you," I begged, tugging on his shirt to bring him up to me.

"Your pussy is the best thing I've had," he told me as I worked to unzip his pants. "I want it every morning, from now on, Alba. Every day when I wake up, I want a taste."

I nodded, as if that would really happen. As if that was any kind of possible reality. But soon I had that cock in my hand and all my focus was in getting it inside me.

"God it's so fat," I was practically purring, my forehead on his shoulders as I stroked him. Feeling the heft of him.

"And I'm going to give it all to you," he promised as he took himself in hand. He rubbed the head to my clit and I bucked from the contact like I'd been shocked by electricity. I needed him inside me. Now. Now. Now.

"I need it," I whispered against his mouth, desperate to have him pounding into me. Then I remembered. "Condom," I groaned.

"I haven't had sex with anyone in at least six months," he said, while he rubbed the head of his cock up and down my slit. Making fireworks go off in my limbs. "And you know my test results." I did know the results, because it was my job to print them out and leave them on his desk.

"Had you been planning this all along?" I asked, resentful that I had to talk about this when I was this turned on.

"I didn't have a plan as such, but I thought it wouldn't hurt for you to know." That was not anything I had the bandwidth to examine when his dick was basically at my entrance, so I filed it in the "to be dealt with later" part of my brain.

"I have an IUD and haven't had sex with anyone but my favorite dildo in at least a year," I confessed, and he looked relieved, even as he growled.

"I hate the thought of anyone getting this." He cupped me possessively before running his fingers along the crease and sinking into me. We both sighed as he sheathed himself inside without quarter. He was big and it stung. I fought to accommodate him, desperate to have him fully inside. I circled my hips until he was all the way in.

"God that's good," I breathed out, grinding my hips into him. The stretch was intense and he had to scoop my ass and press me up to him to get good friction, but I just wanted more. I looked down and watched as his fat cock moved in and out of me. "This is so hot."

He groaned as he pummeled into me. "This is what you need? Hard and dirty where anyone can drive in and see." It was exactly what I needed and I needed it *with him*.

"Your pussy is the sweetest thing I've ever felt," he said hotly against my ear. "Move that ass, baby, give me everything," he urged, as he thrust into me again and again. The way he held me, that stretch that was just on the edge of pain, made my skin tight and my eyes pop open.

"Tell me how I feel inside you." What could I even say? That I felt like everything aligned, that in this moment everything that mattered was inside this small space. Just us. Suddenly his arms tightened around me. Holding me in place while he fucked me so hard that the air got knocked out of me.

"Tip your hips a little," he told me, voice tight, just as he canted his own and then I felt it.

"Oh, God." He was rubbing right on my clit every time he thrust into me, making electric currents fire off in my groin.

"God damn that's sweet. Is it good, is this good?" His hands gripped me tight and I could feel the tension in his body. His skin was slick with sweat and I licked up his neck, needing to taste.

"Make me come, Theo." The muscles of my neck felt like they were going to snap as he moved inside me and worked his fingers on me all at once. "I want you to fuck me over the couch when we get to the penthouse."

"Jesus, Alba, baby," he moaned and fucked harder.

I dropped my head down and kissed him and his tongue swept into my mouth. He licked into me like he owned my mouth and seconds later the orgasm took me.

"I knew it would be like this," he uttered through gritted teeth as his own climax took him. I opened my mouth against his neck as he flooded me. He kissed me for a long time, his hands sliding over my sweaty skin. "Perfect."

It *was* perfect. Exactly like this. Even if I knew that now that I'd had this, it would only be that much worse when I lost it.

## THEO

"You sure you don't want me to stop for something to eat?" I asked Alba as we arrived at our building.

"I'm okay." She'd been quiet since we'd left Miss Susan's property after the hail had stopped. I hadn't been exactly talkative myself, caught up in my own thoughts. Wondering how I was going to convince this woman there wasn't a part of her that wasn't just right for me. I knew there would be no telling her, that I had to show her there was nothing more important to me than seeing her satisfied and happy in every way. And perhaps that message could've come across better if I hadn't fucked her like an animal in a musty shed. "Listen, I didn't—"

"I liked it, Theo," she interrupted, as I pulled the car into our spot. "I liked having sex with you. I don't have to hold back or wonder if you think I'm too loose or whatever. I like that you're rough and that you don't get turned off by how demanding I can be."

"Uh no, I found that hot as fuck, actually." She grinned almost shyly at that and I wanted her all over again. But seriously, what the fuck? "I don't know who you've been sleeping with, but I just need to let you know right here and right now that I love when you tell me all the filthy shit you want me to do to you." I reached for her and pushed her dress up, pressing two fingers at her entrance. I was such a possessive bastard with her.

"Theo, that's..." she protested mildly even as she spread her legs wider and guided my hand inside.

"You still have me inside you," I said hotly, as I pushed in. She fucked into my hand and my dick, which had been half-hard since I'd slipped out of her, went rock-hard again. "This is so tight. I want it again. Going to take you up against the door the moment we get home," I murmured, already caught up in her. "You going to let me in again, sweetheart?"

"Yes," she gasped, her head thrown back as I fingered her. I'd never been like this, fucking in a car, in a parking lot where anyone could walk by. And not even an hour after having her I wanted it again.

A car honked somewhere in the garage, startling us, and I pulled my hand out of her and straightened her dress, but not before leaning over and licking into her mouth.

"Me vuelves loco."

"You also have a very adverse effect on my self-control." She sounded mad about it, but she bit my bottom lip playfully, so it couldn't be too bad. "Thanks for rescuing me today," she said quietly, our foreheads still pressed together. And in that moment I wanted to tell her. That I'd do anything for her. That I loved her. That I'd loved her probably since I'd laid eyes on her. That I wished I could remake the world so nothing bad ever touched her. So nothing bad ever happened in her life to make her think that she deserved anything less than the entire world at her feet. But I only nodded, knowing I had to bide my time, and pressed another kiss to her mouth.

"You're welcome."

"What is that?" Alba said. I turned my gaze to the spot she was looking at, then smiled smugly at the white Volvo SUV in her parking spot.

"That's your rental." She froze midstep and I braced for the fight. But I was not going to lose this one. And I knew that particular look on her face—it appeared when she didn't quite know how to react because she was happy about something she didn't think she should be happy about.

"That—" she pointed at the much larger car parked where her compact should be "—is not my car." She narrowed her eyes at me and crossed her arms, waiting for an explanation. But by now I knew what worked on Alba Duarte.

"That little car is not safe on the roads here," I argued. "I want you to be safe."

"But that's too much," she hedged, but her eyes sparkled in a way that made me think she was very pleased. That primal thing in me pulsed happily at seeing her happy with something I'd done for her.

"Nothing is too much if it means keeping you safe." I tugged her by the hand to the elevator. We got inside and before she could come up with an argument I pulled her to me. "Let me do this one thing for you," I asked, as I peppered kisses to her neck.

"I don't like being coddled, Theo." I almost laughed at the way she told me, like she had to break the news gently.

"Oh, because I hadn't noticed."

"You say it like it's a character flaw," she told me as the elevator opened to the foyer of the penthouse.

I grabbed her by the waist before she could escape and pressed her to me. "I love how fierce you are. How independent and brave. But I also want to do this small thing for you." She smiled a happy little smile as we stepped inside. Even though I'd made lofty promises about a fuck against the door, I knew she had to be hungry.

"Let me make us something quick to eat," I suggested and she nodded, distracted as she looked at her phone.

"Looks like Carrie from Smithson-Napa called me like five minutes ago."

I knew telling her to call back in the morning was useless and just hoped whatever the news was it wouldn't ruin our night. Her phone rang then and she picked it up after one ring. I looked at my watch and saw that it was almost 9:00 p.m.— this was either good news or very bad news.

"Hey, Carrie, sorry I missed your call." She walked away from the door to her favorite leather chair in the living room. I told myself she needed a little privacy to talk business but I felt her slipping from me already.

"I'm glad you like the ideas for the different genre collections." I could hear the mix of relief and tension in her voice. Like me, she probably knew this very much after business hours call had to be about more than just letting her know they saw her material.

"Oh, okay." I didn't need to see her face to know that the other shoe had just dropped. "You want me to make the designs *less* inclusive then?" Even from where I was standing I could hear the woman on the other end backpedaling. "With all due respect, Carrie, I don't know if I agree that the way we have it now it won't appeal to a wider audience. There are—"

Her face crumpled at whatever she was hearing and I had never wanted to inflict violence more than in that moment. Someone was hurting the woman I loved by telling her that her beautiful designs weren't good enough because they didn't fit their small-minded view of the world.

"Sure, a pop of color, but not so much that it isn't relatable to everyone," she echoed woodenly. "I'll work on it." She tapped the screen to end the call and let the phone drop on the couch, her eyes focused on something on the wall. She looked crushed.

Without a word I sat next to her on the couch and brought her onto my lap. And if I needed any more evidence to tell me that this phone call had devastated her, the fact that she clung to me would've done it.

"What happened?" I asked, pressing a kiss to her forehead, grateful that she was letting me be there for her.

"They want me to make the line 'more accessible.'" She twitched the two fingers that were on my chest and shook her head. "I knew this would happen. I thought Yazmin would be more of an advocate, and stand up for my vision, but she wasn't on the call. They liked my design enough to move it to the next round, but they want changes before they take both decks to the executives." The thought of whatever they'd asked made her look sick. "I am not looking forward to facing off with Kayla."

"Are you going to do it?" I asked, suspecting the answer.

"I'm not going to get a chance like this again." She turned those pleading brown eyes on me, asking me for absolution, but I didn't have it in me to judge her.

"Just promise you'll let me take care of you when you're pulling the next round of all-nighters."

Her wobbly smile got a little wider. I leaned down to kiss her and hoped that the next two weeks didn't whittle her down to nothing or I was going to have to crack some heads here in Dallas.

# Chapter Eighteen

## ALBA

"What's wrong with you?" Theo asked as I shuffled out of my room wearing the yoga pants and sweatshirt I'd fallen asleep in after working until almost 3:00 a.m. on yet another round of "tweaks" Carrie had requested.

"Wow, that's exactly what I want to hear first thing in the morning from the guy I'm sleeping with." This would've made anyone else at least flinch, but Theo Ganas was made of stronger mettle than that.

"I hate to point out the obvious, preciosa." God, whenever he said that it was like my bones turned into marshmallow fluff. "But you haven't been doing much sleeping." The way he was looking at me indicated that he was not referring to the sex we'd been having in between me pulling all-nighters.

"I'll rest when this is over, Theo," I told him, annoyed. Because between him and Julia I was getting lectured on working myself too hard every hour on the hour and it was starting to piss me off. "Don't you think I want to relax? How I am supposed to do that?" I asked, heated and frustratingly close to tears from sheer exhaustion. "Half the time I'm trying to fix Kayla's interference on the show and the other I'm attempting to keep up with my business, and this Smithson-Napa collection thing?" I tried not to sound bitter because I knew my problems were ones a lot of people wished they had. But these once-in-a-lifetime opportunities had all turned into soul-killing ordeals I almost wished I could just walk away from. Not that I would ever say it out loud.

"If you'd let me talk to Tina, or to the executives about Chase—"

"No." I cut him off before he could start on that again. My eyes prickled, but I squeezed them shut and gulped from my coffee mug. I didn't want to look at him, because I'd see the worry in his face, and the frustration. "We're almost done, we're literally at the finish line. I just want to keep my head down until it's over." I hated that this was how things had ended up with the show, but it was what it was. Chase and Kayla had turned something that could've been a dream into a nightmare. "It's not like it'll do any good. Chase will just gaslight everyone." Theo clearly did not agree with me, given the death grip he had on his mug and the "I want to make a murder" expression on his face.

And this was exactly what I'd been afraid of. That Theo would get into the cage fight that was my life with me and that it would wear him out too. By this point he had to know that getting me in bed for a few weeks was not worth dealing with the unending drama of my life.

"Why are you here, Theo?" My voice was harsh and breathy, like air was barely squeezing out of my clogged throat.

He always looked so big, so imposing. Like there was no storm he couldn't weather. But I could see that my question put a chink in his armor. He shifted his shoulders like he was bracing for impact.

"You know why I'm here, Alba." His gray eyes, which usually seemed impenetrable, were open now, almost vulnerable, and I wanted to reach for what he was handing me so badly. But I couldn't throw myself on that offer. An exhale skittered out of my lungs and my mind clouded. What would happen after? He'd go back to New York, to his empire, and I would go back to chasing after the next carrot that was supposed to change everything for me until I couldn't do it anymore. I didn't want to admit that this experience had eroded my confidence. That I was beginning to think the only way I could achieve my dreams was by selling them out in the process.

"Theo, I can't be in a relationship. That's the one thing I know for sure I'll fuck up. I am not who you want."

He took a step toward me, but I held up a hand, retreating. Panicked that if he touched me, if he reached for me, I'd fall apart. Because I was tired. I was weak and doubting myself. Sad and disappointed that this show that I thought would be the break I finally needed had been such a struggle. I was mad at myself for getting my hopes up when I knew damn well things like this didn't work out for people like me. That there would be no windfall from this, no offers pouring in. Because this was what always happened: whenever I thought I'd arrived, something happened that sent me back to the start. And worst of all, I was heartsick that I'd stupidly fallen for a man who could not tolerate disorder when I kept my life from imploding with duct tape and hope.

I had to tell him. Just say it, so he couldn't deny that he didn't know.

"The Alba that got your coffee just right every morning and kept your schedule perfectly for two years barely had her life together, Theo," I spat out, needing him to see that he was better off walking away. "You have seen how I am. Chaotic, disorganized. I don't eat right, I forget to exercise, I don't sleep. My routine is shit. Theo, you demand perfection, I am not it." I laughed bitterly, as a hot blur sprung to my eyes. "Fuck," I muttered, swiping under my eyes, and suddenly I was enveloped in him. I shivered as his strong arms gathered me close.

"There's so much I've gotten wrong with you," he said, with his lips so close to my skin they rubbed my temple when he talked. "But I need you to know, that there is nothing, not a damn thing about you, that I would change." Hating myself for needing him, I pushed my face into his chest and inhaled the mix of sleep sweat and hint of cologne on his T-shirt. "Just being around you makes me better, challenges everything I thought I knew about commitment and endurance." I scoffed at that.

"You're an Olympian, Theo." My verbal eye roll came out muffled, but I could feel his head shaking and then he kissed the top of mine.

"Which means I know a champion when I see one." He placed a finger under my chin and gently brushed his lips along my brow. "It's not that you can't win this race, Alba. It's that they keep moving the goalposts on you. All I want is to help. Even if all you let me do is cheer you on." I wanted to soak up his words like a sponge. Let them burrow inside me. Snatch them up and believe them, but I knew better. I knew what was likely awaiting us this morning at the set.

I sighed and tried to pull away, but he wouldn't let me and I was much too weary to fight it. I let him rock me and soothe me like any of this was real until my phone buzzed, reminding me that I had to get ready to get to the set.

"Filming is in three hours, we might as well get this over with," I grumbled, pulling back, and this time he let me go.

"I fucked up by using this show as an excuse to get closer to you."

It was a statement, not a question, and I didn't argue. Because he was right that this had not turned out like either of us imagined. But I wasn't going to let him shoulder the blame alone.

"It looked good on paper," I told him. "I'd probably do it again if I got the chance, despite how much dealing with Chase and Kayla has aggravated me. And even with the bullshit, at least I will get the visibility once the show airs." I shrugged. "And it was a great project. The library turned out beautiful and it's going to serve a lot of families." And I was grateful that I got to work on it. I just wished it hadn't taken so much out of me and that I'd been treated with respect. That I didn't feel so worn out and demoralized by the process. "Also this was by far the biggest project I've worked on and you weren't terrible to be around." I added a grin, to let him know I was teasing.

"*Not terrible* is not exactly a ten, but you did threaten to poison me at the start."

I laughed, feeling the ghost of his smile against my hair.

"Let me take you away for a few days after we finish tonight." He was rubbing extremely enticing circles on my back with those big-ass hands of his. It was so hypnotic I almost said yes without really hearing the question. "A couple of days somewhere quiet. No phones…" God, that sounded like heaven.

"I can't," I told him with honest regret before I slithered away from him. "Besides, don't you have to go to New York for the closing of that Valle Mar deal after we wrap today?" He looked so aggravated I almost laughed. "I have to work on the presentation, anyways."

He narrowed his eyes and crossed his arms like a smartass. "You finished that."

"I need to polish it up one more time," I corrected. "And tonight I have to go out to see a client." His mouth flattened in that forbidding line that annoyed the fuck out of me.

"Don't you dare, Theo." His shoulders only got tighter. "I need to work to pay my bills, and look," I said, throwing my hands up. "I'm glad I didn't stop taking clients while filming the show because neither of us know what Chase is going to do." I should've just walked off to go get ready, but for some reason I hated seeing him all tied up in knots. "I'm just going to get some 'after' videos of the *Evelyn Hugo* room tonight. I'll be here before you head to the airport. I'll drive you." You'd think I just told him I was getting him a puppy for Christmas with the way he grinned.

"Good, you going to let me drive you to the set today?" he asked all low and suggestive. I swear that man's voice was like WD-40 for joints.

"No, I'm taking that couch on wheels you got me. I have that errand to run after, remember," I called over my shoulder, as I walked to my room.

"I'm gonna make you dinner before my flight tonight, Alba Purificacion," he yelled back, and I could hear the grin in his words.

# THEO

I knew there was some bullshit afoot from the moment I walked into the library. For one, it was a million degrees and everyone from the construction to the filming crews were in pandemonium.

My jaw clamped at Chase's belligerent voice rising above the din and I didn't have to see him to know he was probably talking like that to one of the women on the crew. That asshole's favorite pastime was to yell at literally anyone who was smaller than him.

"Hey, Julio," I called to my foreman, who was checking for any last-minute repairs that needed to be done before we filmed the reveal for the local families and staff of the library. "Viste a Alba?" I'd spotted the Volvo rental in the parking lot but didn't see her when I came into the building, which was weird.

"Yeah, she was here just now. She went to get her makeup on I think." His face hardened on the last word, and I didn't have to ask why, because Chase's booming voice took over the space in the next moment.

"Oh, you're finally here."

I clenched my teeth, reminding myself that taking down this fucker would likely only mean more grief for everyone who worked for him. "Kayla and Alba are in the makeup trailer."

"Kayla?" I didn't bother hiding my annoyance, because… this motherfucking guy.

"Tina and I agreed that it would be good if Kayla at least got credit on camera for her help with the design." From the glare that Tina sent in his direction I assumed he was talking out of his ass like always.

"Right," I said tightly, as I watched Alba and Kayla step out of the little trailer. If anything Alba looked paler than she had that morning.

"I'm here." She didn't sound great either; her voice was hoarse, like she'd been crying.

Everything in me wanted to grab her and take her away from this shit show before things turned for the worse.

"Finally," Chase said, exasperated, and that time I could not help it. I stepped up to him and tried my best to remind him that unlike the people he liked to bully, I could beat his ass.

"I'm getting real tired of hearing you yell at people on this set, my dude. Why don't you go cool off before we start?" Chase spluttered, then turned his back on me, but when he spoke to his assistant Mona he at least didn't holler like an asshole.

"Theo, Alba, if you could come here for a moment," Tina the line producer I wished was the showrunner called us over. "The families and the staff are here for the reveal if you want to go introduce yourselves." She pointed at the cluster of about six adults and six kids sitting under one of the tents. "We will hopefully do this without too many takes, because it's only going to get hotter." She turned to Alba then, and her smile was genuine. "The place looks amazing, Alba, you really worked wonders and I know all the hiccups you had." She trained a very unfriendly glare in the direction of Kayla, who was sitting in the air-conditioning scrolling on her phone.

"Thank you," Alba said, and though I could see that the compliment pleased her, she still didn't look great. "We should get started."

Tina nodded and waved a hand to a couple of the crew who were milling around. "All right, let's get the ones with the families and staff first."

I took Alba's hand and almost dropped it from how cold it was. "Jesus, are you sure you're okay?"

"I'm fine." She smiled unconvincingly, heading to the tent. "Let's go meet the families. I think I see the baby you were hanging out with the other day." She was right, my pint-size friend was standing under a tent with his mom. I let it go for the moment and walked over with her.

The moment we began talking to the families things settled a bit. Chase was rude and there was no helping it, but Mona and Tina were running interference. It took a few moments, but we got everyone corralled and soon we were rolling.

Just like Chase and Tina instructed we did our bit, greeted

the staff and families there for the reveal, then guided them up the path to the building. In front the producers had placed enormous panels that would be wheeled to the sides to reveal the library.

Alba was friendly and warm with everyone, but it was hot and every time we got to the part where they were supposed to see the library for the first time one of the kids started crying or one of the foundation staff went off script. By the tenth take, we were all getting irritated and Chase was practically foaming at the mouth. After fifteen tries we finally had it. But instead of letting everyone go cool off and drink some water, that asshole threw a fit.

"Can we get these kids off the set? With them running wild like that we're going to be here all damn day!" I didn't know if Chase meant for everyone to hear that or if he forgot that the mic was on, but everyone froze at his outburst and Alba finally snapped.

"Don't you know how to talk to people like a human being?" she yelled back, visibly seething. Chase twisted his mouth in a sneer, like he'd been waiting for the moment when he pushed her too far.

"On my set I talk however I want, and if you don't like it I suggest you leave." He flicked a dismissive hand in the air, then stalked closer to her. Alba was not going to be intimidated by this clown on my watch.

"I suggest you think long and hard about the next thing you're going to say to her," I responded, getting in his face, ready to throw hands.

"Are you threatening me?" Chase asked in that shrill voice of his.

"Leave it, Theo," Alba said, pulling me back. "Let's just finish, so we can get out of here." Her voice was all slurred and when I turned to look at her she was white as a sheet.

"You—" Chase jabbed a finger in the air, right in the area of Alba's face "—are not going anywhere until we finish filming. Fucking unprofessional." His face twisted with fury. And the only thing keeping me from lunging at him was that Alba looked like she could pass out at any moment. "This shit would not be happening if we would've gone with Kayla."

When it happened it was in slow motion. One moment Alba was swaying like she was drunk and the next she was crashing to the floor.

"Fuck, Alba," I cried, diving to catch her before she hit the concrete, which had to be boiling hot. People were coming at us from every direction asking what was wrong, but my focus was solely on her. "Get out my way, give her room to breathe," I roared, clutching her to me. "I got you, baby," I whispered, running shaky fingers over her damp brow. She looked gray even with the makeup still on. "Where's the medic?" I yelled, turning around to find Chase looking at me like an idiot.

"You did this," I seethed at him, even as I placed her gently on the grass so the medic on set could check her out.

"Me! What did I do?"

"You better pray she's fine," I bit out, turning my attention to what the EMT was telling me.

"Her vitals are good," she told me, still looking at Alba's pupils. "It's probably a bad combination of not enough water and too much sun. Make sure she gets plenty of liquids and lots of sleep and she should be all right. Keep an eye on her overnight, do cold compresses on her forehead. If she gets a fever it might be good to take her to the emergency room." I nodded as a wave of nausea roiled in my stomach. If anything happened to her because of this fucking show...

"Should I take her now, should we call an ambulance?"

The woman gave me that "poor fucker" pitying smile and shook her head.

"This is just dehydration. Electrolytes and some sleep should do the trick."

"I'm taking her home," I told Chase over my shoulder, who gave me a very wide berth when I walked by him. "And she's taking the rest of the weekend off." I didn't wait for anyone to respond or tell me that I'd be wasting the production money by cutting out early. The only thing I cared about was making sure that the woman I loved got what she needed. I brushed a kiss on her clammy forehead as I made my way to my truck, praying this was just exhaustion like the medic had said. Mona caught up with me, looking sick with worry. She had Alba's purse in her hand.

"Here, this is hers."

"Thank you." She was one of like three people who worked for the show who I didn't want to punch in the face in that moment.

"Let me know how she gets on and don't worry about any of this, Tina and I will handle everything." I nodded tightly as she helped me with the door before running back to the tents where the rest of the crew were regrouping.

"I knew I should've kept you home, baby. You scared the shit out of me." Alba tried to smile at me, but she looked out of it. By the time I got her in the car and strapped her in she was coming back to herself.

"What happened?" she asked as I pulled us out of the parking lot.

"You passed out because Chase is an asshole," I said tightly, mad at Chase, at myself, at every person in Alba's life that made her believe that she had to do this to herself. Literally run herself into the ground.

"What?" She tried to open her eyes and winced, then closed

them like the light hurt them. "But we didn't finish filming." She sounded so dazed and it was freaking me the fuck out.

"It's okay. Set is closed for a few days. We can't film if you have heat exhaustion." I stretched my hand to squeeze hers, relieved to find it warmer than before. "Let me take care of you, baby. Please." I would beg if I had to. She looked so fucking tired. Like the weight of the world was on her chest, and I wanted to take it all from her. Take off every brick she carried on her back and smash them into a million pieces.

"I need to..." Her hand slipped from mine and she started moving in her seat, like she was looking for something.

"I already texted Julia," I said in an attempt to calm her down. "She'll go take the videos from that client you wanted. And I have your bag in the back. When I get you in bed I'll go to the drug store and get you an extra-large pack of Doritos to wash down with the electrolytes I'm going to force-feed you all night." She made a feeble sound that I thought was her attempt at a laugh but I was not joking. I wasn't letting her out of my sight or a bed until she'd had twelve uninterrupted hours of sleep. She smiled with her eyes closed, then after a long moment gave me a sideways glance.

"I'm having a really bad day, Theo." Her eyes filled with tears, then two fat ones rolled down her cheeks. My heart felt like it was being torn from my chest.

"Please let me make it better for you," I pleaded hoarsely.

"Okay." She squeezed my hand tight and in the next moment she was asleep. And that was when I knew for sure that I'd die for that woman. I'd do anything, *anything* to make sure she was okay. Without even making the decision, I grabbed my AirPods knowing I didn't want this conversation on speaker and pushed the button on the console to dial the number.

"Are you on your way here?" my father asked me without even saying hello.

"I'm not coming, Dad." The silence that followed felt like the calm before a storm, so I spoke before the avalanche of recriminations rolled in my direction. "I'm not flying to New York today."

"Don't toy with me, Theodoro Anibal, you have a duty to this family, to this business, and I've let you play this game long enough. Don't think I don't know you're down there chasing after that girl that worked for you."

There were so many things I could've said in that moment. Recriminations, rehashed old resentments, but what I wanted, what I really wanted was to be free of my father's business. Of the machine that owned my life before I was even born.

In the last week, talking with Gio and Ivan about their plans had been more rewarding than a decade working with my father. I didn't care about Ganas, not like someone tasked with running it should. I wasn't its future and it wasn't mine. Not anymore. I looked over to the woman next to me, her tired, proud face, prepared for battle even in her sleep, and I could see the rest of my life clearly.

"Dad, do the right thing and let Cecilia take over. She deserves it. She's better than me or you. She's the future of Ganas Corp." I laughed, thinking about my little sister with her head for business. "Maybe even Zoe, if she wants it. I want a different direction for my life."

"You're doing this over some piece of ass in Texas?" my father roared, but his fury didn't touch me. My father had lived his life his way, taken his own path, and now I would do the same. "Is this what I worked so hard for, so that you'd throw away the kingdom I built for you?"

"You still have a legacy, Dad. It's just not the one you envisioned. Cecilia loves Ganas and she'll work to make it something bigger than either of us probably could, you just have to let her. I have to go," I told him as I pulled into the garage. I ended the call and powered off the car, breathing easier. But then a little pained sound came from the passenger side, and my whole body responded to that distress. The only thing that mattered was sitting next to me. I came around the other side, opened the door and bent to kiss my woman on the lips. She fluttered her eyes open and gave me a sweet little smile.

"Hey," I choked out, with a tightness in my chest. I knew exactly where I needed to be.

# Chapter Nineteen

## ALBA

"Why do you keep carrying me?" I muttered testily, even as I pressed my face tighter to his chest. He hadn't let my feet touch the ground yet. Not in the parking lot, not in the elevator.

"Because you passed out like an hour ago," he huffed, like my questions were aggravating him, but I could hear the tension in his voice. "I'm going to put you down to open our door but, Alba, I don't want you getting on that laptop. You need to rest."

"Fine." I wanted to fight him, but my legs felt like wet noodles and I really needed to lie down. He very carefully lowered me until I was upright but kept a strong arm around my waist as he opened the door.

"Our door," I mumbled, and blinked up at him. "I like that."

He made a pained sound and shook his head, which probably meant something, but I was way too out of it to figure it out. "Come on, let's get you into bed, that's what the paramedic said you needed to do, and don't think I won't take your ass to the ER if you don't comply."

"Fine, I'll get into bed. You're so fucking bossy," I whined and he grumbled. "But I'm all sticky. I need a shower." My clothes were stuck to my body from the sweating and then getting in the AC and I had to look like a clown with the makeup melted on my face. "I probably look terrible."

We were walking slowly down the hallway, but he stopped after I said that and looked down at me. His eyes blazed with something that wasn't anger, or even the stoic concern he'd been giving off since we left the set—but whatever it was, it was fierce.

"You're beautiful enough to make my heart stop beating every second of the fucking day." The absolute honesty in his voice made me want cry again. His eyes scanned my face as if he was going over every centimeter. Confirming the facts he'd just stated. "There is nothing, not a hair on you that isn't perfect." His jaw clenched and my stomach wobbled under his gaze. "Do you hear me, Alba?" I only stared back, too unsteady to do anything else. "You're the most magnificent thing I've ever seen. Stubborn, smart, sexy, real, strong, so fucking strong."

"I don't feel strong today," I confessed, as he held me so tight against him.

"You don't have to be, I'll take care of you." The words felt like a vow, and I wanted to snatch them right out of the air and hold on to them. But this was just today. In a matter of days, filming would be over, and he'd go back to his deals and his projects in New York and I'd have to figure out what was next for me after today's debacle. "Let me do this for you, preciosa." The endearment stole my breath, and God, I was weak enough to just sink into what he was offering. If this was out of guilt or just Theo's sense of duty, then I could deal with that later. Right now, for once, I just wanted to not have to fix everything myself.

"Okay." He lifted a hand and rubbed his thumb over my bottom lip. I wanted to kiss him, but I swayed unsteadily instead, making him swear and pick me up again. Once inside the bathroom he sat me down on a small bench next to the shower. I was not doll-sized in any way imaginable, but Theo had no issue whatsoever manhandling me.

"Give me your foot," he ordered softly, as he knelt in front of me. I extended my legs to him and he gripped my calf and slid off my boots and socks while I held on to the bench for dear life. I didn't think I'd ever felt this vulnerable before. But Theo's efficient caretaking was going a long way toward putting me at ease.

"You need help taking off your clothes? So you can shower?" He was speaking so low, like he didn't want to startle me. I nodded, feeling my throat clog. No one had ever taken care of me like this since I was a kid. The last time I could recall had been back when we were still living in Santo Domingo and I'd gotten chicken pox. Every day I was sick Dad had carried me to the tub and let me sit in it to help with the itchiness, rubbed calamine lotion on me and made me laugh until I stopped trying to scratch. But once we got to the States everything changed. My parents became the ones who needed me. Helpless to even ask my teachers how I was doing in school. Unable to advocate for me when I was struggling to adjust to the new classes and language. I'd had to learn to take care of myself *and* of the adults in my life and I never stopped.

Theo stood up and pulled me with him then wrapped my arms around his neck.

"Lean on me, sweetheart." I knew it was only so he could take off my clothes for the shower, but the words pummeled me. I swallowed a sob as he gently, *so gently*, pulled my skirt down and unbuttoned my shirt. I let him carry my weight until I was in my underwear. I could see the hunger in his eyes when he looked at me, but he held himself back, focused only on taking care of what I needed. Not a single touch was suggestive.

Theo was caring for me not because he wanted to sleep with me, but because I needed caring for.

"Sit back on the bench while I turn on the shower, Ma." I gulped again and nodded and soon I was seated inside the stall with water running over my skin. Theo undressed himself down to his briefs and got in with me. He pulled me up and placed me against his chest so that I could lean on him while the warm water washed away the day from my skin.

"Does the water feel okay?" he asked as he ran a soapy loofah over my arms.

"Yeah, it's good, thank you," I whispered, closing my eyes, half asleep as he cleaned me. Showers were a ritual for me, the time when I let go of everything that happened during the day and got my body ready to rest so I could do it again. It occurred to me as I felt Theo's strong fingers gripping me as he lowered himself to wash my legs, my hips, my ass in that brisk and efficient way of his, that as much as I was adventurous in my sex life I'd never showered with anyone before him. It was so strange to have someone, a lover, do this for me. I'd always kept every part of my life in its own compartment. The people I slept with in one box, the job that paid the bills in another. Friends had their own place and my family also I kept apart. I liked it that way, it gave me more control, but Theo had wormed himself into all of it. My bed, my friends, my jobs, even my family knew him now. I'd always thought that anyone who got to see everything, the deck of messy cards that was my life, would run in the opposite direction, but here he was literally holding me up.

"Can you walk to the bedroom?" he asked as we stepped out of the shower, him behind me, holding me up. "I'm going to get you some Tylenol. I put some clothes on the bed for you."

"I can do it," I assured him and he released me reluctantly, but not before planting another one of those gentle kisses on my cheek.

"I'm going to stay there with you tonight, I want to keep an eye on you in case you get a fever." There was no keeping in the relieved breath that escaped my lips.

I shuffled into the room, slid the sleeping shirt over my head and got under the covers. The moment my head hit the pillows my eyes fluttered closed. And even as awful as the day had been I had a smile on my lips as sleep dug its warm gooey claws into me.

"Mm," I groaned when I felt something cool on my forehead. I opened my eyes and Theo was on the bed next to me. Bare chested and solemn. "You're a hot nurse," I teased and he grimaced. "If hospitals had guys like you walking around people be volunteering to be hospitalized." His mouth twitched at that, which reminded me that his mouth was super pretty.

"I like your lips." I lifted a hand, and touched them. "The tip of my pinky finger fits perfectly between them," I told him, before I wrapped my own lips around the straw in the cup he was holding up for me.

"You're going to regret a lot of this in the morning." He sounded amused, as his thumb rubbed circles on my collarbone. I took a few sips of the drink then sighed dropping my head back on the pillow. With my eyes closed I heard him put the cup down on the table and then he slid into the bed with me, his bare skin so warm and hard, a shield against my back. I sighed happily when he gathered me to him like I was something fragile and precious.

"I thought my favorite place on earth was that bakery

in the Upper West Side," I mumbled as I snuggled tightly into him. "You know, the one that sells the Ferrero Rocher cruffins." He made a curious sound behind me and I smiled remembering those rushed mornings when I'd stop by so early the employees would give me one for free because I "clearly needed it."

"I used to go there after getting you your coffee." He made another one of those wounded bear sounds, but I was already drifting.

"The bakery isn't your favorite place on earth anymore then?" He asked the question like he already knew the answer. I turned my head until I could see him, and gazed up at that face that I'd fallen in love with even before I knew the kind of man that Theo Ganas really was.

"I like it here better." I pressed my nose right into his shoulder and he sucked in a breath like I'd punched him. That had to mean something important, something I should probably ask him about, but sleep was coming for me like a lion.

"You made my bad day better," I whispered to him, or to myself, I wasn't sure, then took his hand from where it was flat against my belly. I pulled it up to my mouth and kissed his palm. "Thank you."

"Fuck, Alba." Theo sounded wrecked, out of breath, and I almost asked if he was tired too, if Chase's shittiness had gotten to him like it had me. But I just couldn't stay awake. I'd ask tomorrow.

"I know the rule is that we sleep together when we have sex, but don't go until I fall asleep, okay?" At my request, another one of those pained sounds came out of him.

"There isn't a force in this world that could make me leave this bed tonight." His voice was rough, like he was ready to stand guard for me. I should've told him he didn't have to. That I knew how to take care of myself. But tonight,

I wanted Theo more than I wanted to be strong. The last thought I had before I fell asleep was that what Theo had done for me today felt a lot like love, and for the first time that idea didn't scare me at all.

# THEO

I was sitting in bed with Alba dozing on my chest when her mother's number flashed on my screen.

"Maritza, buenos dias," I said in a low voice, so I didn't startle my convalescent, but the mere mention of her mother had her popping up her head and blinking like a baby owl at me. It was so fucking cute.

"My mom," she mouthed, then frowned. I help up a finger and grinned when she snapped her jaw like she was going to bite it off. Threats of violence aside it was good to see she was feeling better.

"Hi, Theo, just calling to see how she's doing." There was no mistaking the mix of guilt and love in Alba's mother's voice. The two of us had had a long talk the night before and just from that I could sense how proud she was of her daughter and how much she worried about her.

"She's doing better," I reassured her and heard a sigh of relief on the other line.

Alba on her end was making an X with her arm and silently screaming *don't you dare say I'm in bed with you.*

I grinned evilly in response. "Let me get her for you, she's—"

"We were about to have breakfast," I lied, and handed her the phone, but not before whispering something dirty in her ear.

"Hey, Mami, I'm okay, feeling much better," she told her mother, while she pinned me to the bed with a finger. She looked better this morning. She'd barely moved all night and woken up with a sweet smile on her lips. I could make it my mission in life to make sure Alba Duarte woke up every day with a reason to smile.

"Give me a second, Ma, let me call you from my phone." With that she ended the call and glared at me. "How come my mother is calling you?"

"Because I called her yesterday after you passed out on set."

"How did you even know her number?"

I rolled my eyes at that. "First of all you worked for me for three years and had your emergency contacts, so technically I could've gotten it from the old records." She sneered at that, but with all those wild curls around her head, it just made her look cute as fuck. "I called Julia and asked her. After we talked, I told Maritza she could call to check in on you whenever she wanted." Her nightshirt had slid off from one shoulder. The messy bun she'd tied on top of her head had loosened during the night and there was a massive riot of curls sticking up in every direction. She looked mussed, and a little less exhausted, and I had never seen anything more perfect in my life.

"You were really nice to me yesterday," she finally said. She almost sounded confused.

"You needed it." My heart suddenly kicked up in my chest, beating like a drum, but I made myself say it. "I like taking care of you." *I'd make it the sole purpose of my life, if you let me.*

"That's not exactly what you signed up for when you agreed to the friends with bennies thing." I knew why she said that, she still didn't believe anyone would want to put up with "her mess." I'd just have to work harder at convincing her. I reached for her and she came, and that would have to be enough this morning.

"It was my honor and my privilege to do that for you," I

said between kisses. She melted in my arms. I could feel her hard nipples brushing my bare chest, and if I didn't have a bunch of shit to do before we left for our trip, I'd fuck her right then. I pulled away and looked at her for a long beat, my thumb running over that pouty bottom lip. "Call your mom and then pack a bag. Enough for two days."

She frowned then looked at the screen of my phone like that could provide answer. "A bag?"

"Yep." I slid out of bed, then leaned over to squeeze the little sliver of upper thigh and ass visible from where her shirt had ridden up. "I'm taking you to Santa Fe."

"Santa Fe?" She was so fucking cute.

"Yes, I have a house there, remember?" She'd been the one coordinating with the real estate broker.

"I thought it was an investment property."

"It was, but not the kind of investment you thought it was."

"What does that mean? We have to go back to the set."

"Not until Monday," I reminded her, which seemed to mollify her somewhat. "Call your mom, sweetheart," I said in answer, already walking out the room. "The jet will be waiting for us in two hours."

I grinned when I heard a gasp followed by "What jet?"

The moment I walked out of the bedroom I dialed Cecilia's number. My father had left me a dozen messages with escalating degrees of fury in the last sixteen hours and I had yet to deal with that.

"He's getting over it," Cecilia told me the moment she answered.

"Oh." I had no idea what that meant, but also knew that if anyone could get my father to calm down it was her.

"The signing went well, Valle Mar was happy to hear about the show, and it definitely went a long way toward reassuring them that working with us will bring them a new kind of visibility." I winced, thinking about the shit show from yesterday and wondering if this show was even salvageable with Chase in charge. I was starting to think that Alba had been right to fear that this whole thing would end up in disaster. "How is she?" Cecilia asked. I let out a shaky exhale, still feeling the remnants of rage and fear from the day before. "She's better, but she needs more rest. I'm taking her away for a couple of days."

A grunt of approval rumbled in my ear. "Good." A taut silence hung between us for a moment. "Did you mean what you told Achilles about not wanting to run Ganas anymore?" I knew she would ask. Cecilia loved me, I had no doubt of that, but she was also a shrewd businesswoman. She would want to know where things stood for her. And even two days ago, that question would've been harder for me to answer, but now, I was almost certain I wanted out.

"I'm not sure what it'll look like yet, but I know I want to start something that's mine. This veteran housing venture will be the first step. I want to try something new." I knew my father wouldn't give up so easily, that he was biding his time before he came at me again. But it would be harder for him to get his way with Cecilia backing me up.

"Achilles will adapt," she told me with the certainty of a woman who had fought for everything she had and had come out on top. "He knows that he can't force you to run things and that he can only hold me off for so long before I give him an ultimatum." I had no doubt Cecilia would use all the leverage she had to convince my father.

"You shouldn't have to do that. You've earned the right to run this company."

My stepmother scoffed. "As if fairness has anything to do with this? You father loves me *and* his pride is fragile. I will navigate those waters and get what I want. Speaking of, I'm going to start my attack now and catch him while he's still waking up."

"I don't even want to know what that means," I groaned and ended the call with my stepmother's laughter in my ears.

I'd barely gotten started on coffee when my phone buzzed again in my pocket. When I scooped it out, I saw Tina's number flashing on the screen. She'd called to ask about Alba last night, so I figured she wanted to hear how she'd made it through the night.

"Hey, do you have a minute?" Tina was usually the most upbeat person on the set. She didn't even let Chase's bullshit bring her down, so the fact that she sounded like she was in a full panic was not a good sign.

"Sure," I said, putting down the bag of coffee grounds.

"Is Alba better?"

"She is."

"I'm glad," she exhaled, sounding genuinely relieved. I knew she was probably just glad that a major lawsuit was likely not forthcoming, but I appreciated her asking. "Listen, this is still very much confidential, but I thought I'd give you both the heads-up." I stiffened at the ominous tone of her voice. Whatever this was, it would be very bad. "It seems like someone from the crew caught Chase's rant on video yesterday and threatened to release it to the media unless he apologizes." Of course it would come back to that motherfucker. "We're working on sorting it all out, but for now the network has decided to shelve the show."

Fuck. *Fuck.*

"It might be just temporary, but we need to wait until things cool down before making the decision."

From a business standpoint I totally understood the dilemma—it would not be worth the risk of someone outing the showrunner as an asshole and a bigot. The easiest way to mitigate things was to deal with the discontent in the crew before they aired the show. Alba would be crushed. Guilt slammed into me again for bringing her into this fuckery.

"Shit." I pinched the bridge of my nose, trying to think. As soon as Alba heard about this, she was going to find a way to blame herself for it and revert back to form, then probably take on a dozen makeovers to make up for the perceived loss. Goddammit, she needed two days to rest. She deserved that much. "I'll break it to Alba, Tina, okay?"

"Are you sure? I was going to call her next."

"I'll tell her. We'll be in touch on Monday to see where things stand." Probably relieved that she didn't have to be the harbinger of shitty news a second time that morning, Tina ended the call with promises to keep me updated if anything changed.

I was still standing there with the coffee half made when Alba shuffled into the kitchen. Her eyes were bright and she looked lighter than I'd seen her in a long time.

"Here," she said, handing me her phone. "Mami made me promise I'd be off the grid while we're in Santa Fe. I've been ordered to 'let that handsome man take care of me.'" She pursed her lips in feigned distaste for a moment, even as she wrapped her arms around my waist. "She's obsessed with you now and so is my grandmother."

"They're very smart women." I grinned, gathering her into my arms while my stomach roiled with dread from the call with Tina. "You should listen to Maritza, no phone for a couple of days."

I slid her phone into my pocket, dreading having to tell her the news.

"Did you have a good talk?" I asked, and she nodded, and though her smile was a little fragile she looked happy.

"We had a really good talk. Maybe you're magic, Theo Ganas." Her big brown eyes shone and that made my heart tighten. "I figured I'd never see the day when my mother actually encouraged me to go have premarital sex with a man." I chuckled at her horrified expression and pressed my lips to that sweet little spot on her neck I loved. "She said she'll call you if she needs anything." I made a sound of approval and kissed her. Licked into her mouth and wrapped my hands around her hips. Getting lost in her was as easy as breathing. "I think she's right," Alba said, as she rested her face on my chest. "Maybe prioritizing rest a little more will be good for me."

Her words made the decision for me. I couldn't do it. Could not rob her of the first time off she'd had in years. I'd tell her about the show when we got back from Santa Fe. She'd be pissed at me, but the truth was that my telling her would only destroy any chance of her letting herself relax and it would not change anything else. What happened with the show was not up to us.

"I plan to spoil you," I mouthed against her neck, struggling to swallow down my guilt for keeping her in the dark. "You'll be completely addicted to me by the time we leave New Mexico."

"Mm, I like the sound of that." I slid her shirt off her and carried her to the couch without a word, and by the time I was buried inside her, I'd convinced myself that everything but this could wait.

# Chapter Twenty

## ALBA

"This place is crazy," I told Theo as I walked into the sunroom of his huge-ass ranch in Santa Fe. We'd gotten in an hour earlier, and after a very delicious lunch he'd told me to shower and meet him here for a surprise.

He was in his usual jogger and long-sleeve T-shirt combo, but this time he was standing next to a massage table, which faced the enormous window overlooking a valley. The skyline here was breathtaking. That big sky and expansive plains. Felt like I could see across miles and miles.

"Hop on." He patted the table with a very suggestive grin tipping up his mouth.

"Are you serious?" I took a couple more steps into the room, my eyes locked on the setup he'd laid out. He had candles, bottles of oil—he even had music, which when I listened closely realized was not exactly easy listening. "Are you serious?" I sputtered, laughing at how he was grinding his hips to the Bad Bunny song coming through the speakers. He was so different from the man I thought I'd known. And in that moment I felt a little bit more in love. "How is 'Safaera' the proper music for a soothing massage?"

It was a whole fucking scene.

"Extremely serious." He waved a hand over the massage table Vanna White style and I had to smile at his cheesy grin.

"He offers to suck on a girl's ass in that song!" He waggled his eyebrows and winked and fuck. He made me weak.

"Trust the process, Alba Peregrina." He slapped the table, and I almost wished my ass was that leather-covered headrest. "Come on, baby, let's do this. I'm going to give you a massage and then I'll take you to the Georgia O'Keeffe Museum for a private tour."

"Are you for real, Theo Ganas?" I didn't even know why I bothered sounding surprised. We'd been in a *Cinderella* meets *Pretty Woman* live-action show for hours now.

"You would be amazed what can be arranged when you've got a working Amex card and a phone, Alba. Now, come on." He curled his fingers at me, a filthy smile on his lips promising that whatever it was he planned for this massage, a happy ending was for sure in the mix. "Take it off," he ordered and my hands went to the belt of my robe instantly. I undid the knot and slid it off my shoulders while he sent me heated glances. My nipples hardened and my core throbbed, just from having his eyes on me. He grunted in approval when the white terry cloth crumbled softly to the floor.

"No panties," he ordered and my clit responded with enthusiasm at the promise in those two words.

"I'm pretty sure it's illegal to insist that a massage client be naked," I told him then gave a very appreciative look at the bulge in his sweats. I decided I wanted to see how much a little game of hard to get would go in delaying Theo's depraved massage plans. Just to give him a little extra motivation I hooked my thumbs into the elastic of my panties and slid them down a couple of inches. Just enough to let him see it.

"My balance is a little off still," I announced, walking up to him and lifting up until I caught his earlobe between my teeth. "Maybe you can help me take them off." He let out a ragged breath and slid a hand inside the triangle of lace covering, his finger tugging on the thong.

"I'm not going to get distracted before I even start, Alba," he protested, dipping a finger inside. "This pussy's going to be the end of me. Going to give it to you all weekend," he promised in that rough way he had whenever we were like this. "But now it's massage time." He made quick work of getting my underwear off, then grabbed me by the shoulders and turned me around to face the table.

"Hold the edge," he ordered, even as his knees pushed mine apart. "Show me," he urged and I swore I could feel my desire for him dripping down my legs. His big hands palmed me roughly. First the outside of my thighs, then the inside, higher, higher until he was right there.

"Oh." I shuddered out a breath as he sucked on my neck and played with my clit. I could feel the orgasm coming for me already.

"Suck," he said, and pushed two fingers against my lips. "Fuck, I feel like an animal with you sometimes, Alba." He sounded almost confused, but I loved it. Loved that he could be like this with me—that he got me so heated, all I could do was beg for more. I sucked hard, swirled my tongue around the pads of his fingers while he fucked me with his other hand. Without warning he tore his hands from me and I almost cried with frustration.

"On your belly," he commanded, swatting my ass.

I obeyed instantly, too turned on to argue.

"I got derailed for a moment there, but this is supposed to be a relaxing massage." He sounded all put off, but he bent down and kissed the nape of my neck, and along my spine until I was pretty much putty in his hands. He started with my shoulders, strong fingers digging into the tense muscles there. He made his way down my back, kneading as he went. Melting away the tension in my body with every touch.

"This is nice," I whispered as his thumbs worked my lower back. "Thank you," I said, and turned my head so that it was pillowed in my arms.

"You don't ever have to thank me." He'd been a little quiet, tense even, on the way to New Mexico. Since I'd come back from that call with my mother, he'd been off. But he relaxed the moment we got to the house. I'd been in my head too. It was hard to turn off my brain when I was so used to being on the go all the time. But I had promised my mother and myself that I would take these two days to recharge. Theo had been right: there was nothing we could do until Monday anyway.

I sighed and tried to focus on the hands I had on my body and the man who they belonged to. He continued to work in silence, palms sliding over my thighs, my calves, and I couldn't help but notice that my ass was not getting the same treatment. Not one for subtlety when it came to Theo getting me off, I pushed up so that my butt was sticking up in the air.

"You missed a spot," I drawled, to which he responded with one of those sexy rumbles of his.

"I'm saving the best for last, Alba Bellaca," he teased and kept massaging my ankle.

"Calling me horny just spurs me on," I retorted, wiggling my ass for good measure. His hold on my ankles tightened.

"What is it that you want me to do down here, exactly?" He was leaning down now, his lips ghosting the curve of my ass as his hands spread my legs apart.

"If you don't know," I gasped, so horny I was certain I was soaking the towel I was lying on, "then I need to work on my nonverbal communications skills." I drove in the point by spreading my knees farther apart.

When he finally palmed my ass I let out a breath of pure relief. He began a rough massage that was just on this side of painful and had my clit pulsing. I could feel the ghost of his mouth right against where I needed him, but he took his time teasing me.

"Those pink and brown petals," he murmured, mouth so close it brushed my sensitive skin when he talked. I felt myself becoming more engorged, my clit pulsing to the beat of my heart. Ripe, ready for his mouth, his fingers.

"Lick me, baby, please."

"Mm," he groaned, as his fingers moved over my opening. "I'm going to have to reward all that politeness." He ran the tip of his tongue along the crease of my pussy, then swirled it around my clit, making me see stars.

"Oh yeah, that's the spot," I gasped, and his hands tightened on my ass. I smiled thinking I would almost for sure have bruises tomorrow.

"This was supposed to be a relaxing massage," he muttered against me.

"Orgasms are relaxing," I countered, practically vibrating from need.

"Spread it with your fingers for me, my hands are busy." He groped my ass with one hand and pinched a nipple with the other for good measure.

"All hands on deck sex is my favorite kind of sex," I moaned as I reached under me, and made a V with my fingers. In the next instant he was sucking on me again. Relentlessly slurping on my skin and swirling his tongue on my clit until I was panting.

"Oh, God," I heard myself cry, right on the edge, and again he pulled off.

"Don't stop, Theo." I was vibrating with the need to come, my skin on fire.

"Can I give you a finger, baby?" he asked, pressing his thumb to the rim of my ass. The sensitive nerves there sent shocks of pleasure so intense I bucked into his hand.

"Please, please, please," I begged as he pressed inside with oily fingers from the massage. The pressure there combined with the unrelenting suction on my clit had me on the edge of climaxing in seconds. "Oh, you're making me come, oh, oh, I'm coming so hard," I moaned, and he growled. In the next second the flat of his tongue lapped at my clit while the tip of his thumb breached me and my mind shattered. White shards of pleasure exploded inside me, until I screamed. I came and came on his tongue, with his fingers inside me, and the world was reduced to the two of us, this room and the way he could make me feel.

I'd had lovers who had tried the seduction thing, but in the end when we got to it, they couldn't get me out of my head. They couldn't make me lose myself in them, in the pleasure of it. Not like Theo—when he was focused on me like this, there was nothing else.

Once I could think again, I let myself slump onto the massage table, boneless, blissed out, as Theo kept petting. Then I remembered how hard he'd been. I reached back to try and touch him but he moved away.

"You haven't come yet," I babbled into the leather of the table. He only laughed and leaned in to kiss the side of my face that wasn't being squished.

"This was just for you, baby." Fuck me, he was the perfect man. "So how would we rate the service at the Ganas Pleasure Palace?" His voice was full of humor as he leaned to press a kiss on my shoulder.

"Ten out of ten, would recommend," I told him, completely mellowed out from that fanfuckingtastic orgasm.

"I can't wait to read that Yelp review," he joked, making

me laugh, and I felt so fucking happy in that moment, it was hard to imagine it was really my life.

"Take a nap, sweetheart, I'll wake you for the museum," he whispered and covered me with a blanket, but I was half asleep. The last thought I had was: just an hour in and this was already best vacation I'd ever had.

# Chapter Twenty-One

## ALBA

"Oooh, live music," I told Theo as we walked by the bar next to the restaurant where I'd just had one of the best meals of my life. So far the day had been a sexy, relaxing fever dream and I couldn't imagine a better way to end it than dancing. I'd never imagined I could ever take to being pampered, but I realized that what I hated was feeling like I was someone's chore. Like someone doing something for me was an inconvenience. Theo loved spoiling me. He reveled in it, and I wasn't going to lie, I was into it.

"I wouldn't mind seeing you sway your hips in this." He ran his hands over the red halter dress I had on, palms sliding over my sides and hips until they locked at my lower back.

"I could see what kind of moves you have, Mr. Ganas," I teased before pushing up to kiss his jaw.

"Oh, I've got plenty of moves, Alba Serena." He looked down at me with those smiling eyes, like just being with me made him insanely happy. He tucked a curl behind my ear and kissed me again. "If you're not too tired."

I rolled my eyes, because as hot as I found this protective side of him, he had asked me if I was too tired like a hundred times today. "Well, I slept almost fourteen hours straight yesterday and took two naps today. I haven't been this rested since the womb." His mouth twitched at that, followed by a soft swat on my ass.

"You're a brat," he said without any heat, that goofy smile that made my knees weak pulling up his lips.

"You love my brattiness," I told him with confidence, and he leaned in to nip at my neck.

"I fucking love it," he said, before he licked over the spot where his teeth had been, and I was ready for another go at his dick. But he pulled me into the bar instead.

It was more like a piano bar with a small dance floor than a New York City bar. Theo and I found a little table to the side of the stage and he left to go get us a drink. The performer, a Latina with an amazing voice, was belting out "La Llorona," the old ranchera by Chavela Vargas. I was swaying to the music when an older man, who had to be in his seventies, approached the table.

"Would you like to dance, miss?" His accent was unmistakably Dominican, which was a surprise because though there were a lot of Spanish speakers here, they were not usually from the Caribbean. Right then Theo made it back to the table with two glasses of champagne in hand.

"You took too long, Ganas, my dance card is already full," I teased as I let the older man help me up. Was he scowling at the poor old guy?

"You've got competition." I pressed a kiss to his cheek, before letting my dance partner take me onto the dance floor.

"Buena bailarina," the old guy, Sergio, complimented me.

"You're not too bad yourself, old man," I joked and he laughed. "Do you live in Santa Fe?" I asked as he expertly led me around the small space reserved for dancing.

"Almost thirty years."

"But how did you end up here?" I knew there had to be a story there.

"Una mujer!" he cried, making me laugh. "What else? I met my former wife on a tour stop here." I smiled at the image of this guy falling hard for a girl while onstage. "I used to play the trumpet for a salsa band back in the day. We came here in '87. She was one of the servers at this night-club in Albuquerque. It was love at first sight," he said wist-fully, like he was staring right into the memory. "She was Mexican, but boy could she dance a merengue." His face lit up at whatever he was remembering. "She gave me a night I could never forget. We kept in touch and after a few years I decided to come back for her." He smiled again, his eyes bright. "She liked it here, I didn't have much family left by then and this place grew on me."

"That's amazing," I sighed, charmed by the story.

"I managed this piano bar, retired about five years ago, but I still come on the nights this band plays. That's my son on the trumpet." He pointed to the stage.

"Wow." I turned to look at the younger man onstage and could see the resemblance.

"Y donde esta su señora?" His face fell then, and I knew the answer before he said a word.

"She passed a couple of years ago. She was the love of my life. I wouldn't change the years we had for the world."

"Did you ever regret staying here, not going back on tour?" I asked, suddenly needing his answer a little too much.

"I loved music, but *she* was my passion." There was noth-ing in his voice, in the way he said the words, that held even a hint of regret. And as I let him lead me in a bolero I won-dered if that was my fear. That I'd let what I felt for Theo distract me, or that he'd later regret falling for someone who didn't fit his vision for his life. I'd seen firsthand from my parents that love wasn't enough. That the person you love could take everything from you. Ruin you. But maybe the person you loved could give you a life you couldn't even dream for yourself.

"May I cut in?" I looked up to find my very grumpy-looking date standing by us.

Sergio just grinned at Theo's frown and threw his hands up, backing away.

"Te dejo en buenas manos, querida," he told me, and I leaned in to give him a kiss on the cheek.

"Thanks for the dance, Sergio," I told my dance partner before he walked away.

"Do I need to worry?" Theo was trying to be funny, but I could see his jaw was all tight.

"Are you really jealous of a seventy-year-old, Theodoro?" That little bit of possessiveness he was doing was kind of hot though.

"I didn't get the dance I was promised."

I smiled and rested my head on his chest, as he wrapped me tight in his arms.

"I love it here," I whispered and felt his sharp intake of breath.

"I'll bring you whenever you want." His cheek was by my head and I felt like there was nothing in the world that could ruin what I felt for Theo right then. That there wasn't anything that could tarnish what he'd given me with this trip. I turned my head to look up at him and just the sight of him made me feel like the sun was shining inside me.

"Take me home, Theo," I said, pulling him down for a kiss. "Give me a few more reasons to come back to Santa Fe."

## THEO

Never in my life had I felt like I did with Alba. Like I could be burned down to ashes if I didn't have her.

"Thank you for bringing me here," she said in that quiet, content way she'd had since we arrived that morning.

"You're welcome, but it was my pleasure. I like seeing you enjoy yourself." She smiled at that, a sweet and quiet thing, but radiant nonetheless.

It was hard to remember that less than forty-eight hours ago she'd been knocked out from exhaustion. Not with the way her face looked right then. Open, relaxed, those deep red lips tipped up all night. And giving that to her filled me with satisfaction.

There was nothing but her now. I knew the moment I made love to her in that shed that my life was not going to be what I'd thought. That I'd give it all up for her. Not like I'd thought before, that we were a good match because we were both driven and ambitious. Now I knew that my real purpose was to be her resting place. The chest she laid her head on when the world got to be too much.

I stayed by the door watching her, arms by her side as she looked out the window, shoulders loose, face turned up to the sky, and I felt like my heart was being remade, so only she could live in it. And God, I wanted her. Hands aching to touch her, skin tight from need, mouth dry with lust.

"Take off your dress," I croaked, and her back instantly straightened at the order, but instead of coming toward me, she turned around, giving me a great view of her ass. She was wearing a slinky silk thing that moved like water against her skin when she walked. She undid the hooks at the back of her neck, revealing an expanse of brown sugar skin.

"Off, Alba," I ordered, rough and too eager, but I didn't give a fuck anymore if she heard in my voice how bad I wanted her. She tugged down on the sides until she was bare down to her waist, the red lace of her panties peeking out. "Leave on your underwear."

She looked at me over her shoulder in question. "Are we going to play with the new toy?" She bit her lip, and I had to adjust my cock in my slacks. That afternoon after the museum, we'd gone into a sex toy shop and I'd asked her to pick something I could use on her. She'd selected a grinder shaped like a rose. She'd told me she wanted to make herself come with it while she deep throated me and I'd almost disgraced myself in front of the saleslady.

"Yes, brat," I said, taking a few steps toward her to move along the getting-her-naked part of the evening. She bent over and slid the dress down to her ankles. That peach of an ass beckoned me to get down on my knees.

"Up." I gripped one ankle and she lifted the other one stepping out of the dress. My hands slid up her calf, caressing velvety skin. "You're so soft," I whispered, pressing a kiss her thigh, the spot right where the swell of her ass began.

"Theo," she breathed out, asking for more.

"Lean on the glass and spread your legs for me. I want to you lick your cunt." I heard the hitch of her breath as I nosed her. The smooth lips that hid that perfect place. I loved how she smelled, loved how she tasted. "Show me," I demanded and she used her hands to pull her panties aside and reveal her sex to me.

I sucked on her, just the skin of her thigh at first, then the labia. I circled my tongue around her clit and she moaned. "I fucking love the sounds you make when I make you come like this." She gasped as I touched her, taking turns flicking her clit with my tongue and rubbing it with two fingers while she humped my face. She was so demanding, so driven to get her pleasure. No one was keeping Alba from what she wanted. "That's it, sweetheart, fuck I love this ass," I groaned as I palmed a cheek and squeezed.

"Ah." She was making those little mewling sounds. "I'm

so close, lick my clit, baby, please," she begged, and I devoured her. Tilted her hips until her spine arched enough to give me full access to her and I slurped, lapped and sucked until she was sobbing.

"Tell me how much you love this," I gritted out as her pussy clenched on my fingers and her juices flooded my tongue.

"I love it, so much," she cried, as she bucked from her climax. I stood up and pressed my chest to her back, my hands sliding up to her breasts.

I kissed the side of her face, her neck. Plucked on the hard tips while she pressed against me. "I'm not done making you come yet," I whispered in her ear, my hands still playing with her tits.

"Keep making me come, baby," she pleaded, and I thought I'd do anything she asked in that voice. Worn out, fucked out, mine.

"I'm going to put the grinder in here." I cupped her lace-covered crotch. "Gonna make you bring yourself off while you suck my cock."

"Yes," she breathed out, her ass working my dick until I was seeing black spots from holding my breath. I pulled on the spot behind her ear hard one last time before stepping back. Her skin, my hands, the room already smelled like sex, and I was nowhere near done.

I rushed over to the drawer where I'd put the toy after washing it.

"On your knees, Alba. I want you ready to take me the moment I say so." Blood rushed in my head so fast I almost lost my footing. I was practically blind from lust. Only Alba could get me this way. Shaking with need.

"Slide your panties down." She licked her lips, her brown eyes fixed on the toy in my hand. Her red nails scraped the skin of her hips as she tugged the little scrap of lace down. She raised a hand to take the toy, but I shook my head. "I'm putting it on you."

She bit her lip and nodded. Her breath came out in a rush, her pupils blown out. Her eye makeup had smudged a little from my kisses, my hands, and my gut clenched from pure raw want. I slid my hand inside her underwear and rubbed the grinder against her pussy.

"You like that?" I asked and she nodded, her forehead pressed to my shoulder as I played with her. "Fuck into it," I ordered and she did, moans of pleasure escaping her mouth as she ground into the toy.

"So good," she whispered, after I turned on the button making it vibrate. "Ah, Theo." Her voice was tight, like she was on the verge again. The next orgasm came fast and soon she was rocking into the toy as she sucked on my fingers.

"Such a hot piece of ass, Jesus Christ, when I sit you on my dick, I'm gonna blow in a second. Open your mouth." One-handed, I took out my cock. "Going to give it all to you in one go," I warned as she looked up at me, tongue sliding over that plump bottom lip.

"Give it to me," she demanded. I stroked myself and let the tip bump her lips, her tongue snaking out every time it made contact. "I want it." I palmed the back of her head, and gripped her tight, then fed it to her without mercy. She took it all.

"Jesus, baby." I was winded, my eyes rolling in my head as she sucked me. She took me down to the root then let her mouth slide off to the tip and tongued it like her life depended on it. She made these sounds like my taste was the best thing she'd had as I took her mouth hard. "Take me deeper. Fuck, ungh, all the way in." I rammed into her until I could feel the flutter of her throat around the head. She took my balls in one hand, massaging them as she deep throated me, and nothing had ever been this perfect, this dirty. "I'm gonna come," I gasped, and when she pressed a finger to the rim of my ass, I spread my legs for it. The pressure there combined with that mind-blowing suction had me seeing spots. "I want to come inside you, baby," I groaned, hating myself for taking her mouth off me.

She pulled back dazed, eyes glassy from the throat fucking I'd just given her, and once again I thought there was nothing I could ever do, even if I lived a hundred years, that could make me deserve this woman. I helped her up and within seconds had her up against the glass again.

"How much do you like these panties?" I asked tossing the grinder to the floor.

"Not that much…"

That was I all I needed to hear. I ripped them off and was inside her in practically the same breath.

"You fill me up so good, baby."

"It's a fucking miracle to be inside you," I whispered, crazy words, crazy promises sitting on the tip of my tongue. I pistoned my hips into her and threaded my fingers on the cool glass with hers. "Nothing has ever been this good, Alba, I…" I gritted my teeth as we worked toward it together, her ass circling into me as I pushed in and out of her heat again and again. We were plastered together, not even a breath could breach space between us, and I promised myself I would do anything to keep this woman.

"I love you," I gasped, as I pulled all the way out of her body and slammed into her.

"Theo, stop, stop!" she cried out, and it took me a second to understand what she was asking.

I pulled out and she turned around, her eyes blazing. "You fucker, you couldn't wait until I came to tell me that?" She sounded pissed as hell, but in the next second she threw her-self in my arms. Her lips pressing kisses to my face. "I love you too," she confessed, before I took her mouth. Our kiss ignited into roaring flames in seconds. It didn't take much to start a fire when it came to Alba.

"I love you," I told her again, needing to say it as many times as it took for her to believe me. "Every fucking hair on your head, every inch of you is exactly what I wanted, and what I never even dreamed was possible. You are mag-nificent, and have the most perversely perfect ass I have ever seen." That got me a watery laugh and more kisses. My dick was still demanding his finale, so I picked her up and moved us to the bed. I laid her down on white sheets and had to stop to look at her. She was smiling wide, face open, like she'd never known pain. Like what was happening between us had turned on the lights inside her.

"Can I be inside you again?" I asked, hooking my hands behind her knees, so I could sit myself even deeper. She bobbed her head and brought me down for a kiss as I en-tered her again.

"I love you," she whispered again and I felt the words crackling through me as I spilled inside her. The last thing I thought before I sank into the sweet oblivion of orgasm was that I hoped that I could fix things with the show before I ruined everything with Alba.

"I guess you're obsessed me with me then." I was nowhere near recovered from the brain-obliterating orgasm from ten minutes ago, but Alba was unfazed, planting open-mouthed kisses all over my chest.

"Totally obsessed." I nodded with my eyes still closed. "If you keep that up, I'm going to have to fuck you again, Alba." She laughed against my shoulder.

"Like that's a threat." I smiled, but there was a heaviness in my chest. Tonight, these past two days had changed everything, but I didn't know if Alba could forgive what I'd done. I'd make a call to the studios to ask for a meeting the moment we got back to Dallas, but she would still be pissed at me for keeping her in the dark. I'd just fix everything before I told her. Then I'd beg her to understand why I'd done it.

"Why are you so serious?" I did open my eyes then, sitting up when I heard the doubt in her voice. She seemed wary, like she didn't know where things stood with us. I forced myself to smile, even as dread sat in my gut like lead, and brought her in for a kiss.

"I'm not serious, it's just my brain is still buffering from almost getting sucked out through my dick," I teased and I felt that sassy smile against my lips. "That mouth of yours is one of the eight wonders of the world."

She laughed happily, as I nipped on her neck. "I don't know if UNESCO would agree with your rationale."

"Oh, I think I could make a case for it," I joked, not wanting to talk, just wanting to get lost inside her again. I sat back and lifted her so she was straddling my thighs. I was hard and all it would take was lifting her up and I'd be inside. But my woman looked down at me like she was about to talk serious business.

"Did you mean it?" She sounded scared, voice small, like she was afraid to hope.

"I have never meant anything more," I told her truthfully, but I could see that though she wanted to, she didn't quite fully believe me. "Why do you think I came to Dallas, Alba?"

"You came for Valle Mar," she demurred.

"I came for you and I'll stay for you, if that's what you want." A surprised puff of air escaped her lips, and her brown eyes shone with tears.

"I'm scared of being the reason you give up so much only to realize you did it for a hot mess with a big ass."

This woman truly had the power to completely wreck me.

"Alba, I am prepared to spend my whole life proving to you that your big ass and your mess are all I want." She smiled then, a small, incandescent one, and something cracked open inside me. She lowered herself until our lips were pressed together, and when she lifted her hips I slid inside. Locked, as one.

# Chapter Twenty-Two

## ALBA

The moment we got off the plane I knew something was off. After that first night in Santa Fe, the confessions we'd made, I'd never felt closer to anyone than I had to Theo. Like he had claimed my soul. But since we started getting ready to come back to Dallas he'd been acting strange. Preoccupied. I figured it was the same unease that I had of returning to whatever mess awaited us on the set. It had been nice to put my phone on airplane mode for forty-eight hours but we couldn't keep the world at bay anymore.

Not when the show was wrapping up and I had to think of what was next. My stomach sank as I thought about the presentation with Carrie and Yazmin in a couple of days. I liked what I'd come up with despite all of Carrie's requests and changes. But I was not looking forward to facing off with Kayla. And then there was the fact that after this week, we would be done. Theo would have to go back to New York to sort things out with his father. And exiting his role from Ganas would not be an easy thing. As for myself, I'd have to make a decision: even if the thing with Smithson-Napa didn't happen there was potential for good, consistent work here doing Bookish designs. Then there was Theo, who had told me he loved me, but hadn't quite made it clear what he planned to do with Ganas or the veteran project. Everything had seemed so clear in Santa Fe. But all the unknowns were waiting for me the moment I landed.

"Here we are," Theo said, in that terse tone he'd had for hours now. He parked the car in our spot and I remembered that night we'd come back after the hailstorm. Sweet heat pooled in my belly at the memory of how he'd touched me, of what we'd done once we were back in the penthouse.

Smiling I reached for him, running a hand along the inside of his thighs.

"Baby," he groaned and pushed into my touch.

"I was just thinking about that night you got me the world's most boring car," I teased and he grinned. "It's a good thing that you did too," I said after a moment, with his hand now tangled in mine. "I think I can get all my stuff from the set in one trip in this car. I have no desire to see Chase any more than I need to."

The moment I said Chase's name, Theo's face changed. I knew he had to be stressed about going back too. Theo didn't like drama and there was no avoiding it once we went back in to shoot those final takes. Not to mention postproduction and promoting the show. We were a long way away from being done with Chase. Still, for Theo this seemed to be about more than just the show. He seemed distant. I didn't like how he was avoiding my eyes, and a prickle of discomfort settled on the back of my beck.

"Is something wrong?" I asked as we met at the back of the Tesla and he handed me my bag.

He shook his head and I could see it took an effort to make himself face me. "Everything will work out."

"That's an interesting choice of words," I told him and he still didn't look at me. The prickle of unease intensified. Something was wrong and Theo was not telling me. Instantly the memory of my mother's face when she got that call from the IRS telling her the mess my father had left for her to deal with came to mind. I knew this was not the same situation, and Theo wasn't my father, but I couldn't help it. Part of me wanted to have it out right there in the parking lot. Demand to know what it was that Theo wasn't saying. I knew that me passing out had scared him and that he felt responsible for how shitty things had gone with the show, but not letting me know if something else was happening would piss me off.

The moment we got into the penthouse I knew for sure there was a problem. Theo didn't try to kiss me or even look my way, just moved around the room without making eye contact. With a feeling of dread I turned on my phone and within seconds there were dozens of notifications popping up on my screen. It was so overwhelming, I almost powered it off again. Then I saw the messages from the twins from yesterday.

Mitzy Sturm: Honey, we just heard. I am so sorry that the producer was such a scoundrel. We had no idea. We're sorry we weren't here to support you.

I wasn't surprised that they'd been notified about what had happened on the set before we went to Santa Fe. I hadn't wanted to bother them on their trip to Europe and hoped they weren't pissed that all this stuff had happened without them being made aware of it.

Muffy Sturm: Yes, we will make it work. We just wish you would've told us how poorly the man was behaving!

Mitzy Sturm: We heard from Julia that you are taking a couple of days of rest. That's great. And don't worry about the show, we can still have our opening without it and we'll make it a big splash.

I snapped my head up after reading that last text and found Theo standing on the other side of the living room just staring at me.

"So this is weird," I said, as I processed that last line from Mitzy's text. "Mitzy Sturm texted me yesterday to tell me not to worry about the show and that we could have the opening without it." The moment the words came out of my mouth, Theo's face went ashen, and I knew.

"Theo, what's happening?" I asked, as I saw the three missed calls from Mona and the voicemails from Carrie and Yazmin, stomach roiling.

"I have something to tell you," he croaked. The tautness in his voice scared the shit out of me. He was so rigid, standing against that wall. It made me want to brace myself for what was coming. Like the two us were barreling into a head-on collision, and all we could do was hope the impact didn't take us out.

I realized then that even though I thought I'd seen Theo upset, worried, frustrated and even angry, I'd never seen Theo afraid. Whatever it was that he knew and I didn't would ruin things between us. The certainty of that settled on me like a cloak as I readied myself. Theo was about to break my heart.

We stood there in that thick, sickly silence, neither of us willing to speak.

My phone buzzed in my hand and I almost let the call go to voicemail, but then I saw Yazmin's name on the screen.

"I need to take this," I said turning from Theo, who just stood there frozen.

"Oh good, I'm glad I caught you!" Yazmin said briskly

without even a hello. I had my back turned to Theo but I could feel his stare on my back.

"Hey Yazmin, what's up?" I said as cheerfully as I could manage.

"I've been better." She laughed awkwardly and after a brief pause spoke again. "How are you holding up?" I frowned, wondering who'd told her about my dizzy spell.

"I'm fine," I assured her. "Just needed a couple of days of rest and ready to go back into the fray." I heard Theo's footsteps behind me.

"Oh." Yazmin sounded surprised at that. And again my stomach roiled as anxiety churned inside me. "Well, I just wanted to let you know that unfortunately Smithson-Napa has decided to put the bookish collection on hold for the moment." My legs almost gave out then and I let myself drop onto one of the chairs in the living room. My eyes closed and my heart felt like it would explode in my chest.

"I'm sorry to hear that," I said woodenly, not brave enough to ask what had caused them to make that decision.

"Things are just in flux now with Streamflix deciding to shelve the show." I opened my mouth to ask her what the hell she was talking about, but instead I snapped my head up to look at Theo and saw everything clearly. Yazmin was still talking and with effort I made myself listen to her. "I'm sorry this is happening. I think you're brilliant, and the library is truly inspired."

"Thank you," I said through the knot in my throat.

"Alba, I think your ideas and your work are phenomenal and it was a pleasure working with you. I think you're on the cusp of something huge with your bookish concept, truly fucking genius." A little flicker of pride burned in my chest, even as my hands shook from the bomb Yazmin had dropped on my lap in the last minute. My head swam as I tried to make sense of what was happening. The show was *not* happening, apparently. After I'd put everything on the backburner for it. Did Theo know? "On a personal note—" Yazmin's words gave me respite from whatever was about to go down between me and the man I loved "—I just wanted to let you know I've turned in my resignation to Smithson-Napa, and plan to start my own company very soon. So please stay in touch."

"Oh," I responded in surprise. I can't say for sure what I said next. But as soon as I ended the call, I walked over to Theo, my body thrumming with adrenaline, feeling sick with the knowledge that the opportunity I thought would change everything for me was gone. Gone in a matter of days.

"How long have you known?" I gritted out, hating that my voice sounded clogged. That my vision was blurry from unshed tears.

"I didn't want to worry you," Theo pleaded, his hands in front of him in supplication.

"By keeping things from me?" I yelled, furious at Theo's high-handedness. This was so like him, to just assume he knew better.

"One of the crew members took a video of Chase being an asshole to one of the families. They threatened to go to one of the gossip sites with it."

I should've known this was where this would end. "From the moment I met Chase I knew he would do something this fucking stupid." I didn't even know who I was telling this to, Theo, myself, the fucking universe. "But I kept my blinders on, telling myself the opportunity was too good to walk away even though everything in me told me that something about that man wasn't right." Theo made a pained sound, and when I glanced up at him, he looked like he was going to be sick. "You should have told me, Theo."

"I brought you into this and I wanted to fix it before I told you. I have a meeting with the producers; I will take care of it."

"Why do you need to fix it, Theo? You didn't make Chase act like an asshole. You didn't force that person to take the video and leak it. Do you really think it's on you to control every fucking thing that happens around you?" I was screaming and I couldn't stop. The more I talked the angrier I got. "You lied to me," I said, jabbing an accusing finger in his direction. "You kept me in the dark for two days and pretended everything was fine."

"I didn't want to worry you." I almost stumbled from the effect the words had on me. A memory of my grandmother telling my mother over and over again "he didn't want to worry you" after we found out my dad had not paid the taxes for our mom's business for years. That he'd died and left her with debt that almost cost her the business. That took us years to pay back. All because he thought he knew better than her. That by keeping her in the dark he was being her protector, when all he did was fuck her over.

"You knew that the whole time we were in Santa Fe." My voice sounded wooden. Like it was someone else talking.

"Yes."

"You didn't want to worry me so you lied to me instead?" I knew that Theo was not my father. I wasn't my mother. But in that moment, it didn't seem to register. I felt betrayed and manipulated. I was gutted, because I really believed Theo understood me. "You let me believe that I was coming back to the show. Like a fool."

"No," he said, coming closer. He reached for me, but I backed away afraid of his touch. Afraid that it would make me weak again and want to forget how much this hurt. And I needed to remember. "Mi amor—"

"Don't call me that!" I cried, backing away even farther until I was up against the wall.

"I'm going to fix this. I will make it right." His eyes were bleak, and I noticed now that there were shadows under his eyes like he hadn't been sleeping.

"How are you going to do that exactly, Theo?" I demanded, throat straining to speak through the constriction there. "I know this is hard for you to grasp, but you don't actually control the entire world."

"I love you," he said, skittering out a breath. "We can figure this out."

"I love you too, I really do," I told him, standing up straight. Then I let him see much I was hurting. "But I can't be with you right now, Theo."

"Alba, please don't walk away." He kept his fists in his pockets. "What good am I to you if I can't even sort this out?"

"Is that what you think this is about? You giving me a leg up in getting my business off the ground, Theo?" I asked as the blade of his words cut deeper still. "You think that unless you're of use to me I won't love you. Is that it?"

His jaw clenched so tight that I almost winced. I saw the effort he was making to mitigate the effect my words had on him.

"I see things through," he insisted. "I promised you a show and it is what I was trying to give you. Am I supposed to believe that me loving you will be enough? That if I ruin this chance for you that you won't resent me later?"

I stepped up to him and saw the tremors in his arms.

"That's exactly what you were supposed to think. I don't need you to make my career, Theo. I don't even need you to make me coffee. I love you—" I had to take a breath then because the tears were coming now and I had to finish saying this. "I love you because of who you are and how safe and happy you make me. I love you because you're the first person to ever make me feel like I can be strong and vulnerable at the same time. And I will stop loving you not because of what you could not do for me, but because I can't trust you."

His breath hitched then and I wondered if he was going to cry too, but his face just hardened. Every emotion shuttered. His walls coming up right before my eyes, New York Theo. "I'll stop loving you because you don't see me as an equal. You don't let the people you love look like fools. You don't let them walk into a situation that could hurt them unprepared."

"I don't know what to do." He sounded desperate, but I could not give him the answer.

A laugh came out of me, bitter and broken at his question. "You just don't get it, Theo." I turned away from him, swiping my hand under my eyes and grabbing my purse and my carry-on.

"Where are you going?" he asked, but didn't come after me.

"I'm going to Julia and Rocco's. They'll have my stuff out of here before our move-out day."

"You're just going to leave, then?"

I opened the door and left without answering.

# Chapter Twenty-Three

## THEO

"Damn, you're ripe. When was the last time took a shower, my dude?" Julia said as she breezed into the penthouse with Rocco on her heels two days after Alba had walked out. I was supposed to move out the next day, and I had already packed my stuff and planned to go to a hotel until I could find a permanent place.

"How you holding up, man?" Rocco said as he came in to slap me on the back. I shrugged and sank back into the couch.

Julia stood in the living room, turning her head from side to side like she was taking her measure of the place…and me.

"So you're just going to let her go back to New York after I'd managed to get some distance from her family and have her close enough to reinstate our weekly brunch sessions?"

Despite all of my father's money, I *had* grown up in Queens and I knew not to make any sudden movements when a girl from Corona was rolling her neck at me like that.

"Babe," Rocco said with a mix of amusement and admonishment.

"Do you think this is what I want?" I croaked, my voice hoarse from not using it in days. "She doesn't want to talk to me, and I'm not going to force her to."

"Did you apologize?" Julia asked this in a tone that told me it was more of a rhetorical question.

"I tried to, but—"

"Did you try to or did you just mansplain her feelings back to her?" she continued. Rocco moved behind me, and I was starting to wonder if Julia was going to take a swing at me.

"She didn't let me," I explained, my head between my hands as I tried to shut out the way she'd looked when she heard about the show. The way I'd hurt her.

"You do understand that Alba's father left them in so much debt that her mother almost lost everything. Secrets are poison for Alba."

I knew that and the more I thought about it the guiltier I felt about the way I'd handled things with the show. Because as much as it was true that I was trying to give her two days of peace, I was also buying myself time. I didn't want to see her disappointed because something I'd brought her into had ended up blowing up in both our faces. After she'd left the penthouse I had gone straight to the studio and tried to figure out what they were planning. Sarah Billings, my contact, had been vague, but hopeful they could get the show on air, but could not promise when. I'd even called the Sturm twins, who assured me they would apply their own pressure on the producers. But when I'd tried to call Alba to tell her, she'd ignored my calls. She didn't trust that what we'd made in Dallas together would last.

"Have you told her that you're staying here permanently?"

"How did you—"

"She's basically like a hot, Latina, non-racist J. Edgar Hoover," Rocco said, completely serious. Julia preened despite the death glare she was sending in my direction. If I wasn't so fucked up in that moment, I would've laughed.

"I told her." More like I'd implied I would if she stayed

too, which was not the same thing. No wonder she didn't think she could count on a damn thing from me. If I wanted her to believe I was for real, I'd have to start giving Alba a lot more than just lip service. I shook my head, wrecked beyond anything I'd felt before in my life. "I don't even know what I'm doing. I thought we could make a go of things here, but I fucked everything up."

"No, that asshole director fucked everything up," Julia disagreed forcefully. "*You* just fucked up with her. And now you need to fix it."

"I don't know how." I almost wished she'd take a swing at me.

"Yeah you do know, you got your ass over here when she quit. You got here ready to change your life for her, so motherfucker, go ahead and change it." She was yelling now, spitting mad. Rocco went and got an apple from the bowl on the kitchen counter like his girlfriend wasn't gearing up to scratch my eyes out. "Moping around this penthouse isn't it, bro," she said, waving her hands toward the small pile of boxes. "I assumed Mr. Olympics had some kind of a plan once you got her back, but I guess I was wrong."

I'd had a plan but it was fucking stupid and selfish. I came here with the intention to talk her into coming back to New York where we could go back to the balls-to-the-wall, unending grind of our demanding careers. I thought what I wanted was a woman who could keep up with the grueling pace of my life. Whose own life was perhaps more demanding than mine, and yet she thrived.

But now I knew how wrong I had gotten all of it. How high a price Alba paid to keep up with the life and obligations she had in New York. Now I knew what she needed was a man who could see that what she carried on her shoulders would eventually break her. The plan I got here with was no good at all, for her or for me, and I needed to make a new one, and before I lost her.

"All right, but I need help," I finally said, standing up as Alba's best friend stared at me suspiciously. "What I had to give her was no good; I need to come up with something better."

"That's what I'm talking about." Julia rubbed her hands and Rocco grinned at me. "You're going to have to think fast though, because she's planning to go back to the city in a week." I winced at that, but already could see some of the pieces of the plan coming together.

"I'm going to need a real estate broker," I told my new allies. If Alba needed tangible evidence I was in it for the long haul here in Dallas, I would give it to her. Julia winked and threw her arm around my shoulder.

"Don't worry, with your liquidity and my skills, we'll have the grovel of the century squared away in no time."

# ALBA

"Hey, hon," Julia said in that "very careful" tone she'd been using with me since I'd shown up at her apartment after the fight with Theo. "There's someone here to see you." I turned around too fast, my heart giving a sad little flutter of hope. But Julia's eyes darkened, as though she'd realized her mistake. "It's not him, babe," she said regretfully but then I saw my mom's face pop up next to her.

"Mami! What are you doing here?" I screamed as my mother walked into the bedroom and Julia slipped out, closing the door behind her.

"I came to see you," my mother told me as she pulled me into a tight hug. She was shorter than me and felt more fragile every year. But I knew better than to underestimate the strength in those small bones. "When your daughter moves to a new city you go see her." She lifted her face to me and ran her fingers over my brow, my cheeks, as I tried not to cry.

"I don't live here, Mami, I was coming back in a couple of days." My mother gave me one of those knowing looks like she could see right through my bullshit.

"Do you want to move back to New York, Mija?" she asked as we sat on the bed. I reached for one of her hands. They were worn and rough from years of working with harsh chemicals cleaning people's houses and once again I wished things would've been easier for her.

"It's where you are, Mami, I can't just abandon you and Mimita." I knew then, as I'd known for weeks, that I didn't want to leave. But if my mother needed me I would go back.

"Ay, Mija." The soul-deep regret in those two words sliced through me. My mom's brown eyes looked up at me with such sorrow, my eyes blurred. "You need to go where your dreams take you." She shook her head, a bittersweet smile on her face as she looked at one of the sketches I'd pinned to the wall. "We came here to make way for you to do bigger things than we ever could, not to clip your wings with our mistakes. I depended too much on you, mi amor."

"No, Ma, I wanted to help." My mother tsked and squeezed my hand.

"I know you did, you were always so strong, so capable, and I got too used to letting you handle things. But it was too much to ask you." The regret in her eyes hurt, but I knew she'd done her best.

"You were strong too, Mami, and you managed."

"I did," my mother agreed, as she ran the scratchy pad of her thumb over the palm of my hand. "But I don't want a life of just managing for you, baby. I want you to be happy."

A sob escaped my throat at my mom's words, because happiness now looked and sounded like Theo and that was gone. "You shouldn't have to be trapped by my choices." I began to shake my head, ready to disagree and fight her on that. "I am so proud of the woman you are, so strong. But, sweetheart, I don't want to see you bent in half from the weight of what you have to carry on your own."

An image of Theo begging me to let him take care of me pulled another ragged sob from my throat.

"I don't know, Mami. What if I can't make this business work? What if he betrays me?" From the knowing smile my mother was flashing me, it was clear I didn't need to say who the "he" was.

"I don't know the future," she admitted, the put her palm on my face. "But I do know what you do with those bedrooms is amazing. And as for him, there are no guarantees, but there is something to be cherished in a man who can see your strength and your vulnerabilities and love you for them." I was crying in earnest by then, thinking about the way Theo had cared for me that day after I fainted, the eagerness to do even the smallest thing for me. Maybe Theo needed to be needed as much as I craved unconditional support.

"What if he gets tired of how chaotic I am?"

"What if he doesn't?" my mom countered and then wrapped her arm around my waist. "Your father didn't respect me enough to see me as an equal, even when I was the one who provided for our family. He resented me for that. And so he treated the business I'd built like it meant nothing. Because to him, it would've only been valuable if *he* had done it. But that man, he sees your brilliance. He sees you, sweetheart. He's not threatened by your success."

I nodded as tears ran down my face and thought of all the times when Theo had asked me about my work. How he'd gone on social media just to like my stuff. The way he defended me from Chase's dismissiveness.

"I don't know if there's still anything for me here though, Mami," I told her, thinking of the show and the fiasco with Smithson-Napa.

"I don't believe that," my mother told me with a confidence that bolstered me. "The women in our family are sabias and luchadoras. We always figure it out."

"You always did, Mami," I told her, and wrapped an arm around her waist. I came from a long line of warriors. I could have the life I wanted, and I didn't have to do it alone.

"We can come up with a plan, Albita. You and me, we've done it before." We really had. The two of us had fixed the mess my father had left, and here we were. "This time, we have help." My heart squeezed and I wondered if that was still true. I hoped with everything I had that it was.

# Chapter Twenty-Four

## ALBA

"Call me as soon as you're done with the meeting, okay?" Julia told me as I walked into the café where I'd be meeting with Yazmin.

"Okay I will, but don't call again. You love to blow up my phone in meetings," I chastised my best friend, who ended the call with a "whatever you love it." The week before, with my mother holding my hand, I'd called the former Smithson-Napa rep and asked if she'd be willing to talk to me about partnering to make the bookish collection a reality. To my surprise, she had. I'd also called Theo, who had been in New York. He asked that I let him see me when he returned to Dallas. I'd told him I would, but so far he had made no attempt to find me.

"Alba," Yazmin called, standing up to greet me as I reached her table. As always she looked great in a bespoke linen suit and Kelly-green oxfords.

"Hey, thanks for meeting with me."

"Are you kidding?" Yazmin said as we bussed cheeks. "I was *elated* to hear from you. To be honest, I'd been biding my time to call you. I didn't want to seem too thirsty." I smiled at that, hopeful that this could be the door I'd been hoping would open.

"Clearly, I have no such qualms," I joked as we sat down. I quickly took my tablet out of my bag and placed it face-down on the table. "You've seen the concepts I did for the store already," I said with a grimace while Yazmin twisted her mouth in distaste, then surprised me with what she said next.

"I just want to tell you that I thought your designs were brilliant. I can't say too much but I want you to know that the issue was not with what you presented them." I nodded, without pushing for more information.

"Thanks for saying that," I told her sincerely, feeling even better about my decision to call her. Yazmin only nodded. There had to be quite a story there, but that would be for another time. "I do have a few other things to show you."

"I'm ready." She made grabby hands and I relaxed a little more. Yazmin had been the quieter of the two women, and now I wondered if she had been doing her own code switching in that job. Not wanting to show her true self. I knew only too well how that went.

I held up a hand before I launched into things, needing to get one thing out of the way. "I just want to be clear that I'd like this to be a partnership. That if we do this I'd have as much of a stake in it as you. I don't want to license my work, I want to *own* it." My heart pounded as I waited for a response but Yazmin didn't make me wait too long.

"Absolutely, I left Smithson-Napa because I was done with their predatory business practices, always shortchanging creators." The way her brow furrowed confirmed my suspicion that there was a lot of bad blood there. "This will be a partnership." She extended her hand to me and I shook it. We smiled gleefully at each other. "Okay, now that that's settled, can I see the new stuff?" Yazmin begged, making me laugh and in the next instant we were talking business.

"I think we have an absolute winner in our hands," Yazmin told me a while later, as she tapped at the design for a dark blue coverlet with my drawings of pipes and houndstooth deerstalker hats. "I love how elegant it is, and yet it's completely recognizable." A painful pang shot through my heart thinking of the night I'd shown it to Theo.

"That's the idea," I said a little too brightly. It hurt that I couldn't call him after this meeting to tell him about it. "The whole concept is to offer an elevated approach to fandom." I watched Yazmin as she took in what I'd said. Hoping she could see my vision. This was not a concept everyone would connect to. Not everyone respected the passion and energy in the fandoms. I knew it could be a tough sell. But she didn't shut me down so I kept going. "What I mean is that those of us who love a certain universe or fictional world want to be ensconced in it. We seek out art, fanfic, clothes, jewelry, anything that prolongs a connection to that story or characters that mean so much to us." Yazmin nodded, her eyes lit up like she was still with me. "The thing is, that as we get older our tastes change, even if our love for our fandoms stays strong as ever. My idea is to offer options for the stans who have outgrown what's out there."

"Agreed." Yazmin lifted her palm in the air and fucking high-fived me. "Girl, you're looking at a *Buffy* stan for life, I still have those posters in my office," she admitted, making me grin.

"'I might be dead, but I'm still pretty.'" The until-a-minute-ago very formal Yazmin screamed when I recited the iconic line from the first season of *Buffy*. "Oh, Alba, you and I are going to make some magic."

"I think we are," I concurred, with a grin that stretched my face. I was still digesting her words when she pointed at the photograph of the finished *Evelyn Hugo* bedroom suite.

"This is inspired." She traced her finger over the Jeannaret chairs I'd reupholstered in a deep green velvet. The image of Theo carrying them to his truck popped in my head and at this point I just had to let it happen, because apparently nothing that had happened in Dallas could come to mind without a side of Theo.

"This is one of my favorites," I told her.

She looked at it some more, then turned her gaze up to look at me. "I love that you managed to capture the vibe of the story and the aesthetics of it perfectly without needing to have the title of the book in neon over the headboard. It's the essence of the book, but the client can still feel like it's her own."

"Yes." I grinned in agreement, feeling like I'd truly found my creative kindred spirit. "*The essence,* that's exactly it. Convey the vibe of the book and ground it with pieces or colors that are important in the story. For example the green in those chairs is from one of the dresses she wears in the book." Yazmin nodded again, and this time there was a spark in her eye, and I knew we were on exactly the same page.

"So I have a question for you," Yazmin said as she leaned back on the booth and spread her arms wide. She was hot as fuck and if I wasn't desperately in love with Theo Ganas I would try something for sure. "If you could do anything you wanted, think as big as you could, what kind of designs would you be putting out?"

"Wow, really?" I asked genuinely surprised. The question robbed me of breath for a moment, and not because I didn't have an answer.

"Yeah, really. Lay it on me."

I hadn't been kidding when I'd told Theo that no matter how many curveballs I was thrown I'd always keep myself ready for the moment I was called up to make the play of my life. Maybe I didn't know if this thing with Yazmin would

pan out or end up being a letdown like the show, but I had
to try. After all, she was taking a chance on me too.

Trust went both ways and faith did too. I had to take a leap,
and trust that Yazmin was there for the same reasons I was.
Theo had asked me to be on the show because he wanted an
excuse to get closer to me. I knew that now, and the reason
why he couldn't just tell me how he felt was because I'd put
up walls at every opportunity. Told him again and again I
didn't have faith that anyone could love me exactly as I was.

I hadn't trusted him. I hadn't trusted that the show would
work out. I hadn't trusted *myself*. But I had to start. I had to
start because I'd done this. I was sitting at this table because
Yazmin had seen what I could do and wanted to work with
me. Theo had come to Dallas because he loved me, and he
thought I was worth his admittedly extra-as-fuck and over-
the-top gesture.

I was worth all this.

I deserved to have my dreams taken seriously, to have
my talent noticed and given the chance to run with it. I deserved the love of someone who saw all those things clearly
and who wanted them for me as badly as I wanted them for
myself. I finally had the shot I'd been waiting for if I'd just
take it. I leaned in, planting both hands on the surface of the
table and flashed a smile in Yazmin's direction.

"Girl, I'm so glad you asked."

"So how did it go?" Julia's voice boomed in my ear as I
walked out of the restaurant feeling at ease for the first time
since that horrible fight with Theo.

"It was good," I told her and shut down the little voice
in my head telling me this might all fall apart. I knew it
wouldn't, and more importantly, that even if it did, I would
be okay. "Yazmin wants to partner to develop the line, like

she's *in*. She's already got some potential investors she wants me to meet next week."

I had to pull my phone away from my ear at Julia's piercing scream. "What? Eso! Alba Serena eres una fucking jefa!" I grinned at that and walked to my rental with a bit more of a strut.

"She loved the fandom idea. She thinks hiring fan artists to collaborate with furniture designers and come up with full home collections inspired by them is great."

Julia sighed on the other end of the call. "Fuck this is an amazing day for geeks everywhere. Albita, you're going to bring fandom to like a whole new level. You did that shit on your own. No one gave you this," my friend told me, and I let myself absorb the praise for once. "Mira, amiga. Even after that bullshit with Chase, you went and looked for other ways to make your dream happen, someone who saw your genius." Julia always got me with the tears. I had to stop and breathe for a moment, so I didn't start bawling in the street.

"Now that I'm working with Yazmin here in Dallas, I guess I'll have to put up with your annoying ass for a while."

That time I really did lose hearing in my ear for a moment. After Julia's whoops and hollers died down I said out loud the thing I hadn't dared to voice yet.

"This place is going to be home for a while." It was bittersweet to say it, because for me Dallas was Theo too, and it hurt that I might not have him here this time around.

"You're the fucking shit, Alba Serena, believe that." And I was starting to. I was also starting to believe that I needed more than just my job. That I needed someone to love me, to hold me down.

"I am starting to, friend, but I think I want more. I want to be happy too." Theo's face when we danced that night in Santa Fe appeared in my mind. I missed him. The way he could make me forget everything but the two us. I needed him in my life. My work was my passion, but Theo was my heart.

Another of those deep sighs from Julia. "You deserve all of it, Albita, which leads me to the second reason I called you."

"Oh?" I knew that tone in my best friend's voice and it almost always meant she was up to something.

"So, I got you a new client here in Dallas."

"Julia, the last time—"

"I know! I know!" she hedged, interrupting me. "I know the library turned out to be a lot, but hey, it got you connected with Yazmin." And it got me to fall in love with Theo. "It wasn't all bad."

"No." I shook my head even if she couldn't see me, as I leaned on my car door. "It had its moments. What does this client want?" I asked against my better judgement, already breaking my rule about not taking on more than I could handle. But I'd started thinking of settling down here, buying a house, and even with the money from the show, I still had a ways to go before I committed to a mortgage.

"They want you to do their whole house in bookish themes."

I frowned, not even sure what to think. "The *whole* house?" What kind of nut wanted an entire house done like that?

"Yep," Julia confirmed. "And they want you to come see the house today," she added as I got into the car. "Now, actually."

"Now?"

"Yeah, it's not too far from where you are. I'll meet you over there to introduce you."

"Julia, please tell me these people are not some crazed millionaire friends of the twins," I pleaded, because I could not deal with another situation like the library for a long time.

"No," Julia assured me and she did sound sincere. "Not at all, I mean they're rich, but definitely not crazed. Here, let me give you the address. It's like five minutes from where you are." I raised an eyebrow at that since I was currently in Highland Park, one of the nicest areas in Dallas. Julia recited the location and I typed it into Google Maps.

"Hm." I frowned, noticing it was close to that Target Theo and I went to when he first got to Dallas. In fact it was right on that street I loved with the magnolia trees and that cute renovated Craftsman. "What are you up to, Julia del Mar?" I asked as a weird feeling settled in my stomach. "Aren't you at work right now? How are you going to meet me there?"

"What? I'm losing you!" My best friend lied like a fucking pro. "Listen, I'm getting on the road, see you there!" She was gone before I could call her on her obvious bullshit. With an amused huff I powered on my car and followed the directions to the house. I would do this one thing, and then I'd go somewhere quiet and call Theo. I wanted to see him. I wanted to tell him about the good things that were happening to me.

I was so distracted thinking about what I'd say that I got to the house in autopilot. It was indeed the same street we'd driven down that day. In fact it was the same dark blue house with green shutters and a big oak tree in the yard.

I slowed down and parked on the street in front of it and had to press a hand to my chest when I saw the Tesla SUV in the driveway. *Looks like a place a person could be happy to come home to after a long day.*

With trembling hands I pressed Julia's number on the car's touch screen.

"Julia del Mar, what the hell is going on?" I asked, my voice shaking.

"I'm just giving you a little nudge, babe. That's all." Her voice was so full of hope that I couldn't even get mad at her lying ass.

"This is not a client. Is it?" I asked, right as I saw him walk out of the house. A sob escaped my lips when he finally spotted me and his eyes widened with recognition. "Julia!" I cried. Freaking out and swooning all at once.

"Go," my friend urged. "We'll be there later. I love you, friend. Go get your man."

There are those moments in movies when the two main characters finally have their reunion and you think: Would they really drop their phone on the floor of the car and leap out of it like a lunatic? The answer is, fuck yes...well, after they almost crush their own windpipe with the seat belt.

"Fuck this thing," I cried, scrambling to get free. By the time I managed to unlatch myself he was standing by the door of the car. Looking gorgeous and stoic.

I'd been certain Theo was what I wanted from the moment I'd put my mom on the plane back to New York. Before that even—I knew it the moment I walked out of that penthouse the morning after we got back from Santa Fe. When I opened the door and stepped out of the car, he pulled me into his arms and it was like I could breathe again. No, more than that. It was like I could feel the breath coming in and out of my lungs. Like oxygen was returning to my body.

"I'm sorry." My voice was so shaky I could barely get the words out. "I'm sorry, I ran off."

"No." He shook his head as he picked me off the floor. "I should've told you about the show. I was selfish. I wanted more time with you. I should've just said what I wanted, what I felt, instead of letting you guess." He said the words with his mouth pressed to my hair and I almost wept from how good it felt to have him kiss my head again. I wrapped my legs around his waist and let him take care of us, taking us wherever it was he wanted us to go. "I should've told you I loved you the moment I knew. If I had, I wouldn't have put you through all this bullshit with Chase. I keep letting you down." He sounded like the weight of the world was on his shoulders and I would have none of that.

"Put me down, Theo." He slid me down his body like I was precious cargo, but when I looked at him I could see that these two weeks apart had taken their toll on him too. "Look at me, babe." I reached up to cup his cheek in my palm, as my heart stammered in my chest.

"It's not all your fault. Yes, you could've said it, but I don't know if I would've believed you before Dallas. If you'd told me while I worked for you, I don't know if I was ready then," I confessed. "The truth was that I didn't know how to let anyone in. My past relationships I'd set all these boundaries. I kept people away, but you wouldn't let me. You stayed, gave me what I needed, even when I didn't know I needed it. You taught me it was safe to count on someone." My voice came out wobbly on the last part, but the look on his face was brighter, more open.

"All I want is to be the man who can be there to see you soar. You are so fucking strong, for everyone in your life. I want to be the one who is strong for you. Always. I can't think of a better life than one in which I get to be the place where you come to rest."

I gripped the lapels of his jacket and breathed through my mouth. "If you make me cry these eyelashes off, I will never forgive you." He laughed, that deep, happy one I'd only ever gotten to hear in Dallas.

"Happy tears though." He sounded so unsure.

I nodded and he took my face in his hands and kissed me hungrily. I returned the kiss in earnest, my arm tight around his neck as he licked into me. I was running hot in seconds, needing to have more, get what I'd been missing all these days without him. He filled me up. He gave me what I wanted, just like I craved it. And I was so fucking lucky.

"Mi cielo," he whispered as his hands roamed down to my butt and dug in. "I missed this ass. Jesus, baby."

I had to laugh, because he sounded so relieved he got to grope me again. "That's what brought you back then, huh? El culo?"

He groaned hungrily and sucked on my bottom lip in response, his hands still on my backside.

"Perv," I whispered against his mouth. I loved this man, so much. He wasn't perfect. But he was noble, steady, and he didn't give up on what he loved.

"You don't even know." He backed us up against the wall and I was grateful for something to lean on before I sank to the hardwood floors. "Remember when you asked me what was special about you?" he asked and I grimaced remembering that night, the stress I was under and that even after I kicked him out of my room twice, he still kept me company while I worked.

"Yeah..." I trailed off, my heart in my throat.

"I had an answer, but I didn't tell you." He squeezed his eyes shut, regret marring his face. "I should've said you're special because you do everything with your whole self. You're loyal and you take chances even when you're afraid. And you rush home to make Rocco's niece a blanket with little princesses with afro-puffs even when you're swamped with work. You take your grandma food shopping every week even though you hate supermarkets. And you gave yourself to me, this—" He said it as he pressed one hand to my heart and the other to my cheek. "You gave me this fucking treasure even though I won't ever deserve it. You're special to me always, because I knew you were mine the moment I laid eyes on you."

By the time he was done I was clutching to him for dear life as I fought back tears.

"Tell me you believe me, Alba," he whispered in my ear and I nodded, because I did.

With much effort I put a hand on his chest and gently pushed him off.

"Wait a second, Mr. Ganas." I sounded winded, but who could blame me with six foot three of hard-up Dominican-Greek goodness all over me.

"What?" He blinked, dazed and red lipped. Fuck, how could anyone be this hot?

"What do you mean what?" I waved a hand around the empty gorgeously renovated living room. "Whose house is this, Theodoro Anibal?" The moment the question came out of my mouth flames flared up in my belly.

Oh, God, that cocky "I'm about to blow your mind" smile of his did things to me.

"It's mine," he told me with a sweet smile on his lips and he grabbed me by the waist and pulled me tight to him. "And yours." His eyes grew so serious, the gray in them almost pulsing with intent. "I want a fresh start here. I want to build things that matter and I want to watch you create things that make people happy. I want a whole life with you, Alba Serena. Filled with lots of good days and even some terrible ones. But with you. Always with you."

My first instinct was to question it, to let doubt pierce the perfect, perfect thing that I was being given. A fresh start, a life we got to define and build together. A home that we could make ours. I could let my father's shortcomings keep robbing me of having faith in what I was being offered, or I could believe in this, in him. I could have faith in us.

Fuck doubt, it had already taken too much from me.

"I want that too." He kissed me then, like he'd missed me more than air, and I kissed him just as hard right back. When I came back for air I turned my head to look at the big, beautiful room that I could turn into something that was ours. "I'm not doing every room in this house in a book theme, Theo."

He lifted a shoulder then bent down to kiss my forehead, making me melt a little. "As long as you're here I'll be happy." I breathed through the leaps my heart was making into my throat and spotted a frame leaning on a wall. It took me a moment to figure out what it was. Then I gasped.

"Are those your medals?" He smiled that smile that made me glow inside, the one I now knew belonged just to me.

"They are." He nodded and kissed my lips. I was so in love I throbbed with it. "I finally have someone to display them for."

"For me?"

"In part, but for me too. For the me that wants a future that leaves room to take stock. To slow down. For the me that belongs to you."

"I love you," I said, pressing my face to his strong chest.

"I know you do." He held me tight and brought me up for another kiss. "And that is and will always be the greatest win of my life."

# Epilogue

## ALBA

*Two years later*

"There really are ten of you, damn," my as-of-three-days-ago fiancé said, voice full of shock, as he took in my cousins.

"I told you." I laughed as he pretended to pick his jaw off the floor. "You're such a drama queen. It's not even that unusual; a lot of Dominican families do the same-name thing, Greek families too," I reminded him and he bent down to kiss my forehead in answer.

"Baby, look what you did." His voice was redolent with awe as he looked around the room my work had built. Pride and overwhelming gratitude filled me at his words. We were standing right inside the new flagship store for Bookish Living, the lifestyle brand that Yazmin and I had launched together a year earlier. The drop of our first Rom-Com bedroom line—the original version that had been too much for Smithson-Napa—had been such a success that within hours we'd had investors coming to us with massive amounts of money. In the end we'd partnered with a Latina-owned firm as our first big investor. That partnership led to things I could not have dreamed of.

"I honestly have to pinch myself sometimes," I admitted as my man tucked me tighter onto his side.

Today we'd unveil five new collections at this first store and there were plans to open ten more across the country. We'd built this place to be a literal dream for book lovers. They could buy anything from stemware from our Cozy Mystery collection to complete bedroom sets inspired by popular fantasy series. We also had a bookstore focusing on genre fiction, and a café and wine bar in-house. Next month we'd roll out a full line of book-themed furniture designed by a team Yazmin and I had put together. There were already talks of adding a few apparel lines. A true book lover's playground. I was so proud of what we'd done, but more than anything I was proud of the life I had with Theo.

My man had made some big changes too. He'd fought for his stepmother to take over the helm of Ganas and decided to pursue his own passion, which turned out to be building affordable green housing for low-income families in Texas. The veteran housing project had just been the start, and together with his two partners they'd raised millions to continue housing those in need.

"I'm proud of us, baby," he told me and I smiled as his lips pressed a kiss to my brow. I turned in his arms, trying to get a little bit of quiet before we had to join our friends and family.

"Did you ever think we'd end up here?" I asked, still marveling at what we had. A home, a life, a found family that held us down, work that lit us up.

He turned his head to the side in that way he did when he wanted to think something over, and my heart pounded in my chest, just overflowing with love.

"I knew that you were what I wanted and wherever that led me, that was where I'd go."

"Liar," I shot back, unable to keep the silly grin off my

face, making him laugh. "You were ready to do one of your classic Theo Ganas decrees and drag me back to New York."

"Okay," he admitted, as his cheeks flushed red. "Maybe that was part of the original plan, but in the end all that mattered was you." We grinned at each other like the saps we were and he lowered his face to mine, close enough that our lips bumped against each other. I swiped my tongue over that bottom lip I still loved to play with, and he groaned, pressing me to him. That hard, strong body that I'd learned not just to lean on, but to depend on anchoring me. "You've given me everything I ever dreamed of," he whispered against my mouth, so low and fierce, like he was feeding me the deepest truth in his soul. And now, here, in his arms, I believed it.

"I love you and our life," I told him, wobbly and awash with happiness. "Even if you've forced three demon dogs on me."

He pressed a laughing kiss to my mouth and shook his head. "The demons you buy steak for every week."

"My dogs are bougie, just like me," I reminded him, before I kissed him for real. Happier than I ever thought was possible. Literally standing in my wildest dreams, with the man I loved beside me.

"There you are!" Julia exclaimed, exasperation clear in her voice. "Girl, what are you doing necking back here? The ribbon cutting ceremony is about to start and you know how José gets if we get behind schedule." I'd brought José over to Bookish as our publicist and the man took his job very seriously.

"You're interrupting!" I told my best friend, who scoffed like I was an idiot and started clapping in my ear.

"Uh, let's go! The champagne is gonna get warm. And you." She pointed at Theo. "You're supposed to be helping, not grabbing ass behind bookshelves."

The Theo that I'd worked for in New York would've probably bristled at that. *This* Theo, the man who took days off to stay in bed with me and our dogs. Who surprised me with my favorite doughnut in the middle of the day. The man who I was planning to spend the rest of my life with. *This* Theo only smiled as he slid his hand into mine, his eyes shining with mischief as he turned to my best friend.

"I can't help myself," he said with a wink, and I fake swooned.

"Dummies," Julia said with a shake of her head and walked off.

"Are you ready for this?" Theo asked, and I nodded before tugging him down for a kiss.

"Baby, I was born ready."

★ ★ ★ ★ ★